BEAST MASTER

NATE TEMPLE SERIES BOOK 5

SHAYNE SILVERS

ARGENTO PUBLISHING

COPYRIGHT

CONTENTS

THE NATE TEMPLE SERIES—A WARNING

ate Temple starts out with everything most people could ever wish for—money, magic, and notoriety. He's a local celebrity in St. Louis, Missouri—even if the fact that he's a wizard is still a secret to the world at large.

Nate is also a bit of a...well, let's call a spade a spade. He can be a mouthy, smart-assed jerk. Like the infamous Sherlock Holmes, I specifically chose to give Nate glaring character flaws to overcome rather than making him a chivalrous Good Samaritan. He's a black hat wizard, an antihero—and you are now his partner in crime. He is going to make a *ton* of mistakes. And like a buddy cop movie, you are more than welcome to yell, laugh and curse at your new partner as you ride along together through the deadly streets of St. Louis.

Despite Nate's flaws, there's also something *endearing* about him...You soon catch whispers of a firm moral code buried deep under all his snark and arrogance. A diamond waiting to be polished. And you, the esteemed reader, will soon find yourself laughing at things you really shouldn't be laughing at. It's part of Nate's charm. Call it his magic...

So don't take yourself, or any of the characters in my world, too seriously. Life is too short for that nonsense.

Get ready to cringe, cackle, cry, curse, and—ultimately—*cheer* on this snarky wizard as he battles or befriends angels, demons, myths, gods, shifters, vampires and many other flavors of dangerous supernatural beings.

Consider yourself warned...

DON'T FORGET! VIP's get early access to all sorts of Temple-Verse goodies, including signed copies, private giveaways, and advance notice of future projects. AND A FREE NOVELLA! Click the image or join here:
www.shaynesilvers.com/l/219800

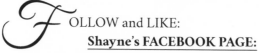 OLLOW and LIKE:
Shayne's FACEBOOK PAGE:
www.shaynesilvers.com/l/38602

I try to respond to all messages, so don't hesitate to drop me a line. Not interacting with readers is the biggest travesty that most authors can make. Let me fix that.

CHAPTER 1

It was madness, bullets, arrows, and even a spear, flying every which way, pelting antique portraits of long-deceased family members, priceless vases, and other worldly *objets d'art*. A nearby glass-paned cabinet of curiosities was struck twice in quick succession.

The cabinet was filled with dozens of random artifacts – an antique pair of spectacles, a watch, several figurines, a bullet casing, and a shot glass – to name a few. Another bullet winged off the corner of the cabinet as I ducked. Luckily, it didn't break, the glass made of something stronger than your typical window. Magical glass, apparently.

Amazingly, nothing had been broken.

Yet.

But dozens more cabinets filled my ancient mansion – Chateau Falco – and they were now all in danger of being destroyed. Dean was going to kill me.

But there was no time to wonder what my Butler would say about the damage.

All that mattered now was *surviving*.

I saw a lock of red hair behind the couch and unleashed a barrage of bullets at Ashley Belmont. In rapid defense, her fiancé – donned in a crisp navy blue suit and tie – rained down bullets on my position, sending me ducking back behind the furniture. An Alpha werewolf like Gunnar was not so easily taken down. Especially when someone was trying to plug their fiancée with bullets. At least neither of them had shifted into wolf form.

We had been friends, once, but no longer.

This was war. But my magic wouldn't help me now. It was off limits.

I caught the swish of a dress out of the corner of my eye as Sonya and Aria – affectionately known as the Reds when together – silently closed in on the Alpha werewolf to cover me. The twin teenagers gripped overly large pistols in each dainty hand, fingers resting on the triggers as their eyes danced with feral instincts. Which looked comical given their cute dresses. They weren't lethal *only* because they were female teens, but because they were *also* weredragons, and the crimson glint in their horizontal-pupiled eyes – like demonic goats – dripped with murderous intent. I quickly rolled to my left, finding new cover behind a Guardian statue. The stone sentinels were also useless in this battle; they no longer knew friend from foe.

The world had been turned on its head, pitting friend against friend. I thought about bringing this one to life just to up the chaos factor, but knew it wasn't a good idea. As soon as I upped my arsenal, my enemies would do the same. And for now, we were evenly matched.

I nodded at Achilles as he stalked the shadows with two short spears that somehow complemented his pressed jeans and cardigan. He barely acknowledged me as he hunted for the missing assailant. But I didn't have time to join his search, because out of nowhere, Tory – wearing a racy green dress – shouted out in glee, discovering my hiding spot. I bolted down the hallway as she levelled a ridiculously large shotgun my way, and began unleashing round after round, her bullets hammering into tables, the wall, and even smacking the Guardian's nose to no effect. One of Achilles' spears sailed from the hallways, but she dodged it at the last second, swinging her shotgun around. She pointed it down at the legendary Greek warrior's feet and began to unload. He panicked on instinct, hopping up and down frantically. But one of the bullets scored a direct hit to his heel and he collapsed, spear falling to the ground beside his now lifeless body.

A legend had just died.

But there would be no pyre.

Not today.

Tory belted out a shout of triumph at slaying the infamous warrior.

Then she began yelling for Gunnar to intercept my flight, but Othello emerged from the shadows directly behind her, wearing a nice black dress.

"Die," the international hacker grinned, unleashing an arrow from point blank range straight into Tory's kidney. The ex-cop (thanks to me) gasped, collapsed, and rolled onto the ground with sounds of anguish, managing not to flash the whole room in the process, despite wearing the low-cut green dress.

I smirked in relief at Othello, who quickly melted back into hiding.

I dove behind another couch, only to find myself directly behind Alucard – master vampire, and onetime friend – who was fidgeting anxiously with his pistol, cursing lightly. "Fucking jammed!" he hissed to himself, not noticing my arrival. The body of Greta's literal Guardian Angel, Eae, lay before him, eyes closed in death. Even now, he had a smugly pious and judgmental look about him. The undertaker-like suit only added to the effect. I would have laughed at the irony of a soldier of Heaven being slain by an agent of darkness, but my gun slipped from my sweaty palms and clattered to the heated marble floor. The vampire rounded on me, startled, but still managed to use his superhuman speed to aim his gun at me. I leaned to the side, just in the nick of time, and his bullet flew wide.

On reflex, I stabbed him in the damn forehead with my knife. His eyes glittered with disbelief from beneath the dagger, no doubt stunned at my choice of targets, before they fluttered closed and he collapsed like a sack of potatoes. I dismissed his body as just another casualty of war, and risked a quick peek over the edge of the couch, trying to discern who still survived.

A bullet whizzed past my ear, and I ducked back down.

I knew the Reds were closing in on my once-best-friend, Gunnar, but his beau, Ashley, wouldn't let them get away with it. I still had Othello and the Reds on my side, against Gunnar, Ashley, and the Huntress, whom I hadn't seen for some time now. I ducked back down, thinking furiously. *Where is she?* I thought to myself, remembering Achilles had been trying to flush her out before he had been slain.

Just then, I heard a loud scuffle as one of the Reds screamed in fury, "Die, wolf!"

I attempted to load my gun, but spilled the fistful of bullets on the ground. Cursing my clumsiness, I risked another glance as I fumbled a few stray bullets into the chamber. Aria was standing in plain sight near the fireplace. Gunnar and Ashley peered around opposite edges of the same couch, teeth shining in the lamplight. I tried to shout a warning, but I was too late to help the tween.

The wolves unfolded from their crouch to hammer her with way too many bullets. She groaned and grunted, falling to the ground. Sir Muffle Paws – all twenty pounds of my adopted Maine Coon kitty – chose that moment to dart between Gunnar's legs, and he flinched, reacting instinctively as he unloaded his gun at the feline.

The cat bolted under a table with a hiss, and a flash of movement behind the panicked wolves let me see that Aria's sacrifice had not been in vain. Sonya stood silently behind the mutts, a pistol pointed at each, like a female James Bond villain. "Bad puppies," she cooed before squeezing the triggers of both semiautomatics. Bullets sprayed the wolves, sending them flipping over the couch and into a chair. Ashley landed in Gunnar's lap with a loud expulsion of air as she died. Gunnar stroked her face one last time, a sad smile on his bearded cheeks before his eye closed and he let out a drawn-out death-rattle. Sir Muffle Paws darted out from beneath the table, glanced up at the fallen wolves, and then pounced up to land on Gunnar's chest, settling in for a nice nap before his body cooled.

Heartless little bastard.

I stood, winking at Sonya, only to see her eyes shoot wide as her gaze flinched behind me.

But I could tell by the look on her face that it was too late.

"I've waited a long time for this," a cool voice murmured in my ear as I felt the barrel of a pistol press into the base of my neck.

I sighed, dropping my hands in defeat.

Death entered the room, studying the fallen bodies with a detached look on his face. The Pale Horseman of the Apocalypse was, of course, no stranger to death. Literally. He leaned to the right to get a better look at my murderer. "Dead to rights," he murmured, a dark grin briefly flashing across his face. I had seen his mask before, the skeletal one, and it was downright terrifying. "Dinner is ready," he added. Then he turned without lifting a hand of support, and left the room.

He had once been my friend, but even he had turned against me this day.

"Time to die, Maker," the Huntress whispered before pulling the trigger.

CHAPTER 2

*T*he bullet hammered into the base of my skull, and I flipped over the couch, landing on a luxuriously soft pillow with a bajillion sequins that sliced through my tough, manly skin. Like a freaking decorative cactus. And it briefly made me think of Indie, who was partial to the Martha Stewart torture devices known as throw pillows...

I sighed. I hadn't wanted to think about Indie, my fiancée, but there it was.

In my dying breath, I glanced up at my murderer, who was grinning victoriously, pistol raised in the air. "I win—"

A Nerf bullet struck her right in the forehead and Othello burst out laughing. The Huntress blinked in surprise, staring down at the fallen bullet, and then a tiny smile swept over her stunned look. "No, *I* win," Othello roared. The Huntress turned to Tory – who had just emerged from the shadows – and the rare look of joy on the assassin's face made the whole thing worth it. Her smile turned hungry, suggestive, as she openly admired Tory's cleavage.

Tory blushed, which made me smile.

Everyone began climbing back to their feet, chuckling and grinning as they patted each other on the back. We were all dressed up, foregoing street clothes for the day. After all, it was a family dinner, and Dean kind of required it. Speaking of Dean, I rolled off the couch as I spotted him entering the room, face a mask of disapproval at the mess of bullets and toy guns strewn across the living room. He didn't say a word. I strode over to Othello to give her a big hug.

"My lady hath avenged my death. How shall I ever repay you?" I laughed into her neck, chuckling as I pulled away, still gripping her by the shoulders.

She rolled her eyes, covering a faint blush at our brief physical contact. "How about you carry your weight next time. I saved your ass twice. And I'm just a *Regular*." She used her fingers to mime quotation marks in the air at the last word.

I opened my mouth to argue, but Sonya and Aria sauntered up to us. I couldn't quite place how I could tell them apart, but after spending more time with them lately, I had acquired some kind of sixth sense about it. Also, Aria was more emotional than her sister, Sonya. More outspoken and rebellious. Sonya was less fiery, and more prone to mix up her words a bit, so that totally innocent statements could often be interpreted in a crude manner. Which was just fun, fun, fun for me.

True to form, Aria took center stage. "She has a point. I had to sacrifice myself to give us a shot, and you did *nothing*. It took two teenagers and a Regular to save your as—"

"Language," Tory belted out.

"But—" Aria began to argue.

"Don't argue with me," Tory warned, tone now a pitch darker. I hid my smirk. Tory was doing well as a new mother.

"She's right! There's nothing wrong with a little ass!" Sonya began to defend her sister, repeating the curse word, and giving me a perfect opening for an object lesson in embarrassment.

Tory snapped a finger, her eyes pulsing a bright green like tiny fires, ruining my chance.

The tension in the Reds' shoulders immediately evaporated and their faces went slack with unconditional obedience. "Yes, Mother," they murmured in unison.

Othello looked from the once-fiery Reds to Tory with a shiver. "That is incredibly unfair," she said. One part of me thought it incredibly impressive, but another part of me was cowering in fear that she could so easily control the two teenage weredragons – creatures that harnessed mind control powers of their own – without even the slightest effort.

This was in addition to her already creepy super-strength that allowed her to *Hulk Smash* anything and everything around her. And now that she had these new *green* powers, the metaphor was even *more* appropriate.

Her new abilities were thanks to me bringing her to a fight she had no business being in, but I had been desperate, and had needed her strength.

During my fight with the Brothers Grimm a few months ago, Tory had lost a lover – the mother of the Reds who now stood before us, mute and obedient as Labradors – and had decided that the only acceptable cure for her grief was to stand by my side as I battled a veritable army of Grimms – supernatural assassins from beyond our world.

Tory had lost an arm during the battle, and a woodland sprite fighting alongside us had decided to cast the last of her powers into my friend before she succumbed to her own injuries. Tory had regrown her arm within minutes, bone and tendon melding with vines, branches, roots, and a pulsing green glowing power. The savior sprite hadn't survived, whether from her own injuries, or her choice to grant her powers to Tory, I didn't quite know.

Shortly after, Tory had been volun-told – not *volunteered* – to stand in for the dead sprite in a trifecta of power with the two other surviving sprites – seeing as she now commanded their fallen sister's powers – and together, they managed to imprison the leader of our enemies, the legendary Jacob Grimm. Since that time, Tory had shown remarkable powers at controlling, well, *creatures*. She had already been inhumanly strong before, able to lift cars, shatter trees, you name it. Like a pint-sized Incredible Hulk. But now she did it with glowing green eyes.

And after the battle, she had shown an entirely new affinity for wood.

Heh.

Whenever she touched a wooden bannister, or tree, or tabletop, the wood was likely to suddenly begin sprouting new growth: leaves, branches, or even moss. She had also managed to control the inner beast of Ashley – Gunnar's fiancée – who had then been struggling with her new powers as a werewolf – again, thanks to me bringing her into my fight against the Grimms. She had been unable to determine friend from foe, harboring only an instinct to kill any and all threats. Whether it was the unpunctual mailman or the pizza delivery guy casting a disappointed frown at a low tip.

Tory had also managed to control the powers of my own fiancée – a newly-minted Grimm – during our altercation with Rumpelstiltskin, or Silver Tongue, as he was more commonly known.

A particularly clever person might begin to notice a theme here.

I had brought each of my friends into a deadly battle, and that battle had *changed* them.

All of them. And often not in good ways.

I vanquished that brief flash of guilt, and pondered Tory again, recalling the times I had seen her use her new abilities.

She had nullified Baba Yaga's magic, and then things had gotten even stranger.

My Master Vampire pal, Alucard, had been off the blood-drinking bandwagon for a few days, trying to become a better-behaved monster. During our fight with Rumpelstiltskin, he had gotten his ass handed to him, and an injured and semi-conscious Tory just happened to be lying nearby. His instincts had kicked in, and he managed to take a quick sip from Tory's wrist in order to regain some of his strength to rejoin the battle.

But it didn't pan out like anyone had anticipated, least of all, him.

He drank for a few seconds, but then a sudden explosion had sent him cartwheeling a dozen paces away. He came to his feet, newly energized, and… sparkling.

He now no longer had a thirst for blood. And he seemed to be pretty much in her thrall – by choice or obligation, I wasn't quite sure which.

As if to emphasize this, the once-vampire approached us now, unconsciously checking Tory with a concerned look. Even though it had all just been a harmless Nerf battle. Alucard wasn't a Revenant or anything, still the same old snarky vampire… except, I wasn't sure if he *was* a vampire any longer.

Even though he now sometimes sparkled. *Heh.*

"You stabbed me in the forehead! What the hell, Little Brother?"

I rolled my eyes at his annoying term of endearment. "It was a reaction. Next time I'm killing you, I'll try to be more heroic about it." I turned to Eae, who was glaring at the vampire. I hadn't seen him approach. "You were literally less than useless, Feathers. You find it ironic that a vampire killed you? Because I find it *immensely* satisfying," I teased.

His scowl deepened. "Would never happen in real life."

Alucard flashed an arrogant grin at the Angel before turning back to me. "Practice makes perfect, and stabbing someone in the forehead – although surprising – is not as effective as you would think. It's one of the hardest bones in the body. Likely, your dagger would have slid right off, injuring me, sure, but not killing me."

I shrugged. "I'll try to remember that."

"That's the point of all this, Maker. Practicing for the real thing. So that we don't have any major casualties," Achilles added in a grouchy tone. "For example, every time your friends have aided you in your vendettas." He turned to Tory before I could even try to argue the valid accusation. "Nice shot. A bit melodramatic, but it's good practice to aim for known weaknesses."

Tory dipped her head, accepting the compliment with grace.

"And here I thought we were just having some fun," Gunnar chimed in, his beefy arms wrapped tightly around Ashley, whose eyes were practically closed as she rubbed her cheek against his forearm appreciatively.

I often took my aggression out on my dog when pissy. "That was a pretty dramatic death. Thinking of going into theater?"

Gunnar flashed a toothy grin at me as his only response, his stupid man-bun looking good on his large bulk. Like a Viking.

"War is not fun," Eae argued, frowning in disapproval.

"It is if you win," Othello chimed in. Achilles grunted in agreement.

Eae had a distant look in his eyes. "My brothers had a war once..." his Heavenly gaze rested on each of us for a millisecond. "It was not *fun*."

The silence grew for a minute as everyone absorbed the severity of his reference. The Angel War that had cast those Angels allied with Lucifer down from Heaven. Or Eden. Or whatever the real story was. "Well, who invited Buzz Killington?" I muttered.

He glanced at me sharply, but finally let out a slow nod of embarrassment. "Yes, it was long ago. My apologies. I believe it is time for us to break bread. The Horseman is growing impatient."

"Alright, let's go. Death makes a mean turkey. But we should probably pick up first, then—"

I glanced at the room and saw that all the bullets and toy guns had been picked up already.

Dean.

"He's a freaking ninja," Alucard murmured. I nodded, glad that he hadn't chosen that moment to berate us all for disrespecting my ancestors' paintings with stray bullets. I was sure that I would hear about it later, though. In depth.

"Friendsgiving," Othello smiled, snatching up my hand before tugging me on towards the dining room. My friends filed after me, Ashley's gaze discreetly settling on Othello holding my hand. I shrugged back, feeling a brief pulse of anger at the silent judgment.

Indie was gone. With no word. No letters. And in decidedly unpleasant company.

My grandfather. I shook off my testosterone-laden reaction as we headed to the dining room. I wasn't about to let Ashley's subtle look ruin my day. Things like this were important. The glue to our friendship. Not just death and destruction, but simple things. Like Friendsgiving.

And Nerf wars.

CHAPTER 3

*W*e entered the dining room to find that Dean and Death had been busy.

The long table stretched before us, laden with steaming bowls of mashed potatoes, green beans, salad, covered baskets of freshly baked rolls, plates of butter, pitchers of gravy, a smattering of other covered dishes, a dozen unopened bottles of expensive wine, as well as a half dozen crystal decanters brimming with already-poured wine. Steam curled around the massive turkey centered on the table, and my mouth instantly salivated at the savory aroma. China plates, expensive silverware, and crystal wine or highball glasses sat empty before each seat, waiting to quench the untamable thirst of my table of monsters, legends, and famed warriors.

Sir Muffle Paws darted between my legs before hurling himself up onto a side-table that held a ritzy silver saucer with fresh cream. I rolled my eyes at the opulence granted to the filthy feline.

But, hell, why not? It *was* Friendsgiving.

"You spoil that mangy fur-ball too much," Gunnar smiled.

I nodded back absently. I didn't mention that – in my own private way – treating the cat like royalty made me feel like I was treating Indie like royalty, because she loved that little beast unconditionally. The cat was getting bigger fast. Not super heavy or anything, but in height and length. I shifted gears away from Indie, not wanting to ruin my mood.

Dean had gone all out, dusting off the priceless dinnerware that had sat unused for far too long in my home, Chateau Falco. After a rough few years, the halls of my mansion finally had guests again.

And it felt...

Nice.

Dean wore a freshly pressed tuxedo and stood in the entryway leading to the kitchen, hands clasped behind his back, looking extremely pleased with himself.

Everyone began taking their seats. I unbuttoned my coat, and chose the practical throne at the head of the table, an ornate, ebony-stained wooden chair – complete with Druidic carvings from top to bottom. My dad's old chair. The back stretched well over my head, but the gaudy throne was surprisingly comfortable. Death sat at the opposite end of the table, looking out of countenance in his black suit. He sat in an equally pompous white throne, but this one was carved in feminine, Fae-like adornment. My mom's old chair. I briefly considered the irony of him, the Pale Rider, in a white chair. But that brought up other memories of the White Room, and the Mad Hatter whom resided there. I still didn't have a solid explanation for Death's relationship with the Mad Hatter. Or of the exact dangers associated with the Hatter. Just that Death hadn't been pleased I had met him. Or that I had *continued* to meet him. But now was time for celebrating.

I smiled to myself, eyes slowly absorbing every aspect of the scene before me. Here I was, hosting Friendsgiving with a truly terrifying assortment of Freaks.

To my right, after a few empty chairs, sat the Reds, followed by Tory, Alucard, and finally, Achilles, next to Death at the far end of the table.

Opposite Achilles, sat Othello, then Eae, Greta, Gunnar, and Ashley. Two pairs of empty chairs sat on either side of me. "Where did the Huntress go?" I asked, curiously. Everyone looked around, surprised to find her absent. My gaze tightened. She was an elusive one, and had likely snuck off before things grew too... intimate. I counted the empty chairs, and then turned to Dean. "We're dropping like flies. Where's Raego and—"

As if on cue, Mallory entered the room with Raego in tow. Midas and Tomas followed behind them, and they all stared, enthralled, upon the aged bottle clutched in Mallory's fist. A Macallan Lalique sixty-two-year-old single malt scotch. I had only tried it once in my life. I knew we had a stash of Macallan fifty-year bottles around the house, but I hadn't known about this treasure. It was upwards of $30,000 per bottle. I wondered how many more could be lying around in some forgotten storage room in the 17,000 square-foot mansion.

Mallory paused, noticing that everyone was already seated and staring at his posse expectantly. He turned to Dean with a guilty grin. "Sorry, Dean. Didna' know we were seating yet." Dean dipped his head in response, and the tardy guests took their places on either side of me, various stages of light chastisement on their faces.

"Where's Famine?" Alucard asked, deadpan.

Othello smirked absently, but then seemed to grow mildly alarmed at the thought of another Horseman joining us, as if, perhaps, he really was on his way.

"Friendsgiving is not really his... thing. Neither is *food*..." Death replied in a cool tone that darted from Alucard to Greta, then back again, as if warning him against being rude in front of the deeply religious Regular at the table. Alucard looked only slightly ashamed. I caught Death shoot a deeply considering gaze at Othello as she idly tucked a stray hair behind her ear. Like a lion catching a gazelle stumble in his peripheral vision. I wasn't sure exactly what was going on there, but it had seemed like the two had kind of hit it off when they first met. Back when she had died.

Long story short, I had hunted down my parents' murderer – a renegade wizard – who had kidnapped Othello to use against me. I had borrowed Death's mask, brought Othello back to life after the wizard killed her, and then promptly burned him alive.

Emphasis on *alive*. Slowly. With Othello by my side.

Shortly after, I found myself in a courtroom with Angels, Demons, and the other Horsemen.

It had been a big misunderstanding. Akin to a Biblical parking ticket.

I swear.

Death first met Othello at the renegade wizard's funeral pyre, and the two had seemed to flirt back and forth a bit. Or at least had whispered together in dark corners for a few days.

I wondered if it was possible for the two of them to share romance, or if Death was merely interested in the Regular's presence at my table of mostly Freaks. Or, maybe it was because he could taste the death on her. I shivered at that.

Othello noticed his gaze and blushed, basically admitting that *something* was going on between the two of them.

Greta broke the silence, seated beside her Guardian Angel, Eae. "Now that you are done playing games, let us say grace."

"Grace," Alucard murmured, reaching for the potatoes. Tory looked at him with lightly flickering green eyes, and his hand went rigid, frozen. He turned to her, grinning sheepishly, before withdrawing his hand. Tory nodded, then turned back to Greta. Her eyes shifted back to their normal, already bright-green shade. Just not glowing any longer.

"Thank you, child. Although I won't pretend to understand how you control such dark forces." Tory smiled back politely, not taking offense, and not offering an explanation. Upon meeting an actual Angel, Greta had received a crash course in the supernatural, and although she had accepted it with aplomb, she was still less-than-thrilled to be in the presence of some of the 'evil' guests at the table. Especially Death, one of the Four Horsemen. She cleared her throat, lifting a glass of wine, eyes flicking briefly to each person. "Now, it is apparent that the table represents many different... cultures and faiths." She shot a questioning look at Eae, who nodded back in approval. "However, since I arranged this dinner—"

Dean cleared his throat softly, barely even a sound, but Greta blushed.

"My apologies. Since *Dean and I* worked together to arrange this... *Friendsgiving*, I think it's only fair to honor my beliefs..." her eyes darted around the table, both a challenge, and a... well, a look of concern.

Drama, I thought to myself, masking my grin.

CHAPTER 4

*B*ut Death ruined it, responding with a warm smile. "Of course, Greta. That is an excellent idea. I additionally propose that we each state what we are thankful for." His icy gaze took in Mallory, who was urgently fumbling with the bottle of Macallan. He finally got it open and poured glasses for those interested. Mallory handed me mine first, to which Raego rolled his eyes. I stuck my tongue out at him. Finally, everyone ready, Greta cleared her throat again.

"Dear Heavenly Father..." she began, reciting the well-known prayer. I let her words wash over me, not particularly religious myself, but still respectful, and somewhat admiring, of her faith. Hell, she had a freaking Guardian Angel sitting next to her. It wasn't like I could deny the Almighty, but I felt like a fraud trying to worship Him *after* the proof had been shown to me. Seemed kind of backwards. Like cheating. Was it considered faithful worship if I already had the proof? So, I had decided to continue being myself, hoping that God understood my position.

I studied those at the table with silent pride. I had gathered this motley crew of Freaks to join me for Thanksgiving. Except, several had prior engagements, or didn't celebrate the American holiday, so I had chosen to host a *Friendsgiving* instead, a few weeks prior to Turkey Day.

And for the most part, all my loved ones were here.

Well, except one.

Indie, my fiancée.

I squashed that thought down deep, holding its metaphorical head underwater until it drowned a messy, spluttering, gasping, fitful death. Which made me feel only marginally better.

I focused on those present, genuinely appreciating the diverse group, almost wanting to shake my head in disbelief. Greta finally finished her prayer, and for the most part, we all responded with *Amen*.

A few obvious exceptions were Alucard, Midas, Achilles, and Mallory.

I didn't know much about Mallory's background, and had been strongly encouraged not to pry. The Greeks were understandable. They worshipped Mount Olympus, the Greek Pantheon of Gods and Goddesses.

Alucard was a vampire. Kind of on the *no-fly* list with the Almighty. He was particularly sensitive to religious items. It wasn't too long ago that Greta's squad of Bible School children had effectively taken him hostage when they tried to host a bake sale at my bookstore, Plato's Cave, which he had very briefly managed for me. Looking at him now, I could tell he was on edge, waiting for something bad to happen. I had also frequently used religious flyers from Greta to prank him. One touch of the mailer and he was basically Tasered by Heaven.

"I am Thankful for my Father, and His gift of Eae to aid me on my spiritual journey," Greta said after a pause. "I ask that he guide me on our upcoming mission trip to Guatemala."

Eae nodded in agreement.

I almost grunted, but bit my tongue. Eae hadn't been a *gift* to Greta. He had been cast down for a mistake during my courtroom appearance over the Biblical parking ticket, forced to spend his Heavenly *Time-Out* on Earth. He had wanted to find someone to protect that was close to me, so that he could point the finger at me the next time I made a mistake, maybe earning him early parole from Daddy. Smug bastard. I hoped that mission trip took a good long while. Give me a little breathing room from his judgmental eyes.

"I am thankful for my journey to Earth, to better learn your mortal ways," Eae stated piously.

"I'm thankful to have met Death," Othello said softly, then she let out a giggle, likely realizing how ridiculous that would have sounded at any other dinner table.

Death smiled in response before turning to stare directly at me. "I am thankful for my new *Brother*."

And an abrupt shiver shot down my arms. The room grew quiet as everyone read between the lines. He was referring to his belief that I was the *fifth* Horseman of the Apocalypse, the Horseman of Hope. He had called me that long ago, while standing beside his Brothers – War, Famine, and Pestilence during my courtroom appearance. None of his brothers had argued, though they had laughed about it a bit. I could never tell when they were joking. But Death seemed to remind me of that conversation on a fairly regular basis.

Like now.

I dipped my head politely, avoiding staring too intently into his icy eyes, and ignoring the thoughtful looks from the others at the table.

Achilles cleared his throat. "I want to thank Dean and Death for preparing such a lovely meal, and inviting me to this feast." He held up a finger, "But I would also like to thank everyone for defeating Silver Tongue, releasing me from my bond." He turned to me. "And Nate, for partnering with King Midas to set up our... *book club*." He winked at me, and I grinned back, shrugging my shoulders. Several others murmured their agreement with identical boyish grins. Greta looked confused.

He was referring to the Fight Club I had set up with King Midas at the Dueling Grounds, the Minotaur's *sanctum sanctorum* – or *inner sanctum*, for those not bored enough to pick up Latin as a hobby. The Dueling Grounds was on a different plane of existence than our regular world, and allowed those battling there to fight to the death without *actually* dying. It gave these gods and warriors a place to hone their skills without lasting harm. It had been unbelievably successful, and although none were supposed to talk about it, many loose lips had shared the information. Achilles and the Minotaur had kind of taken over the management of the fights, and had come up with some rather grim punishments for those who didn't follow the rule of silence.

I shivered at the memory of a few nights ago when two such individuals had been informed of the Fight Club without official invitation from Achilles.

They had been nominated as target practice for anyone who wanted to take them on. Repeatedly. For the duration of one month. They were tossed into the ring, and one by one, every single warrior who wanted to was allowed to kill the defenseless rule-breaker. The guilty had to accept the punishment without future reprisal. Only to be punished once again at the next meeting. Until Achilles deemed them properly chastised.

Silence had quickly been restored. And now it was by invitation only.

Alucard spoke next. "I want to thank Nate for letting me join his family..." I found it uniquely cute to see a pale, undead vampire blush. Then again... he didn't look as pale as usual, no doubt thanks to whatever had happened between him and Tory. Despite usually being a snarky guy, he spoke this with the utmost sincerity. I smiled back, deciding not to rib him as much. It was true. During the Grimm War, he had turned against his fellow vampires to help me, essentially declaring his own people his enemy. He had literally given up his life to become my friend. "Tory's kinda cool, too," he added, grinning at the Reds, "because she keeps these two gingers from stealing my soul."

Tory rolled her eyes, and the Reds tried to glare at him, but were having a hard time fighting down their smiles. Tory gave him an affectionate pat on the wrist before speaking. "I want to thank Nate for giving me a family. Without him, I wouldn't have met these two beautiful women, and their equally beautiful mother, Misha. Although our love was brief, I have gained two beautiful daughters, and a whole table full of friends, after a lifetime of loneliness." Her eyes were misty as she finally lowered them to her lap.

The Reds forgot Alucard in an instant, speaking in unison with varying forms of how much they loved Tory, despite her new ability to force them to obey her parental... *guidance*, which elicited a smattering of chuckles from the table. The three hugged each other, sobbing and smiling. Mallory watched with a faint grin, but to me it looked haunted.

Raego piped up, snapping my attention away from my bodyguard. "Nate gave me a nation to rule." He said with a nod of respect my way. "Even if one of his friends has managed to swipe up two of my subjects," he growled playfully at Tory.

She simply shrugged, returning a grin.

Mallory lifted his glass, thick Scottish accent marking his words as he spoke. "To Macallan. Only reason I stick around this dusty ol' pile of a mansion is because of Master Temple's stash," he smirked.

I leaned forward. "The stash you have refused to show me, even though it supposedly belongs to me."

Mallory feigned confusion. "I'm sure I've told ye where it is, Laddie."

"Yes, several times. But miraculously, whenever I go to check it out in person, the stash has coincidentally been relocated. No doubt to a safer location."

Mallory shrugged, leaning back with a look of dramatic surprise.

Midas cleared his throat. "To good returns on investments." He winked at me. Achilles chuckled, nodding in agreement.

"For steady work, and for giving his trust to an ex-assassin." Tomas, the British dragon hunter smiled, face serious. He obviously no longer hunted dragons, unless Raego hired him.

Now, he mostly did odd jobs for us. In fact, I had used him recently to ferret out some information a little out of my jurisdiction. But that was kind of hush-hush. And Othello and I still needed to speak with him about his recent travels to Germany.

"For *Family*," Gunnar grumbled, discreetly touching the tattoo on his wrist, the tattoo that let he and his fiancée control their werewolf form. "And for introducing me to Ashley, and handing me a pack of loyal wolves on a... silver platter." He chuckled.

Ashley smiled at him, clutching his beefy arm in her dainty hand. "Yes, for *Family*. And for giving me this handicapped stray puppy to take care of."

Alucard burst out laughing, and Gunnar grumbled warningly at her, his lone eye doing a miraculous job at scowling. He had lost an eye battling Wilhelm Grimm. The Grimm was the reason Ashley was now a werewolf. He had suckered Gunnar's pack into turning her. Which had taken him some time for him to forgive. Ashley kissed him on the beard, grinning at him until his glare melted away.

Everyone turned to me, and I idly swirled the glass of scotch, thinking.

I took a breath, forcing a smile on my face as I banished the first thought that came to mind. "For joining my family, and standing beside me when I lost everything. For protecting each other, and for helping me fill Chateau Falco with laughter, joy, and tears after my parents were killed."

I didn't mention Indie. Or Ichabod.

And everyone seemed to silently note it. I lifted my glass, trying to hide the sudden influx of power coursing through my veins, threatening to shatter the glass in my fist. This happened whenever a strong emotion struck me. A Dark Presence rumbled close to the surface of my resolve, eager to destroy something, and the masterfully-worked silver eagle-headed cane holstered to my belt throbbed warmly. Right now, it was just the head of the cane, but if I lost control, or consciously *thought* about it too intently, the handle would become a full-fledged, cane sword. Magic can be kind of neat like that. I mastered myself, forcing the Dark Presence back deep down into the cane, and let out a soft breath. The warmth at my hip gradually subsided, no one the wiser. Everyone drank.

I opened my mouth to tell everyone to load up their plates, but I was interrupted.

The doorbell rang.

A frown split Dean's face as he pulled out his phone to check the video camera at the front door. His frown deepened further before he shot me a look. I nodded and he left. But everyone had instinctively reached for their weapon of choice.

I waved off their concern. "Don't worry. We're fine. Now, let us eat." After a few seconds, everyone tucked in, serving themselves since Dean had stepped away. I sipped my drink, ignoring the food.

Apparently, I was doing a bit more than sipping, because Mallory refilled my glass a moment later, eyes concerned. I nodded in appreciation as I leaned back in my chair, waving off his concern with a subtle look. Death was watching me thoughtfully, but everyone else was enjoying themselves as they murmured approval of the food.

I kept a smile on my face, determined to focus on the *now*.

Not Ichabod and Indie, who were nowhere to be found.

The cane handle at my hip murmured whispers of dark entreaty for my ears alone, attempting to fan the flames of my rage. But I was used to it. If I touched it, the sword was liable to flare into existence from the ornate handle, and the dark voice would grow more persistent. I kept myself under control, casually smiling and responding to any questions shot my way. Dean silently reentered the room, face tight as he shot me an imploring look.

I stood, and everyone in the room froze, noticing Dean's return.

"Easy, everyone. Enjoy the meal. I'll be right back. The Guardians are back online. We're safe."

They didn't look satisfied, but complied as I left the room. I was kind of thankful for the distraction, but who the hell would just show up at my house in the middle of the day like this?

CHAPTER 5

*D*ean was patiently waiting for me in the hallway, hands tucked behind his back.

"What is it?" I asked in a low voice, but loud enough to be heard over the laughter and chatter in the dining room.

"Someone is here to see you."

My heart fell into my stomach, suddenly reconsidering Dean's trepidation. I opened my mouth to speak, but Dean forestalled me.

"It is not Miss Rippley," he said softly, clearly reading the terrified look on my face.

"Oh." I ran a shaky hand through my hair, heart now beating wildly at the brief thought that Indie had stopped by. "Well, who is it then? How did they get through the gates?"

Dean watched me. "Those answers will be clear in a moment," he replied slowly. Then he turned on a heel, leading me towards the sitting room where he usually left guests upon entrance to the ancient mansion known as Chateau Falco. The home had been in my family for centuries. I wasn't concerned that this mysterious stranger was already inside my home. Dean was an experienced Butler. He had the means to judge friend from foe, threat from not a threat.

But we also had redundancies. For starters, anyone wishing me harm wouldn't have used the front door. They would have simply tried to blow up the place.

And anyone wishing me harm wouldn't have been able to even walk through the front door, after the recent upgrades I had put into place. I had done the same thing to my bookstore, and that had already come in handy when a Russian witch had decided to pay a visit. I had been left alone after Indie decided to go train with Ichabod, and that spare time had left me a lot of time to tinker with my new powers.

To study and practice from the book Ichabod had left me. The educational text from his own childhood on how to use the Maker power.

Which, thanks to my parents' foresight, I had been unknowingly given access to. Until now, Makers had been extinct, hunted and slaughtered by pretty much any and every supernatural tag-team imaginable.

For we were rumored to be a wee-bit dangerous.

Wizards could use magic. Shape elements. Wield the fabric of life that existed all around them.

But Makers... well, we had *Made* wizards. Allegedly.

I wasn't entirely up to speed on the potential of my new powers, but thanks to the Grimm War, I had inadvertently freed my ancestor from a centuries-long prison sentence. Hundreds of years ago, my ancestor, Ichabod Temple, had banished the Grimms to a Dark Realm. But he got sucked away with them, and had been their prisoner ever since. Which had been about 426 years that he was forced to work for them. Until I had unknowingly released a handful of them from their prison. During the fight, my girlfriend – now fiancée – had been turned into a Grimm. And after barely defeating the bastards, I had come to realize that Ichabod wasn't a Grimm, but was actually a Maker, like me. And he was my ancestor.

But we hadn't spent much time around each other.

And he had stolen my fiancée. To train her in the use of her new powers before they turned her into a raving psychopath, hell-bent on murdering any Freak within a dozen feet of her. Because, well, that's what Grimms *did*. And thanks to me, she was the last Grimm.

At least in this world. The others were still locked away in their Dark Realm, thankfully.

Anyway, before Ichabod had taken her away, I had shown him the book I had received from Rumpelstiltskin – a book teaching the ABC's of being a Maker. And what did I find inside? *Ichabod Temple*, written in childlike handwriting. His childhood schoolbook on being a Maker, if you will. It wasn't an all-inclusive text, but it set up the groundwork for me, and I had always been a good student, able to extrapolate to areas of my choosing after a rudimentary understanding of the principles. And one of the first things I had wanted to learn was how to better defend my home. Now that I knew the ancient mansion held vast secrets of her own – more than I had originally even known – I had wanted to make sure she was impregnable.

I also had a literal army of guards hidden in plain sight.

Dean paused outside the door, turning to address me. He straightened my dinner jacket, plucked an extra Nerf bullet from my coat pocket that I had stored away in case I ran out of ammo, and then tugged my sleeves. I rolled my eyes, and his face portrayed a brief smile before he entered the room, holding the door for me, face now solemn.

"Master Temple, at your request," he announced.

I entered the room to find a wizened old man seated on the couch to my right, a glass of chilled scotch in his shaking palms. The reason for his fear was the man seated directly across from him in the other couch, idly polishing a crackling spear of electrical power like a live bolt of lightning.

Mallory.

The room was dim, the majority of the curtains drawn, and the Tiffany lamps did little to pierce the gloom. Dean's face was a carefully-controlled mask, but I knew he had obviously prearranged this scenario. He and Mallory must have had a failsafe in place, and had chosen not to share it with me. This momentarily infuriated me, but I released the grip on my sword cane, and the darker emotions evaporated. Not *my* fury, the *cane's* fury.

The Dark Presence inside of me.

Composing myself, I considered the situation more rationally. It actually wasn't a bad plan. They were looking out for me. Even though the other redundancies made this a waste of their time. Still, it was nice to see that they cared so much for my safety. And their actions were not the true cause of the loose grip I had on my temper. That was the Dark Presence inside of me. A seed of knowledge, or the soul of a demon, that was buried deep inside the Maker's ability that had been forced onto me by my parents. Their parting gift to me before they had been murdered.

They had the best of intentions…

Highway to Hell… by ACDC rang in my ears at the thought.

And they hadn't asked me, or even *told* me about it beforehand.

Mallory was grinning as he casually continued to polish the deadly weapon on his lap. "Master Temple," he grinned politely. "I didna want yer guest to feel lonely. Hope ye don't mind..." I kept my face neutral, even as a new thought briefly struck me. He had beaten me here, even though he had been sitting at the table when I left the dining room. I kept the shock from my face, and spotted movement near the fireplace.

A stone griffin the size of a Great Dane casually snapped a spare log from the fireplace into two pieces between his razor-sharp beak. He flicked out his wings with a sharp *crack*, dove onto a piece of wood, and then flung it into the fireplace. Like a cat playing with a toy mouse. With a thought, I cast a whisper of power at the fireplace and the log instantly flared to life as if it had been burning for hours. The guest flinched at the sudden fire.

Mallory yawned, then took a sip of his own drink. The griffin tore into the other piece of wood, lying down to worry it like a dog with a bone. Another motion revealed three other griffin Guardians prowling the room, staying out of the way, but their stone eyes watched the guest with loosely restrained threat.

"Thank you, Mallory. I trust that our *guest* has received all courtesies in my absence?"

Another one of the defenses of Chateau Falco was that none entered without accepting *Guestright* from Dean on my behalf. This prevented them from directly harming me through trickery. It wasn't an exact magic, but worked pretty darned well when it came to most supernatural factions. Neither could harm the other without probable cause, lest the offender lose a considerable chunk of their powers, whatever flavor they may be.

Mallory chuckled. "Aye. I was just entertaining him. I was telling him about the lesson ye always rattle on about. How ye can achieve anything in this world with just two things." He ticked off a finger for each as he continued, "Leverage and lubrication." He winked at the guest. "Isn't that right, Sir..." he leaned forward. "How rude o' me! I never asked yer name!" His eyes glittered intensely.

I watched the guest, his eyes dancing with barely concealed alarm at the overwhelming display of power before him. Dean silently walked the perimeter of the room, idly patting one of the Guardians on the neck as he passed. He finally halted directly behind the guest, out of sight, a psychological ploy.

Jesus. Bad cop and silent, creepy cop.

Mallory and Dean must have practiced this a dozen times judging by their performance. They were treating this like an interrogation. Unless... they knew something about this guest that had them on edge. But then... why would they have let him in?

I cleared my throat, and Mallory turned his piercing glare from the guest to me. He chuckled as he stood to his feet. "Of course, Master Temple. Apologies. I'll just wait over there with Dean. I need to ask him when he last fed yer pets." He winked at the guest. "They get mighty hungry." Then he took his spear and walked out of sight to stand beside Dean. The crackling sound of his spear caused the man to twitch now and then. Especially after a few errant sparks landed on the carpet, smoking like fallen embers. Dean's face crunched in disapproval at the damage, but he remained silent.

I took Mallory's old seat and faced my guest. He was an older man. Not old as in frail, but old like he was in the prime of his life. He looked *hard*, with two noticeable scars on his face, and his eyes were cold, distant, and... hopeful. For all of that, he still looked dangerous. Maybe Dean and Mallory's display hadn't been a bad idea after all.

His hair was pulled back into a ponytail, and he wore dark working-man jeans, boots, and a thick flannel shirt, sleeves rolled back to reveal meaty forearms that were pebbled with faint scars. Like knife wounds and burn marks. He was tall, too. He took another sip of his drink, and then slowly set it down onto the table, as if trying not to startle me. His shoulders were subconsciously bunched forward at the sensation of Dean and Mallory standing out of sight behind him, and his peripheral gaze subtly tracked the Guardians as they prowled the room.

"Are you finished trying to frighten me?" he asked in a deep, scratchy baritone, as if overcoming a cold. It wasn't fear. Or, it wasn't *just* fear. His voice was raspy, strained with some unspoken emotion.

"*Trying...*" Mallory chuckled.

I ignored Mallory, and nodded at the man. "Precautions..." The guest nodded back in patient understanding, although obviously not pleased at the situation.

"Understandable."

But I let my face slowly morph into a darker, more aggressive visage as I dimmed both the fireplace and the few lights, casting the room into an even more intimate, foreboding darkness. "I like to cover my bases when it comes to uninvited wizards entering my home," I warned in a low growl.

Some of the Guardians began to purr, as another let out a light, hungry screech, like a velociraptor from those *Jurassic Park* movies. The sudden crackling of Mallory's spear punctuated my next words.

"So why don't you tell me, oh nameless wizard, why a member of the Academy would dare interrupt my dinner…"

CHAPTER 6

*T*he man blinked back, eyes hard. "Rufus. The name's Rufus. And you can cut the theatrics. I already know you're powerful. It's why I'm here," he growled defiantly. "If you're going to kill me, just do it already. Then at least I'll know you're just like the blood-sucking Academy, despite your recent activities implying you're *oh, so different* from those cowards."

He took a long drink of his scotch, slamming it back down as he panted, eyes smoldering with hatred at mention of the Academy, the ruling body of wizards. And no friends of mine.

I watched him. "Blood-sucking. Cowards… Explain."

"I came here to ask for your help. The Academy wouldn't use me to wipe their ass if it indirectly resulted in saving my life."

I burst out laughing, eliciting a small smile from him. "Well, that's an image. And why would the Academy hold you in such high esteem?"

"They don't tolerate dissenters. The bastards." I nodded, motioning for him to continue. "How much do you know about chimeras?" he asked, tone guarded.

Mallory's spear crackled loudly as if he had ratcheted it up a notch. "Well, feck me sideways!" he blurted.

I glanced at him. "Tone it down back there or join us. Dean, can you get me my drink? And a *real* drink for Rufus? I'm sure Mallory chose from the bottom shelf when offering a beverage."

Mallory grumbled a bit, but finally complied, choosing to occupy a chair to my right between the guest and myself. Dean left, but was back moments later with the hallowed Macallan. He poured a fresh glass for Rufus, which Mallory didn't approve of, judging by the glare he shot at the guest. The man took a cautious sip, but I noticed that he waited until after I had taken a drink first. He was wary. And clever. Even looking out for poison.

As if I would ever poison someone.

Rufus' face morphed into a look of pure astonishment as his gaze darted to the glass in his hands. Mallory grinned in response to Rufus' reaction. The wizard actually blushed, barely hiding his smile.

"What in the hell is *this*?" he asked eagerly, turning his eyes to the bottle in Dean's fist. "Sixty-two-year!" he exclaimed. "I didn't know they made such a thing..." he took another sip, savoring it now.

I cleared my throat. "Thank Mallory. He doesn't tell me where he keeps it."

"I wouldn't either!" the man smiled. Mallory grinned lightly, the sparks winking out from his lightning bolt to reveal a regular spear. He propped it up against the chair and leaned back, crossing his ankles. He wore tight, pressed slacks and a wool vest, a brilliant tie underneath. His neat, thick beard rested on the tie's knot, and he looked fresh out of a GQ photo shoot. His Johnston Murphy shoes gleamed as I allowed the fire and lighting to return to normal. I unbuttoned my own coat as I leaned back, crossing my legs too.

"So, chimeras... bloodthirsty monsters. Trifecta of death. Head and body of a horned goat, chest of a lion, and venomous snake for a tail. When one creature dies, one of the others takes over. Stab the lion in the face, and the beast falls to all fours, thrashing at you like a carnivorous goat. The lion head breathes fire, snake spits venom," I waved a hand, "a bunch of other nasty rumors, but I've never seen one. What about it? Is there one terrorizing my city?"

The man tightened his lips. "Not exactly."

I frowned. "And why wouldn't the Academy help you take out a chimera? I seem to remember them taking out nests of them throughout history. Quite ruthlessly, actually. This sounds right up their alley."

The man responded with a pained look.

"Wait, are you asking me to help you *protect* one of these monsters?" I asked in disbelief. "No way. Those things are out of control. Untamable. You're better off letting the Academy handle it. I'm definitely not in their good graces. I don't need any other reasons for them to be gunning for me. The Grandmaster especially doesn't need any other reasons to hate me."

"She's... just a kid." Mallory looked as if one of his lightning spears had struck him in the nuts.

I sympathized with him.

I stared at Rufus. "Well, fuck me..." I finally answered, expelling a long breath. I couldn't turn down a... "Wait, did you say, *kid*? As in, *human*?" I asked, frowning.

He nodded back, face pleading. "Yes, chimeras are *weres*, just like your dragons."

I stared back, at a loss for words. "Great, you're telling me you want me to protect a..." I almost couldn't say it without shouting in disbelief, "were-chimera from... wait, who are we protecting this violent little child from again?"

He took a long drink. "Well, that's where it gets complicated. We'll be *protecting* her from the Academy." He took another long drink, and I found myself doing the same as I began to ponder the horrible consequences this discussion would lead to.

But wait, there's more...

"First, we'll need to *rescue* her from the Beast Master."

The glass shattered in my fist and Mallory jumped to his feet, spear suddenly in his fist again, crackling with power as he stared out the only window not obscured by a curtain, as if expecting an attack at any moment.

So, Mallory had heard of him too.

"The Beast Master is in St. Louis?" I stated, incredulous.

Rufus nodded back, face grave. "Yes."

"Feck this, Master Temple," Mallory muttered. "He's bloody certifiable."

I was nodding. "From what I've heard, that's not giving him enough credit." Dean delivered me another drink, using a wet rag to scoop up the larger pieces of glass. Blood liberally poured down my arm, staining my shirt, although the wound wasn't life-threatening or anything.

Rufus cleared his throat and I glanced at him. "Need my help?" he offered cautiously, staring at my injured hand. I frowned down at it, considering his offer. Mallory growled warningly, but I nodded. Let the wizard feel a bit helpful, extend my trust. I had, after all, terrorized him up until this point.

It was a good thing Gunnar hadn't been here. Or half the other guests at my table. They would all be prime candidates for the Beast Master. The monster collector.

Rufus cautiously approached, extending his scarred hands towards my palm. Mallory stepped closer in warning, his spear crackling with hunger. I waved him off, staring at Rufus, ready to kill him if he did anything untoward. Not that he could, really, thanks to the Guestright situation.

Not if he wanted to continue breathing.

Still...

Rufus was almost touching my hand when the door burst open in an explosion of splinters – one of the hinges flying into the room to strike a Guardian in the beak – as a huge white werewolf flew through the opening to strike Rufus in the chest, knocking him into a bookshelf. He struck with a solid *thud*, head smacking into the wood hard enough to instantly render him unconscious. Gunnar gripped the man's throat between massive jaws, growling murderously. A small black werewolf padded into the room, yawning lazily as she assessed the scene. She trotted over to me, curling up at my feet and settling down contentedly. Raego strode in, swirling his drink in the glass as he nodded politely at Mallory. "Gentlemen."

Tory walked in behind him, eyes a forest green as she studied each person with a calm, detached look on her face. The Reds entered behind her, in full dragon form, claws scratching the marble floor as they flanked her.

"So, who's the new guy?" Alucard drawled, petting the dragon's scaly neck to the right of Tory.

I rolled my eyes in frustration and concern for Rufus. "Thanks, guys, but we're fine here. Although I think Gunnar just killed my *guest*." Then the severity of those words hit me. Shit. A *guest* had been harmed in my home. Now that I probed deeper into my power, I noticed a huge vacuum that was suddenly inaccessible to me. Gunnar attacking Rufus had indirectly made me break Guestright. He and Ashley wore *family* runes on their wrist – to help them control their ability to shift at whim – so by extension, they were part of Chateau Falco, too.

Part of my family.

And Gunnar had broken a promise I had made to a guest.

I needed to fix this, promptly, without harming Rufus, and hopefully somehow earning his forgiveness for the misunderstanding.

Gunnar growled in response, carefully loosening his stranglehold on the unconscious wizard. Mallory looked pleased, grunting approval at the army that had saved me from being healed. "Little crowded in here. Why don't we head to my office? I think we have something to talk about with the guest you guys almost killed."

Gunnar stared back at me with his icy werewolf gaze, and I shivered. What was it that made his glare so intense lately? Was it an Alpha thing or was it merely because he only had one eye?

"Gunnar smelled your blood and took off like a Beagle," Alucard offered, helpfully.

The werewolf growled in response, and Alucard grinned. I frowned at the vampire. "Shouldn't you have been the first one to smell blood?"

Alucard's smile disappeared in a blink, eyes growing distant, but he managed a shrug before silently exiting the room. Mallory picked up Rufus' body. "I'll take care o' the wee lad. After ye, Master Temple."

Everyone turned to me expectantly.

"Whoever knows where my Macallan is, go grab another bottle of it." I counted the people around me, knowing they would all want drinks after hearing this. "Two bottles." Then I left the room to head to my office. I needed to give everyone an update on the newest monster in town, one who was legendary for kidnapping monsters of all flavors. Monsters exactly like my friends.

And how we were going to go poke a stick in his eye to save an equally dangerous chimera.

From my good friends, the Academy, the strongest wizards on the block.

CHAPTER 7

I sat behind my desk, pondering my friends, and considering the reactions they were likely to have at Rufus' request for our help. Death and Achilles sat near the fire, conversing lightly. Eae had taken Greta home after things went south, fearing for her safety.

Big chicken.

Dean stood unobtrusively near a bookshelf, awaiting any requests my guests may have had. He had told me that Midas and Tomas had also taken the hint that it was time to leave. Gunnar taking off like a rocket in the middle of dinner, right after I had gone to meet a guest, had soured the festive mood of our elaborate Friendsgiving dinner, and I could tell it annoyed Dean to have been so close to normalcy – only to have it dashed to pieces by an uninvited guest.

Mallory stood behind my desk, glaring at everything and nothing, like a bodyguard.

Which he was.

And he looked even less pleased whenever his gaze settled on Rufus. On the other hand, Dean *did* look somewhat pleased at how everyone at least had drinks in their hands, and that the Chateau was effectively entertaining guests again after such a long hibernation. Even if the mood had been muted. It was his livelihood as my Butler. And he took his responsibility very seriously. Seeing everyone content, he nodded at me. "I will leave you to your business, Master Temple. If anyone needs anything, I will be cleaning up with Miss Othello in the kitchen. Just use the intercom." He pointed at the wall, and then left the room.

My palm throbbed lightly, but it wasn't bothersome. It had already stopped bleeding, and was now crusting over. I would worry about it later.

The monsters sat before my desk, padded chairs pulled up to seat everyone comfortably. Ashley was still in wolf form, nestled up on the floor in front of Gunnar, who had shifted back to his human form. Raego stood off in the shadows beside Alucard, watching, not speaking. Every now and then, the Dragon King glanced at his watch, as if debating whether or not it was time to leave. Dean had mentioned something about him having business to attend to, but I hadn't really been paying attention, other than the fact that he was going to make an appearance at the dinner.

Alucard simply looked bored, idly picking at his canines.

The Reds sat on either side of Tory, two judgmental teenage girls. Which was almost more intimidating than their dragon forms.

So, Rufus had awoken to find himself surrounded by my friends, a crew of monsters who had no mercy or sympathy on their faces. In fact, they had quite the opposite look.

"Why don't we start from the beginning? My friends smelled blood and reacted understandably. Thank you for the quick response," I nodded at my friends, "but he was under my protection as an honored guest." I turned to Rufus. "My apologies for that. They meant only to protect me. They didn't know you were a guest."

Rufus nodded tightly, injury now healed thanks to Mallory using his mysterious powers to remove the large knot on the back of his head. It had taken some forceful conversation to get my bodyguard to obey my request. I wasn't quite sure what Mallory was, and had been politely encouraged not to pry. So, I hadn't. For the time being. But the day would soon come when I could no longer stand in ignorance. He had juice. And he worked for me as a bodyguard of sorts. I needed to know his story. Despite any agreements he had made with my father. "I think everyone needs to hear what you told me. Please." I leaned back, motioning for him to proceed.

"Yes, well. There's a truly vicious creature in town. One who kidnaps Freaks and uses them for his own purposes. He primarily focuses on children, likely finding it easier to control them, break them. But I've also heard it on good authority that he has no problem taking on full-grown Freaks."

Gunnar frowned. "And what does he do with his victims? Murder? Ransom?"

Rufus frowned. "No. He kidnaps these children to use in his colosseum. A fighting arena. To the death. He sells… a form of entertainment to certain groups. They hire his menagerie of Freaks to battle each other to the death during certain rituals, celebrations, or feasts. He's quite… sought out."

Gunnar looked absolutely disgusted. "How many Freaks are we talking about?"

Rufus shrugged. "Two-dozen? More? Who knows? As many as he wants. He likes to collect different kinds of Freaks so that the fights are truly… memorable." He rubbed his fingers, indicating *money*. "His M.O. is to abduct three Freaks in each city he visits. Leading up to his show. To replenish his… inventory."

Gunnar was frowning, but Alucard beat him to it. "Wait, you're trying to tell us that one man can control more than two-dozen Freaks? Simultaneously? That isn't possible. They would team up and overwhelm him."

Rufus smiled sadly. "That's why he takes children. He… breaks them. Not their flavor of Freak, but the *child itself…*"

Tory gasped, instinctively reaching out for the two teenagers, the Reds, who sat on either side of her chair, clutching her knees. The girls looked scared, but I noticed a faint glint of defiance in their eyes. I spoke up, backing Rufus' story before emotions ran wild. "I've heard of him before. He's called the Beast Master, and just to be clear, it's rumored – from reputable sources – that even if all his… *pets* were adults, he could control them just as easily. He simply chooses children so that he can raise them in the ring. A life of violence. Makes for better entertainment, and why he receives top dollar." I let that sink in for a few moments. "So, for example, he could walk into this room and have you all eating out of the palm of his hand. Easily." Sounds of protest erupted, but I ignored them, turning to Rufus with an arched brow. "Do I exaggerate?"

He shook his head. "Even the Justices stand wary of him."

That shut everyone up.

Sure, we had nut-tapped the Academy Justices a few times and come out on top, but we still respected their ability. Hell, I had accidentally kidnapped their leader once, and I was still concerned about their impending retaliation. More so, now. To hear that even they feared the Beast Master put things into stark, crystal-clear perspective.

Tory spoke. "Okay, he's in town, and he can control Freaks. What is your involvement in the matter?" she asked, tone serious, her old cop skills rising to the surface. Her eyes seemed to grow darker, a lush, deep green, and I felt a power begin to enshroud her. Which was not an old cop skill of hers, but an entirely new ability. An ability to persuade.

Rufus shook his head angrily, scooting his chair back from her. "What *are* you? Get out of my head!" He was breathing heavily, scowling at her. His glare shot my way. "Guestright, you say? Pah!"

Tory looked embarrassed. "Please. I'm sorry. I don't quite know how to control myself yet. It's an ability that I'm only just learning. Truly. I meant no harm. It just… happens sometimes. When I'm particularly emotional." She shrugged sadly. "Kids. Maternal instincts…"

Rufus eyed her warily before grunting. "Just keep it to yourself," he warned. She nodded, holding out her hands, placating. "They took a girl…"

"A Freak, you mean…" Alucard drawled, fingering his vampire canines as if digging for a piece of flesh stuck there from the last wizard he had eaten.

Rufus nodded. "Aye. But still a child."

"Well, what is she? I'm *dying* to know," his fangs glistened.

I'd had enough. The situation was bad enough without him snarking off. I had a real problem right now. My power was drastically affected by my accidental breach of Guestright. Rufus had been attacked. In my home. Despite our silent pact. I needed Rufus on my side, not alienated further.

"Seriously, Count Sparkula, no one thinks a vampire's clever usage of the word *dead* is as funny as you seem to think. Especially not after what happened with you and Tory…" I added, growing impatient. I needed everyone to pay attention. Hearing that a child was involved had hit me deep in the core, and I had lost my usual sense of humor. Also, I needed to rectify the broken Guestright, and Alucard's hostility was only making that harder, even if he had the best intentions. Simply put, Rufus was not one of us, and Alucard was reminding him of this. The problem was, Alucard wasn't considering the full implications of what had already happened thanks to their intervention to save me upon sensing my blood.

Alucard huffed, scowling at me briefly. "Fine, Little Brother. I can see my rapier wit isn't appreciated among Plebeians. I'm going to go get some sun," he muttered under his breath. The Reds shot me withering glares, but I ignored them after months of practice. Teens. One could only hope to

37

weather the storms of their wrath. Rationality was a concept that applied only to other creatures, not to the two who believed themselves to be the center of the universe.

Rufus looked entirely confused as the once-vampire stormed out. "I don't get it. Was he joking about getting some sun? And why did he call you Little Brother? You're no vampire, I can see that much."

I sighed. "The name is a term of endearment. The rest is a long story. Our vampire friend made a poor choice, and, well, I'll let him share with you if he wants to. Not my place to talk about it."

His gaze tightened. "That won't work. I'm asking for your *help*. I want to make sure I'm not asking for *trouble* instead. This child's life is on the line. What does..." he managed not to laugh, "*Sparkula* have to do with Tory? Did she do something to him? Should I be concerned?"

Tory opened her mouth to answer, but I interrupted her. "I understand your position, Rufus, but that truly is not my place to talk about."

Tory leaned forward. "It's okay, Nate. Thanks to our battle with the Grimms, I now have a new ability to..." her voice trailed off as the answer dawned on her, thinking back on what she had done in recent events. "Well, tame beasts, among other things." she answered, surprising herself at the revelation. I nodded thankfully at her. "Isn't that coincidental?" she added thoughtfully, eyes distant.

"If I didn't know better," Rufus began, looking suddenly wary, "I would seriously consider the possibility that *she* was the Beast Master, or at least in league with him." Tory opened her mouth to argue, but he held up a hand. "Easy, like I said, your reaction to a child in danger put proof to your words. Also, I know the Beast Master is a man. I've seen him. And he doesn't have partners." He shrugged, voicing his next comment neutrally, "And I can see that you are just as in the dark about your power as I am."

She frowned, but gave him a tight nod. Aria squeezed her knee affectionately and Tory smiled down at her, brushing a stray lock of hair from her eyes.

"So, tell them about the kid," I pressed.

He sighed. "A chimera. Technically, a were-chimera. She—"

"Aaand we're done here," Raego's voice cut through Rufus' explanation. I had forgotten he was even here. He was prone to lurking in the shadows, watching, studying, waiting. A lack of social skills did not even brush the surface when describing Raego. I had once considered him quite insane, in fact. But since then, I had met some truly *mad* people. Everyone turned to him, but Achilles had heard the word and stood from his chair to approach.

"Did you say chimera?" Achilles asked slowly.

Rufus nodded. Achilles shook his head in disbelief. "Well, you can consider yourselves fucked. The dragon is right. Those things are nasty. Trust me, a Greek would know."

Rufus' head cocked to the side. "Wait, you're Greek? Where are you from?"

Achilles chuckled. "A country long dead, wizard. Don't worry yourself about it. Just trust me when I say that chimeras are bad news." He shot me a meaningful look, and then turned to walk away.

"He looks familiar..." Rufus said.

I shrugged. "He's one of those foot models. Always showing off the latest shoes. I mean, look at those calves." I pointed at him as he walked away.

"If I was a pair of shoes, I'd want him inside me," Sonya said distractedly, eyes locked on his tight jeans. Then her face flushed as red as her hair when Aria and Death both burst out laughing. "I didn't mean—" she tried. "He just has nice legs, perverts!" she screamed in desperation. Aria managed to console her between fits of laughing snorts. The Heel had momentarily stiffened at the comment, before striding up to Death and punching him in the arm, hard. Anyone else would have stumbled, but Death didn't even quiver.

Rufus was chuckling softly at the teen, not noticing that the man Achilles had just punched hadn't moved a muscle. Instead, his gaze looked forlorn, as if remembering a daughter of his own as he smiled at Sonya. He caught me watching, cleared his throat with mild embarrassment, and then spoke. "I used to work for the Academy. Not as a full-blown Justice, but part of their military arm, nonetheless. We were tasked with taking out a nest of chimeras. We succeeded, but after everyone left, my sole responsibility was to clean up all trace of our presence. A glorified janitor. I... found a child. Three or four years old. Too young to shift, but she was clutching her dead mother. She looked up at me, eyes glistening with confusion, fear, terror, asking me for the answer to her question... *why?*" his voice trailed off, rasping. I heard the Reds intake sharp breaths, murmuring softly to one another in sad tones. "That look destroyed me. I cast a sleeping spell on her just to get her to stop. Not being a warrior, and perhaps a coward, I lied to my officer about it. They had questioned my use of magic, which they had sensed from outside. I told them I had put one to sleep, so that she could die without further pain. They bought it, laughing at my weak stomach. We left, but I returned later that night. And…" he managed to look both ashamed and proud, "took the girl home. I retired from the Academy, telling them that the most recent mission had been too much for me to handle. I was the laughing stock of the Academy for quite some time, but coming home to that sweet orphan, seeing her smile and clutch to me like her savior… well, let's just say that the Academy won't be pleased to hear about my betrayal. As in, an immediate death sentence. And I would do it all over again." His voice was fire at the end.

Tory and the Reds were sobbing softly, clutching each other tightly. Ashley groaned as she stretched, dozing at Gunnar's feet in full wolf form.

"She only recently began shifting, but she isn't violent. Sure, there have been some tough calls, but she's still only a twelve-year-old child. Just like any other *were* learning their lineage." He eyed the Reds meaningfully, and they nodded back, before casting their gazes at the rug on the floor.

"So, how was she kidnapped? If no one knows about her, how did the Beast Master discover her, and why the hell is he in St. Louis?"

His bloodshot eyes lifted to mine. "Well, that's where you come in."

CHAPTER 8

I frowned. "What do you mean, that's where I come in?" I asked.

Rufus eyed each of us. "You and your pals here have caused quite a ruckus in the supernatural community. Took out some Grimms, spat in the Academy's face… allegedly." He flashed me a faint smile. "Word gets out," he explained. I nodded, neither confirming nor denying. Which basically was as good as admitting to it. "Took out a demon. Took over the local werewolf pack. Allied with the Obsidian Son." He pointed a thumb over his shoulder where Raego stood in the shadows. Raego grunted noncommittally. "Just to name a few eventful nights."

I nodded. "As you said. *Allegedly*. But what does that have to do with anything?"

"It's attracted… attention to St. Louis. The Beast Master is always looking for new toys. And you seem to be collecting quite a few specimens lately." His eyes drifted to each face. "Not that I see any of you as specimens, but *he* certainly does. And he doesn't like to share."

This seemed to calm my friends down a bit. A tiny bit.

"He's come here to collect some new pets? And he coincidentally found your girl?"

Rufus nodded. "No one knew about her. Hell, *she* didn't even know her potential until recently."

I waited, there had to be more to the story.

Rufus sighed. "She was volunteering at a soup kitchen. That was the last anyone has seen of her. Of course, no one thinks it's anything other than an Amber Alert." He scowled.

Now that he mentioned it, I had noticed quite an increase in Amber Alerts over the past few days. Now that practically everyone's phones alerted them about one when it happened, it was impossible not to notice. Surely, they hadn't all been Freaks kidnapped by the Beast Master.

And as far as I recalled, almost all of the children had been found. Although, now that I thought about it, I seemed to remember hearing quite a few newsreels where the parents had said something had been… *off* about their children. They had put it all down to stress from the abductions.

But a slimy thought began to creep into my head. I squashed it down. I had enough to deal with as it was. I didn't need to add saving every child in St. Louis to my laundry list.

"What makes you think the Beast Master is behind it, and not that she was simply kidnapped?" I asked with a frown. Gunnar was nodding his agreement. Raego merely folded his arms, still frowning.

Rufus chuckled. "Because any Regular who happened to kidnap her would no longer be breathing. Intense emotions bring about the shift at that age. Instead of an Amber Alert, we would have heard about a murder spree."

Well, that was a good point.

"Pegasus took out one of the first chimeras. Attacked it from above," Death interrupted, shooting me a meaningful look. "The aerial assault was particularly effective," he added.

I frowned at him, knowing what he was getting at. "Yeah, well, Grimm can't fly."

Death shrugged. "Just a fun fact."

Everyone stared at him, wondering if he was joking. But the Horseman had eyes only for me. He was constantly trying to get me to acknowledge my gifts. The job offer his Brothers had offered me. To be a Horseman. Rufus saved me from responding.

"Then there's this." He pulled out a flyer from a pocket, tossing it on the desk. Mallory darted ahead of me, protectively grasping the paper before I could touch it. He hadn't moved for some time, merely watching events unfold, so his sudden motion startled all of us.

"Really, Mallory? I think I'm safe from the deadly postcard," I muttered. "I'm not Alucard."

"It's the small things ye need to look out fer, Laddie," he chided. Studying the paper for a second, he finally handed it over, judging it non-lethal.

I stared down at the flyer. It looked like a *Ringling Brothers* advertisement. Except it cryptically alluded to some beasts that truly weren't possible, and there was no location given for the event three nights from tonight. It simply said, *Inquire through standard channels.*

Which meant the supernatural community.

Achilles was suddenly back at the table, reaching for the flyer.

I handed it over. He grunted after a few seconds. "A bloke dropped off a hundred or so of these at my bar yesterday."

I blinked at him. "Why would he give them to you?"

He shrugged back. "Pretty typical. My clientele attracts all sorts." He eyed me up and down. "You should know."

"Wait, now I know who you are. You're Achi—" Rufus began in disbelief.

"Easy, boy. Don't hurt yourself."

Rufus' eyes darted to me. "He's… that's…" he finally let out a breath. "Christ! No wonder everyone's so nervous about you. Dining with *him* of all people?"

I chose not to mention any of the other names in attendance, fearing his reaction to discover that a Horseman of the Apocalypse stood a dozen feet away. I shrugged in answer, turning to Achilles. "So, your chimera is one victim. Which means I have three days to save two new victims and get the chimera back—"

Rufus cleared his throat, shaking his head. "Three new victims. My girl was taken from Chicago, not St. Louis. I followed the Beast Master here. His thugs chased me off before I could learn their base of operations, so I came straight here."

Mallory's head swiveled to stare out the window in alarm.

Rufus flushed. "No one followed me. I swear. I took the long way." Mallory continued to stare out the window like a sniper.

"Of course," I muttered. "That means I need to save one new kid each night, then take out the Beast Master at his circus…" I said absently, thinking. "Or I can take out the Beast Master early, save your chimera, and hopefully prevent him from taking anymore hostages." Rufus nodded, not catching my sarcasm. "Do you know where this is going down?" I asked Achilles.

He nodded. "Sure. And anyone else who pays the ridiculous cover can also know."

Plans were already spinning in my head, adrenaline filling my veins. I would get to test out my new powers against a truly dangerous foe. I had been practicing, and if I had to admit it, I was kind of eager to see what I could do in a fight. The cane throbbed warmly at my hip, agreeing. "Or you could just tell me," I said to Achilles. He was silent, so I turned back to him. He simply stared back. "Right?"

He shook his head. "Not without payment."

I frowned. "You're kidding. You're going to make me pay you to save a child?"

He shook his head again. "The money doesn't go to me. It goes to him. The Beast Master. And I do need to keep up appearances." I began to argue, but he held up a hand, forestalling me. "I swore an oath. One of those pesky magical ones you can't get around. And if you continue with this mad quest, you're going to need me on the inside in the future." He grunted. "If you *have* a future after this."

I growled under my breath, closing my eyes as I silently argued with the Dark Presence that was suddenly encouraging me to murder Achilles for the information. Forcing him back to silence, I sucked in a deep breath, and opened my eyes to find Achilles staring at me with sudden concern. "I'm fine." He didn't look convinced, and neither did the others, judging by the silent looks I caught in my peripheral.

"You were muttering something."

"I already told you. I'm fine," I snapped. "So, I need to get some money. How much are we talking?"

He told me. And it wasn't standard US currency.

"Okay, wow. I don't think... I don't keep that stuff lying around."

He shrugged. "Let me know when you've got the coin."

I sighed in resignation, wondering how in the hell I would get that type of money on such short notice. I knew my friends couldn't help, even with Gunnar's pet accessory business booming. Because we weren't talking dollars. "Once I get the funds, we have him."

"Right. Fat lot of good that will do you," Achilles muttered. I frowned. "Did you miss the part where he had over two dozen Freaks bound to his will? And that's just counting the prisoners. Not his thugs. Those Freaks he's had under his thrall for so long that he trusts them to work for him without chains."

I slumped in my seat. "Well, sure, we have a few wrinkles to work out, but at least we will know where he'll be."

Achilles growled. "And the crowd of several hundred twisted sons of bitches. The ones who paid good coin to see a bloodbath. Think they'll like you strolling in to crash their party? It will literally be you against hundreds. And don't forget, he hosts events for all types of monsters. Even a mysterious group you've had encounters with in the past, and aren't supposed to talk about. It's fair to guess that some of them will be present." He turned his back on me, muttering angrily to himself as he walked back to Death. I shivered at the thought. He was talking about the Syndicate. The group who had employed the Brothers Grimm. And Rumpelstiltskin. "And forget about the circus," he continued. "You still need to stop him from taking any more kids." The Horseman watched him, murmuring soothing words to the warrior.

Unruffled, I turned back to Rufus. "Ignore him. He's a Negative Nancy. His foot must be bothering him." Rufus blinked, his gaze darting back to Achilles across the room. I turned to find the Myrmidon flashing me a cold smile as he drew a finger across his throat. I grinned back, waving my injured hand at him. "Love you too, Heel."

Raego let out an annoyed breath. "Would you please get that sorted? You're flinging blood flakes everywhere. And we are *not* going to help you on this suicide mission." I glanced at my hand. He was exaggerating, as it was now dried and crusted over, but he had a point. I turned to Mallory, but then hesitated as a thought struck me.

Yes, this would be perfect. Maybe give a little trust to earn a little trust. Negate the breach in Guestright by extending an olive branch.

"Rufus, would you mind healing me?"

Rufus paused for a beat, glancing guardedly at Mallory. "As long as I'm not going to be tackled into another bookshelf or Tased with his lightning stick."

I grinned back. "They'll play nice. Won't you, boys." Grumbles answered me. "See?"

Rufus still looked wary as he leaned forward to take my hand in his palm. He studied the small wounds thoughtfully. "Yes, this isn't bad at all. Just an inconvenience, really."

I felt the warm tingle of magic delve deep into my hand, repairing the damage done, but then the power ratcheted up to a level that was way too intense for a simple healing spell. Then it was gone. I saw the guilty look on Rufus' face before he pulled away, the spell over before I could stop him, especially with my powers weakened due to breaking Guestright earlier. The Dark Presence inside me screamed with an almost feral fury. I slid back in my chair as Mallory jumped atop the table, his crackling lightning spear sizzling against Rufus' neck.

"What have ye done, wizard?" he roared. Gunnar had jumped in front of Ashley, who had woken suddenly at the abrupt chaos. Her confused growl punctuated Mallory's threat.

"I… bound him. No harm. As long as he helps me find my girl," the man admitted.

CHAPTER 9

I gritted my teeth. "Well, isn't this just magical. Trust. Curses. It makes one feel so appreciated," I spat. That hadn't gone as planned. At all.

Rufus carefully pointed a finger at Raego. "He just blatantly said that you weren't going to help. I *have* to protect my girl."

I stared daggers at the man. "And that would be relevant if you had asked *him* for help, not *me*," I shouted back. "Did you think I was just going over plans out loud for the hell of it?"

"Let's just say I press a little harder with my stick. What happens then, wizard?" Mallory growled, a hungry, slightly psychotic gleam in his eyes.

"He loses a significant portion of his power," Rufus answered slowly, careful not to jostle the tip of the spear on his throat.

"Doesn't that sound familiar," I grouched, remembering the Academy's first attack against me. "Let me guess, this lasts three days." Which meant it lined up almost perfectly with the event at the circus.

He blinked. "A little bit longer. Almost four days. How did you guess?"

"It seems the Academy is partial to this particular spell. Tried it on me once before."

Rufus' eyes shot wide open. "Impossible. I invented that spell. None of them are strong enough to duplicate it."

I stared at him, sensing the blockage of power between me and my

47

Maker ability. It was different than the first time. Stronger, but different. For example, this time it was limiting a different type of power. Before, I had been a wizard, a like magic to Rufus' spell. This time, the spell was battling an alien power, a Maker's power. For all of that, it was still doing its intended job. I could sense the reservoir of power, and knew I was limited only to that. And that as it was used up, it would no longer replenish. Until I concluded my end of the bargain.

"They used seven Justices to duplicate it," I answered him. Rufus' eyes grew thoughtful before he finally let out a small nod.

"That might work."

"No, that *did* work. They ended up taking my wizard's power. Luckily, I had a backup plan, and it only expedited the growth of my Maker's ability," I answered cryptically.

"Except they didn't," he said, looking at me as if I had told a joke.

"They didn't *what?*" I whispered, frustrated at his bizarre statement, and ready to kill him for cursing me. Except that would only guarantee my loss of power.

"They didn't take your wizard's power." The room was silent as a tomb. "I mean, sure. For all intents and purposes, it's dead and gone." He held two fingers together, squinting his eyes as he used a high-pitched voice to say, "there's a *teeny* bit left. Just a fragment of a fragment, practically dead and decayed." He watched me curiously. "But it's still there." He seemed to sense the mood in the room, turning from face to face. "Are you saying you didn't know this?"

"Yes. That's exactly what I'm saying." A small part of me had risen up, suddenly excited, only to hear that it was ultimately a bust. As good as dead. My heart was beating faster though, imagining being a wizard again. None of this stupid Maker stuff. I needed to change the topic.

I leveled him with a furious glare. "What happens if I comply, or if I don't?"

"Well, if you don't, you lose your power." I opened my mouth to argue, but he was already shaking his head. "Even though you are a Maker, I was thorough in my research. It would work just as well on you, the dragon, or even Mallory – whatever he is. Doesn't matter the target. I was a bit of a coward," he admitted truthfully. "Not much for battle magic, but this kind of stuff?" he motioned at the situation. "Yeah, I'm *beyond* good." He kept his hands on the arms of his chair, remaining motionless. "And none of this *decaying seed of your power left over* business. It would be gone. Entirely." He wasn't saying it to be rude, just one practitioner critiquing the failed attempt of another practitioner. "But if you help me, the spell evaporates."

"So, you're extorting me to help you rescue a murderous monster, from another murderous monster who would like nothing more than to kidnap my friends, to eventually protect her from yet *another* group of murderous monsters that control every wizard on the planet. By holding my power hostage."

He nodded slowly, face torn. "Yes," he answered, obviously shamed.

I gave him a few seconds. "Are you seeing the flaw yet?" I hissed.

He blinked, not comprehending.

Aria finally piped up, voice full of venom. "He means, you idiot, that you came to him for help because he's powerful." Her shoulders heaved as her eyes began to shift to red, and her fingers became dragon claws. "And the first thing you do is curse him... limiting that *power*..." she hissed. Tory placed a palm on Aria's wrist as the teen took an angry step. Tory's eyes flashed green, and Aria was suddenly back to herself, still shaking with anger, but wearing a confused look on her face. Sonya embraced her in a soothing hug.

Rufus cast his eyes down. "She's very... important to me. I already helped murder her parents. Even if I didn't hold the blade, I was party to it." His eyes grew far away. "I can't fail her again. I had no choice."

"And what about our conversation made you think I wouldn't help?" I all but shouted.

He blinked. "Well, you broke Guestright, and every single one of your allies is warning you against helping me. And they tried to kill me."

My mouth clicked shut. And the series of unfortunate events clicked into place at the same time.

Of course.

There was no way he would have been strong enough to overcome me if Gunnar hadn't broken Guestright by attacking him first. Even with him touching me, he wouldn't have been able to do it without that breach of etiquette. I rounded slowly on Gunnar, who looked suddenly embarrassed. The Dark Presence was screaming inside of me, and I realized I was muttering out loud. But not to argue with it.

To *agree* with it.

"Um, I'm sorry?" he offered with a wince. "Best of intentions?" he clarified, staring at me with an alien look of fear on his face at my incoherent mutterings.

"*Bad* puppy," I snarled, slowly climbing to my feet and taking a threatening step his way.

"Right, Ashley and I need to go for a walk really quick. Catch up later?" And he exploded into wolf form alongside his fiancée, tearing out of the room in a blur of fur. Dean had the unlucky fortune to be stepping back into the room right when the wolves were fleeing the mad Master of the mansion.

They bowled over him with a yelp of surprise, but didn't help him to his feet before disappearing from sight. Which only stoked my anger.

"Some friends," Rufus murmured.

My rage cooled for a brief second as Death crouched over Dean, helping him to his feet. Seeing a little civility helped center me. Death spoke softly into his ear, then leaned back, listening as Dean mumbled a response. The Horseman nodded before guiding him over to Achilles near the fire, and settling him down into a chair. Then he left. I noticed he was carrying a black box with a purple silk bow on it before he disappeared from view. Achilles chuckled softly to himself, shaking his head as he watched the Horseman leave.

As he left, my rage seemed to reignite. I closed my eyes, breathing deeply as I coaxed myself back down, shutting out the alien voice inside of me that was raging for blood. It had been getting stronger lately. I opened my eyes and shot Rufus a scathing look before turning to Mallory. "Bind him, but don't kill him. Put him in the dungeon. I will have questions for him later. Right now, I don't trust myself to be civil. And my to-do list is suddenly full."

Mallory glanced at Raego instead of answering me.

Raego got the hint. "Right. I'll take him down to the dungeons. Hopefully he does something epically stupid so that I can mind-fuck him," the dragon king chuckled darkly.

Sonya piped up. "I haven't seen a good fucking in a while." Tory gasped, and Sonya suddenly realized she had cursed. Then she replayed the rest of the sentence in her head. "I mean, I just want to watch!" she said urgently.

"Not any better, sister." Aria was clutching her knees, gasping with laughter, and Tory looked like she didn't quite know what to do. Which statement to correct.

"I meant, how are we supposed to learn if we can't watch?" Sonya argued.

"You figure it out, child," Achilles chuckled at his double-entendre.

Sonya threw her hands in the air, giving up.

Rufus' face was pale at the exchange.

"I'll join you, lizard," Achilles finally said, climbing to his feet. "The magic man seemed interested in Greek history. Perhaps I can share the... *finer points* with him," he enunciated. "I need to get back to the bar anyway." Dean, apparently recovered from his tumble, also stood.

Mallory turned to me, so I nodded. "Fine. I'm going to go get some fresh air. Maybe hunt a hound or two," and I stormed out of the room, ignoring the looks from Achilles and Dean.

"He has a dungeon here?" I heard Aria whisper to Tory. I couldn't tell if it was eagerness or disgust in her voice. I didn't care.

There was a pause before she answered, and I was almost out the door. "This is a dangerous place, child. And Nate Temple is a dangerous man. Just because he is our friend, we mustn't forget..." I ignored the rest of her answer, my mind a furious tumble of rage as I left the room to step outside. I very deliberately did not touch the cane at my hip.

CHAPTER 10

I continued mumbling dark profanities under my breath as I stormed through the halls of Chateau Falco, my vision faintly pulsing blue, as it sometimes did when my passion began to overrule my reason. Or when my magic was dangerously close to cutting loose. It happened more often now, thanks to – what I had decided to call – the Dark Presence riding shotgun in my sword cane. Except the dark influence wasn't entirely restrained by my cane any longer. I was finding myself more amiable to its influence, even when I wasn't consciously choosing to do so. Which meant the cane wasn't as good of a defense as I had originally thought. And the blue vision was much more erratic now. I could be just as crazy without my world turning blue. I needed to learn more about my powers, which meant I needed Ichabod to hurry his ass up and get back from his training session…

With Indie…

I growled, anger rising back up at the sudden emotion. I was glad I had stowed my sword cane in my rooms, realizing that if that darker voice inside of me said just the right thing, right now I was liable to listen…

And might eagerly oblige the violent little psycho.

I took a deep breath, closing my eyes as I stepped out onto the roof. I had discarded my jacket on a random chair before heading up here. I absorbed the cool air in hopes that it would calm my mood.

"Of course, you can't cut loose with your magic and burn everything to ashes. That would be melodramatic."

I pondered my statement, and decided that since I was all alone on the roof, it was entirely acceptable to argue with myself out loud. "Although justified, it's still an overreaction. And cutting loose now would only open the floodgates about Indie. She's gone, which makes you trigger-happy, and outside of the Dueling Grounds, cutting loose here could be a potentially fatal idea. For everyone. Especially now that you're cursed."

"But *fun*."

I nodded, eyes still closed. "Fun, possibly. But after Doofus zapping you with his spell, you could very quickly burn up all of your reserves, leaving you defenseless when you go to save the girl."

"From the bloodthirsty circus Freaks."

"Yes, them." A faint smile tinged my lips. "This is helping. You're a good listener."

Someone cleared their throat and my heart fell into my stomach as my eyes shot open, frantically searching for the source of the sound. My fists crackled with raw, violet electricity, my fingers throbbing at the arctic chill suddenly coating my skin. And the world pulsed blue as if I was suddenly wearing tinted glasses.

I saw the cause of the sound, and blinked.

Alucard lay on a lawn chair, Ray-Ban sunglasses on his face, clad in only a pair of silk boxers, his clothes folded neatly beside the chair. He was propped up on an elbow, watching me with concern. I blinked again, looked up at the noonday sun, then back at him, my jaw now hanging open.

"You're sun tanning," I stated, the blue tint to the world fading away from my vision.

He pulled off his sunglasses. "You're talking to yourself. Literally. Full-blown conversation with responses, snark, and logical reasoning. Either that, or there is someone else up here with you who sounds a hell of a lot like you. Because I don't think you were telling me that *I* was a good listener. You didn't even know I was here."

"You're sun tanning," I repeated, dumbly.

He sighed as if giving up on me, and slid the sunglasses onto his nose before leaning back into his chair, folding his arms above his head. His chair was near the edge of the flat roof, which my mother had also sometimes used for sun tanning when she didn't want to waste her valuable time heading to the Olympic-sized pool on the grounds. I strode closer, staring in amazement as his skin literally did seem to sparkle, albeit faintly. Almost as if he was simply wearing some of that shimmery women's lotion. I pinched his skin, wondering if it really was some kind of lotion.

"Hey!" he grunted, glaring at me. "What the hell?"

"You really do sparkle. Just like—"

"Say it and die," he hissed.

That made me smile. "You know this is going to end poorly for you, right? I absolutely cannot keep my mouth shut about this. You really are Count Sparkula." He stared at me. "You know, Count Dracula, and Sparkles. I combined the words." He didn't react. "It's funnier when I explain it all out like that," I added.

He groaned, letting out a final jerk of his head, accepting his fate. "So, what rattled that last bolt free?" he asked after a pause. "The one barely keeping your sanity in check. The one that is apparently forever lost now." He slid his sunglasses down to peer over the frame at me. "In case I'm being too obtuse, I'm telling you that you're bat-shit nuts." He slid the glasses back in place and leaned back, absorbing the frigid sunlight as if it was a balmy summer day.

"Scoot," I commanded, kicking the chair in polite encouragement for him to quit taking up all six feet of the lounge chair.

He tumbled off the chair with a curse, rolling a few paces, and I realized my toes throbbed a little where I had kicked the chair.

Okay, maybe I had given him a little more than *polite encouragement*.

"Sorry," I mumbled. "Think I'm a bit unhinged."

"I'll say," he grouched, picking up his sunglasses and inspecting them for damage as he climbed to his feet. "What the hell happened down there? Did Indie show up and confess her undying love for Dean or somethin—" His comment was abruptly cut short with an entirely new sound from his throat. "*GACK!*"

His bare feet were frantically kicking my shins, and I realized I was holding him by the throat over the edge of the roof. And the purple power was back, crackling around my fist as it seared his skin like bacon. His eyes were wide, but I felt entirely calm. So calm that I carefully lowered him back to the safety of the roof and took a few slow steps back, shaking my head as I forcibly released my power. A faint burned ring in the shape of my hand circled his throat, but it quickly began to heal. I looked up at the sun, then back down to see it striking his flesh, watching as it knit back together right before my eyes.

"You're like Superman," I murmured more to myself.

"You're like Lex Luthor mixed with the Mad Hat—" his face paled. "The Scarecrow," he corrected, eyeing me warily. "What the fuck was that? You really are bat-shit nuts!"

I nodded guiltily. "Perhaps. Short fuse."

"*No* fuse," he clarified, eyes fiery. He took a few deep breaths before sitting back down in the chair, motioning for me to join him. "Tell Count Sparkula your problems," he offered in a resigned growl.

I smiled faintly. "Yeah, that's gonna stick." He rolled his eyes, and I told him what had happened downstairs.

He was silent for a long time before answering. "That sucks incredibly hard."

I nodded, idly studying the grounds around Chateau Falco. "Tell me about it."

"Well, Gunnar is an idiot."

I shrugged, letting out a long breath. "Yeah, but how could he have known? He smelled blood, and reacted. In most cases, it would be better to react than to play it cool. Blood outside the body usually isn't a good thing." I glanced at him. "At least I know *I* don't prefer it."

Alucard's fangs flashed instinctively at the mention of blood, but he looked embarrassed as he snapped them back into place. I knew for a fact that blood literally held no appeal for him any longer. I had heard the term *Daywalker* applied to him from someone who would likely know. But neither of us knew exactly what that signified, and his body had spent a long time reacting to the thought of blood. Kind of like Pavlov's dog. *Hear bell, start salivating.*

Or, *mention blood, turn into bloodsucking monster.*

"Don't take this away from me." He leaned over to his clothes, placing his glasses down as he fumbled with his pants. Expensive glasses safe, he finally turned back to me, face a grin. "Cyclops is an idiot. Your sanity literally cracked as a direct result of his actions. Say it."

I grinned, repeating the words.

He closed his eyes, as if relishing the words. Then a tinny voice interrupted the silence. "*Cyclops is an idiot. My sanity literally cracked as a direct result of his actions.*" I blinked, staring down at the source of the sound.

Alucard gripped a pen in his fist, as if willing to protect it from all dangers in the world. Like Gollum with the One Ring. His eyes danced with glee and I burst out laughing.

"You *recorded* me?" He nodded eagerly. I patted him on the back, instantly recalling that he was practically naked. Which was weird since I was wearing my dress shirt and slacks, sans coat. It was a hetero-man rule – two men had to be in identical states of dress to embrace. I cleared my throat. "You're picking up my bad habits." I grinned, flicking my gaze at the pen.

He nodded. "It's the only way to keep treading water around you."

I was silent for a time, gazing out at the rather impressive view of the Chateau's estate. I had done this many times with my parents. Simply absorbing our beautiful home. Alucard followed my gaze, sighing. "Pretty cool place, huh?" I said.

He nodded. "I'll say. You're a pretty lucky guy, Nate. Never forget that."

I murmured my agreement as my eyes continued to rove the property, finally coming to rest on the gargantuan silvery white tree that now stood near the gardens. Where we had battled the Brothers Grimm. And where Indie had died and been brought back. The tree had torn free from the earth, shooting well over a hundred feet into the air to mark her grave. I still didn't understand what that symbolized, but knew there had to be more to the story than that the sprites had done it as an honor to Indie. Alucard's eyes followed mine, and I heard a soft intake of breath.

He opened his mouth to say something, but I cut him off, fearing he was about to say something about Indie and ruin my mood. "Thanks, Sparkula. I think my head's clear enough to not murder everyone downstairs."

Alucard closed his mouth, nodding silently as he watched me, his features now a sad attempt at masking the questions bubbling underneath. "No problem. I'll be down shortly. I'm just going to sit here for a few more minutes. Need to juice up, since you stupidly agreed to help the extortionist wizard. And turned my neck into bacon." But he was smiling. I grunted, turned my back, and headed towards the door leading inside. I heard the press of a button behind me, followed by the recording of me blaming my mental breakdown on Gunnar. I rolled my eyes as I heard Alucard chuckling to himself mirthlessly.

Then I heard him press the replay button.

I strode inside, feeling marginally better. "Right, time to go figure some stuff out," I murmured as the door began to shut behind me. "Nothing's going to mess with me this time. I'm ready. One with my mind. At peace. Cool, calm, and collected..." I murmured in false encouragement to myself.

I heard Alucard hiss in alarm, and then a powerful blow to my shoulder sent me tumbling down the stairs and into the hallway below. My forehead skidded across the wooden floor with a loud *screech* to finally hammer into the leg of a side table. A vase wobbled and tipped over, dumping a million gallons of water onto my face. I gasped in surprise, jumping to my feet and whirling in a blur, ready to fight back.

The vase was floating before me, and my hands instinctively knocked it away to shatter on the floor. Barbie, the silver sprite who had helped me defeat the Grimms, hovered in the air before me, all of a foot tall, cute as a button, and a tiny frown on her face.

As usual, she was gloriously naked.

"Hey! I saved it. Why did you knock it back down to the ground?" She snapped angrily. She folded her arms, only managing to emphasize her breasts. She was a sex sprite, so I was entirely sure that she did it on purpose, using the motion to lift them up for better view.

I was distantly concerned that the Dark Presence hadn't reacted in any way. Things like this usually brought him to the forefront of my mind, screaming that everyone needed to die by fire or something particularly violent. He must have been napping.

A similar-sized sprite flitted about beside her, but this one was an aged crone, reminding me of a piece of old driftwood. Her skin, wings, and clothing were entirely black, like dark ink. I stared at them. "You!"

"Us," they responded in unison, cocking their heads curiously. Barbie turned to her inky compatriot. "Is this perhaps a mortal game where we shout pronouns back and forth?"

The aged black sprite shrugged, tapping her lips thoughtfully. "If so, I've never heard of it. And don't understand the point of such a game. But it makes sense, in an idiotic mortal fashion. Yet another useless pastime."

I snapped my fingers to get their attention. They snapped back. "Perhaps he's trying to communicate with us," the old sprite stared at me quizzically.

Barbie nodded. "Yes, I've heard of this one. I think they call it *shah-rayds*."

"You almost killed me!" I finally shouted.

"Perhaps you should pay more attention," Barbie snapped.

"Yes, we did call out your name." The crone frowned. "We did call out his name, didn't we?"

Barbie nodded in response, studying me with a frown. "I'm sure we did. Almost sure. Yes, we most likely did." I blinked at them, imagining a fly swatter in my mind before quickly vanquishing the thought. After all, with my Maker power, I could literally do such things and they would pop into existence.

Most of the time. But I didn't dare waste my now-limited powers on such a trivial action.

"Unless we didn't." Barbie amended. She swept closer, right up into my face and prodded me with a silver finger. "We're not here for you. So maybe we *didn't* call out your name. What do you have to say about *that?*" she snapped.

"Jesus, calm down. If you're not looking for me, why did you almost kill me?" I finally answered, deciding it wasn't doing my patience any favors to sit here and argue with the Lilliputians.

"We are looking for the conduit. The pretty one."

I tapped my lips feigning a thoughtful look. Payback time. "I know where the ugly conduit is, but not the pretty one," I replied, deadpan.

Barbie scowled at me, weighing my words. "I don't want the ugly one. I was perfectly clear. I want the pretty one."

I shrugged. "Then I cannot aid you."

"Impossible mortals. Honestly, you would think they would make more sense sometimes."

Before I could respond, the two sprites sailed past me, shouting Tory's name. I cursed under my breath. If they knew the name of the person they wanted, why hadn't they simply said so? Damn fairies. Still, I wasn't exactly optimistic about their sudden arrival and their sudden interest in Tory.

CHAPTER 11

I tore after the pixies, muttering silently in my mind, *I don't believe in fairies.*

But I didn't dare say it aloud. Just in case. I didn't want them falling dead, after all. Not really. I heard Alucard pounding down the stairs after me, urgently shouting my name as he struggled to pull his pants on while running. I shouted encouragement for him to hurry, but didn't slow down for him.

Shouts of alarm burst out from the office as the pixies zipped through the open doorway. I followed them inside to find everyone on edge, fangs, claws, and guns out, ready for war at the sudden intrusion. Luckily, no one had actually tried to kill anyone yet. I held out my hands in what I hoped look like a *wait* gesture. I did a quick scan of the room, checking for attendance, and who was the most likely to be in danger if things went south. The sprites were tiny, but they had *juice.*

Mallory stood near the wall by the massive window behind the desk, watching, waiting, looking ready to break something as he clenched and unclenched his fists repeatedly. I knew his lightning spear was readily available, even if it was currently unseen. It could do that. Dean, Raego, and Achilles had escorted Rufus to the dungeon and had not returned.

But Gunnar and Ashley *had* returned, and stood close enough to the doorway that they could leave in a heartbeat if I still seemed to have their names on my Most Wanted List. But I didn't have time to concern myself with them.

The sprites hovered before Tory. The Reds were hunkered down, ready to pounce, but Tory was holding her hands out to calm them. Othello sat stiffly in one of the chairs, having returned from her kitchen clean-up in my absence. She probably hadn't ever seen a fairy before, and I noticed that she was clutching the box I had seen Death holding. A gift? The Huntress leaned casually against the far wall, now back in her typical tight-fitting, hunting leathers, eyes glittering as she watched the spectacle. She had come back from her brief hiatus at dinner.

"Stop!" I commanded.

"Stop what?" Barbie asked without turning to me.

"Oh, don't bother with him. His head is cracked. I heard it from the Daywalker outside."

"Ah, that's right." Barbie replied, as if suddenly remembering.

"Okay, I'm here. You're all safe now." Alucard muttered, bursting in the room after me. It still annoyed me that vampires didn't typically get winded from exhaustion when exerting themselves. "What the hell happened to your *face?*" he asked me, alarmed. I idly touched the red skin on my forehead with a scowl. It stung. He shook his head. "Never mind. Now, what the hell is going on?" he said, scanning the room for danger. He saw the sprites surrounding Tory and pointed a threatening finger at them. "You!" he shouted.

"Us!" they shouted back, then burst into high-pitched squeals of laughter. I decided I was going to call the black one *Inky*. Barbie smiled at Inky with a knowing look. "See? It really is a game. We'll practice later so that we can best these mortal swine." With that, they turned to Tory, faces and voices animated. "You mustn't use your powers," they said in unison.

Tory blinked. "What?"

Barbie zipped closer, tapping her head with a silver finger. "Not cracked, just dim." She zipped back up beside Inky and focused on Tory again, speaking slowly. "You mustn't use your power. The power of our sister."

Tory blinked. "Okay. I can try."

"Do or do not. There is no *try.*"

"Star Wars? Really?" Othello gasped in astonishment.

"Okay!" Tory exclaimed in frustration. "Perhaps you could explain it to my *dim* mortal mind. Why mustn't I use the powers your sister gifted me."

"Oh, this one's not dim. She's *clever*," Barbie grinned.

"Yes, it is why our sister gifted her the power."

"That, and the conduit was missing an arm."

"Perhaps. She did always have sympathy for wounded beasts."

"But everyone was wounded that night, so perhaps our sister was wise beyond her years."

"Pah, wisdom. What good did it do her?" Inky snarled.

Barbie nodded in agreement. "Sympathy is for the weak. Grammarie is a strong gift. More than she would give to a wounded beast."

Tory's face was growing dark with impatience, and her eyes began to flash a deep green. Barbie shrieked. "That! Stop it. Right now!" She threw a fistful of silver dust at Tory, getting it in her eyes and sending her into a coughing fit.

"Hey!" I yelled, suddenly terrified that they had harmed Tory.

"Straw! Grass! Quit your braying, mortal mule!" Inky was suddenly in my face, slapping me violently. It felt like a swarm of wasps stinging me, and I began to shout back, thrashing about wildly in an attempt to protect my eyes. She was gone before I could make contact, and the Huntress burst out laughing. I scowled at her for good measure.

"*Hee-haw!*" she bellowed at my annoyed look, laughing all over again.

Before I could respond, Tory growled, rubbing furiously at her eyes. "What the hell is wrong with you! You just bedazzled me."

The sprites shared a look, seeming to ask each other, *what the hell is the mortal wench babbling about?*

Tory finally wiped enough of the fairy dust from her eyes, which luckily had not harmed her, only infuriating her. "Now, what the hell is wrong with me using the powers your sister gifted me?"

"Because the Queens are looking for you," they answered in tandem.

The silence was a physical presence in the room. You could have heard, well...

A fairy fart.

CHAPTER 12

*O*thello spoke softly. "Queens?" she asked. The Huntress had grown suddenly tense. And Mallory stood so still that he almost appeared to be a statue. Which couldn't be good. The Reds now looked more relaxed, seeing that they weren't actually under attack from the fairies. But they didn't look pleased at the conversation. And they kept shooting thoughtful looks my way. Equal parts wariness and interest. I wasn't sure what that was about, other than maybe they still held a grudge for me being rude to Alucard. Or because I had blabbed about my dungeon.

Barbie noticed the Huntress' reaction. "She understands. Tell the mortal swine in common speak. Make them see." She danced furiously about the Huntress' head, plucking at her shoulders and shoving her forward a step. Surprisingly, the Huntress took this very calmly, eyes distant as she was prodded forward. The Huntress had ties to the Fae. I wasn't sure how, exactly, but the first time I had met her she had commanded a Gruffalo from the Fae realm.

Yes. A real fucking Gruffalo. Like the children's book, but scarier.

A lot scarier.

"The Queens... of Fae—" she began.

Inky quickly interrupted. "No names, please."

The Huntress nodded. "Right. The Queens of Winter and Summer. They command the Fae in a unique partnership. They split the year in half, then pass on the responsibility to the other during the solstices." She turned to the sprites. "They are after Tory for using her new powers?"

The sprites raced towards each other, arguing softly before separating. One was nodding, the other was shaking her head.

"Yes."

"No."

I waited as they glared at each other. Finally, Barbie held out a hand for Inky to continue.

"Upon the death of our sister, we were summoned back to the Land of the Fae. They requested news of this world, and where we had been, and what we had done. They had sensed a great disturbance in the forces here."

"Jesus," Alucard muttered. "Fairies really do love Star Wars…"

I sighed, collapsing into a chair. Then I jerked my head, realizing Alucard had just uttered the name of the Son of God. And he was still standing. He didn't appear to have realized his choice of words. He had *definitely* changed. "The Grimm battle," I said to the sprites, not wanting to draw attention to him.

Inky nodded. "Grimm *War*," she corrected, then burst into a fit of cackles. "Grimm War… Grimmwar." The emphasis finally made me get it.

I rolled my eyes, growing impatient, and justifiably alarmed. The Queens were serious business. "Yes, Grimoire, very clever. Now, what about the Grimm War concerns the Fae?"

"Why, *us*, of course. We involved ourselves in mortal schemes, calling upon our gift of Grammarie to cage the vile beast. And the conduit has used her powers since."

"What is Grammarie?" Ashley asked politely.

"The art of making things seem," Gunnar murmured, and was immediately slapped upside the head by Barbie. He growled at her. She shook her fist back at him, making Ashley burst out laughing. His hair hung in a mess now, his man-bun disheveled.

Inky was eyeing Gunnar with a frown. "Why does he decorate his head in such a fashion?"

Alucard laughed hard. "Yeah. The man bun trend needs to die. In a fire. With multiple casualties." Gunnar scowled at him for a moment before turning back to the sprites.

Barbie put her hands on her hips, glaring at the room. It was hard to take her seriously since she was naked, but I gave her points for effort. "*Glam-*

ourie is the art of making things *seem. Grammarie* is the art of making things *be,* filthy hound." I burst out laughing, and she spun, leveling a finger at me. "The Maker also wields Grammarie and Glamourie, just like the Fae." And I shut up. Immediately.

"Nate's a fairy!" Alucard hooted, before the sprites attacked him in a pincer movement, slapping the sparkle right off his face. But all I could do was stare vacantly, dumbfounded.

"No, that can't be right. All wizards can do similar things…" I began, but it felt hollow even as I said it.

"No, they can do only mild reflections of what you can do."

"Is that how you change your size? Grammarie?" I asked thoughtfully.

She weighed me up and down with a serious face. "Yes."

"Why do you choose a smaller form?"

She rolled her eyes. "When one is larger, more energy goes to power the body, taking away from the brain." She shot me a sharp look, and Aria burst out laughing. "That's why trolls are mindless beasts," she said, matter-of-factly.

I smiled. "Which means that a cockroach would be smarter than you…"

"Don't be ridiculous, mortal man-child. I am *Fae.*" Her argument held literally no merit, but I let it go, simply pleased that I was annoying her. "With training, you could learn such things. If you survive that long. But don't worry, the Queens, or one of them at least, will likely capture you to fit you with a leash before you need to worry about that. Then she will train you properly before releasing you again."

"I will not be fitted for a leash," I growled defiantly.

Inky shook her head sadly. "Such fight, you will need it to maintain your sanity amongst her other pets. Such is the price of knowledge, Maker."

I dropped the topic, knowing I would likely pin them to a bug box if they continued. "That was months ago. If they wanted me so badly, they would have already come for me."

The sprites were shaking their heads. "They can't. Not yet. But they have begun stressing the barriers to ease their entry into your world."

"What?" I demanded, almost hyperventilating now. The Huntress looked about ready to bolt.

"They are too powerful, so they have begun sending their henchmen into your world, to familiarize your world's barriers with our presence."

I blinked back. Everyone was silent. I remembered the Amber Alerts, and shivered. Alucard approached, handing me a drink. I took it blindly, and instantly began to finish it in one pull. Then I hesitated, and took only a sip. But a big one. I had experienced what happened when my emotions got out of control. Especially if it involved alcohol. My mind was a dangerous place. I was almost entirely sure that a stray thought could come to life if I wasn't careful. It had happened once before. And now I had a name for it, if the sprites were correct.

Grammarie.

"That doesn't make sense. The Fae used to come here all the time. Stealing children, turning bridges into troll-booths," I waved a hand, "and other general nuisances."

"And you appeased us with milk and honey, and hard iron, before collaborating with forces better left untouched…" Their eyes tightened with disapproval at the last.

I nodded with a glare. "I have some hard iron to show your queens. Tell them that," I said, wondering what her last comment had meant.

The Huntress and sprites all gasped at my disrespect. "Inappropriate," Gunnar agreed.

I took another drink, ignoring them. Alucard placed a hand on my shoulder in support. "What does this have to do with Tory?" he asked politely.

"She has taken gifts from our sister. She is now one of us…" They shared a look. "Kind of. I think," Barbie finally muttered. "Semantics. Her using her power is a beacon that will call them directly to her. They want to… *speak* with her." They looked at Alucard with hungry smiles. "And her pet," they added.

"No," Alucard and the Huntress growled at exactly the same time. The Reds suddenly sported dragon claws, irises a brilliant crimson shade with the telltale horizontal pupils that marked them as dragons. They stared at Tory and Alucard protectively.

"Then don't use the power!" The sprites hissed right back, but their words were aimed only at Tory, ignoring everyone else's reaction.

It was silent as everyone marginally calmed down, the Reds losing their claws, but still anxiously watching their adopted parents. "So, the evil queens are trying to break in to take Tory, and they will also take Nate, if he's not careful," Gunnar concluded. "And the sparkly one, whatever his name is. I never remember the names of henchmen." Alucard's fangs snapped out instinctively as he sneered back at the werewolf.

"The Gateway protects you. For now," Inky rasped, looking displeased at the words.

Everyone shared a look, waiting for elaboration. Inky sighed, and then zipped to the window overlooking my property to point at the gargantuan tree. The metallic white bark glowed in the sunlight, and the metallic razor-sharp leaves glittered in golds and silvers, looking as if...

They had been painted with the colors of Summer and Winter.

I shivered.

"But... the tree is only here thanks to you..." I finally said.

They nodded sadly, turning to me. "To buy you time..." Barbie murmured.

"To say goodbye..." Inky finished.

CHAPTER 13

*M*allory growled. "Well, this is what we call FUBAR. Fecking Queens—"

The sprites were on him in a blur, but they struck an invisible dome of power surrounding him, rebounding in a flurry of wings and hisses.

"Don't. Just don't," he muttered, clutching his spear, although it wasn't crackling with power.

"Nice stick," Barbie drawled. "Can I touch it?"

Mallory grinned like a wolf. "Be my guest, tits. I mean, *toots*."

Barbie grinned back voraciously. Sonya was frantically pointing at Barbie and looking for one of the adults to notice that she had also made an inappropriate double entendre. No one paid her any mind though, so she folded her arms with a loud *huff*.

I was suddenly very nervous. "Everyone calm down. What *exactly* is that tree?" I *knew* there had been something more to the tree than a mere headstone for Indie. The Huntress was now staring out the window at the giant tangle of limbs, as if seeing it for the first time. Perhaps she hadn't ever paid attention to it before.

The sprites were shaking their heads. "That is irrelevant. We are forbidden—"

"No. You will answer."

They stared at me defiantly, then the look morphed into frustration. "We. Cannot. Bound to our Queens, we are."

I finally let out a sigh. Fucking Queens. Fucking Fairies.

"Tell me what the Queens have done to stress the boundaries. Have they taken children? Give me someth—"

Barbie suddenly squealed in terror, slamming into my head and grabbing me by the hair. Sir Muffle Paws flew through the air where she had been hovering, landing lightly on his feet. I hissed in pain as Barbie tugged and yanked at my scalp in an effort to get away, or to at least use me as a human shield. I hadn't even known Sir Muffle Paws was in the room with us.

I heard the Huntress laughing. Possibly one or two other voices.

"Filthy feline!" Barbie shrieked, tugging tiny fistfuls of my hair out by the roots. Sir Muffle Paws – the size of a cocker spaniel – saw the sprite was now tangled in my hair, and decided collateral damage was entirely acceptable in his hunt to catch the shiny fairy. He dove at my face. "Gah!" I yelled as Barbie used my skull as a launch-pad to flee out the open doorway, ripping out another chunk of my hair in the process. Inky wasn't far behind her. Sir Muffle Paws struck my chest with four sets of claws backed by a solid twenty pounds of force, and then launched himself after the fairies with a less than gentle slash of his claws. He disappeared around the corner, leaving me panting, chest on fire, and hair like a foreclosed bird's nest.

"So…" Gunnar began. "Fairies. The Beast Master. What else do you have going—"

Dean uncharacteristically bustled into the room, interrupting Gunnar. "Sprites in the main corridor," he announced with an alarmed frown. Then he took in my appearance, and his frown deepened. "What happened to your forehead?" I growled as Sonya chuckled. "Right. I see you are already aware…" He cleared his throat, subconsciously straightening his tuxedo. "Master Temple, I think you need to see this. I have been fielding calls all morning, deflecting lawyers and—"

I held up a hand, discreetly eyeing our audience. Dean let out a breath, straightened his coat again, and nodded with a slightly embarrassed look. They didn't need to know about my side project, and why Dean was fielding my calls. Othello hid her face behind her drink, pretending to take a big gulp of her whisky. She immediately choked on it as it went down the wrong pipe.

"What is it, Dean?" I asked, annoyed that she had only managed to draw attention to the comment and herself. The Reds had rushed over to her and were patting her on the back. Gunnar turned from Othello to me with a calculating frown.

Dean saved me by plucking up a remote off a nearby table and turning on the TV. He switched it to the news, and everyone but the Reds – who were still doctoring Othello – watched in confusion at the chaos on the screen. The news was replaying video footage of the baggage claim area of the St. Louis Airport.

But people were running, screaming, and causing general mayhem as a woman in a trench coat suddenly appeared on the screen. She stalked past the luggage carousel carrying a sword that dripped crimson liquid.

My heart stopped as I leaned closer. The footage was grainy, but not many carried an umbrella sword. Alucard hissed in recognition of the unique weapon. His old weapon. Then she was gone.

"Indie…" I breathed.

Sonya, apparently not watching the TV, sounded suddenly excited. "Yay! Indie's back! *Ow*, Aria! What the hell was that fo—" Her sister must have punched her, realizing what was happening on the news, but I didn't turn to see. Because I couldn't peel my eyes from the screen.

A man with white hair appeared, calmly following in Indie's wake, eating peanuts out of a paper sack in his hand, not a care in the world on his recognizable face. Then he, too, disappeared from the camera's angle.

Ichabod.

"Well," Alucard murmured. "She's missed dinner. That's… unfortunate."

Dean cleared his throat, breaking the stunned silence after Alucard's comment. "Agent Jeffries has also called numerous times."

"What have you told him?" I whispered, feeling like I was in physical shock, as if having just survived a serious car accident.

"That I was unaware of the situation," he answered carefully. I managed to nod back, thankful he hadn't tried to lie. Agent Jeffries had the unique ability to sense lies.

"If he calls again, tell him I'll… call back soon. That you just showed me the news, and that I was equally… unaware." He nodded and left, pulling out his phone as it began to ring. I simply stared out the window, feeling numb, not seeing anyone in the room as my mind raced with questions.

Othello clapped her hands loudly, speaking in a commanding tone. I didn't even flinch at the sound. "I think everyone needs to leave. Now. I'll keep you updated, but I think everyone has their marching orders." I snapped out of my daze to see Othello point a finger at Tory and Alucard. "Don't use your powers." She turned to the Reds. "Keep your parents from doing anything stupid." This elicited a round of laughter, but I couldn't move; even a facial twitch was beyond my abilities at the moment. "And maybe everyone should find some iron. Just in case." Everyone murmured agreement and said quiet goodbyes, risking discreet glances my way. Which I didn't acknowledge.

Gunnar patted me on the shoulder as he and Ashley left. "I'm sorry about…" he sighed, getting no reaction from me. "Look, just let me know about the circus Freak. Once…" he waved a hand at the TV, which was still playing, "you figure this out. We're here for you."

I felt Ashley staring at me intently. I might have mumbled something back, nodding absently at her concerned glance. But it was equally as likely that I just stared at her. I walked up to one of the chairs near the fireplace and sat down, staring out at the unnatural tree through the large window. I had tried carving the bark once, but the wood had resisted any attempts to mar the surface. The sprites had called it a Gateway. Staring at the tree only emphasized the video footage we had just watched, because this was where Indie had died and been resurrected. It sparkled in the noon sunlight as the room grew silent.

The door clicked shut and I turned to see Othello slowly walking to the chair opposite me, not making eye contact. She poured a fresh drink, glanced down at the black book on the coffee table, and picked it up.

Or, she tried to.

But it didn't budge.

I waved a hand. "Sorry, off limits," I whispered, still replaying the footage of the airport in my head, even though the TV had moved on to some reporter talking about terrorism with no facts at all to back up her claims.

Othello watched me, waiting for an elaboration, but after a long pause, seemed to accept my silence. She poured me a fresh drink, pressing the cool glass into my hand. Then she glanced down again at the cover of the book, *Through the Looking-Glass*. "Off limits to me, or…?" she pressed.

I think my face managed a semblance of a smile as I met her eyes. "No, everyone but me." She nodded once, then took a sip of her drink, staring into the fire. After a few moments, I spoke again. "Thanks. For getting everyone out of here. I... didn't feel like company anymore."

"I know."

I sighed, a true smile split my cheeks as she didn't get up to leave. "But, no, you can stay."

She didn't look at me, but smiled anyway. "I know."

I leaned back in the chair, taking a sip of my drink.

Othello cleared her throat. "The suspect's name was R. Stiltskina..." I shot a sharp look at her, and she pointed at the TV. "I spoke to Dean. He's waiting outside in the hall. Pacing." She glanced at me. "He's nervous about... your reaction. Or lack thereof..."

I nodded, setting down my glass, realizing that my drink was gone and I was desperately thinking of refilling it. "It's his job."

"No. The way he looks at you... you're like a son to him... It's not just his job."

I ran a hand through my hair. "I know. I'm being dramatic."

She shrugged. "Understandable." She hesitated. "May I ask a question?"

I nodded with mild resignation after a few moments.

"You asked if the Fae had taken children. Why?"

I sighed, rubbing my temples as I leaned forward. "Just something they used to do. And it feels like I'm getting more of those Amber Alerts than usual."

I heard a sharp intake of breath and looked up to see a horrified look on her face.

I nodded. "Yeah. They used to take kids. Switch them out with Changelings – or Fae. Then they had a plant that would be raised in our world, able to wreak havoc later. And they would raise the mortal child in a world of monsters. Twofer."

She shivered, and then straightened her shoulders resolutely. "Let's go for a walk."

I laughed. "Just like that? My terrorist fiancée rampages an airport with a bloody sword, without letting me know she's in town, and... you want to go for a *walk*?" I asked, smiling despite myself.

She nodded. "It's not that *I* want to go for a walk, but that it might be nice for *you*. I figured you could do with less crazy. Walks are the opposite of crazy." She paused. "And I do miss this rambling old pile."

She didn't comment on our past dalliances. That we had once had a *thing* together, and that she had spent a fair share of time here. And I wasn't about to bring it up either. She knew we were over. That I loved Indie. That I had proposed to her. That she had said yes. But then... "Fine. Let's go." I grumbled, more to myself, as I halted my train of thought. Apparently, I didn't know my fiancée all that well if she was making a terrorist debut at the local airport, under an alias that was obviously a message to me.

R. Stiltskina.

Very close to *Rumpelstiltskin*, whom she had helped me vanquish.

She wanted me to know she was here. But she hadn't reached out to me.

I stood, holding out my hand. Othello downed her drink, poured another, and then poured me a refill. I began to protest, but she calmly held the drink out anyway. I sighed. One more couldn't hurt. Thinking about our walk, I had an idea.

"Let me show you something..." I said, leading her out of the office and past Dean, who simply stared at me holding hands with Othello as I led her into the depths of my mansion. I wasn't going to do anything stupid.

Even if Indie was a terrorist wanted by the FBI.

And that she hadn't called me.

And that I was holding hands with an incredibly beautiful young woman I used to have relations with.

But I could still sense the question in Dean's eyes.

And to be honest, a small, small part of me ran with the idea. And it wasn't the Dark Presence. It was all Nate. I ignored it, and decided to just relax and have a good time with an old friend. Things were going to get hectic soon. I needed a break. A diversion.

Nothing more...

CHAPTER 14

I opened the door to Ichabod's office beneath the sublevels of the mansion – an area not shown in the blueprints – smiling at Othello's excitement. "This is incredible!" she gasped.

Her eyes quested the room, taking in the skulls, candles, a globe, naval navigation equipment, and various other random collectibles – as if we had entered the room of Indiana Jones. Or Sherlock Holmes at 221b Baker Street. Bizarre paintings and faded newspaper clippings decorated the walls in a random hodge-podge that could only make sense to the original inhabitant. Other than cleaning up the place, I hadn't touched a thing.

It felt… soothing. Tranquil.

And I didn't know what was dangerous to touch.

Othello darted to one of the bookshelves, scanning the dozens of titles, then gasped as her eyes caught upon the adjoining room full of priceless gems sitting about like so much trash. I had left the door open. Actually, it was a bookshelf that doubled as a concealed door. I hadn't bothered hiding anything, because no one even knew about the sublevel, or how to get here. Well, no one outside my circle of trust, anyway. Dean and Mallory knew. And Ichabod and Indie. But I had a pair of Guardians roaming the halls just in case.

But now that Ichabod and Indie were supposedly back in town, and bloodthirsty terrorists, perhaps it would be wise to conceal the treasure.

Ichabod had supposedly gifted me the treasure – collected fortunes from a misspent youth – to use to build an army, buy favor, basically a war chest. But I didn't really want to go to war. I sighed. With the two suddenly showing back up in St. Louis under a bizarre terrorist-type display, who knew if his plans for the gems had changed? After all, my last talk with Ichabod had revealed his burning vendetta to hunt down and destroy the elusive Syndicate – a group that had employed the Brothers Grimm and Rumpelstiltskin. They were so elusive and dangerous that we weren't even supposed to talk about them.

And Ichabod had a real hard-on for taking them down. He had made it his life's purpose after surviving the Dark Realm with the Brothers Grimm. It was fair to say that whatever he was doing in town tied into the Syndicate somehow. I let out a breath. I would deal with the gems later. Or have Dean or Mallory hide them with the Macallan. Even I wouldn't be able to find it after that.

I sat down in the chair behind the desk, and lit the fireplace with a thought before considering my curse. Using magic was not smart now. I only had a limited supply. I needed to remember that until I figured out how to rescue the girl. A chimera. A very dangerous little girl.

"So, what's up with you and Death?" I asked distractedly.

Her shoulders tightened before she turned to face me. "I'm not sure. Do you think it... unwise?"

I thought about that. And the gift box I had seen both of them with. She must have left it upstairs, because she didn't have it now. "Honestly, I have no idea. I think he's a good guy. As good as any of us are, I guess. Still, he is a Horseman."

She was nodding, mind distant, as she sat down before me. But she changed the subject before I could press further. "What do you need from me, Nate?"

I frowned.

"Everyone seems to be thinking about themselves, and not about you. It must be terribly traumatic for you," she teased, smiling as she idly tucked a strand of hair behind her ear. She was still wearing her formal clothes, not having had time to change after Rufus' arrival. She wore it well, looking relaxed, and scandalously beautiful. Which I absolutely did not need to notice.

"How about you just make sure the deal goes off without a hitch."

She nodded, face growing serious. "Everything is going according to plan. We still need to talk to Tomas about what he found." She paused, looking up at me. "Well, don't you worry about that. I'll take care of Tomas. You just sit there and try to look pretty." She grinned. "If you think you can manage that." I chuckled as her eyes drifted to the gems in the other room. "Am I correct in assuming that this treasure will provide the necessary capital?"

I nodded. "Yes. I'll need you to liquidate it. Cleanly. Discreetly. Check with Dean later, just in case I decide to move it... since we have guests in town."

She shrugged, not elaborating on my reference to Indie and Ichabod. "Of course. Sticking with the same name you mentioned?"

"Grimm Technologies, for the public. But I'll probably still just call it Grimmtech for short."

She nodded. "The paperwork all to your satisfaction?"

I smiled, nodding.

"Then I think we're set. But what else do you need? Not for business. What do you, *Nate*, need?" she asked, emphasizing my name. "Not the billionaire tycoon. The man." She took a sip of her drink, watching me.

I thought about that. For a good long while, ignoring the faint whispers of the Dark Presence urging lewd ideas in my ears. Which wasn't good, in and of itself. The cane was several floors above us, yet I still felt his influence. "A friend," I managed with a whisper. Sir Muffle Paws sauntered into the room at that moment, likely having followed us after failing to catch the sprites, and deciding to hunt down the larger, dumber humans as an afternoon snack.

Othello nodded. "I can do that," she offered with a pearly smile, eyeing Sir Muffle Paws. "Where did you buy a lynx? And why?"

I smiled. "He bought me, actually. Saved a bunch of Bible School Students from a warzone."

She blinked. "Is he... magical?"

Sir Muffle Paws flicked his tail into the air, and turned his back on her. I frowned at the cat.

"Not that I know of. He just helped the little girls feel safe during an attack outside my shop." Then I smiled. "Actually, it was Baba Yaga who attacked me," I said, remembering her penchant for Russian folklore.

"No way," she exclaimed, leaning forward eagerly.

I nodded. "Her house is actually her shadow. A Familiar of hers. Creepy as hell. Walks around on those chicken feet and everything."

She was shaking her head regretfully. "Incredible. I miss all the fun."

"She wasn't... fun." I rolled my eyes.

"If you say so. Tell me, since you need a *friend*, what can I do to help you out? Seems like you have a lot on your plate."

I nodded, mind turning over recent events. I had no idea what I was going to do about the chimera, other than find a way to make a substantial amount of money, fast. Then convert it to the chosen form of currency for antiquated supernaturals, which wasn't truly that common these days. Most just used cash. At least in my circles. Lucky me, I had nothing else going on in my life. Except for protecting Tory from the Queens.

And dealing with Indie.

I rubbed my temples, thinking, and an idea tumbled out almost immediately, thanks to talking about Baba. A predatory smile cracked my cheeks. "I need you to make a phone call. He won't answer if I call. Set up a meeting. Here. In a few hours." I calculated the time in my head, knowing that the Beast Master would likely make a move tonight. "You can tell him it's to meet me," I said, a smile beginning to stretch across my face.

She watched me curiously. "Okay, who am I calling again?"

I told her. And about our past.

She blinked. About three times. "He's real?" I nodded. "And you want me to just call him..."

"Yep. This will be fun."

"If you say so..."

CHAPTER 15

*M*allory spoke in a low tone, even though no one was around us. "Squeeze the trigger, don't pull," he whispered, eyeing the gates of Chateau Falco in the distance through a set of binoculars. It was an hour before sundown, so the sun rested behind me, not blinding my vision.

I nodded. "I know. I *have* handled a gun before, Mallory. And there's no need to whisper."

He ignored my last comment. "This ent' a gun. Tis a wee bit different from yer pistols and whatnot," he chided.

"Okay. Got it. I don't know dick about this, and you know everything." I rolled my eyes. "Now, can we hurry up already?"

The rooftop was silent as we waited, giving me time to replay my conversation with Agent Jeffries an hour ago. I had called him to appease his concern, and to answer his questions honestly. Hearing me outright tell him I had no idea what Indie was doing in town was huge, because he could discern truth from lies. Literally. Some kind of ability of his. Telling him these things out loud would remove all doubt in his mind. Which would prevent a SWAT team from kicking down my door in the next few days. I was his only lead, so without that call, he could have made my life a living hell. Thanks to our conversation, I now had some breathing room. But he had made me promise to check in with him often, no doubt so that he could repeat his same questions, to make sure my circumstances hadn't changed.

Which meant I really needed Indie and Ichabod not to reach out to me. Because if they did, and if Jeffries later asked me about it, he would catch me in a lie. Not answering his call would be as good as admitting I was aiding and abetting a fugitive.

He hadn't given me any further details on the attack at the airport. Other than the knowledge that a few security guards had been harmed, but were expected to make full recoveries from their sword wounds. Jesus. What the hell had she been thinking? She could have very easily shifted her appearance to just waltz through the airport, no harm done. But she hadn't. Which had to mean something. And she had used a name that would catch my attention quicker than a streaker at a Cardinals game.

Mallory let out a sharp breath, snapping me back to the moment. "Target in sight and approaching the kill-zone. Calling Dean now," he whispered to me before murmuring into a walkie-talkie. I heard Dean respond in a dry tone as I focused on the Op.

At least, that's what the pros called this kind of thing.

I stared through the scope, relaxing my shoulders as I lay on the frigid rooftop. The thin blanket wasn't enough to keep off the chill, but it was better than nothing. I let out a measured breath, and locked in my sights. Or however the pros said it.

Listen, I looked through the lens thingie and aimed my metal fire-stick.

The gates swung open at a glacial pace, and a figure stepped into view, pausing for just a moment as he listened to the speaker beside the gate, Dean saying something to him.

Right on schedule.

I let out a controlled breath, and squeezed the trigger. The cannon in my arms exploded, jolting my shoulder hard enough to likely leave a bruise. The figure flew backwards a good ten feet, somersaulting into a nearby bush. I watched him through the scope, struggling to climb back to his feet. He crouched, scanning the horizon, wary of another attack. I saw a faint glint near his head as he used his own binoculars to spot his attacker.

Little old me.

I stood, waving belligerently.

He was motionless for a moment, and then very slowly unfolded to a standing position. But he didn't take a step. He just stood there. His gaze flickered to the intercom beside the gate again and then he unloaded a full clip at it, emitting an arc of sparks. Then he began storming up the drive with murderous intent.

Mallory only watched me with a thoughtful frown.

"Reckon we ought to go talk to him."

I smiled and turned to head back inside the mansion to meet my old friend. Dean was waiting at the bottom of the stairs inside the house. "Judging from the intercom's state of disrepair at the gates, I'm presuming your brilliant plan worked?" he asked scathingly.

I nodded, brushing past him with a smile. "Thanks, Dean."

"There are ways to make friends, and then ways to make enemies. I think you may have misunderstood the lesson. And you seem to have forgotten you are no longer a billionaire."

"We'll see about that," I winked to both statements.

Moments later, Mallory and I were outside, slouching against the columns of the covered parking area leading up to the front door.

A man strode up the last hill of the drive, coat tattered where a giant hole marred the center of the fabric, right over his heart. His face was a storm cloud, and his lips were tight with fury.

"Hi, Van," I said jovially.

He stopped ten feet away, and continued to glare. He took a deep breath, let it out, and then repeated the motion before speaking, voice quivering with rage. "Your social skills… leave something to be desired," he finally said. Although he was furious, he was also very, very cautious. He had seen me and my friends during a fight with his old master, Rumpelstiltskin. It hadn't ended well for him, but at the same time, my actions had released him from his bond to the monster.

So.

Was he pissed right now?

Yes. Yes, he was.

But did he remember how dangerous I could be?

Yes. Yes, he did.

And that was the only reason he wasn't trying to murder me right now.

"You're immune to weres, right?"

He stared at me as if I had struck him in the forehead with a rock. "What happened to your forehead?"

I managed to restrain myself, needing him more than I needed a sooty stain where he currently stood. "Lycanthropy. You're immune to it, right?" I asked, ignoring his comment. "If you're clawed or bitten, you don't acquire the fun, homicidal menstrual cycle at the full moon, and all that."

He continued to stare, his anger at me sniping him so profound that his face didn't quite know how to express itself. "Yeah. Sure," he finally grumbled, staring at me as if I had been speaking French.

"Okay, that's good. I need a babysitter. Your name came up. Good references."

His mouth opened once, then closed. "What?"

"If you can handle it, I'll consider us even."

"And what if I already consider us even?" he asked.

I shrugged. "Then I guess I'll just reacquaint you with Silver Tongue."

He flinched. "He's still *alive?*"

I nodded. "Much to his displeasure. I'm sure he would love a long talk with an old friend though. Maybe even a sleepover…" I let the threat build in his mind for a few seconds. "You interested?" I asked, face blank.

He finally let out an exasperated sigh. "Fine, you son of a bitch. Fine. After this, we're even."

"No. If you do a satisfactory job with this – of which I am the judge – we're even."

He growled back, "Fine. What's the job?"

This next part was risky. There was always the chance that he would double-cross me, but I needed an inside man. Someone to scope the place out, and give me better chances of surviving. "I need you to go to a job interview with the Beast Master."

He stared at me like a fish out of water for a few seconds. "The fucking Beast Master is here?" I nodded. "Do you have any idea what you're messing with?" he asked softly.

I shrugged. "Kind of. But I need you to do it anyway." I wasn't stupid enough to tell him about my curse, and my dwindling magic. Let him think I was as juiced up as he remembered. "Listen, I just need a man on the inside to give me a layout of his facility. You're immune to weres, which makes you my prime candidate. You don't actually need to do anything dangerous. Just observe, and get me information."

"Nothing dangerous. Just get a job with a lunatic, spy on him, and then give the information to his enemy. Nothing dangerous at all." He threw up his hands. "Working for him is kind of a long-term job. He doesn't just let people leave, you know."

I smiled at him, leaning forward conspiratorially. "If I have my way, that won't be a concern for long." I paused. "You are both connected to the big players. The Syndic—"

He blazed through the space between us in a nanosecond, and clamped his hand over my mouth. Mallory hissed, practically dancing on the balls of his feet, ready to kill. But Van wasn't attacking. His eyes were wild. "Easy, kid. Neither of us has protection any longer. With Stilts gone, saying that name could be hazardous to our health." He met my eyes until I nodded, then he withdrew his calloused hand and stepped back.

"Okay. What I was saying is that you both have connections with... *them*. Use your hatred for me, and your extensive track record of hunting down Freaks to win him over. You're in town without a job, thanks to your previous employer... shutting down operations, which was thanks to *me*. Tell him you want nothing more than to stick it to me by helping the Beast Master – for a brief window while he's in town – to steal some of my citizens. Then you're done. Unless the Beast Master has a better offer later. He'll bite. If not, make him. I *need* someone on the inside."

Van's gaze wandered the grounds as he searched for an excuse. I let him, nodding discreetly at Mallory who looked the exact opposite of comfortable with the situation. Finally, Van turned back to me and nodded. "Okay. But after this, we're done."

I nodded gratefully. "Thank you." I began to turn away, and then paused. "Oh, Van. Few other things. Can you keep an eye out for... the Grimm?"

He studied me. "Your fiancée? *That* Grimm?" He asked with a frown. I nodded. "Sure. Did you misplace her?"

"Something like that."

"Did you check the kitchen?" he grinned. I didn't smile back. "Just keep my eye out? Because I don't think she's going to like it if she finds me tailing her. As in, she'll take my eye," he added dryly.

"Oh, she definitely won't like you tailing her. That's why I need you to be sneaky."

"Fine. We done?"

"Almost. I also need to see Baba Yaga."

He threw his hands up in frustration. "What the hell, man? Do you need me to wipe your ass, too?"

My glare tightened. "Remember who you're talking to..." I threatened with a harsh smile. "This is your way out of my crosshairs." I plucked a bullet from my pocket, holding it up to the light. "Speaking of crosshairs, I got some fancy new bullets the other day." And I tossed it to him. "You can have this one. I have more boxes of them upstairs."

He caught it instinctively, studying it. His face grew pale as his other hand absently touched the hole in his shirt. Where I had shot him. He looked at me, face emotionless.

"Bone and claw, right? The only thing that can harm you…"

He nodded, face tight, as he pocketed the bone-tipped bullet I had tossed to him.

"I listen, Abraham, and I plan ahead. Be thankful I didn't use this bullet a few moments ago. Call it a gesture of good will."

He didn't look happy, but finally sighed. "You can find Baba in a warehouse in Soulard. Not far from your bookstore, actually." He rattled off the address. Which was in fact alarmingly close to my bookstore, only a few blocks away. And I didn't like that one bit. One, because she was in my city – even though it was fortuitous right now. Two, because out of the whole city, she had chosen a spot in my backyard. Van continued, watching me thoughtfully. "But be careful. She's… not right in the head after our last… meeting."

I frowned. "Okay. Go get that job. Be persuasive, Van. This will benefit you just as much as it will benefit me. And Achilles will probably be your best bet to get information to me."

"What?! He wants to kill me!"

I rolled my eyes. "Don't be such a drama queen. You brought that on yourself." He was fuming, panting heavily as his fists flexed open and closed spastically. "Listen. Everyone knows you hate each other, so no one will be stupid enough to think you're working with him. Also, it is totally believable that – working with the Beast Master – you would need to be in contact with a local bartender who sells tickets to the show. This isn't a request. Anything else will give you away."

He let out an exasperated sigh. "Any way you can tell me why I'm risking my life again? Why are you picking a fight with the Beast Master?"

"I need to save a chimera."

His jaw practically hit his chest. Then he began to laugh. "You're fucking insane. Bat-shit insane. I'll do these things. And do them well. And then, we're done."

I nodded, ignoring his accusation. But the Dark Presence inside me didn't ignore it, and began railing against my resolve to kill this murderer once and for all.

Van left between one blink and the next, simply disappearing from my sight, which infuriated the Dark Presence inside of me. Mallory scowled at the spot where he had been, and let out a grumble of disapproval. "What next, Laddie?"

"We go question a prisoner. Then I go see the witch so I can hopefully save a kid tonight."

Mallory's responding grumble was altogether hungrier and more approving this time.

CHAPTER 16

I threw a pitcher of chilled ice water at the sleeping form. He woke with a startled gasp, jumping up and down, panting, eyes wide. He saw me and his hands flashed to the thick bars of his cell. He leaned forward. "How *dare* you imprison me!"

"The way I see it, handing you over to the Academy would put me in their good graces, and rid me of a nuisance." I held my phone out so he could reach through the bars. "Go ahead, call Jafar, Captain of the Justices." I feigned a sudden look of embarrassment. "Oh, wait... I *killed* him." I smiled at him. "In that case, phone a friend. I'll wait." I began tapping a foot as I leaned against the bars with one shoulder.

The man glared back. "And how much good will that do for you, seeing as you will no longer be a Maker if you don't help me?" he replied smugly.

I didn't let my frustration show on my face. But I was seething. Little bastard should have known I was going to help him. If he had done his homework, like he said he had, he would have known. But instead, Gunnar had attacked him, and the man had responded by extorting me to help. Or risk forfeiting my power.

"So, we are at an impasse. I need you, and you need me. Neither of us is happy about it. I understand that." He nodded his begrudging agreement. "Now, if you want to get out of this cell, you will release me from the curse."

He stared at me for a good long while, and then shook his head. "I can't," he said, dropping his head. After a few moments, he looked back up at me. "But even if I could, I wouldn't. I need you to save my girl, and after everything that happened, I don't know if you'd help me. Call it cowardice." He shrugged. "I don't care. I'd do worse if it promised her safety."

I sighed, understanding his position. Things had gotten out of hand, and I wasn't sure if I would have reacted differently in his shoes. I hadn't really thought he would be able to simply cancel his curse. Things like that usually required some predetermined action to be fulfilled to nullify the magic spent on the spell. No free lunch. "Worth a shot." I tapped my lips in thought as Mallory smiled darkly at my prisoner. "Fine. Counter offer. Make an oath to do whatever I say, no matter what. For the duration of our rescue attempt. Once you touch hands with your... daughter, the spell is restored. Period. No negotiations."

The man watched me for a few seconds before finally sighing. He nodded. "I swear to abide by the conditions you just stated."

"Not so fast. We're going to make this binding. I have trust issues."

I nodded to Mallory and he pulled out an archaic set of keys to open the cell door, glaring the whole while at Rufus. He let the man out, shoved him before me, and said, "Kneel." Then he very politely held a pistol to the base of his skull. "This is how I say *please*."

Rufus didn't look happy about it, but complied.

"Ye will use yer magic to make this oath legit. Swear it on yer power. And make it convincing. Tryin' to break free gets ye a bullet to the brain pan. No hesitation." He chambered a round, the sound loud in the stone chamber. "The second time I ask ye to repeat it will be through a bloody mouth, and I always found it hard to speak with loose teeth. So, try to get it right the firs' time, boy." Mallory smiled before looking up at me. "Or don't," he added.

Rufus nodded, meeting my gaze, and took hold of his magic. I felt faint tingles on my arms as he swore his oath. Perfectly. No wiggle room. I felt the power settle around both of us like a warm blanket. Then he wisely released his power, and the sensation on my arms faded away. The Dark Presence murmured uncomfortably at the magic that had briefly touched my skin. I soothed his concern with a murmured response under my breath. When I looked up, Rufus was watching me with a frown. I shook off his look, frustrated that I had spoken out loud.

"We're both in the same boat. You renege, you lose your power. I renege, I lose my power."

He nodded, and climbed to his feet. "What do you need me to do?"

I studied him. "You're going to stick to Mallory's hip. Do whatever he asks. Make him tea. Tuck him into bed. Wipe his ass," I added, remembering Van's comment. I prodded Rufus' shoulder with my finger, hard. "*Whatever* he asks. And you'll do this without a glimmer of disrespect. When I need anything further, I'll let you know. For now, you're his girl Friday."

Mallory smiled approvingly. And I left to go meet up with the iron-toothed nightmare of a Russian witch, Baba Yaga.

CHAPTER 17

I knocked on the door of the old warehouse, shrugging deeper into my coat. I had my cane handle strapped to my belt, but other than that I was unarmed. I was here to ask a favor, and couldn't risk picking a fight with the old hag. I didn't have enough power, and frankly, she was pretty goddamned powerful, and I wasn't sure what would work on her, magically speaking.

I had once fought her in a street, raining down hellfire on her, and it hadn't fazed her in the slightest. I didn't have the power to waste getting in a slugfest. Also, honey had worked better than a stick last time. I just needed to be sure I limited my drinking around her, lest I bring a horde of monsters to life.

And you can't spell *Russian* without including the letters for *vodka*.

The door clicked as the lock disengaged, but it didn't actually open, which was creepy. She knew I was here. Little tendrils of detritus whispered around me in tiny cyclones of cool November wind as I patiently waited. Was I just supposed to walk in? I waited another minute, listening to the sounds of the city behind me, cars whizzing by on the streets outside the alley, sirens blaring in the distance, people shouting at one another.

You know, city life. Night time in St. Louis. I just hoped I wasn't too late to save a kid.

"To hell with this," I muttered, and pushed the door open. Nothing tried to bite my face off, so I tentatively extended my boot through the threshold, surprised to feel no resistance. At least she hadn't rigged the place to blow upon my entrance. "Baba Yaga?" I called out softly, but urgently, pushing my voice into the dark space. No one responded. I pulled out my phone and activated the flashlight, shining it into the murky gloom.

Crates, boxes, an old forklift, and even a few makeshift beds were tucked here and there. The building had long since been abandoned, long enough for squatters to occupy the space.

But there were no squatters now. Baba Yaga had seen to that.

I wondered why she was still in my city, and not in Russia, the Land of Optimism, Friendliness, and Big Dreams.

I had a feeling I was about to find out. Van's warning about her not being the same since our battle whispered darkly in my ears. Foreboding. What had he meant?

"Baba?" I called out again, louder as I closed the door behind me. Dim streetlamps shone through several filthy windows in the back, but other than that, the place was dark, gloomy, and threatening. I pressed on, searching for the old witch, wondering if Van had lied, or been mistaken. I let out a breath, trying to avoid any stray pieces of glass, blades, trash, or any other obstacles underfoot. Hell, I wouldn't have been surprised to trip over a body. Or a pile of bones. My breath fogged before my face, and I shivered. Was it getting colder?

I walked for a full minute, studying my surroundings. It was an old factory of some kind. Conveyor belts and ancient machinery filled the space. Metal racks, shelving, and broken crates created a landscape of the industrial world. I was familiar to it, having grown up around my father's company, Temple Industries.

I heard a faint rustle behind a shelving unit and tensed. Then I caught the whiff of a slaughterhouse, as if the smell had been masked up until this point. "Hello? Baba? I'd recognize that cologne anywhere." She didn't respond, and I began to grow nervous. "It's me, Temple."

"I know it's you, boy. Anyone else would be a pile of ashes right now."

I smiled, rounding the corner. "It's good to see you, Baba—" but I stopped, eyes wide. Baba was huddled over her Familiar, who was lying prostrate on a pile of pallets. The smell struck me like a slap, making my eyes water in an instant. Full-blown decay. Now that I was closer, I could hear his breath rattling. Let me clarify.

Baba Yaga lived in a house on chicken legs that could move about her forest. The thing was freaking *alive*.

But before I had met her, no one had told me that her house also doubled as her *shadow*. The thing was literally a creature that followed her around. Like Secret Service for the old, deadly crone. It was a frighteningly tall mass of torn, soiled, faded dark robes. It smelled like rotten meat more often than not, and had giant chicken legs that peeped out from beneath the robes. It also had the head of a giant Renaissance doctor mask. You know, those ones with the long, beak-like noses you see in old movies and video games. Its eyes were deep pits of swirling magic, and it was a violent, deadly, horrifying monster.

Home, sweet home.

Except now, it wasn't a violent, deadly, horrifying monster.

It was… dying.

A spider web of cracks decorated the bone mask, and those cracks glowed with a crackling, violent violet light. I grimaced. That would be my fault.

Baba was hunched over the figure, holding a cup to its face, where its mouth should have been, although I hadn't ever seen what lay beneath the mask – and definitely didn't want to – I had never seen a mouth. Still, it was obvious that she was tending to him.

And that it wasn't working.

"Should I come back?" I asked softly.

She slowly unfolded from her patient, set the cup down on another pallet, and turned to look at me, face devoid of any human emotion. The blank look that signified a rage so deep that the face couldn't depict anything, so remained utterly dead instead. Her iron teeth glinted from the purple light emanating from her Familiar's bone mask. The injury I had given it. Or him. Or her. Or whatever gender it identified itself as. The world was a confusing place these days. I wanted to make sure I was being respectful of the sanctity of gender-identification for real estate.

"Should you come back?" she repeated in a raspy hiss. "Why on earth would you ever want to leave?" She began slowly walking towards me. Her eyes locked on my forehead with a brief frown that slowly shifted to light amusement at my suffering. It still stung a bit. She continued. "After all, you and I have so much to discuss. You…" her voice caught, but she quickly regained it, "broke my house. Damaged my home with Outerfire. A force powerful enough to overcome your clever Dueling Grounds, permanently harming my Familiar."

I had no idea what Outerfire was, and judging by the look on her face, she wasn't open to explaining it. I swallowed, suddenly realizing I had grossly underestimated the situation. She was beyond irrational, and I had just waltzed on in like an old friend. "Listen, Baba. Things got a little out of control that night. We all tried to kill each other. Repeatedly."

"Because you started a fight. With my master. Putting everyone in danger. Which we still are. Do you know who he *worked for*?"

I nodded, taking a step backwards, stumbling over a piece of wood. I caught myself, and tried to maintain my breathing, to discard my fear. "Listen. Everyone fucked up that night. But I didn't know the severity of what I did to your house, or else I would have personally come here to make it right."

She laughed darkly. "Oh, you would have *loved* that. To swoop in and save the day. No, I think I would like to see if your *blood* will heal my house. I'll need quite a lot of it, I'm afraid." And her hands erupted in flames as she began to advance on me.

I stood my ground, avoiding staring at the fire. Instead, I put on the arrogant, powerful face of a Temple. And sneered back, bluffing. "Sure you want to try that, witch? In another plane of existence – where according to the rules of the universe, no one should have been permanently harmed – I still managed to fatally wound your house." She slowed. "So how much juice do you think I can wield now? Here? In *our* world? I've learned a lot since we last met…" I didn't let loose a fanfare of magic. One, because I didn't dare risk wasting it. Two, because sometimes the best threats are the ones left to the imagination.

She watched me for a few moments, breathing heavily. Then she shrugged. "He's dying anyway. You may as well end both of us. I prefer to go down fighting." And she took another step.

"As fun as that sounds, I propose a better alternative."

"You have a few more seconds where I will be able to hear your voice. Then come the screams."

"Life. Healing. A future," I pressed, growing nervous beneath my calm façade.

The flames winked out. "What?"

I nodded. "I will heal your house. Reunite you. But I need a favor."

Her eyes tightened. "I don't do *favors*."

"Consider it an exchange then. Wipe the slate clean."

"Pah. Like you've done with Van and the Huntress," she snarled. "I won't be your friend. Your ally. Your Freak on a leash. Been there, done that."

I shook my head. "I'm not asking you to. I need your help finding someone. Well, technically, I need your help finding some targets, and stealing those targets before my opponent can get to them. And in exchange, I'll heal your Familiar."

She frowned back. "What do I know about tracking people? You already have a pack of dogs for such things," her voice trailed off, and then her gaze snapped back to me in realization. "*Children...*"

I nodded. "I need to save them before they can be kidnapped. I don't have any specific targets, but I know the type of person my opponent is hunting. He's a collector. I have other sources working on it, but their information might come too late. Or not at all. You, on the other hand, might be able to tell me where and when it will happen... *before* it happens."

Honestly, I had no idea if such a thing were even possible. But if anyone knew dark magic, and children, it was Baba Yaga. Worst case, she could possibly identify where she would go if she was looking to abduct children, and I could at least feel confident that the Beast Master thought the same way as the witch, and I might get lucky. If this didn't pan out, I would have to rely on Van. Which would take time. And that was even *if* he was successful getting the job.

She began to laugh. Hard. Then she turned back to her Familiar, striding over to him to check his pulse, listen to his breath, lick his nose (gross), and lay a comforting palm on his chest. I let her do this in silence. "You mean to take on the Beast Master..." she chuckled softly.

"Yes."

"Okay."

I blinked. "That's it? You're not going to run away screaming?"

Her misty gaze rose to mine and she shook her head. "He took something from me. A long time ago. Someone dear to me. And I despise who he works for." She shot me a meaningful look, implying the Syndicate. "And these aren't Regular children, but Freaks. I draw the line there. You heal my Familiar, and I'll help you prevent more kidnappings."

I hesitated, deciding to play a risk. "I can't heal your Familiar yet." I sucked in a breath. "Wait, did you say *more?*" Was I too late?

But she had only heard my first comment. "Then you shall die. I knew you were a liar." And the fire was back, her fingers now claws of flame, itching to grip my throat.

"No, *listen.*" I swallowed, realizing I had to tell the truth. "I was cursed. My power is limited at the moment. Once it's used up, it's gone. The only way I can get it back is to defeat the Beast Master. If I use my power to heal your Familiar, I stand no chance stopping him." Another thought hit me. "Stopping *them,*" I added, referring to the Syndicate in hopes that it would sway her decision. I tapped my chest, then held out my arms. "See for yourself."

She didn't even hesitate, despite the frown on her face. She strode right up to me, and punched me in the stomach. Except her hand turned misty and went straight *inside* of me. I grunted in discomfort as her fingers twisted, pulled, and prodded at my very soul.

The Dark Presence roared in outrage, and I found myself struggling to keep him in check as well as survive the horrible sensation. I managed, barely, to calm down the creature inside of me.

The physical feeling of her hand inside me was that of my stomach instantly turning into a commercial laundry machine. All in all, unpleasant. But I gritted my teeth, and suffered her mild payback. She stepped back with a satisfied grunt. Then looked up at me appraisingly, and I could tell the she had sensed the creature residing inside of me. But she didn't comment on that. "That's nasty magic." She turned back to her Familiar, studying him in silence for a few moments. "You're telling the truth, but I refuse to help *you* now if you cannot help *me* now."

I sighed in defeat. I would have to do this the old-fashioned way. Relying on Van's word. A man who had recently tried to kill me. "I understand." I turned to go, then called over my shoulder. "Know that once this is finished, I will come back to heal your Familiar. I swear it."

"Then will be too late..." her voice was a whisper.

My feet stopped. Goddamn it.

I was forcing myself to take another step when her voice called back out. "Wait."

I turned to face her, and saw her eyes suddenly dancing with hope.

"There might be a way." I was entirely sure that I didn't like the sound of that. "Ganesh."

I just stared at her for a moment, not understanding. "I've never met him."

She strode closer, suddenly eager. "You own the Fight Club."

"I don't know what you are talking about..." I replied lamely, reminded of Achilles' punishment for talking about the Fight Club.

"Don't play games, Maker." And I was suddenly airborne. I landed in a moldy, rotten, stained stack of pallets that smelled like the target of a decades-long pissing contest. They crunched and cracked under my weight, and the urine smell intensified. Baba's sympathy for my plight was overwhelming.

Meaning, she kept right on talking. "Ganesh has a belt. It healed him once, and is said to have healing powers for anyone who wears it." I scrambled to my feet, gagging at the stench, eyes watering as it combined with the already disgusting slaughterhouse smell.

"Like I said," I wheezed, getting as far away from the pallets as possible. "I've never met Ganesh." I stepped on something squishy, and when I looked down, I saw wriggling... things erupting from an old take-out bag. I shuffled a few more steps away, taking a deep breath. "Or any other elephant men. You expect me to just stride up to him and, what, de-pants him? Take his belt? He'll gore me alive, and then eat me."

"He attends the fights. He is friends with Asterion."

"What fights?" I attempted to sound sincere.

"Don't deny it. Van told me everything. Before Achilles incorporated his strict rules."

"Fine. I still don't think I have any chance of stealing his belt."

She shrugged. "That is my price. Get the belt. I'll help you save the other children."

I sighed, having no idea how I was going to make this work. I had enough on my plate already. But I had no choice. "Deal. But what do you mean, *other* children?"

"The Beast Master has already acquired his first victim from your city. A red dragon."

My heart stopped. The Reds. I had to call Tory. Now.

Baba turned away, calling over her shoulder. "Tick tock, Temple. Tick tock..."

"She's the fucking crocodile, and I'm Captain Hook," I muttered.

"I can still hear you…" her voice drifted to me as I exited the building.

But all I could think about was the Reds. Had they been taken? And I also had to figure out how to pickpocket a Hindu God. Well, more precisely, how to de-pants him and nab his belt. Easy-peasy.

CHAPTER 18

*I*t was early morning, an hour before dawn, and I sat in my office, thinking. I had immediately checked in with Tory after meeting Baba, and had been relieved to hear the Reds were safe. Although my call had almost given her a panic attack.

But hearing the teens were safe had only brought up more concerns.

I had called Raego to ask if any of his dragons had gone missing.

They hadn't.

Which was weird, because there were no rogue loner dragons in the city. Raego had made sure of it. He was kind of a Type-A personality in his domination of other dragons, and since he was the Obsidian Son – the ruler of all dragons everywhere – he would have known. Not having anything else to go on, I had chalked up the current score.

Beast Master – 1. Team Temple – 0.

Othello was fast asleep after spending most of the night fielding phone calls and reviewing legal documents. She had also caught up with Tomas. After arguing with me for ten minutes about not being tired, she had abducted Sir Muffle Paws out of spite on her way to bed. I could still remember his protesting purrs as he was dragged away, rubbing his chin against hers in a last-ditch plea for her to release him, sheathing and unsheathing his claws into the meat of her shoulder like he was trying to hit the Chakra that would make her magically release him. I was pretty sure that's what it had all meant anyway. I didn't understand cats, but I was observant.

I would find out what Tomas had discovered later. Right now, I stared at the screen in front of me, reading up on Ganesh, eyes tired, but body wired. I was on borrowed time, and didn't have time for sleep.

Three days, and I had no more power.

So, Ganesh.

I had called Achilles, rather than going to the Fight Club and risk being tossed into the ring. I had expected to have to fight him to get the information, but Achilles had been surprisingly forthcoming. In fact, creepily forthcoming. Before I had even managed to ask about the elephant-headed god. I replayed the conversation in my head.

Achilles picked up the phone. "Heel, speaking." The bar in the background had sounded busy.

"Hey. It's me."

He hadn't missed a beat in replying. "Right. You'll find him at Forest Park at nine in the morning."

I had paused. "Well, that's mighty precise. And I didn't even tell you who I'm looking for, or that I was even *looking* for someone…" I had said, slightly alarmed.

Achilles had chuckled. "Trunk-face asked about you, said you two needed to talk. Told me his travel plans. That you would be calling."

"Right. I guess I'll go to the park then."

"You do that." And then he had hung up.

Which had set off all sorts of alarm bells in my head. Ganesh was looking for me, and knew I would be looking for him. Which kind of heavily implied that he would also know I intended to steal his belt. But how had he known? Baba Yaga *had* said his name out loud. Perhaps he could pick up on things like that. He did have big ears…

Or maybe it was entirely coincidental.

I chuckled mirthlessly. Right. Coincidence.

So, I had decided to research him. Not knowing much about the Hindu pantheon, I had skipped the books and gone straight to the web. I had even found myself on Wikipedia trying to learn more about him. His origins were mixed, his stories were varied, and he had a billion different names. Some stories spoke of him having a broken tusk, some didn't. And I read a few completely different stories about how he had broken his tusk. I read at least three stories about how he lost his head, and how he had received an elephant head transplant. From his dad. From a party guest. Or possibly from some random dude in the elephant-head-selling business. But I had also read that he had been born with an elephant head.

Contradictory, to say the least.

So far, here was what I believed to be true, whether it was or not was yet to be determined.

Ganesh had the head of an elephant, and the body of a large pot-bellied man. His skin was likely a reddish hue, and he was known as being the Lord of Obstacles. I found stories where he assisted people in the *removal* of obstacles, and stories where he *placed* obstacles in the way of those who needed to be stopped. He was a Hindu God, son of Shiva and Parvati, and the stories about him were both varied, and wild. For example, he rode a mouse named Krauncha.

Yep, that's right. A large elephant-headed god riding a mouse.

Don't ask, because I have no idea how *anyone* could use a mouse as a getaway vehicle, let alone a huge, elephant-headed Hindu God. Why not a horse? Or a dragon. Supposedly, since mice could sneak into almost any crevice, Krauncha aided him in removing any and all obstacles by being able to *get to* any and all obstacles. I began reading a story on the screen about him beating his brother in a race. With his stupid mouse.

I let out a frustrated breath, not finding anything particularly useful, or even particularly believable, and took a drink of the water on the table. I scowled at it for good measure, and poured myself a Macallan. I took a contented sip, and leaned back in my chair, swiveling so that I could stare out the giant window at the massive tree standing well over 100 feet tall. It had grown. Thickened up. The canopy filling out with more of the razor-sharp metallic leaves that seemed unaffected by the season. The *Gateway*, the sprites had called it.

Whatever the hell that meant.

It emitted a faint glow in the moonlight, an otherworldly glow, like those bioluminescent fish in the deepest parts of the ocean. Its silvery bone-like bark seemed to pulse stronger where moonbeams touched it, but it still glowed in other places, just not as strongly. It was the world's tallest glow-stick.

A silhouette dashed behind the trunk, only noticeable thanks to the glowing tree's contrast.

I grunted in shock, almost spilling my drink as I lunged to my feet to press my face up against the window, squinting out at the nighttime scene. The Dark Presence inside me growled territorially. I ignored him. Was I seeing things? After a few seconds of nothing, I began to calm down, convinced I was merely sleep deprived as I settled my drink down with a concerned thought. Maybe I had *Made* the thing appear without realizing it.

Stranger things had happened. I really needed to further my training with Ichabod on my abilities. I was aces in a fight now, at least, but there was a whole world of *finer points* I needed to get a grip on. Or I would be liable to bring deadly creatures into this world that were a *zero* on the friendly scale.

But then I saw the silhouette again. The Dark Presence inside of me instantly muted, which couldn't be a good sign. The figure slunk back into view from behind the tree, and I could see it clearly for the first time. A pale albino humanoid figure, except much too tall, and limbs way too long. Like a scarecrow. It wore straps of a leather-like material crossing its chest, and large pirate-like boots, but that was all I could tell from this far away. It seemed to be searching for something.

Then I saw another one. It slunk up to the first creature, leaned forward as if to exchange a few words, and then turned away, looking frustrated as it, too, began searching the grounds of my estate.

I was bolting out the office door and tearing down the stairs before I consciously realized it. I nabbed up a sword from one of the cabinets, knocking over a vase – which brought Mallory stumbling out of the living room with his lightning spear, ready for a fight. He wore no shirt, only his tight-fitting slacks sans shoes. He took one look at me, my sword, and then followed as I turned to flee towards the front door. He didn't say a word, but I could sense the violence building inside him as he chased me, ready to fight whatever the hell had me so on edge an hour before dawn. Rufus was safely locked away in the dungeon, his new temporary living quarters.

I flung open the front door and raced towards the tree, Mallory hot on my heels. We neared the old Gardens, and I finally got an unobstructed view of the base of the tree. I skidded to a halt, eyes dancing about wildly for any motion, but there was nothing. A raven cawed in alarm at my sudden arrival, but other than that, the grounds looked like they always did.

But other than the raven, still cawing angrily, the scene was deathly silent. It reminded me of a particularly bad ice storm in my youth. It had been so quiet that I had clearly heard trees groaning under the weight of the accumulating ice. From hundreds of yards away. But no sounds of life. Just death. And pain.

But this time there wasn't even that.

Just.

Silence.

And us panting from our fast and furious sprint.

No one was here. I raced over to where I had seen the creature, walking the circumference of the giant bone-colored trunk, shielding my eyes from the mild glow, searching for footprints or any sign of the creatures I had seen. Mallory was following me, not speaking, eyes vigilant.

With no other ideas, I reached out to the Dark Presence inside me, hoping he had a comment.

What was that thing?

My question seemed to echo down a vast tunnel, and I received no response. But I could sense him watching through my eyes.

Hello? I pressed. Still, it didn't answer. *Not so talkative now, are we...* I muttered.

I finally let out a growl. There was literally nothing to see, and my buddy didn't – or *wouldn't* – comment on the matter. I stared at the ground behind me and saw that my own feet had left footprints in the frosted grass, so it didn't make sense to find no other tracks. There should be something here, proving the existence of whatever monster had been lurking here.

I turned to Mallory. "Something was here. Two somethings, to be precise."

He stared back at me, nodded, and then did a quick search himself of the grounds. I waited, staring up at the tree with a pensive frown for a moment. "Where are you?" I asked out loud, and then began aimlessly searching behind bushes, shrubs, and tiny rises and valleys in the grass, pretending I knew what I was doing. I knew exactly dick about tracking. But I could fake quite a lot, and right now, I could sense that my mental state was on the line as I caught a few considering glances from Mallory. I even searched for holes in the ground, or traces of magic. Perhaps they had Shadow Walked here, or something similar. An icy shiver shot down my spine. Hell, they could have been Fae hunters searching for Tory.

Mallory approached me, eyes neutral. "Nothing here, and nothing's been here in a good long while, Laddie. Trust me," he said softly, almost with regretful tone at the risk of offending me. "What did ye see that sent ye off in a tizzy?"

I described the creatures to him, hoping to hear a *ye gad, Holmes!* But his face remained blank. "Any idea what they were, or where they went?"

He took a breath. "Ye sure ye saw anything?" he asked carefully.

"Yes." I looked around at our fruitless search. "Despite evidence to the contrary." I looked at him, concern showing on my face. "Fae?" I asked.

He glanced around, thinking. Then shrugged. "Dunno, Laddie. But I don't think so."

I nodded, frowning at him. He was bare-chested, and covered in old, silvery scars. A lot of them. Some thick, some razor thin, but if I had to count, I'd say close to a hundred in total.

Just on his chest.

"Aren't you cold?" I asked.

He shook his head with a tired smile. "Fresh air in me beard. That's all I need."

I stared at him in disbelief for a second before glancing down at my watch. "No way I'm getting any sleep after that. I need to go out. Keep an eye on," I waved a hand at the grounds around us, "and Othello for me while I'm gone?" He nodded in answer to both questions. "Thanks," I said as we began heading back to the Chateau, me following behind Mallory. After a few seconds, I spoke softly. "You believe me, right?"

His response was a millisecond too late for my taste. "Aye, Laddie..." he murmured.

I didn't argue with him. But it hurt to hear the doubt in his voice. But I didn't have time to get in touch with my wounded pride. I had seen *something*. And I would find out what it had been.

The raven cawed again behind me, tickling my memory, but it drowned under the weight of my current concerns.

It was time to go get cleaned up, eat, and go meet Ganesh.

I ignored the sinking feeling in my chest about Ganesh wanting to speak with me, too. And how the hell was I going to get his damned belt? As I followed Mallory, I quickly analyzed what I knew about him. He liked wagers, to eat, to write, and... *races*.

A mouse... My eyes widened as a thought hit me. Then I grinned, pumping my fist at the sky with a triumphant *hoot*. I raced past a startled Mallory, and headed up to my room. I pulled open the nightstand and withdrew something Indie had left behind. The black and red item glinted in the lamplight. I didn't think she needed it anymore, not after her shift into a Grimm.

But it could prove plenty useful to me. I also made a phone call, hoping my idea would work.

CHAPTER 19

*T*ory rubbed her tired eyes. "You woke me up at the crack of dawn to attend a so-called sausage party," she grouched. I grinned from ear-to-ear. "So where is this glorious mecca of well-hung gentlemen?" she continued sarcastically, holding out her hands as if hoping to be showered with dongs.

"I have to admit, you sounded surprisingly eager for someone interested in—"

"Say it and die," she snarled.

I shook my head as we continued walking through the crowd of people towards a large tent staked into the frosty grass. Outdoor space heaters stood inside dozens of smaller tents, and open fire pits were never far from sight. Also, it wasn't as cold as it had been lately. Coat weather, yes, but not below freezing or anything.

Missouri, the bipolar weather location of America. It could go from seventy degrees to thirty degrees the next day. Or the same day. Even in November.

Kegs, food trucks, loud speakers, and even a few carnival games dotted the gathering.

I glanced at my phone. We were only a few minutes late, because parking had been hell. An Amber Alert had gone off on my way to pick up

Tory, but it didn't seem to be anything related to my current problems. Some relative accused of taking his own child over a custody debate.

I hoped.

We finally approached the largest tent and pulled the makeshift canvas door open to duck inside. A roar of chanting and applause rolled over us. We waved our wrist bands at a man behind a booth. He nodded back after a quick glance down at our hands. "They're almost finished. Hurry on in before it's over," he urged, letting us pass. His eyes hesitated on me for a moment as I walked past, as if recognizing me, but he didn't say anything. I was used to it. I had been a celebrity in the past, thanks to my parents' company, Temple Industries. But it had closed down, and been sold to a German company, coincidentally right around the time the Brothers Grimm decided to ruin my life.

It had upset many families with relatives who had worked there. Now, I was a celebrity for entirely different reasons. Something that rhymed with *one of the most hated people in the city.*

Tory's head darted back and forth at the screaming crowd, mouth open in disbelief as they finally tracked to the stage. We continued walking down the center aisle, rows of chairs extending to either side before us, leading up to the massive platform. It was standing room only now, every chair occupied. Still, it wasn't difficult to navigate the center aisle because everyone was so focused on the event up front. We finally reached a bottleneck close to the action. "One minute remaining!" A voice bellowed from a cheap loud-speaker. The crowd exploded with renewed cheers and shouts as Tory and I watched the competition.

Cheap plastic tables had been jammed together and covered with even cheaper tablecloths to stretch the entire width of the platform, and nine people sat behind the tables, heaps of steaming wieners resting on plastic platters before them.

"Ever seen so many wieners in one place?" I yelled at Tory loud enough to be heard over the crowd's cheers. "It's just so beautiful!"

She rolled her eyes with a faint smile.

The people on stage were demolishing the hot dogs before them as fast as possible while a digital clock ticked down above their heads, showing less than a minute remaining.

The contestants were doing an impressive job, especially a kid at the far end of the table, maybe ninety pounds soaking wet. Most of them were large, middle-aged men. But there was one young girl in the center, trying desperately to keep up with the machine of an eater beside her. Judging by the stack before her, she wasn't even close to her competitor. This was the man the crowd was focused on.

A tiny god in their local hot dog eating contest.

Ah, irony.

He was a young man of average build and Indian descent. He wore sweatpants, sandals, and a T-Shirt that said, *Namaste, Bitches,* with a depiction of Ganesh in his traditional meditative yoga-like pose. I could see this clearly, because where everyone else was leaning forward, eagerly shoving hot dogs into their mouths, he was leaning back in his chair, legs crossed beneath the table, looking about as unconcerned as a cow chewing grass. He was holding a platter of hot dogs in one hand, and using his other to literally shovel hot dogs – bun included – into his mouth at a remarkable speed, easily twice as fast as the girl beside him, who looked rather green at the gills. And he was doing this with only one hand. I was pretty sure that he had four hands when in traditional form.

Because the man adored by the masses was Ganesh, Lord of Obstacles.

And, apparently, Lord of Hot Dog Eating Contests. But, wasn't eating certain kinds of meat against their customs? I'd just have to ask him about it. You know, question a Hindu God about his own customs. Right.

The crowd continued to roar, cheering, and encouraging everyone on for the last stretch, but the struggle was real. The contestants were exponentially slowing down, looking about to burst. The funny thing was, the Indian man didn't look the slightest bit concerned. Or full. As if he could literally do this for hours. Days. Months. *Centuries.* In fact, he didn't look like he was even trying that hard. If anything, he looked to be restraining himself.

I pointed at the Indian dude, turning to Tory. "That's our guy." But Tory was already staring at him with a frown. As I looked back to the stage, I saw that the Indian man was staring directly back at me, still shoveling food down his throat, but more focused on watching me than eating. There was no question he would win. He could stop eating right now and still win. I nodded back politely, and he did the same.

"Stop!" A voice on a loud-speaker announced. "Please give a big round of applause to today's contestants." Everyone did. The participants slowly climbed to their feet, some grinning, most looking nauseated. The tally was 63 for the Indian guy. The closest competitor was 47.

I leaned toward one of the guys beside me. "How long was the competition?"

He chuckled. "New to this?" I gave a guilty shrug. "Me too. Ten minutes. They have to eat the bun and all. Crazy, man. I don't know how they do it."

I nodded, shaking my head. "Thanks."

"No problem. I was looking up the record, and I saw that it's 69. Your friend could totally beat it with practice."

I frowned at his words, but answered politely. Maybe he had seen us exchange a nod. "If you say so. Take care," and I turned back to Tory, only to find the Indian man holding her hand in his palm, and raising it to his lips for a polite kiss. I instantly grew alarmed that a Hindu God was touching Tory.

"Namaste," his baritone voice was like molasses, deep dark eyes seeming to probe into her soul. He released her hand, his tanned skin a reddish bronze color. Tory smiled, her cheeks blushing, and she sucked in a sharp breath of joy.

He turned to me, extending his hand. Seeing no ill-effect from Tory's contact, I traded grips with him. His skin was rough, and warm, emanating a deep heat, as if he had been lounging close to a bonfire for a long while, or had just stepped out of a hot tub. That heat abruptly traveled up my arm and deep into my chest before spilling down towards my belly, invigorating me. The sensation simultaneously flowed down into my legs and up into my head, leaving me feeling oddly euphoric and well-rested, which was much appreciated after getting no sleep the night before. He let go, and I was sure it had only been a brief second, but the sensation remained. Tory was staring down at her own hand, smiling contentedly. "Let us go for a walk," the man chuckled, his great big belly wiggling beneath his strained shirt before he turned to leave.

"Okay," I answered, guiding Tory's shoulders to follow Ganesh, wondering exactly what I had gotten myself into.

CHAPTER 20

*W*e walked, and walked, until the elephant said, "I can hear thoughts, rumbling around in your head. Troubles you have, obstacles you face, just know that every leaf has its place," he said softly, slowly turning to face us.

No one was around us any longer. In fact, I hadn't seen anyone for quite some time. We were in a corridor of trees, like a hallway in a building, the trees looming over us to form a canopy of sorts. The majority of the branches still held a stubborn contingent of leaves, providing us with intermittent shade.

As Ganesh turned, his form rippled, and before us suddenly stood a nine-foot-tall giant of a man. His four thick arms and two legs resembled tree trunks, but pudgier. His skin was textured like an elephant, dry and leathery, and his belly hung out alarmingly far, but didn't seem to get in his way. In fact, I was sure that he could outmaneuver me with the slightest of effort, despite his bulk. He wasn't overweight. He was exactly the weight he wanted to be. Needed to be.

I briefly noticed a tattoo etched into his leathery skin above the black hole of his belly button, but was immediately distracted by a long, thick scar that stretched from end to end of his stomach, reminding me of my purpose here. As if sensing my attention, he was abruptly wearing elaborate crimson robes, gold embroidery decorating the edges, and a golden silk sash tied it closed, the knot resting above his belly. Oddly enough, I noticed that the knot on the sash was beautiful in and of itself, like a piece of art.

If I had tried to hug him, I would have gotten only a face full of belly. The front of his belly. Unable to wrap my arms around his girth.

He was a Hindu God.

As my eyes trailed up, I came face to face with his massive elephant head. A large, scarred trunk rested in a relaxed curl atop his belly, faintly resembling the all-important *Om* symbol – pronounced *Ohm*. In my research, I had read that *Om* meant *ultimate reality, soul, entirety of the universe, truth, divinity, supreme spirit, cosmic principles*, and *knowledge*. And his trunk typically rested in a shape that vaguely reminded his followers of this Sanskrit symbol, even though the symbol was way too complicated for a trunk to duplicate. Even a god's trunk.

But I wasn't stupid enough to voice *that* out loud.

His eyes were a deep, deep reddish brown, swirling like melted strawberry chocolate from those *Lindt* commercials. Scars marred his face in several places, even through his thick, leathery skin, and a ruby the size of my fist was embedded into his forehead, skin folded around it so that it looked to be a natural part of him. His curtain-sized ears were pierced in a dozen places each, and I caught a few nicks around the edges, wounds of some sort. One aged ivory tusk emerged from beneath his trunk, decorated with two golden bands an inch from the tip. The bands held Sanskrit symbols of some flavor, and although I couldn't read them, I could sense the magic emanating from them. Like tiny waves of heat. The other tusk was broken off in a jagged fracture, now weathered and aged like the rest of his tusk.

And his skin was a deep, deep red, like the darkest of red wines catching light in the glass.

"You're beautiful..." Tory whispered in awe.

His ears quivered in appreciation as he replied with what I took for a grin beneath his trunk.

"It's an honor to finally meet you in traditional form." I glanced behind me warily before turning back. "Aren't you concerned someone will see you?"

He shook his head, his ears flapping at the motion, an amused expression on his elephant face. "None can see us until I allow it. Neither will they see you two. They would walk right past us without the faintest idea we are here," he replied confidently. "We need to speak."

What the hell? We were invisible? I hadn't felt even a flicker of warning that he had actually used magic on us. Then the skeptical part of me began to remind me how dangerous it was that this god wanted to meet me, and had suddenly made it impossible for me to scream for help.

"Nothing is the matter, is it?" I asked.

He chuckled, the sound beginning deep down in his belly. "Far from it, Maker." And he continued to watch me.

"You sure ate a whole lot of wieners back there. With practice, you might even take the world record," I said, growing uncomfortable under his gaze. Then, before I could stop myself, I blurted out, "Are you even allowed to eat hot dogs?"

The silence was like a thick blanket for a few moments. Then he chuckled. *"Allowed..."* he murmured, amused. "I changed my plate to *tofu* hot dogs before the competition began." He eyed me thoughtfully. "But I do admire your attention to detail."

What the hell? He had *changed* them to tofu? Just like that? But I didn't have time to ask.

"And I don't need *practice*. I ate an entire feast once. The other guests' food. The furniture. Chandeliers. Utensils. Decorations. Everything. Then I threatened to eat the host. Despicable, greedy Kubera. Vain fool..." his eyes grew fiery for a moment before the look of calm returned. I had come across that name in my research. Kubera was the God of Wealth in Hindu religion. Ganesh cleared his throat. "I am an incredibly patient person, but I do believe you need to ask your question with some haste. That way we can haggle down to an agreeable price." Two of his hands motioned scales tipping back and forth, but the other two rested comfortably on his belly.

"I... wait. You know why I'm here? But you told Achilles *you* wanted to speak with *me*."

"I wanted to speak with you about what you wanted to speak with me about," he answered calmly, eyes blinking slowly as his trunk curled and uncurled absently.

Tory laughed, so I shot her a quick glare to put her in her place before turning back to Ganesh. "That would mean you have some kind of foretelling ability..."

He shrugged. "I see obstacles. Both those that need to be overcome, and those that must be placed. Past, present, *pah*," he tooted his trunk loudly, and I almost ruined my underwear. "What is *time*, anyway?" He noticed our startled and confused looks, so waved off our concern with one of his four hands. "*Obstacles*," he reminded himself, getting back on track. "For example, the one that was placed on you was necessary. To keep those around you safe. You are not at peace. You are wild, unpracticed, and emotionally unbalanced at the moment. You should thank Rufus for aiding you with the gift of an obstacle."

"But he's always unbalanced," Tory offered.

I shot her a scowl. "You're not helping," I warned, and she folded her arms with a smug smirk. I turned back to Ganesh. "*Thank* him? Are you serious? His action could be the downfall of me saving the girl."

Ganesh shrugged. "Maximum effort. Overcome it." I stared back in disbelief. There was no *way* he was aware of the *Deadpool* reference he had just made. That would be ludicrous. He winked at me, and I remembered him saying he could hear my thoughts rumbling around in my head. "*Francis*," he murmured, and I burst out laughing. I couldn't help it.

"Okay, Wade Wilson. Fine. Obstacles. I may be unbalanced, and maybe you think that's a benefit for Team Temple, but I don't see it that way right now. The way I see it, I was extorted to help someone, even though I was going to help him anyway."

"Then perhaps you must prove yourself to this man, despite his poor assessment of the situation. Be the bigger man, so to speak. You have a lesson to learn. An obstacle to overcome."

"Yeah, if that lesson doesn't get us all killed first." He continued watching me. As previously arranged, I silently encouraged the Dark Presence inside of me to begin reciting nursery rhymes. It did so without argument, for once, filling my head with a steady flow of words. Ganesh grunted, cocking his head slightly as he emitted a brief honk from his trunk again, agitated.

I had brought Tory with me for a reason, and had shared my plan with her in the car, but now I wasn't so sure how successful it was going to be with him able to read my thoughts, despite my futile attempt at distracting him with the Dark Presence's continued recital of nursery rhymes filling my brain. Hell, my plan might not even be necessary. I could tell that Tory was growing uncomfortable, because she was wringing her hands. I didn't dare look at her. If Ganesh could read our thoughts, I needed to keep him distracted. Now. Act first. Think later. My motto.

Or, in the famous words of Deadpool, *Maximum effort.*

"Okay, I don't suppose you can just give it to me?" I asked, implying his healing belt. He shook his head slowly, studying me thoughtfully as one of his hands moved to his broken tusk, stroking it absently like one would their chin when thinking intently about something. "It figures. Alright, I propose a race. If you win, you give me the belt. If I win, I get the belt," I said quickly.

He chuckled, belly quivering beneath his robe. "Nice try. I win, I get the belt. You win, you get the belt."

I smirked. "Worth a shot."

He nodded. "A footrace. I haven't raced in ages..." he began to stretch his legs, as if warming up for a jog.

I held up my hand. "Not footrace." I pulled out my pet unicorn's feather. Grimm's previous owner... or *partner*, had been the Minotaur. Grimm was Pegasus' brother. I don't understand how the genes worked, but Pegasus got wings, Grimm got feathers and a gnarly horn.

And technically, I think Grimm belonged to Indie now, but I knew for a fact that the feather still worked. Unlike his famous brother, he wasn't pretty, and he wasn't cute.

He was a killing machine. And my feather could call him up like a cell phone.

Ganesh hissed, stepping back. I called his name in my head, and A bolt of black lightning hammered into the grass a dozen paces away, tearing through the canopy above us. Twigs and leaves rained down from above.

And suddenly, before us stood Grimm. The black feathered horse was huge – like one of those Budweiser Clydesdales, and around his neck was a mane of feathers not dissimilar from a peacock. Except they were also black, with brilliant red orbs on the tips, and they were currently flared out, almost seeming to rattle in warning like that venom-spitting dinosaur in *Jurassic Park.* Or a demonic peacock's tail.

Grimm's massive barbed horn pointed at us, and silver fire flickered on the grass beneath his hooves. I turned to Ganesh with a grin. "Where's your Mickey Mouse?"

He was staring at Grimm with familiarity, but still seemed surprised that I had been able to call him. And that he had obeyed. Ganesh was eyeing the feather in my fist, his meaty hand caressing his trunk thoughtfully as the other one continued rubbing his broken tusk. Good. At least the Minotaur hadn't told him about Grimm. I was pretty sure the two were old friends. "You do indeed have a mount... *Horseman.*"

I stared back, masking my surprise behind a calm face. How the hell had he heard about that? Were the Riders notorious gossips, or had he broken through the Dark Presence's ramblings to read my thoughts again? I didn't acknowledge his comment. Because I didn't actually agree with it, but also because I didn't know *how* to respond to it.

"You propose to race me. You atop *him*, and me atop my Krauncha," he stated flatly. I nodded, more than anything, curious to see this legendary mouse of his to better understand the physics, or magic, behind it. "Very well..." and he began to chant, his voice physically vibrating in my chest. And the trees behind me began to rattle and quake much too loudly.

Shit.

CHAPTER 21

A rodent the size of a Mini Cooper tore the trees in a blur of motion, somehow not disturbing the foliage around him, despite the sound. He landed before Ganesh, nuzzling the god with blood-soaked fur near his mouth. "You've been eating, Krauncha."

A voice *exactly* like Morgan Freeman replied to Ganesh. "Just some pests, nothing innocent."

"That is well."

Tory murmured under her breath, staring at the… *mouse*. I couldn't help it either. The thing was huge. Still proportionally a mouse, but it wore leather bracers around its paws, and the claws were long, yellow, and razor sharp, judging by their crimson-stained tips. Fangs much too large protruded from his jaws, and his whiskers were like concertina wire. He wore a huge saddle strapped to his back, sporting a noose and an axe hanging in holsters for easy access. Its eyes glistened like a ruby on an obsidian sheet of velvet.

The beast faced Tory and dipped his head. "My lady."

"You're… perfect," she said.

I turned to her, frowning. "Perfect?"

The mouse stilled in an instant, and then slowly cocked his head as if curious. "Thank you, my lady. You see me clearly…" he said, sounding impressed. Ganesh was watching Tory curiously as well. What the hell could she see, that I couldn't?

Ganesh turned to me. "Mount up, Temple. This will be fun."

I turned to Grimm, who looked decidedly uncertain. "What is the meaning of this. Did you summon me to play games?" he demanded.

"No, I summoned you to help me *win* a game." I climbed onto his back, no saddle for me, and ignored his continued grumblings. He stomped a hoof, sparks flying out beneath it like a blacksmith striking glowing steel. Ganesh was astride his mouse, grinning at me. As I approached Ganesh, and the imaginary line he had chosen as our starting point, I risked a quick glance at Tory, nodding imperceptibly.

She nodded back, but the look on her face didn't inspire confidence.

Ganesh was speaking, pointing to the end of the tunnel of trees we stood in. "First one there wins." I nodded, gripping Grimm's mane in my fist since I didn't have reins or a saddle. "Tory, if you would please count down from three. We begin on *one*." She nodded, and I prepared for the worst, but hoped for the best. This was a calculated risk. I needed his belt to get Baba's help. And I needed Baba's help to try and save the next kid. The Beast Master had already kidnapped one Freak. Well, two if you counted the chimera.

I couldn't risk him capturing any more people. One, because it only created more people to try and save when we went for the chimera – which would be hard enough as it was – and there was no way I would leave a victim from my city behind. Two, because more victims potentially meant more enemies if the Beast Master could truly control them in full. The more people he kidnapped, the more monsters I would have to fight on my way in and out to save the chimera. The more *kids* I would have to fight, and potentially *kill*. And I wouldn't have enough magic to simply cut loose and let the cards fall as they may. Not until Rufus got his hands – literally – on his chimera.

Tory jolted me out of my thoughts. "Three... two... ONE!" Grimm took off like someone had hoofed him in the stones, and I was screaming for dear life to simply hold on. Ganesh and his mount tore up earth beside me as we raced neck-and-neck. Ganesh was grinning like a madman beside me, hooting and hollering, and even letting out another squeal from his trunk.

Then Krauncha's legs locked up for a moment, causing him to skid into the earth, and I gained the lead. The mouse let out a hiss, shaking his head in confusion, and then pressed on.

But then it happened again. I glanced behind me to see the mouse bolting forward, then abruptly skidding to a halt again, as if having a fit of some kind. Still, they were only a dozen paces behind me, and I had seen how fast the beast could move. Ganesh's face was clouding over with frustration and confusion as he urged on his mount.

I crouched lower and continued on towards the finish line. I heard a loud shriek behind me as Krauncha broke free from his malady and raced after me, eyes furious.

"Uh, Grimm? Pour on the speed. He doesn't look happy."

"Well maybe you shouldn't have let a fledgling Beast Master mess with an ancient beast's mind," he muttered dryly, but he did pour on the speed, flames licking the frosted grass beneath his hooves.

Even still, Krauncha and Ganesh were rapidly gaining on us. The mouse still flicked his head back and forth, as if shaking off a swarm of bees, but for the most part, continued to pelt on, despite the random moments when his legs locked up or spastically twitched. Ganesh's face was tight as he also leaned forward, both struggling to remain in the saddle and to dig his heels in for more speed.

I leaned forward, almost at the finish line. "Come on, GRIMM!" I roared, kicking his sides instinctively. We raced across the finish line, neck-and-neck with the mouse, but Grimm's pearlescent horn broke the line first.

Before I could celebrate my win, Grimm promptly ejected me from his back with a violent motion. I flew, flipped, and landed on my ass, bouncing several times as my teeth clacked together, biting my tongue with a sudden flash of pain that tasted of copper. I sat up, heart beating wildly at both my triumph and my new aches.

"Don't *ever* heel my sides again..." Grimm warned murderously from right next to me, even though he had thrown me a good dozen feet. His horn hit my chest like a baseball bat, knocking me down onto my spine, which somehow managed to strike the only rock in the entire park. I hissed in pain, rolling over a few times until only frosted grass lay beneath me, but I was sure the rock had drawn blood. I stared up at the beautiful crimson and yellow canopy for a few seconds, panting from both pain and excitement. Then Ganesh was suddenly looming over me.

I smiled sheepishly at him. "Go, Team Temple?"

He didn't smile back. One of his hands held the noose over his shoulder, while the other held his axe. The two other hands were folded on his hips in a most disapproving manner. He let out a quick, frustrated honk from his trunk, closed his eyes, and I distinctly heard him murmuring, "*Ohmmmm…*" in a deep, calming baritone. The Hindu chant used during meditation rituals. I risked a peek at Krauncha, who split his glare between myself and Tory way back behind us. The mouse lifted a paw as if considering going back to take a bite out of her, but Ganesh suddenly snapped his fingers. I flinched instinctively, because it sounded like a freaking wrist-thick tree limb suddenly exploding. I saw the mouse lower his paw out of the corner of my eye, but I didn't dare take my eyes off Ganesh, ready to fight if necessary.

Ganesh opened his eyes and stared down at me again, noose still clenched in one of his fists as he now swung it back and forth in a steady *swish, swish* sound. I wanted to melt into the ground under that godly glare.

Then, ever so slowly, his face began to stretch into a smile, wider, and wider until he began to chuckle to himself, and then pat his belly in great deep bellows, interspersed with more trunk-honking. He wiped a tear from his eye with one hand while the other extended out to help me to my feet. I took it, wary, and he pulled me into a great big hug.

Look, basically, I head butted his great big Buddha belly with a loud slap. And he held me there like a mother protecting her child. And that same warmth and euphoria as I had experienced earlier washed over me again, and I found myself laughing. He patted me on the back a few times, rattling my teeth, and then pushed me back to a respectable distance, wrapping a massive palm around the base of my neck as he guided me back towards Krauncha.

"Your little Beast Master… very clever. I was so focused on racing that I didn't even think to check for trickery. It's been so long since I had a good race. I must thank you."

I nodded in relief. "My pleasure." I looked up to see Tory approaching astride Grimm. He came to a halt beside the mouse, dipped his head respectfully, and then freaking knelt low to let Tory down. Polite jerk. Where was his ejector seat when it came to *her*?

Grimm gently nudged Krauncha with his muzzle, drawing him away to speak in private. The mouse stared at Tory for a good long while before Ganesh cleared his throat. The mouse blinked, and then let out a frightening toothy smile at Tory. "Do not fear me. I'm not upset with you, my lady. I'm upset with myself for not seeing the power coursing through your veins sooner. It was well done." And he dipped his head at her politely, then followed Grimm, murmuring words I couldn't quite catch in his awesome Morgan Freeman voice to My Little Pony.

I growled, and Tory blushed, hearing the sound. She smiled, shrugging. "It's my dimples, I think. People," she glanced at Krauncha, "and beasts, I guess, have a hard time staying mad at me. I struggle on as best I can, despite this heavy burden." She winked before sidling up to me, playfully nudging me with her hip. Ganesh burst out laughing as Tory draped an arm around my shoulders, and planted a big fat kiss on my stubbled cheek. I glanced down at her and she theatrically batted her lashes at me, causing Ganesh to roar again in great big honking laughs.

"Okay, you're cute. Dimples and all. I get it. But at least Grimm could have catapulted you before he saw your dimples."

Her expression grew thoughtful as she turned to the elephant-headed god. "Ganesh, I've had an epiphany, no doubt thanks to your presence, and the fact that you help me feel at peace. When someone is genuinely nice to another person, I think I'm just beginning to understand that the other person will reciprocate that same demeanor..." her gaze flicked my way. "Actually, that other person will generally reciprocate *whatever* action you show them. This is just a theory, mind you, but I do seem to have evidence to back it up." She held up a hand to mimic blocking my vision as she used her other hand to point a finger at me. Ganesh roared in laughter, plucked her up in his massive arms, and settled her on his shoulders like a dad with his daughter. She squealed in delight and I rolled my eyes.

"Can you just give me the belt now? I get it. I'm an asshole."

Ganesh carefully set Tory down, who was smiling from ear-to-ear, and then turned to face me. He quickly shot one hand beneath his robes – which looked *wildly* inappropriate, let me tell you – and withdrew a giant scaled belt from beneath his giant belly. The buckle was the size of a dinner plate, and the belt itself was as wide as one of those boxing champion belts. And it looked ridiculously heavy.

So, of course, he tossed it at me.

I yelped, throwing up both arms and firmly planting my feet, but the belt shifted in midair, leaving me to catch what looked like an expensive snake-skin belt.

"What's so special about your belt?" Tory asked, grinning at my over-reaction.

Before he could respond, I felt a sudden warmth wash over me, as if someone had poured warm oil over my head. It flowed all the way down to my toes, and then was replaced by a cooling sensation. And my previous injuries itched for a moment before fading away.

I gasped as the sensation faded away entirely.

Ganesh folded down into a sitting position, crossing his legs, identical to every Ganesh statue everywhere, not acknowledging my reaction, although Tory was staring at me curiously.

Not knowing what else to do, we sat down before him, even though I had already read a version of the belt's origin story. "I was once traveling when I injured my stomach. Sliced it open entirely, as a matter of fact. I killed this snake – more like a dragon than a snake – and bound my wound. It healed me. Since then, the belt has been sought by many to cure injuries, ailments, and diseases. Nate needs this to cure Baba Yaga's pain."

I held the belt in my palms, blinking wonderingly.

Ganesh chuckled. "It changes to suit the wearer." He looked up at the trees above. "If you want to heal the Familiar, you'd best be on your way. Time is almost up for the creature." He locked eyes with me for a long second. "Take heed." I nodded, momentarily frozen. "You may also have need of the belt in the days to come. Like you just experienced, and for other reasons... You will need assistance with all the pain that must be healed. And that healing starts with *your* pain..." he said, levelling saddened eyes with me. But he didn't give me time to ask what he meant before he continued. "There is no harm in using the belt, as long as you do not abuse this gift," he added in a meaningful tone. "Even the briefest touch from my belt is enough to delay lasting harm for the Familiar. For three days." He nodded once, and looked about to leave before another thought hit him. "One more thing. I think it goes without saying, but I must get my belt back. I know the desires of such an artifact, and that many would want it, even abuse it." He didn't point fingers, but I couldn't help but feel like he was referring to my character. "For example, if one were to give the belt away, or put it in an extremely well-guarded Armory, the rightful owner would then be obligated to burn those buildings down to their foundation..." He levelled me with a calm look despite his threat. "Even if one were compelled to steal the belt by a... close friend."

And I knew beyond a shadow of a doubt that he was referring to both Baba and her *House*, and the Dark Presence inside me. I knew the latter, because the Dark Presence instantly grumbled unpleasantly.

Ganesh smiled, and stood, nodding his head as his great big trunk curled and uncurled restlessly. He shook our hands, and then began walking over towards his mount, Krauncha. "We shall meet again, Temple, Tory. I do not wish to be here when they show up."

His hand touched the mouse, and they disappeared.

I turned to face Tory, wondering what the hell he had meant. "You no longer have a skid-mark on your face." She grinned, jarring my train of thought. "You do have the most interesting companions," she murmured, wrapping her arm through mine and leading me back the way we had come. "Let's go see your witch."

"There she is! Get her!"

And we turned to see that Grimm had abandoned us, and two tiny green goblins were suddenly firing arrows at us from a dozen paces away.

And I suddenly realized why Ganesh had bolted.

CHAPTER 22

I threw a violet dome of power up around us, and the arrows struck with sizzling crackles of electricity. The sudden drain of power was enough to make me shiver as my vision abruptly pulsed blue from calling upon my power. Something so simple shouldn't have exhausted me so much, but thanks to Doofus, I wasn't playing with a full deck.

At least there were only two of them.

I threw a quick javelin of the purple power at the closest goblin, but it deflected at the last second, a wooden cuff at his wrist suddenly flaring with blue light, somehow repelling my attack. Tory was shouting something at me, but I didn't hear the words against the sound roaring in my ears, like crashing waves. My power was struggling against the curse. Like trying to force an ocean through a pipe.

I growled at the hideously pale green-skinned figures, all of four feet tall, and looking malnourished. They looked like identical twins. Entirely bald, and wearing sleeveless pelts that hung down to mid-thigh. The drain of power was making me slightly dizzy, as if I had been at it for hours. I wheezed, opening a gateway behind one goblin. Sparks flared into existence around the circle, and were immediately sucked into the darkness like a draining bathtub. Then I hammered him with a blast of air to send him screaming into the darkness as the other goblin continued firing arrows at my shield.

This, too, was deflected without any effort from the goblin.

Although he did dart away from the gateway as fast as possible.

Tory was suddenly standing beside me and threw her hands into the air. Tree branches rained down on us as if a tornado had just touched down, the explosion of twigs, bright leaves, and earth swirling about us like a hurricane, causing the goblins to halt their attack to shield their eyes. But my shield protected us. Tory's eyes were green fire.

Living fire.

I noticed a large branch on the ground, and with a burst of power, picked it up to swipe at the goblins like a game of whack-a-mole. I missed the first time, but swung again in a lateral motion, sending one of them flying towards the gateway.

He hit directly on the ring of fire surrounding it.

And was abruptly torn in half.

His upper body went screaming into the darkness while his legs flopped onto the ground, twitching for a moment before they turned into a pile of compost that was sucked up into the vortex of power Tory was somehow controlling.

"And it burns, burns, *burns...* the ring of *fire!*" I cackled madly as the Dark Presence tried to take over my power, judging me unfit. I fought back, still grinning.

The surviving goblin gasped in terror and turned to flee. But branches and vines suddenly lashed out from the corridor of trees, stabbing through his chest, legs, arms, and even his neck as if he had been struck with a dozen arrows all at once. He cried out as he fell, thick green blood marking the wounds before he, too, turned into a pile of compost.

I let go of my power immediately and forcefully gripped Tory's arm, suddenly terrified.

But she didn't stop. I squinted my eyes and shouted her name three times, using her true name as the fires in her eyes grew brighter, like a venomous snake or a nightmarish monster.

"Tory Marlin, Tory Marlin, *Tory Marlin!*" The vortex instantly stopped, and the debris rained down around us. The canopy was destroyed.

Tory wobbled slightly, and then her now normal eyes fluttered closed, and she collapsed.

I caught her before she struck the ground, but I, too, was dizzy, so I fell to my knees with her in my arms. I panted heavily, struggling with sudden exhaustion, but was relieved to feel her breathing normally.

"What the hell?" I whispered to myself, stroking her cheeks in wonder.

I gently settled her onto the ground and approached the remains of the goblins. The smell of compost was fresh and pungent, but inside each pile was a wooden wristband, etched in whorls and curlicues of an alien language. "You seeing this?" I asked the Dark Presence inside of me.

Yes. Fairy make. Typical armor for those who hunt wizards.

I frowned. "They have a regular crew of wizard hunters?"

They did in the old days. Seems the Queens reenlisted them.

I opened my mouth, but a voice interrupted me. "Who... are you talking to?"

I discreetly pocketed the bracelets, not wanting to leave them out where anyone could find them, and turned to see Tory staring at me with terrified, and concerned eyes.

"No one. Just thinking out loud," I said with a faint grin, hiding my troubled thoughts at the Dark Presence's answers.

She nodded after a second. "I'm so sorry, Nate..." she sobbed. "I should have reacted sooner. I didn't mean for you to use your power."

I waved off her concern, approaching. "Don't worry about it. Didn't take up very much power at all," I lied. "Can you stand?"

"Yes."

"Then let's get the hell out of here," I said, extending a hand to help her to her feet. "And I think we just had our first reaction from you using your powers. Just like the sprites warned."

CHAPTER 23

I sat in my study, staring out the window at the large silvery tree, waiting impatiently. I had sent Tory home to check on the Reds and to get some rest from our sausage party. Hell, I could use a good rest after our fight with the goblins. I felt hollowed out, as if my soul was starving. I guessed that Othello was still sleeping, because I hadn't seen anyone upon my return.

I growled to myself, impatience getting the better of me as I waited on my guest. Where was she? I needed her help, and I needed it *now*. It was early afternoon, so if she got me the information soon enough, I could gather the crew and set up a trap. Maybe even catch the kidnappers, or even the Beast Master himself, if he participated in these abductions. I fiddled with the wooden bracelets in my pocket as I waited, the Dark Presence growling in displeasure at the contact. They didn't feel any different from regular wood, but their ability to nullify magic definitely put the Dark Presence in a mood, and I could sense that he was examining them like a scientist, despite his grumblings. I ignored him as I focused back to the matter at hand. If she would just hurry the hell—

"Where is it?"

I jumped, spinning in my chair. Baba knelt before my desk, cheeks stained with fresh tears as she begged without shame. And my office suddenly reeked of offal, blood, and death.

The Familiar towered behind her, hunched low as it glowered in my direction. It was almost as if Baba was experiencing the same pain as her Familiar, as she was clutching her abdomen and grimacing. The Familiar had already had bad posture, but now…

The Familiar was practically folded in on itself, barely standing. And the violet glowing cracks were brilliantly lighting up the room, almost as if a force was trying to break free of the bone mask, like a chick trying to break free from its egg. And Baba didn't look to be doing too well either.

I stood slowly and approached the pair. I began to unbuckle my belt, and her hands began to reach out for it pleadingly, like a beggar on the street reaching out for a coin.

And that's when my Butler walked into the room. Dean took one look at me unbuckling my pants, then at the gnarled, old woman kneeling before my crotch. He didn't even acknowledge the Familiar.

He blinked.

He blushed.

His mouth opened once, then clicked closed.

Then he turned on a heel and left without a word.

Baba didn't even notice. She stared at the belt hungrily, desperately, hope brimming in her eyes as she clawed for it in desperation.

I groaned, imagining how *that* must have looked to Dean.

"This isn't a show. Give me the belt," she whispered. "He doesn't have much time. *I* don't have much time."

I nodded, pointing at the couch. "Put him there. This is specific magic. I can't just hand it over. It doesn't work like that." Baba's eyes instantly grew skeptical, but I kept my face open and honest. "Well? Hurry up, if you want me to help him!" I urged.

That made her move. She groaned to her feet, stumbling slightly, and touched the Familiar's shoulder. The creature hissed, and was instantly lying on my couch, breath wheezing with pain at the sudden motion. I walked closer, began to murmur unintelligible things under my breath, and placed the belt over the Familiar's body, careful to make sure I touched both his body and the mask.

The room suddenly flashed purple and then yellow, and the cracks slowly began to tighten closed. I continued chanting, closing my eyes, and papers began flying about haphazardly. The Familiar was locked rigid, gasping for air, and Baba was frantically wringing her hands, tears streaming down her face.

I pulled the belt away suddenly, and the Familiar went slack, motionless. Several seconds went by before it sucked in a large gulp of air, gasping for a few more seconds before falling back asleep with one word on its lips, "Missssstressssss..." Baba shoved me out of the way and collapsed onto his chest, hugging him tightly. Then the room was silent, except for her sobbing and his breathing, which sounded heavy, healthy, and deeply, deeply asleep.

There wasn't even a trace of a rattle in it anymore.

Cracks still marred his bone mask, and in places, a bit of purple still shone through, but the cracks now looked old, and mostly healed. Still, I knew this was only a temporary reprieve. Baba lifted her head, placed a hand on the Familiar's chest, and then slowly turned to face me, cheeks still wet.

"Thank you..." she whispered. She took a deep breath, glanced back at him, and studied his mask. Then she turned to stare at the belt in my hands. I had to force myself not to jerk it away instinctively. She cocked her head, as if I had done just that. Then she lifted her gaze to mine. "Why does he still appear injured, although greatly healed?"

I decided to be honest. Like I said, I didn't have time to go picking fights with everyone. "He is not fully healed yet. Although he is perfectly safe for the time being."

She began to breathe harder, faster, and her shoulders began to tighten. "I... see..."

I held up my hands, and coincidentally, the belt. "Too much right now would kill him for sure. Trust me. Trust *this*." I waggled the belt. Her eyes tracked it like Sir Muffle Paws watching a laser pointer on the wall. "He just went through a great shock to bring him back from the brink of death." She flinched. "Oh, yes. You weren't imagining it. He was *this close* from dying," I held up my thumb and forefinger, barely a space between the two. "He needs to recover from this, and then we will complete the healing. In three days. You have my word."

She watched me warily, skeptically. "And this just happens to give you what you need without giving me what I need," she said in a threatening whisper.

I shook my head, then hesitated. "Well, yes. Technically. But I swear I will make this right."

"Give me the belt, and I will see that he gets the proper rest before healing him completely."

"You don't know the words."

She watched me patiently. "That was gibberish. There was no power from you. It was all the belt. Do not test my resolve, or my intelligence again, Maker," she hissed.

"Fine. You're right. There was no spell, but Ganesh gave me strict orders to keep it in my possession."

She was quiet for so long that I began to grow a twitch every time she breathed, fearing an immediate attack. She took a slow, confident step forward, gaze unflinching and unblinking. "Know this, Maker. If you deceive me, I will wait exactly three days, and then visit you. You say my Familiar will survive that long. We will visit you while you sleep. And we will slowly, deliciously, peel the skin from your hide. I will use the last of my power to keep you alive. I will use a rusty old knife to tear the flesh from your bones, not daring to risk diverting any of my power for such a trivial task. Because, you see, I want you to experience the pain I have experienced. I will make you watch my Familiar..." she took another step, eyes dancing with madness. "Gobble. You. Up. And *then* we will move on to your organs. He will drink your blood while digesting your innards." She poked a finger at my chest, enunciating each word. "While. You. Watch."

I swallowed audibly. "You could have just said, *thank you for healing my friend*," I muttered.

She pointed at my desk and a lance of fire bolted from her gnarled fingernail to burn a message into the wood. Thin tendrils of smoke rose from the surface as the fire winked out. I turned back to her, but they were both gone, leaving me alone in my study. I rushed over to the desk to find an address and a time burned into the wood. Only one, not two. Damnit. At least it was a start. I began to put the belt back on, but a shadow startled me, causing me to look up in alarm. Dean stood in the doorway, watching me put my belt back on. I jerked it back out of the loops in my jeans more forcefully than necessary as his eyes scanned the mess of paperwork on the floor and desk, as if one wild party had gone on in the few minutes he had stepped away.

Goddamn it.

"I see you are... finished," he said carefully, face devoid of any emotion, showing only duty.

"Dean, it wasn't—"

"You need not apologize to me, Master Temple. Othello was searching for you earlier. I informed her that you were…. Entertaining a female companion." My jaw dropped to the floor, but he continued on. "I understand that Indie has been gone quite some time, Master Temple." He cast his eyes down, ashamed – of himself or me, I wasn't sure. "Please call on me if you need anything further." As an afterthought, he called over his shoulder. "I cleaned up the vase you broke earlier this morning. It had been in your family for over 100 years. Your mother was particularly fond of it…" he said, sadly. And then he left.

Stab. Twist.

"Dean!" I shouted, but he didn't return.

I sat down heavily in the chair, staring at the belt in my fist for a long time. Then I turned to stare out the window, and began to drink straight from the bottle. Proprieties be damned. For all intents and purposes, Chateau Falco had a resident GILF lover. I took another long drink, and stared out the window for a few moments, fiddling with the belt and the cuffs.

Ganesh had told me that I needed healing. That I had a lesson to learn from all of this. Obstacles to overcome. But what could a healing belt teach me? I was running low on magic, so wasn't sure the lesson was related to magic. I decided to wander the halls, let off some of my anger.

Yes, walk, drink, and clear my head. Hopefully, it would help me *learn* things.

Like Tyrion Lannister and the famous quote of his.

I drink and I know things.

Perhaps I could drink and *learn* things. Like how to rescue a shifter child tonight.

I kept the bottle in my hand, but I did tuck the belt safely into my safe rather than wearing it. Along with the magical cuffs.

Just in case Baba decided she wanted to jump me and steal it since I had admitted to her that I was limited in my magical defenses.

Better safe than sorry.

CHAPTER 24

I had been walking the halls for quite some time when I came upon a dim section of the house with full length windows stretching down the hall. I was on the upper floor, and it granted a stunning view of the grounds. I paused, staring out at the scene, gaze resting upon the silvery tree for a few moments. The wind blew forcefully, causing the massive branches to sway back and forth, knocking a few of the razor-sharp leaves free. I watched as they lazily drifted down to the ground, and then flinched in surprise as a pale creature darted out from behind a bush to smack it out of his way. He scowled down at it, stomped on it, and then began sniffing the air. His fists flexed at his sides, and then he began walking towards the base of the tree. Not wanting to lose him from my sight by running outside, I did the next best thing. I began fumbling with the latch on the window so that I could yell at him.

The glass window opened, providing me with a fresh, unobstructed view of the tree. As I looked up to open my mouth and shout, I stopped.

He was… gone. I blinked, eyes questing the bushes and trees for any sign of movement.

What the hell?

The cold wind began to howl louder, but I didn't care. I crouched down to my knees, out of view, eyes peering over the windowsill, and spent a good five minutes studying the tree, waiting for him to come out of hiding.

He must have heard me open the window, and had seen me. If he saw I was no longer there, perhaps he would come back into view. I took another sip from the bottle, waiting. I heard a door click behind me and glanced back sharply. Dean was exiting one of the storage rooms. He turned to find me kneeling below the open window, bottle of liquor in my hand, obviously acting mischievous. I grinned at him in embarrassment.

He blinked, glanced past me out the window and the cold wind rushing inside, then settled patient eyes on me. He opened his mouth, thought better of it, nodded at me politely, and then slowly backed away. He disappeared down the hallway and I heard him quickening his speed. I realized I was still grinning like an idiot.

He could write a book about his experiences here, and make millions.

I turned back to the window with a sigh and, realizing that the skulker wasn't going to reappear, stood with a frustrated *huff* and pulled the window closed. As I was reaching for the latch to lock it in place, I glanced through the glass one last time and saw him again. I was already shouting as I pushed the window back open.

The moment the window swung free, leaving only empty air between me and the creature, he was suddenly gone again. I stared in disbelief. There had been no puff of smoke, no magic. He was simply gone. Then I frowned, slowly turning to study the window. I reached for it and began to close it again.

And the creature was suddenly visible. But... only when looking *through* the glass.

As I was staring through the partially-open window, stunned by the observation, a particularly strong burst of wind caught it and slammed it closed, shattering the glass to rain down upon me. I fell on my ass as one of the pieces sliced deeply into my forearm. I leaned back with a hiss, glancing down at the bleeding wound. I crouched on the thick carpets, surrounded by glass shards as I heard heavy feet pounding my way. I ignored them and my wound, and crawled over to the large piece of glass that had cut my arm. The edge was stained with my blood, and it was about the size of two of my hands put together. I picked it up, gazing at it wonderingly, watching as my blood dripped down the surface.

I held it up to the tree...

And there the creature stood, studying the grass at his feet, entirely unaware of me.

I heard a gasp and a muffled curse behind me.

I turned to find Dean and Mallory staring at me, eyes practically bugging out of their sockets. I held up the bloody glass for them to see, more blood dripping freely down my arm as the wind rushing into the house blew my hair in every which direction. "The glass. It lets me *see* things," I whispered, more to myself than anything.

Dean sucked in a breath, and Mallory's mouth dropped open as they stared at me in horror.

"I know. It blew my mind, too," I said, grinning at the marvel of magic and construction used in building my mansion.

They shared a concerned look, and then Mallory grabbed Dean by the shoulder and forcefully stormed him back down the hall, out of sight. I frowned, but was too enamored with the amazing fact that the windows of Chateau Falco were freaking *enchanted*.

I jumped to my feet and stared out at the tree. Nothing.

Then I held up the glass and peered through the bloody surface. And saw the limey bastard still skulking about. "I've got you now," I whispered, and began to laugh.

I carefully set down the glass and tore off my shirt, using my teeth to bind the cloth to my wound. Then I picked up the large piece of glass and began barreling towards the front door. I bolted past Dean and Mallory, who stared at me with obvious alarm, but I ignored them, laughing wildly as I shouted, "I got him, Mallory! The glass. It's all in the glass!"

Othello, wrapped in only a thick towel, was exiting one of the bathrooms. I stumbled into her, but quickly caught myself, suddenly terrified I would drop the glass. I leaned my back against the wall, staring down at the precious item to see that I hadn't broken it. I looked up to find Othello staring at me with horrified eyes. I was grinning like a mischievous teenager, shirtless, covered in blood, and holding a sharp pane of glass.

Her towel had dropped to the ground, and she stood utterly nude before me, pale skin exquisite and unblemished. Her breasts heaved as she stared from me to the glass, and she was very obviously cold, but she didn't seem to care as her eyes locked on the blood.

I grinned. "It's okay. The glass is safe. It lets me see things that aren't there," I whispered. Then I realized I was wasting time. "I'll be back in a bit. Put some clothes on or you'll freeze that cute little butt of yours right off!

Damn your luck, Death!" I shouted, laughing as I ran down the hallway again.

I raced out the front door and made my way to the tree, careful to keep the glass at my side so I didn't drop it. I reached the trunk of the tree, and with a nervous sigh, held the glass up in front of my face. The creature was abruptly visible, only a dozen feet away, and this close, he looked like a pure killing machine. Leather straps crossed his chest, holding long, milky white knives. His eyes were a frosty blue, like chips from ancient glaciers, and he scanned the ground in search of… something. Long, reptilian hands ended in white, scaly claws, like an albino lizard, and his legs and feet looked to be reptilian too, like a dinosaur. At least, judging by the calf-high boots covering them.

His elongated jaws also jutted out like a reptile, with inky black fangs ending in jagged, pointed teeth.

And he didn't see me as I took a few cautious steps closer.

I stopped and watched him for a time, stunned at the unknown creature, but also growing uneasy as he didn't seem to notice me. I was only six feet away from him now, and openly watching him. Before, I had come out here to threaten him, declaring to know what he was doing on my property, but now that I saw him up close…

Not only was I reconsidering how badly that conversation might go, but I was also growing a little nervous about what he was doing, and why he hadn't acknowledged me at all. Did he even see me? Did he know where he was? Did he know I was here? And the Dark Presence had decided to take another nap, so he was of no help.

I cleared my throat.

The hole where his ears would be – again, like a lizard – might have constricted in my general direction, but other than that, he kept right on searching. Frantically. Desperately.

What the hell was he looking for?

"Excuse me. What are you doing here, Scaly?" I asked, the proper balance of command and curiosity.

He froze, and slowly turned to face me, eyes narrowed as they locked on the piece of glass between us. He took me in with a gaze that let me realize he was not in the slightest bit concerned for his safety. Then he looked past me, and around us. Seeing no one, he turned back to me, leaned closer, and waved slowly, as if wondering if he was imagining things.

I waved back with a light smile.

"You sseee meee," he hissed, spine straightening.

I nodded, still holding up the glass before us.

"If you can sseee meee, I can eatss youss…" His nightmare jaws opened up with a hungry growl, and he launched himself at my face.

I shouted on instinct as I dove clear, managing to drop the piece of glass in my fright. It shattered on the ground, and I found I was alone again. My head darted every which way, terrified that now that I could no longer see him, I was about to die an unseen, horribly violent death from those black teeth or his white knives.

But I saw nothing.

And nothing happened.

As I spun in slow circles, searching for the lizard-man, I spotted Dean, Mallory, and Othello watching me from the driveway. They looked concerned, and considering.

They shared a look with each other, and then turned away, leaving me alone.

I took one last look at my surroundings, saw the pieces of glass on the ground, and shivered. I stomped on them for good measure, and began trudging back up to the house, wondering what the hell was going on, and wondering how I was going to tell anyone about it.

After all, the second the beast knew I could see it, it had been able to attack me. But the second I dropped the glass, nothing had happened. Almost as if the beast *couldn't* do anything to me if I couldn't actually see it. What the hell?

CHAPTER 25

I walked into Shags, a barbershop, a few hours later, and found him seated at a chair. He tracked me as I walked inside, but he didn't move his head, allowing the barber to continue uninterrupted. I sat down in one of the unused chairs opposite him. It was past dark now, and the place was closed for business.

For all but a select few.

We didn't say anything, but I could see the calculating look in his gaze, no doubt eager to hear any updates about tonight. I stayed silent as the barber continued to work, having taken one look at me, and receiving a calming murmur from his customer that it was okay for me to stay. I rolled my eyes. As if anyone would have been able to kick me out anyway.

After my run in with the goblins and my introduction to the creatures snooping around my tree, I had gone back to my office to search for answers. And to heal my wounds with Ganesh's belt. I had decided to leave the cuffs and belt locked away for now. I didn't want to risk losing them in a fight. Hell, I had even swung by the Armory to check with my dad about the windows. I hadn't shared details, not wanting to terrify him, but if anyone had known about the enchanted glass windows, it would have been him.

I had hoped.

Of course, he would know nothing about the tree, seeing as how he hadn't been alive when the tree came into creation. And I had yet to share too many of the details about that night with them, not wanting a lecture, and not wanting to remember any of the details: The Dark Presence now living inside me, the one I had temporarily partnered with to kill the Brothers Grimm.

It never tended to go well when you told someone that you had an imaginary voice inside of your head, urging you to do dark deeds. Or that you had seen creatures no one else could see. But my father had been less than helpful, only wanting to see me use my Maker ability, and to talk about the educational text that Ichabod had left me. He was fascinated by anything happening in the real world. My engagement. Wedding plans. My Maker power.

I left in a hurry, because none of these things were pleasant conversations at the moment.

I hadn't seen Mallory, Dean, or Othello since coming back inside, but to be honest, I hadn't wanted to talk to them anyway. I had too much going on to worry about their feelings.

So, I watched the werewolf get his hair cut.

The barber finally stepped back, appraising him. "Satisfied so far?"

Gunnar glanced in the mirror, turning his head side to side so his one eye could see it all, and then smiled.

"On to the other one, then?" Gunnar nodded.

I frowned. What were they talking about?

Gunnar loosened his shirt collar, and abruptly shifted so that his head was in wolf form. I glanced down at his hands, and saw that they were lightly furred, meaning he had done the next to impossible shift that only Alphas – or really powerful werewolves – could do. Part man, part wolf, remaining in a bipedal state.

The barber took one calming breath, and began to trim Gunnar's thick, snowy white wolf fur.

I burst out laughing. "Really?"

Gunnar slowly swiveled his eye my way, and gave a slight nod between cuts. "It chafes in this form. Especially around the neck where my collar is."

"Halloween is over, so why are you planning on walking around as a wolf-man?"

He shrugged slightly, careful not to interfere with the barber, who was leaned down over Gunnar's neck with a pair of scissors, cutting carefully. He cursed a few times, reached into his drawer, stared down at a new pair of scissors, and then sighed, resuming with the first pair of inadequate shears. Apparently, wolf fur was harder to cut than human hair, and he was already using his sharpest pair.

"I find it more necessary than you might think," Gunnar murmured, tilting his head back to expose his throat. "In this form, I can maintain rationality while utilizing the strength of my beast. If only the most powerful werewolves can do this, I figure there must be lasting benefits. It also serves to remind everyone who I am. Both my friends, and my foes," he added with a light growl. "I don't need anyone else getting attacked while someone is looking for the Alpha. This way there can be no mistaking it. Anyone wants trouble, they know exactly whom to come to."

I blinked. "You're saying that you are getting your fur trimmed so that you can be a more recognizable target."

He shrugged. "That's one reason. Like I said, the clarity of this hybrid form is quite... thrilling." He smiled through wicked fangs, causing the barber to flinch a bit, thinking he had nicked the werewolf. The man didn't look the slightest bit alarmed at cutting a werewolf's hair. Just that he might have cut him. Then again, it was after hours, so the man had to have known this would be a special visit. Maybe he was a wolf, too.

I watched in silence as the maybe-werewolf-barber continued trimming Gunnar's ruff. His icy blue eye tracked the barber's scissors in the opposite mirror, ready for an attack in this vulnerable position. The barber finally stepped back. "This should help with the... discomfort of mortal clothes while in your Alpha form." He leaned in, made another quick snip that only would have bothered a perfectionist, and then tossed the shears into a glass jar full of a blue antiseptic solution.

Gunnar stared in the mirror, nodding finally.

The barber took off the cape around Gunnar, used a blow dryer to get the last of the loose fur away, and then stepped back again. Gunnar unfolded from his chair, Tee bulging and stretching over his massive wolf-man bulk. He saw me staring and grinned.

"I'm convinced that *Under Armour* was designed for werewolves, by werewolves. The spandex material is perfect for accommodating my shifts." It looked like he was wearing a Batman costume, so perfectly defined were the contours of his musculature underneath the thin fabric.

The world was unfair. He must have understood the look on my face, because he grinned.

He paid the man, hopefully for two haircuts, and then followed me outside. "Jeffries called me earlier. Told me you two spoke." Gunnar said carefully. "I backed up your statement."

I frowned back at him, not sure whether to be angry or thankful. Jeffries and Gunnar had worked together in the FBI, so his confirmation would go a long way. Then again, Jeffries didn't *need* confirmation. He could sense lies. Which meant I was kind of angry that he felt he needed to back up my statement.

Ashley saved me from answering as she rolled the window down from inside a shiny new silver Yukon Denali XL. Silver car for a werewolf. I rolled my eyes at the arrogance, but was mildly proud. Ashley studied him with a hungry smile, and then whistled in approval. I shook my head with a grin, turning back. Gunnar had flung a pea coat around his shoulders, and was shoving his arms through. He popped the collar, striking a dramatic figure in the dark night. His white wolf head stuck out above the black wool coat, lone eye squinted as his body struck an arrogant pose for Ashley's benefit. She hooted and hollered, even honking the horn once. White furred claws peeked out from Gunnar's sleeves – again, a hybrid of wolf and man – sporting long obsidian claws, but more in the shape of a giant man's hand, not the paw of a full-blown wolf. He looked absolutely terrifying.

And intimidating.

And... *Royal.*

"Alright, GQ. Let's go. I need to talk with you about my BM problem."

He frowned back, finally opening his long wolf jaws to reply. "I don't want to hear about your bowel movement issues, however fascinating they may seem to you."

I scowled. "The *Beast Master*," I clarified, rolling my eyes.

He frowned, looking suddenly uncomfortable. "Look, Nate. No one wants to catch this punk as bad as me, but I have something that needs taking care of tonight. Pack business." He walked up to me, placing a giant claw on my shoulder. "Why don't you take a night off, and we'll plan a hit for tomorrow night, or a way to break into the circus and save everyone. Maybe call in a few cards for help. I think everyone is mutually vested in the outcome of the Beast Master. You just need to remind them of it."

I opened my mouth in disbelief, and then closed it. "You're... *busy?*" I asked, dumbfounded.

He nodded, looking guilty. "It shouldn't take long. But this is vitally important, and..." he looked truly uncomfortable now. "You seem a little bit out of sorts lately. I think the... *Grimm* business is getting to you. And the *family* angle." He emphasized the word, referring to Ichabod. "And maybe a whole bunch of other stuff you haven't allowed yourself to process."

I stared back in disbelief. "What are you *talking* about?"

He gripped my shoulders tighter in his arms, and stared at me intently with his lone eye. "You were talking to yourself on the roof. Alucard told me about it. And I've caught you – a lot of times, now – muttering to yourself as you grip your cane." I instantly released the handle in my fist, unaware I had been gripping it. He noticed, nodding as if to prove his point. "Then you were caught unaware by Rufus, which I didn't think was possible for you. Then the news with Indie..." He shook me gently. "Take a night off, man. Find your center. We can't have you going off half-cocked. *Kids* are involved this time."

Seeing the hollow socket and scar where his other eye had been reminded me that when I had taken dangerous *adult* monsters into a fight, even they hadn't been well-enough equipped to survive it unscathed. What would happen if kids were involved? And if I was half-cocked like he thought?

I sighed in frustration. "Look, you're right, but these kids don't have time for that. One of them is in danger. Tonight. Hell, we may already be too late! An Amber Alert went off earlier." Gunnar nodded, grimacing. "So, my personal sense of *peace* doesn't really factor into the equation. The fucker took someone last night. A red dragon." Gunnar winced, at least it looked like a wince on a wolf. "But I have reason to believe that the Amber Alert wasn't our target. Just another Amber Alert. Like the handful we've seen over the past few days." I trailed off. "I hope."

He let out a long breath. "How many wackos are kidnapping kids these days?" He growled angrily, shoving his hands in his pockets. "Fine. I'll be finished shortly." Ashley honked her horn lightly, as if to emphasize this. He frowned at the car, but nodded before turning back to me. "Let Ashley and me take care of tonight. Tell us where the kid is, and I'll be sure he's safe. Or she." His face looked calculating for some reason.

I was already shaking my head. "No. I'm going with."

He studied me like a petulant child. "No. If you want my help at all, then you need to go back home. Take a breather. This Maker thing is too dangerous for you to be out of control with it. You're also emotionally unstable when it comes to kids in danger. Or women. I'll take care of this. Go home."

I could feel the command. He was trying to use his Alpha power on me. Which meant that I knew he wasn't going to back down, no matter what I said. And this tipped my patience down a dark, bottomless hole where it died. "Fine. I'll take a break. But if I feel calm in an hour, I'm going in. I'll call you to see if you're done with your club meeting. Must be awfully important for you to choose it over a kid's life," I growled, turning my back on him. "I would hate to inconvenience your dinner plans just to save a life."

God chose that moment to bitch slap me. One second I was lifting my foot to storm away, the next I was pounded into a pile of empty trash cans a dozen feet away. I jumped to my feet, the dark voice whispering into my ears, ready to destroy everything around me, and sort out the facts later. Ashley was staring through the windshield of her idling SUV, eyes wary over the werewolf claws now gripping the steering wheel.

Gunnar stood staring at me patiently, his hand still extended from where he had punched me. His eye trailed down to my hip meaningfully. I realized I was gripping the sword cane with tight knuckles. I released it as if it was scalding hot, and cast my eyes down in shame, panting as I fought against the Dark Presence. It submitted with a disappointed grumble. A few seconds later, I looked up to find Gunnar staring at me from his giant wolf head, arms folded.

"Fine. You're right. I'm a little stressed right now. Maybe I should go take a break."

He nodded. "I'll call you when I'm finished, but I don't think I'm going to change my mind. Ashley and I will take care of this one. You can join us tomorrow. Text me the address."

I wanted to lay waste to the SUV, slam him into the building, light the street on fire… and I began to snarl a threat at the Dark Presence inside of me for thinking such things.

But only a silent laughter echoed up from my soul. I shivered, understanding dawning.

Those thoughts had been all me.

I gave a short, harsh nod, and turned on my heel. I reached the end of the street, rounded the corner, and once out of sight, ducked into a shop entrance, hidden. I watched for a few minutes until I saw the SUV drive past me, and then out of sight.

I plucked out my phone and made a call.

"Oh, this ought to be fun…" a silken voice answered.

"I need a wing…chick. You free?"

"Only if you promise death, screaming, and destruction."

I smiled. "I know how to show a girl a good time, if that's what you're asking."

CHAPTER 26

*W*e were ducked behind a dumpster in a filthy alley outside of another soup kitchen. "You sure you can identify a Freak on sight? Without them doing anything?"

The Huntress looked distracted. "I stalk. I hunt. I kill."

I guessed that was a *yes*.

I watched the constant flow of filthy bodies in and out of the building. "I don't think they're going to try a smash-and-grab with all these people around. That would be stupid. We go in silent. Like the *G* in *lasagna*."

The Huntress slowly turned to me with a condescending frown. Then, without looking, she whipped her bow into position, aimed directly above us with an arrow already drawn, and loosed it before I even had time to widen my eyes. The arrow hissed up towards the fire escape, and a raptor-like scream split the night amidst a blur of feathers. Then a man crashed down the fire escape with loud bangs and clangs, to land inside our dumpster. The lid promptly crashed closed, effectively trapping him. The sea of homeless people near the soup kitchen began to scatter like a herd of cats fleeing a charging dog, shouting, yelling, and stumbling over each other in their haste.

I stared at the Huntress, ignoring the mayhem. "What the hell was that? That was *not* silent!"

"A werehawk of some kind. Probably not a werepigeon," she added dryly.

A fucking *werehawk*? How could she be so calm about that? And surely there was no such thing as a werepigeon… Her face gave me nothing to go on. "Well, let's go question him!" I blurted.

She shook her head, calmly studying the screaming people running about the entrance to the soup kitchen. "He's dead."

I hissed. "Well, what the hell was the point of that, then?"

She opened her mouth to answer, but her eyes instantly grew distant, and she hissed, jumping to her feet to pelt down an alley without waiting for me. "We're not alone! There are more!"

And I heard it. The sounds of violent fighting from an adjacent alley. I cursed, tearing after the Huntress. I didn't want to rely on the power and knowledge of the Dark Presence any more than I absolutely had to. I silently promised myself to only use him as a last resort. I felt him growling in disappointment at my mental promise as I forcibly shoved people out of my way, tripping and stumbling into a brick wall.

Which saved my life.

A vampire flew right past me, fangs snapping closed on my coat rather than my throat, ripping off a large chunk of fabric. I skidded to my knees, spun, and unleashed a wallop of purple power, angled up at the sky. I had practiced this one all by myself, and was proud of it.

A small wave of violet electricity uppercut the vampire, and upon contact, latched onto his ankles and turned into the equivalent of a Looney Tunes rocket, spraying sparks as it carried him screaming high up into the night sky. A small supernova exploded above the opposite building where the werehawk had been hiding, marking the vampire's demise. I grew momentarily dizzy as I watched the explosion, and the delayed *thump* suddenly hit me in the chest like a giant feather pillow, knocking me onto my ass. It looked as if some big idiot had set off a commercial-grade firework.

Except for the screams.

But the Ultraviolet explosion had incinerated all evidence of the attacker.

I climbed to my feet, shook off my dizziness, and scanned the area for immediate danger. Seeing nothing, I tore off after the sounds of fighting, racing through the alley to find a small opening between buildings. Brick exploded past my ear as a werewolf crashed into the corner of the adjacent building, falling to the ground in a pitiful whine. I looked up to find a fucking Gorilla staring at me.

Except his fur was blue.

Really blue. And crackling with static electricity. And his shoulder sported three arrows. Not that it seemed to faze him at all. Hell, blue arcs of electricity even trailed up to the tips like a Tesla experiment before fading away.

His eyes blazed with blue fire, and he roared at me, the sound like a physical burst of pressure. I held up my forearm on instinct, but no magical power came at me.

I lowered my arm to see a half dozen wolves suddenly pepper him from all sides in a coordinated attack. The gorilla grabbed one by the ruff of the neck and threw him into another wall, seeming to laugh at the puppies nipping at his thick fur. Another dove at him, and he hammered his giant fists down into the pavement, using their length to lift his body high as he tucked his giant legs up. The wolf's jaws snapped shut on empty air as he skidded beneath the gorilla. The damned dirty ape stomped down on him, and I heard bones break.

A white-furred beast of a man slammed into the gorilla, claws slicing open the monster's cheek before the ape went flying into the wall. The building shook, and several metal poles broke free from the fire escape above, slamming into the pavement near the gorilla. I blinked at the werewolf's familiar coat, which was now shredded. The other wolves darted clear, leaving my friend to face the gorilla alone as it scrambled to its feet, screaming at the white one-eyed werewolf.

I seethed with rage, briefly entertaining joining forces with the gorilla to smack the shit out of my best friend. "Meeting, eh?" I snarled, vision now pulsing blue at the combination of my emotions and my power.

He didn't reply, but his shoulders did twitch in guilt as he continued to stare down the gorilla.

I saw a group of figures fighting in the alley behind Gunnar, and then heard a sharp scream.

Two sharp screams, to be precise.

A little girl, and a grown woman.

"GUNNAR!" Ashley screamed in a desperate wail.

"NATE!" the Huntress yelled almost at the same time from the same direction as Ashley. Gunnar shot me a panicked look, but the gorilla wasn't having any of it. He had picked up one of the metal poles, and was barreling towards the Alpha werewolf. They met in an explosive thud as Gunnar dodged the pole, and I heard him growling in a strained roar. "Get the girls, Nate!"

I didn't have to be told twice.

I ran straight at the fighting hulks, watching as Gunnar's eye shot wide in confusion, but then I used a boost of power to catapult myself over them. I looked so cool.

Then I landed wrong, on top of one of the other injured werewolves, eliciting a sharp yelp of surprise, and a quick slash of claws on my leg that felt like fire. I crashed to the pavement, shot a blast of power at the wolf as he instinctively attacked the body that had just crashed into him. The wolf went sailing straight into the gorilla, knocking him off balance for Gunnar. The wolf grunted again as it struck the blue gorilla, and then sailed off into one of his brethren. The wolves hunkered low, growling at me, but I ignored them, scrambling as I dizzily tore off after the sound of the screams. I heard the slamming of car doors, and the repetitive *thwack, thwack, thwack* of the Huntress' bow and arrow.

I rounded the corner to the sound of screeching tires at the far end of the alley. Arrows riddled the side of a retreating van, one even stuck in the tire, which had gone flat as a result.

But that wasn't enough to stop them. The van disappeared from sight, and the Huntress cursed, rounding on me. "Took your damned time!" she yelled, taking an aggressive step towards me.

I threw my hands in the air. "You forgot to mention the fucking scene from *Jumanji* back there!" I yelled right back, then my eyes shot wide and I whirled back around, realizing Gunnar was still fighting the gorilla. If we could catch him and question him, maybe we could find out where Ashley and the kid had been taken.

But I came face-to-face with Gunnar, striding towards me, claws dripping dark blood, and two or three wolves shadowing him like deadly sentinels. His eye was ablaze, and his muzzle was bloody, whether the blood was the gorilla's or his own, I wasn't sure. His coat was tattered and burned, hanging freely from one shoulder, the other side simply gone. He shook it off, not even looking as it fell to the filthy pavement, leaving him in the now equally tattered and burned spandex shirt I had seen him wearing at the barbershop.

He stopped a dozen paces away, broad chest heaving as it stretched the spandex. The wolves beside him whined, hunkering low in shame.

"Where is she?" he demanded, licking the blood from his lips.

"Gone," the Huntress spat acidly.

His shoulders went rigid, but I shot him my own scowl. "How was your meeting?" My voice also dripped venom, and he had the rationality to briefly look mildly ashamed. Very mildly.

"Unsuccessful resolution," he snarled.

"You lied to me."

His fists flexed. "Not really a priority right now, Nate."

I took a menacing step forward, fist clutching my cane, which suddenly flared to a full-blown sword, a warning that I was about as close as I could be to drawing on the Dark Presence deep inside of me. The Dark Presence groaned with excitement. I released it, barely, and took a deep, calming breath. "Actually, it kind of is a fucking priority," I said, the world tilting oddly for a second.

"I don't have time to deal with your temper tantrums right now. I—"

"Will admit that the reason your fiancée is in the back of the Beast Master's van is a direct result of your arrogance!" I interrupted with a shout, the dizziness fading.

His claws actually began to shake, and the wolves beside him hunkered lower, ready to eat my face. The enemy of their Alpha, no longer a friend.

"I—"

"Was a fucking idiot. Repeat it. Now." I roared. "You thought you could swoop in and save the day, and your fiancée is now as good as dead in the back of a filthy van."

I didn't even have time to move. His claws were suddenly around my throat, and he was holding me against the brick wall. The Huntress had an arrow aimed at the base of his skull, eyes as pitiless and cold as ice chips, but that would do me no good.

"Call off your wolves, or I'll have a shiny new pelt," she murmured calmly. I saw that she was actually grinning with anticipation.

The wolves yipped and barked in frustration, unsure what to do. I stared down into Gunnar's lone eye, and didn't flinch. I poked him in his stupidly large chest, fingers poking through the holes in his *Under Armour* shirt, enunciating each word with a firm prod. "This. Is. Your. Fault." His lips curled back into a snarl, ready to eat my face. "You better let go, pup," I warned.

We were too heated, too in the moment to remember our past. That we had been friends.

"And what if I say, no?" he whispered darkly, eye no longer that of my friend, but of the local Alpha. "*No one* talks to me like that. What if I simply say, *no*, and let my pack teach you a long-deserved lesson?"

I smiled as the Dark Presence murmured a single word in my head. "Underestimate me. That ought to be fun." And I slapped the palm of my free hand over his rune tattoo, focusing on the word the Dark Presence had whispered. It didn't need to be spoken aloud, and I didn't want anyone else hearing it. Plus, my silence would make this look all the more impressive.

An arc of blue power hammered into him, and he slammed into the brick wall on the opposite side of the alley, suddenly human as dust and debris rained down on him. He groaned as he unsuccessfully tried to stand. His wolves decided it was finally time to retaliate.

"You bring the claws, but I bring the terror," I snarled, lost in an ocean of blue, not even caring that I was dizzy and that the world seemed to tilt crazily.

I threw up a sizzling curtain of violet power, and the wolves hammered into it.

The result was akin to a swarm of bugs hitting a bug zapper, except it didn't kill them.

Those unlucky enough to be in front touched the shimmering curtain, and an explosive *zap* of power sent them cartwheeling back into the alley and out of harm's way, or into their brothers and sisters behind them. None of those who had tried attacking me were even in wolf form any longer, all of them forced back into human form. The dark whisper in my head murmured approvingly. I shut it away and released the cane that I hadn't realized I was holding again.

As soon as I let go of the cane, a bucket of frigid water seemed to dump over my head, and I suddenly felt unbelievably exhausted. And much, much weaker. The dizziness made me want to vomit.

But I didn't let any of that show on my face.

Gunnar climbed to his feet, and I felt the Huntress staring at me in awe.

The remaining wolves smart enough not to have attacked the magical shield stared at me with pure hatred. Gunnar looked even angrier.

"Whenever you're ready to admit your stupidity, and save your fiancée, you know where to find me. But know that there will be a reckoning for this..." and I motioned for the Huntress to follow me as I turned my back on my best friend. I called out over my shoulder, rage practically dripping out or my pores. "Or you can just wait until Fight Night to see her in action."

The Huntress was staring at me, but said not a word. She simply nodded in approval, and followed me, glancing back now and then to make sure we weren't followed.

I wouldn't have minded a little following. I was amped up and ready to do some more damage, despite my exhaustion. Friendship be damned.

CHAPTER 27

*O*thello stared at me. "Wait, *what?*" she whispered incredulously.

I sat in my chair, fingers tapping the cover of the book in my lap, *Through the Looking-Glass*. I didn't know why I was holding it, other than the tempting thought to speak with the man on the other end of the book, see if he knew anything that could help. Or maybe just to go visit him for a spot of tea and some pleasant background music to my current mood.

The soothing sounds of Rumpelstiltskin's anguished wails under the tender-loving-care of the Mad Hatter.

The Huntress answered for me, interrupting the mental image. "The wolf betrayed him, and lost his lady-love in the process. And from what I gathered… lost a friendship, too." She didn't sound the least bit concerned about it. Just a statement of fact. The Huntress was one cold cookie. I was pretty sure I was her only friend. I glanced at her icy gaze, and bit back a shiver. *Friend* may be stretching the definition of our relationship.

But she *had* been there for me last night.

More than I could say about Gunnar.

I fidgeted with the wooden cuff on my wrist, the one I had taken from the goblins. I had decided to start wearing it after the alley fight yesterday, assuming with my limits, that it was an added protection I desperately needed with the curse and violent dizzy spells that now plagued me when-ever I tried using my powers. Worth the risk of losing the cuffs. Who knew, perhaps the BM had wizards in captivity and it would come in handy for our next fight.

And I would make sure there was another fight.

And I would use the cane to make one hell of an introduction. The Dark Presence growled approval at the fires burning inside me.

I had also used Ganesh's belt to heal my wounds, because, why not? He had told me it was okay to do so. I noticed no one was speaking, so looked up.

Othello seemed to be debating her response, shooting a meaningful glance at Mallory, who was leaning against the wall, frowning as he intently listened to the conversation. Rufus sat in silence, close to Mallory, subtly realizing that if he opened his lips, someone would bite his head off. This was a family matter. "I think you may have been too hard on him," Othello finally said.

I slowly turned to look at her, and wondered what about my face suddenly made her flinch.

"I mean... he *was* simply trying to help, right?"

I shook my head. "He *lied* to me. That's not *helping*. He told me he had pack business to attend to, and that he would call when he was finished."

Mallory cleared his throat. "With all due respect... wouldn't ye call what he did... *pack business?*"

I turned the age-old Temple glare on him. "If *pack business* means *betrayal*, then yes. Be productive, or leave, Mallory. I won't say it again."

He frowned, looking properly chastised as he averted his eyes. But not before shooting Othello a not-so-discreet glance.

The Dark Presence growled territorially.

Othello reached out and touched my hand atop the book. I flinched back, and power instantly covered my arm, spitting sparks onto the table. Othello yelped in pain, and flinched away. I let the power go, as well as my fist around the cane handle. Her eyes saw the motion, and shot wide with an inner hurt. Like a puppy kicked by his owner. Not understanding how they had earned their master's wrath, and still wanting nothing more than to go and lick his hand. I'm not saying Othello wanted to lick my hand, but that look did make me feel like utter shit.

"I'm not feeling very... *touchy* at the moment," I said softly, my tone apologetic.

"I like him like this," the Huntress grinned, crossing her legs on a stool.

"Not helping," I muttered.

Othello pleaded again, but kept her distance this time. "He was an idiot. That's true. But maybe he's just concerned for your..." she trailed off, face flushing as she struggled to find the right word. A *nicer* word for whatever she had been *about* to say.

I leaned forward. "My *what?*" I spat, icily.

"Sanity," the Huntress chuckled. "I think she was going to say, *sanity.*" I rounded on her, couldn't think of anything to say, so turned back to Othello with the obvious question on my face.

"Well-being," she finished softly. "I think he was just concerned for your well-being."

"I don't need a babysitter." I could feel the rage building up inside of me, threatening to break free and do some real damage. Cut loose. "Everyone, out," I gasped in a forced whisper, fighting the urges pressing against me as the world began to shift to blue shades. I spun my chair around to stare out the window, trying to think calm, non-homicidal thoughts. I heard everyone get up to leave, so cleared my throat. "The Huntress can stay." There was a meaningful pause before I heard the shuffling of feet again. Finally, I heard the door click closed. I could sense the Huntress' presence behind me, but didn't turn as I spoke. "What do you think?"

She was silent for a time. "I think you're at a Crossroads." I turned to her with a frown.

"Explain."

She was staring down at her bow in one hand, eyes distant. "You're in a dark place right now. Your woman betrayed you. Or abandoned you. Or whatever you want to call it. With your grandfather. Then a fellow wizard cursed you. Then your friends betrayed you. And the only one sticking up for you is the unhinged murderer you battled not a few months ago." She smiled sadly as she looked up, fingers idly drumming her bow. "You're in a dark place. A crucible."

I let out a sigh of frustration. "Well, what do you propose?"

She leaned forward, staring into my face intently. "*Survive* it. Whatever survives the crucible will be stronger, more resilient, more powerful. Make peace with your darkness." Her eyes grew distant, and I shivered as she leaned back, staring out the window at the morning sunlight. I hadn't mentioned anything about darkness, or the psychopath riding shotgun in my mind. Still, her words struck too close to home for my liking. "Or you give up. Give in. Admit defeat. Be burned to ashes." She shrugged. "But I suggest that you keep walking. Nothing wrong with a little darkness. It conceals your secrets," she glanced pointedly at where my cane handle lay concealed at my hip. "I prefer the darkness. It lets you see people as they truly are. Takes away disguises. Character is who you are in the dark. Or who you are when no one is watching."

I studied her thoughtfully, ignoring the Dark Presence's pleasant agreement from inside the cane. Inside *me*.

I finally nodded. "It doesn't change anything. I need to save the chimera. And the others. With or without help." I shot her a hopeful look. "You in?"

"I'll look at my schedule," she murmured. "But I think I can move some things around." An idea crossed her features, but she masked it well, continuing in what she considered nonchalance, "As long as you can set up a... date with Tory." The Huntress had been fantasizing about Tory ever since their first encounter outside my family mausoleum, our first real battle against the mysterious woman before me. The interest hadn't been mutual, but Tory had changed lately. And she was grieving. I had caught more than a few subtle glances between the two of them over the past few months. And now that I thought about it, her sudden interest in spending more time around me began to make a lot more sense. I had chalked it up to the fact that we had so handily defeated her a few months ago, and that she now harbored a begrudging respect for a worthy adversary. *Ally with power.* No one truly knew the inner workings of the Huntress – friend or foe – but I was pretty sure she was right where she belonged.

By my side. And friends helped other friends set up dates, even if by subterfuge.

I smiled. "I'll see what I can do."

She nodded. "So, where is the next target? The Beast Master typically takes three per city before moving on. Baba have any ideas, or just the one?"

I sighed. "Just the one. And I don't think Baba will be willing to give me another. But I've got an insider who might be able to help. I don't think the Beast Master will move until tonight. We have a bit of time, because he's got some new... warriors to welcome into his fold," I added with dark thoughts.

Ashley. And three new victims. The chimera, and two from my city.

Well, Ashley was Gunnar's problem. They had both knowingly lied to me, so although I didn't want any harm to come to her, I was too furious to see things any other way right now. Ashley had known of the deception too, so her abduction was solely a werewolf problem, not mine. My job was to get the kids, and the chimera. Gunnar could clean up his own house.

"So, where to next?"

"The bar. I need a drink."

Her eyes glittered as she smiled with her teeth. "Little early, but okay."

"Maybe I'll get Tory to give us a ride…" I said casually. Her grin was hungry.

CHAPTER 28

I pushed the new door open, a steel-reinforced piece I had paid for.

After I had, well, demolished the old one in a hissy fit.

A scarred, blonde-headed man stood behind the bar, watching us as he polished a glass. His forearms were thick, but not overly so. He wore a flannel shirt, sleeves rolled up to reveal his forearms and scarred knuckles. I could see the tendons and the veins flexing and moving beneath his skin with each movement, revealing the strength of the man tending bar. His eyes tracked my movements like a tiger hunting prey. Quite a few patrons filled the bar, drinking quietly as they murmured softly to each other. It didn't typically get wild until much later in the evening, but the place was practically booming compared to normal. Upon seeing me enter, a few stood, downed their drinks, and then left. A few more left as the Huntress walked in behind me with Alucard in tow.

"Bad for business, you three," the man behind the bar growled with a soft grin. "Did he win?"

I cocked my head to the side for a moment as I approached. Confused. Then I realized he was asking about the hot dog contest. I nodded, chuckling as I sat at the bar, my accomplices flanking me with confused frowns of their own at the Heel's question.

Achilles' eyes narrowed slightly, but he nodded back. His gaze flicked to the Huntress and Alucard, nodding politely to each.

"I'm in need of some entertainment," I said.

"Tough to find when you're a billion—" he stopped, and a dark grin washed over his face. "Sorry, when you're *used* to being a billionaire, but suddenly find yourself down on your luck. I truly feel just *terrible* for you."

I rolled my eyes. "I manage."

He met my eyes. "So, you came to my bar. As you can see, entertainment seems to flee when you arrive. And I was having such a *lucrative* day…" His eyes flicked to the door leading into the back, where two heavy-chested men stood, arms folded, scowling at life in general as they guarded the door.

Myrmidons. Achilles' famed warriors, and sackers of Troy. I frowned, but stayed on point. "I was thinking something a bit more… antiquated."

He set down the glass, casually looked around at his remaining patrons – who were studiously ignoring us – and turned back to me, voice low. "Not really the kind of thing I discuss with non-paying customers," he said.

"Then how about you be a good bartender and quench our thirst?" I added, rolling my eyes.

He folded his arms. "It's always amazed me how no one has put you in your place yet."

His Myrmidons were suddenly, silently, paying much closer attention to me and my friends. The Huntress waved at them, invitingly. I grinned back at Achilles. "It's not for a lack of trying."

Achilles grunted, and poured me a scotch. The Huntress got a white wine – which I was surprised this type of bar carried. It was known as a *Kill*, due to the grave potential of dying here. One of the most dangerous types of bars out there. I hadn't expected white wine to be on the menu. Achilles handed Alucard a bag of blood. "Fresh from a young donor. People pay top dollar for that to use for blood transfusions. Filling their bodies with the blood of a young person." He rolled his eyes. "Idiots."

Alucard didn't take the blood. "How about a scotch, like Nate."

Achilles blinked. "You mean both?"

"No. You can keep the blood. Just a scotch, please."

We were all silent for a few beats before Achilles poured Alucard a scotch, weighing him with a thoughtful look.

The vampire *truly* didn't really like blood anymore if he was turning down a fresh bag.

Well, Daywalker, not vampire. I hadn't taken the time to research it in depth, because I hadn't wanted to draw attention to him. For example, if Daywalkers were so rare, me asking for details on one would absolutely guarantee that Alucard would get flagged, which could mean the Academy coming to town, or else a gang of vampires. And the way he now acted like a father to the Reds, I wouldn't just be putting him in danger, but the whole family. And I couldn't do that.

And now the Fae wanted him for his powers. I thought about Tory, and how the hell she had done whatever she had done to forever change Alucard that night we fought Rumpelstiltskin.

She had used those newfound powers to save our bacon that night. She had whipped the women into order, controlling their previously out-of-control beasts, and pointed my girls – Indie, Ashley, and herself – at our enemies. The Huntress now sitting beside me being one of those enemies, alongside Baba Yaga and Van Helsing. And now they were all helping me.

Alucard feigned nonchalance as he took a sip of his drink.

"Now that we're all paid up, where can I go to see a particular violent form of entertainment. Tomorrow night, to be precise," I asked, leaning forward.

Achilles scanned the bar, pretending to wipe off the bar with an old rag. "Not the payment I was referring to, Maker. And you know it."

I sighed, opening my mouth to attempt to guilt-trip him, but the Huntress spoke first. "How about this?" she asked, slapping a stack of money onto the table. It was $10,000, still in the bank wrapper that said so.

Achilles didn't even look at it. "No. Wrong form of currency. Do you three not listen? You heard what I said at the mansion."

The Huntress shrugged, shooting me an apologetic look as she pocketed the stack of money. Oh well. She had tried.

"I don't have time to run to the Vaults," I finally said in a low tone.

Achilles shrugged. "Then it looks like you'll have a pretty uneventful night." He folded his arms.

I threw my arms up. "Achilles, come on! We're talking about *kids*, here."

The Myrmidons shifted. That was all, but I calmed down, placating them with an apologetic look. Achilles nodded at me, his resolve breaking slightly. "I get that, Temple. Really, I do. But I have to pay the Beast Master in Gold, and the Vaults are too ritzy for my deposits. Ask too many questions. Which means that I can't simply take her cash," he pointed a thumb at the Huntress, "and exchange currency. They won't let me. And if I try to pay the Beast Master's cronies in cash, they will know something is up. Which you don't want." He leaned forward, not angry with me, but a desperate look in his eyes, urging me to do what had to be done. "So. Go to the fucking Vaults. Now."

I stood from my stool, nodding in resignation before turning my back on him. It didn't matter that he was right. I couldn't risk drawing attention to myself or Achilles. Or else the Beast Master could just up and kill Ashley and the chimera, possibly fleeing town before I could get to him. Or changing venues, or a million other things. Then, I would find myself without power, totally helpless, and no longer a certified member of the supernatural community.

Which would basically be an invitation to every creature I had once pissed off that it was high time for a little payback.

But I didn't have to like it. Might as well make this quick. But I had another problem with going to the Vaults. One I hoped the Huntress could help with. "You guys ever been to the super-secret, I'm not supposed to talk about it, Freak's Bank of St. Louis? Otherwise known as the Vaults?" I said to my crew.

I caught brief shakes of their heads as I pushed open the door leading back outside. "I'll need your cash. I'm kind of strapped right now. But I should be able to repay you very soon. If we survive, of course."

She arched a brow at me. "Looks like I'll need to protect my investment over the next few days, then," she smiled, handing me the money. I leaned in and gave her a quick kiss on the cheek, which made her flinch, and then blush in confusion, unsure how to take my response. She was like a wild animal, and I wanted her to get more familiar with being human. I nodded at her gratefully, and then turned away as I heard a horn honking at us from a few cars down.

Tory leaned out the window of the SUV that had dropped us off at Achilles' Heel. "Did you get it?" I could see the Reds in the back seat as we approached.

I shook my head in defeat. "Plan B. He didn't take the bait."

Sonya squealed in delight from behind Tory. "We get to see Nate's magical money spot!"

Aria's groan was perfectly audible, and Tory's face went crimson.

Alucard just shook his head, shooting me a desperate look. I chuckled, as we climbed into the SUV, listening to Aria tease Sonya.

As Tory pulled out into traffic, I admired the interior of the car. Tory noticed my assessment and shrugged. "Gift from Raego. After..." she sighed, "everything went down. Figured I would need a bigger car to take the girls around town."

I smiled. "That was very nice of him."

Tory shot me a grin. "He also wanted to buy something he knew you couldn't. Made him feel like the bigger man. It's what he said, anyway." I laughed. "Where to?" she asked, grinning. I told her. She shot me a curious look, not understanding, but she followed my directions, knowing my penchant for skipping on details.

This would be... interesting.

CHAPTER 29

*W*e pulled up to the DMV and parked in back. The Reds gazed in eager anticipation at the disheveled building. No longer caring about the super-cool wizard's bank, but now imagining a future visit to this hallowed place where they would earn their first taste of true freedom.

A driver's license at the DMV.

"I don't get it," Alucard said.

I smiled, and climbed out of the car. I waited for them to join me, and then began walking to the dumpster. "This one was closest. Some of them are more… elaborate." I stopped in front of a brick wall, careful not to step on anything squishy near the dumpster, recalling Baba's hideout. A wall of tall trees blocked the view of the street, and consequently, all traffic.

I turned to my friends to find them all frowning at me. Except the Huntress, who looked bored. "Been here before?" I asked, surprised.

She nodded. "I'm an assassin. How else do you think my clients pay me? I don't accept checks. Or PayPal." She grinned at each of us, especially the Reds. "It also lends a certain prestige among the community. They see me enter the bank, they know someone has been taken out. *This cute little thing offed some badass monster again.* For some reason, I get quite a bit of respect from the employees. I have no idea why…" she winked. The Reds stared at the Huntress as if seeing a Rock Star in person for the first time.

"I still don't understand. The DMV is the epitome of evil. Satan's Asshole, as I once heard it nicknamed. Why would there be a secret bank here?" Alucard asked.

"Because *no one* ever wants to go to the DMV. Anonymity, but still centrally located. Hidden in plain sight. The other branches are also equally dreary government building types." And I turned to knock on the brick in an exact, complicated sequence.

The wall shimmered, and was suddenly an antiquated oak door with a glass window that read *The Vaults – no soliciting, dragon fire, or Fae.*

I frowned at that, never having really paid attention to it since it hadn't ever applied. But this time I had two dragons and someone who might be considered a Fae with me.

I could read the uncertainty in their faces as they shared the same thought.

But instead of talking about it, I pushed open the door.

And we entered a twinkling, ebony marbled throne room. Dozens of black pillars stretched all the way to the ceiling, a good seventy feet above us, despite the DMV only being single-storied. The ceiling was stained-glass windows from end to end, absolutely breathtaking as the colored light shone down on the lobby, reflecting off the black and gold flecked marble floors. There were maybe a dozen people inside, and several of them frowned, recognizing me or the Huntress, I wasn't sure. They looked concerned, so it could have been either of us.

Twin lion statues crouched on either side of the three steps leading up into the lobby, and they sniffed the air as we passed. "No fire, my sweets..." one of them snarled politely at the Reds.

The girls flinched, obviously not having noticed they were alive.

The other sniffed the air, and tensed. He cocked his head sideways and sniffed some more. Then he shook his head with a confused look, and stared at us with distrust. I began to grow very nervous until the Huntress stepped up. "I'm here to make a withdrawal."

The other lion started upon seeing the Huntress. "Of course, my Lady Huntress. I didn't recognize you in... such company," he added, very respectfully. He turned to Alucard, and pointed a paw at a covered hallway leading towards the teller line. "The vampire will want to use the Hallway of Blood, of course." I hadn't ever known what the covered hallway was for, but I had also never entered the Vaults with a vampire. It made perfect sense. They couldn't stand sunlight, so of course they would need a safe way to get to the teller line.

The Huntress gave the lion a curt nod, and strode up the short set of stairs, heading towards the solid row of old-school wooden teller windows beyond the vast lobby. The marble floor was decorated with carved runes. So many, that they seemed decorative, as if creating their own piece of art.

Or one hell of a defensive spell.

As the Huntress stepped into the light from above, I slowed, paying very close attention. Alucard gasped as her form… shimmered into something else entirely.

You see, the glass above wasn't just decorative, as the lions hadn't just been decorative. And as I was sure the Hallway of Blood hadn't been purely decorative. And why I was certain the runes on the floor were not just decorative. They were all safeguards and defenses.

The Huntress was suddenly a fur-clad shadow with orange eyes atop a fiery steed of living vines and tree bark. She clutched a bow in one fist, and a hood cloaked her from forehead to rear, falling over the horse's rump like a waterfall of quivering shadows.

The Huntress, in her true form. The second she was out of the light, she returned to her normal-looking self. She hadn't even slowed, continuing on to grab a spot in the line.

But the other customers definitely noticed, and for obvious reasons, let her take their places, moving her up to the next spot in line behind a disheveled, hairy man speaking urgently to an unseen person behind the teller line.

The Reds hadn't noticed the Huntress' transformation, focused on the scenery itself – the ornate carvings in the obsidian walls around us, depicting battles, landscapes, and glittering kingdoms and castles. Which meant they hadn't noticed when the light struck them, and two adolescent-sized red dragons burst into view for the other customers.

Tory turned to blink at me, stunned. I shrugged, and motioned her forward. She did, and a faint green fog began to form around her, then snap back out of view. The veins on her arms flashed golden, and remained that way, but the green fog momentarily flickered back into place before disappearing again, as if not quite sure whether it should reveal itself. I frowned. I had never seen the spell falter, but apparently, it didn't quite know what to do with Tory.

Alucard watched with sudden interest, before taking a breath and striding into the sunlight.

One of the lions grunted in disbelief, no doubt fearing that a customer had just tried to commit suicide in the lobby. But what they saw instead silenced them completely.

Golden rays of light burst free from his suddenly tan skin, like the spines of a porcupine...

Alucard was a *porcu-shine*.

Which definitely trumped *Count Sparkula*.

But all jokes aside, Alucard looked stunning. Like a god come down to earth. Apollo himself making a deposit.

He glanced down curiously, but of course the spell couldn't show you yourself. He shot a questioning look at Tory who was staring at him in wonder. Then she clasped hands with him, smiling as her eyes grew damp with sheer appreciation at his previously unknown beauty, and she led him out of the light. The Reds were oblivious, now standing beside the Huntress and bickering back and forth lightly, like teenagers do.

I pointed at the teller line, noticing the Huntress had sidled up to another window beside the disheveled man. My friends all turned to look, and I quickly made my way through the light, not wanting them to risk seeing a Maker in true form.

One, because I wasn't sure what I would look like.

Two, because I had a Dark Presence inside of me, and absolutely didn't want them seeing something horrific.

Alucard quickly spun around, no doubt realizing that he had a chance to see me in my true form, but he was too late, as I was already out of the light. He was beginning to scowl in understanding of my deceit when the alarms started going off, great booming bells that seemed to vibrate my very vision.

And silver warriors began dropping from hidden alcoves up in the ceiling – once just presumed to be decorative metal statues, blindfolded and with scales in one fist and a sword in the other to signify *honesty* at all cost.

But now I realized the truth.

They were guards. Just like every other beautiful thing in this place.

And they were bristling with weapons, and staring at me.

The lions roared, and the Hallway of Blood slammed shut with great big iron bars, as did the entrance to the Vaults, and a grid that suddenly block-aded the ceiling above us.

Time to panic.

CHAPTER 30

I remained very, very still, but I was ready to unleash hell if they attacked.

But the statues raced past me, straight to the teller line.

I let out a sigh of relief, heart beating wildly for a moment as I clasped my knees. Alucard had his fangs out, and Tory was suddenly staring at me with fiery green eyes. They widened for a moment as the warriors raced past her, and she spun to locate her girls.

The Reds.

I followed her gaze to see that the Reds were now in full dragon form, and the Huntress was crouched before them protectively, hissing at the disheveled man at the next window.

He had pulled a creature from out behind the teller line, and was holding him by his throat, shouting incoherently. And I realized that he was a werecat of some sort. Some kind of jaguar or something, judging by the partial shift revealing a black-furred feline with massive teeth. He spun, clutching the teller to his chest as a hostage. "You will give me the money. I have to save my girl from the Beast Master!" He roared, ducking a head protectively behind the hostage in his paws. Not just any werecat.

An Alpha werecat.

Then his words struck me. The *Beast Master*... What was he talking about?

It clicked a moment later. This must be the father of the girl I had seen kidnapped in the alley. And apparently, he was collecting money to buy his girl back. Whether he was that foolish, or if the Beast Master truly did accept ransoms was yet to be determined. Before I could ponder it, I sensed a power building off to the side, and spun, but too late to stop her.

A green flash of light exploded around Tory, and twin spears of green lightning slammed into the Reds from a dozen paces away.

But it didn't harm them.

Instead, they instantly shifted back to human form, eyes stunned as they were abruptly yanked back to Tory against their will, sailing over the space between like puppets on a string.

Several of the warriors suddenly rounded on Tory, swords out, while the others surrounded the Alpha werecat at the teller line.

Her secret was out of the bag. She was a Fae of some flavor. In a place that didn't allow Fae.

Then another thought hit me. She had just used her powers, and the sprites had warned us—

The front door of the Vaults suddenly exploded inwards, and a fucking mountain troll roared into the air, clutching a club as big as a car. His wild eyes locked on Tory, and he slammed his club into one of the lions, pulverizing it in a single blow.

Fuck.

Her powers had drawn the Fae.

Not wanting to use my magic, I picked up a fist-sized hunk of marble and threw it as hard as physically possible at one of the warriors surrounding Tory.

I missed, and it clipped Alucard right in the head, knocking the porcushine to his knees.

Hey, sports hadn't really been my thing as a kid.

The warriors spun, lips peeled back as they faced me, blindfolds looking like ninja masks now that I thought about it. I waved urgently, then stopped, remembering they were blind-folded. Goddamn it. "Look. I don't know if you can see me or not, or even understand me, but you need to get us out of here, or else everyone is going to die. The troll is after *us*."

They cocked their heads, and spoke as a single voice from every throat, a dry, dusty hiss. "No Fae."

BEAST MASTER

I waited for more, but they continued to stare at me. "She's not really *Fae* Fae, but more, *I slipped and landed on a Fae, and was tainted with their powers,* kind of Fae." They continued to stare at me, and I threw up my hands. "None of your sensors picked up that she was Fae, which has to mean at least something to you..." I added, hoping against hope.

The Huntress chimed in. "They are my guests, and have no personal business here. I will vouch for them, with my deposits as security..." her eyes scanned the damage to the building as the troll began stomping up the steps, the other lion now a broken pile of rubble also. The thing was ancient. Skin like rock, and covered in warts and scars where his toga hung loose. His yellow eyes were locked on us, and he looked eager to smash first, ask questions later. "And to pay for the damages, of course."

The warriors dipped their heads once, and then began to back away. I held up a hand. "Wait, I need to open a gateway to get us out of here." I knew from their account opening statements that gateways – or any form of travel into and out of the bank – were prohibited. Which I hadn't properly appreciated at the time, because I hadn't known how to travel like I did now. Because it had been an Academy secret. Or, at least I hadn't known about it. Only the main entrance was allowed for ingress and egress. Which was currently blocked by a goddamn troll wearing a fur toga. "The troll will leave if we do. Otherwise we have to throw down right here, and risk even more damage to the building." I eyed the customers, all too terrified to move as they stared from the twelve-foot-tall troll to the hostage situation. "And to prevent any casualties." The lead warrior nodded once, and flung a hand at me. A cloud of silver dust struck me in the chest, and I suddenly felt something tug loose in my chest. Which was likely some kind of previously unfelt block on my power that settled over my shoulders upon entrance to the Vaults.

Which was pretty goddamned cool, if I hadn't even noticed it.

The floor shook as the troll roared again. I hastily threw a gateway open, leading us back to Achilles Heel, the first location that popped into my head. I dove through the opening, shouting, "Come on!"

I landed on my knees on the other side of the gateway, and was instantly dog-piled by my friends. The troll screamed in outrage from the Vaults before I yanked the gateway closed. Stars flashed in my eyes at the use of my dwindling power, and I struggled to breathe as everyone climbed off me.

After a few awkward moments and accidental grabs of flesh, I took a deep breath. I opened my eyes to see a pair of boots only inches away.

I slowly climbed to my feet and found myself staring at Achilles. He didn't look happy. "Where's my money, you fucking lunatic?"

My shoulders sagged in despair. All that time and risk, and we had nothing to show for it.

CHAPTER 31

*T*he Huntress shoved a small velvet sack into Achilles' chest. "Here it is," she said.

I stared at her, and she shrugged. "You guys were too busy dilly-dallying, so I just went ahead and made the withdrawal. Honestly, I can't take you guys anywhere. Like a herd of toddlers," she shook her head.

Achilles hefted the sack, satisfied with the weight of the *tinkling* sound, and then tossed it without looking. One of the Myrmidons at the back door caught it, and then disappeared into the back room. And I finally realized why they were there. They were guarding all the gold for the Beast Master's show.

Achilles was nodding to himself. "Aye, that'll do. And preferable to come from you rather than him," he said to the Huntress. He pulled down a bottle from one of the top shelves, and poured himself a drink. Then began absently wiping down the bottle as his gaze discreetly shot around the room, verifying we were alone. Our abrupt entrance must have sent the last customers fleeing.

Sonya and Aria stormed up to me and shoved me from two different directions.

"You threw a freaking rock at our *dad*," Aria growled before rounding on a heel and storming away to a side table. I followed her to find Alucard sitting at a table, forced to be Aria's patient, even though I knew the blow hadn't really bothered him long-term. He scowled back at me anyway.

Sonya cleared her throat beside me. I had forgotten all about her.

"I'm sorry, Sonya. I didn't mean—"

"You're supposed to keep us safe when things go bad. Not hurt us." She looked on the verge of tears. Realizing this, she rejoined her sister. I watched, heartbroken at her tone. It had just been a rock. I hadn't hit him with a truck or anything.

The three slowly turned to glare at me, and I took a step back instinctively. Alucard was suddenly very, very paternal as he stared at the man who had made his daughter cry. And the girls looked murderous as they stared at the wizard who had hurt their dad.

Jesus.

It wasn't like the rock had actually hurt him. Freaking psychos.

I turned away to get back to the adult table, and found Tory in my way. She prodded me with a very powerful finger, knocking me down into a chair. "Hurt my family again, and we'll have words." Then she stomped off to check on them.

The Huntress burst out laughing, clapping loudly for all to hear.

I ignored her and shot a pleading look at Achilles. "I need a drink. Right now."

He nodded, motioning me over to the bar with a wry grin.

I climbed out of the chair and approached the bar, sitting on a stool beside the Huntress, who still found the situation extremely comical. Achilles slid a glass of scotch my way. "What the hell did you do? Pinch her ass in front of a priest?"

The Huntress choked on her drink, snorting out her white wine.

I grinned, shaking my head. "I accidentally hit the porcu-shine with a hunk of marble when we were trying to get away from the mountain troll."

Achilles glanced at Alucard thoughtfully, remembering the vampire's new interest in sunlight, and then burst out laughing, suddenly putting it all together. He downed his drink between laughter, then poured himself another, muttering, "Porcu-shine," under his breath several times. I didn't dare glance back at the Brady Bunch for fear of being attacked, but could imagine the hateful looks we were getting.

Achilles wiped his eyes, sighing, as he turned back to the Huntress. "Okay. The quarry, tomorrow night, seven o'clock." He replaced the bottle of liquor from in front of him back up on the shelf, and then gave us pointed stares.

"Don't we need tickets?" I asked.

Achilles shook his head, staring only at the Huntress. "No, Huntress. The fact that you know the location is enough. I give the Beast Master his gold – in person – and a list of who is coming. His guards take care of any... party-crashers." He leveled the Huntress with a considering look. "It's surprisingly efficient. Kind of similar to our own... *book club*, just more *fatal*."

"Okay," she said, nodding her head.

"Now, it's probably time for you guys to finish up." He continued in a lower whisper, practically breathing his next words. "Tonight's the last night before the show. Which means the Beast Master has one more night to abduct an extra kid for the fights. Another toy for the more... *experienced* pets of his to dismember."

I shivered at that. Ashley was in his clutches. Would she become a toy, or could she hold her own against monsters who had spent years in the pit? There was really no way to tell, but Gunnar needed that information.

"You should find a way to get this information to... the Alpha," I whispered just as low.

Achilles didn't even blink, speaking in a normal tone now. "Already paid for the information. He was here late last night. Before he joined us at our book club."

I stared at Achilles. "He went to the... *book club* last night?"

Achilles' eyes went distant for a minute as a small smile escaped his lips. "Truly magnificent show. He was something else." He settled his eyes on me. "I wouldn't want to get in his way. Well, *I* would, but if I was anyone *else*, I would stay clear of him. He was... singular in his appetite for violence. Refreshing to see, actually. Earned some respect from the crew. Even *my* crew." He was referring to his Myrmidons. Like the two still standing guard near the back door.

I discreetly assessed the men, warriors to the bone. Myrmidons didn't pass praise on lightly, so if Gunnar had gone to the Fight Club and cut loose enough to impress the Myrmidons, Gunnar was playing on a whole new level.

Because the Beast Master had taken his fiancée. Woken up a sleeping giant.

Achilles cleared his throat. "I think you may want to reconsider your plans."

I shook my head. "I'm not scared of the wolf." I recalled the rune I had deactivated on contact. I hadn't known it was possible, but the darker voice inside of me had whispered just the right advice, and I had responded. Since Gunnar's control rune was tied to my family, I could literally turn it on and off. "Trust me."

Achilles was shaking his head. "I'm talking about the Beast Master. And saving a bloodthirsty chimera." He leaned forward, pretending to clean a spot on the bar before me as he murmured in a low tone again. "The Beast Master is getting ready for a big show. And I'm not talking about the one here in St. Louis. He has a... prior obligation for a certain group we both have knowledge of. The one I tried to warn you about earlier."

I stared back at him, and finally understood. I opened my mouth, but he cut me off.

"Best not say it aloud, but, yes. *Them*."

"*That's* why he's filling his ranks. So, he can provide, what, a party? For *them*?" Achilles was referring to the Syndicate. When I had heard that the Beast Master worked with them, I hadn't considered that he was *currently* working with them. But it made perfect sense now. Achilles had warned me that the Syndicate would likely be in attendance at the show, but I had shrugged it off as merely a *possible* threat, an argument to throw me off my game and keep me safe. Now, I saw it for what it truly was. A very literal, factual, and *likely* warning to leave the Beast Master alone.

I was entirely sure the Syndicate wouldn't want me to crash their party. Not after taking down their army of Grimms a few months back – well, part of their army. Yeah, saying they wanted me dead was putting it mildly.

If that hadn't been enough to earn their hatred, I had met Rumpelstilt-skin a few months later.

Rumpelstiltskin had spent centuries making deals with all sorts of people – power of different flavors in exchange for their soul or some other precious commodity they cherished above all else. Rumps had also been the Syndicate's enforcer, commanding the Grimms, but when I had taken him down, all of his commitments had been dissolved. Like with Achilles here, and even myself and the Huntress. Hell, even Baba Yaga and Van Helsing had traded their souls to Rumps. Depending on the agreement the individual had made, some of his... past clients had kept their powers, regardless of his absence from my world now.

Because he was currently vacationing with the Mad Hatter. A truly horrifying punishment.

And I began to hope that maybe the Syndicate hadn't yet heard about that part.

CHAPTER 32

I frowned. "I haven't seen any embers or sparks," I murmured to Achilles, referring to the telltale residue left behind by members of the Syndicate, marking their presence.

Achilles shrugged. "*They* aren't here. Yet. The Beast Master is getting ready to entertain them. Not sure when. Or where. I'm not really on their VIP list any longer, for obvious reasons."

I nodded. "I'll keep my eyes open." I stood to leave, all my accomplices following me.

"I provided the Huntress with the same information I would to any paying customer."

"Scared of reprisal, Heel?" I grinned.

He shook his head. "No, but I do have a reputation. And that reputation will come in handy in the future. Like it did to the *Huntress* just now," he enunciated her name, making it blatantly obvious that he hadn't given the information to *me*.

"Understood," I nodded. Before turning to leave, I asked him another question. "How's your... friend? The one with the box?"

His face grew harder. "Complicated." I sighed. Yeah, if any girl could be described as *complicated*, it would be Pandora. Before I could leave, he called out. "If anything is on your mind, perhaps Eae could help. Or... Hemingway. That family is a good bunch of listeners..." he added cryptically.

I frowned at him. "What are you talking about, Dr. Phil?"

He motioned me forward. I approached close enough so that only the two of us could hear. "I'll say it a bit more gently." He leaned over the bar, folding his arms. "You're acting fucking insane lately. I've been around you only a few times in the last week and have caught you talking to yourself each visit."

I frowned. "I'm just stressed. Not really talking *to* myself. Just muttering angrily out loud."

Judging by the look on his face, he didn't buy it. "Okay, how about this? When every single one of your friends is moving to a different beat, and instead of talking to them, you create a *Dark Team Temple*," he motioned at my current crew, "you might want to reevaluate your decisions."

The Dark Presence bucked up angrily. "I don't tolerate betrayal," I whispered.

He shrugged. "Even if that betrayal is possibly the *right* thing? You know, because *you* are the problem?"

I blinked. "That's... impossible." I glanced back at my crew for a second to find them all watching me with concerned eyes. I smiled back weakly, realizing that Achilles may have a point. *May*. I turned back to the Heel. "Because I'm infallible," I said with a straight face.

He stared at me incredulously. Then I smiled. He let out a breath, shaking his head. Then he shoved my shoulder, sending me on my way. I nodded, and then headed towards my friends.

"Few other things," Achilles called from behind me. "You have a meeting scheduled at Dick's Sporting Goods. In an hour. Something important, supposedly." I turned, frowning. But his disgusted scowl basically answered my question. There was only one person that could elicit such disgust on Achilles' face, and delivering a message *for* that person was even more degrading. I nodded in response. "Oh, and if that troll shows up, I consider it common courtesy for you to resolve the situation. If I have to do it, I'm putting it on your tab." He paused. "In case that wasn't clear, I'm speaking to you, Nate. Not the Huntress. She's a respectable customer."

I wanted to throw something at him, but he had a point. I turned to my friends. I had to get to that meeting. "Right. We need to get back to the Chateau. I have wards in place that will hide us. Or protect us. Don't want the troll stopping by here. It wouldn't be fair to Achilles."

"You mean you don't think you can handle it. Or that you are scared of

Achilles. Or that you couldn't afford to pay him back if he had to take care of it." Alucard smiled in delight.

I scowled back. "Yes. Pretty much all three of those. Let's get in the car."

"Shouldn't we use a gateway?" Sonya asked absently, practically drooling as she stared at Achilles. I shot Alucard a frown, indicating Sonya's blatant ogling. He shrugged back helplessly.

I muttered under my breath as I stalked out of the building. I couldn't afford to use my magic to make a gateway when a car would suffice.

I stood on the sidewalk, scanning the street with a frown. Aria stepped up beside me, whispering for my ears only. "That's what Sonya was trying to tell you. We left the SUV at the Vaults."

I groaned, and although I wanted to destroy something, I reached out with a hand, and squeezed Aria's forearm in a silent *thank you.*

Without another word, I opened a gateway, using my rage to instantly shut down the Dark Presence who stirred deep inside me, and stepped through the swirl of sparks to enter my study. I didn't speak, letting the others figure it out on their own. They had walked through enough of these to not need a tour guide.

Once the last of them stepped through, I let the gateway drop, and collapsed into my chair, exhausted even at such a brief use of my magic. It wasn't just the use of my limited power though; it was the constant internal struggle with the Dark Presence. He wanted to show me things, and in time, to take over me completely if he could manage it.

It was an exhausting dance.

I turned to Alucard. "I need to see your old friend for a chat. Care to join me?"

Alucard's eyes tightened. "Can I kill him?" Apparently, he had understood Achilles' cryptic comment too. I hated it when other people understood my plans ahead of time. The look of surprise on their faces was like crack to me. Oh well.

"No, not yet," I sighed. "He's working for me."

Alucard and the Huntress shared a look. "Just curious, Nate, but have you noticed that you seem to be allying yourself with untrustworthy people, and distancing yourself from those you've cared about for quite some time?"

I kicked my feet up on the desk. "I'm not going to talk to you about Gunnar. He made his bed. And I read him a bedtime story. Enough said."

The Huntress actually laughed at that. "It was rather impressive, Sparkula. You should have seen it."

"Don't call me that," Alucard growled, but his heart wasn't in it.

"Yeah, he prefers porcu-shine, now," I sneered.

Tory actually let out a laugh, having been the only other person to see Alucard's true presence under the spelled glass at the Vaults. "Oh, that is so *cute!*"

Alucard hissed at me. I smiled back, but noticed the Reds glaring at me with calculating, mischievous teenaged eyes. The look was basically a promise that I would regret what I had just said. Drama queens.

Before Alucard could start swinging, Tory walked up to him and led him to a chair. She pushed him down into the chair as Sonya used a nearby decanter to dampen a cloth. Tory accepted it and began wiping away the blood on his face. He let her, continuing to study me. I made a whipping motion with my hand, smirking at his immediate reaction.

"Want to talk about your buddy, your pal, the stray dog?" Alucard asked, eyes hard.

The dark voice inside me responded instantly, territorially and I unclenched my fist from the cane handle, not realizing I had grabbed it. The Huntress watched my hand, then shot me a look, as one would a particularly skittish horse, trying to calm them down. Alucard looked pleased.

"Fuck calm," I snarled. The voice inside me purred approvingly at the rage burning inside of me.

And I wasn't holding the cane handle.

CHAPTER 33

I stared up at the sign to the store above me and burst out laughing. Someone had vandalized the sign, crossing out the *G* and replacing it with a *W* so that it said Dick's Sporting *Woods*, rather than Dick's Sporting *Goods*.

Alucard chuckled beside me. "Nice."

"I don't get it," the Huntress said, frowning.

"It's teenage boy humor," I shrugged, striding inside. The Huntress made a direct shot for the hunting section, aiming for the compound bows and hunting arrows. I smiled. It was where we were supposed to meet anyway.

She looked like a kid in a candy store, dancing from item to item, practically skipping.

Alucard mumbled something under his breath, but was smiling distantly as his eyes stalked the customers, searching for my contact. He wasn't happy about this errand.

"Tory made it home alright with the Reds?" I asked absently.

He nodded, still scanning the crowd. "Yep. Getting rest, just like you commanded, Master Temple," he said, dryly. I turned to shoot him a dark look, but suddenly grinned instead.

"Dead," Van murmured into the vampire's ear, suddenly pressing the barrel of an airsoft gun at the base of Alucard's spine. It was still in the box, but he had snuck up on us without us knowing. A familiar smell permeated the air and I grinned wider. Alucard, on the other hand, did not.

"Garlic?" I asked casually, pointing at his other hand. It clutched a paper sack of almonds, smelling strongly of cheese and garlic.

"Personal favorite of mine," he smiled, openly chewing a large mouthful, staring straight at Alucard.

Alucard took one perfect step, dug his hand into Van's sack of nuts – *heh* – and withdrew a large handful. He shoved them in his mouth, staring down Van Helsing the entire time. He didn't blink as he chewed. "My favorite, too," he grinned darkly, before slapping the bag free of Van's hand. Van stared in surprise at Alucard – a vampire – eating garlic, but then his face grew darker at the spilled almonds on the floor.

"You owe me three dollars."

"How about I take you out for drinks instead? I know a little place, off the beaten path, very quiet, not a lot of customers. Practically *no* customers, really." He winked. "But you have to bring your own drinks." He took a step closer, eyes seeming to shimmer a golden hue. "But I already know which one I'll bring. That is, if you can make it, of course."

I burst out laughing at the look on Van's face. He scowled at the two of us. "I'll just take the three dollars, Twilight."

Alucard let out a dark laugh. "Rain check, then."

"Okay, penis-measuring contest concluded. Did you get a job?"

He shot one last look at Alucard, then me, as if verifying it was okay to speak in front of the vampire. I nodded. "Yes. I got it. Wasn't easy."

"What, was there a written test or something?" I rolled my eyes, then looked off to make sure the Huntress was still relatively close.

"No, but I did have to kill a Freak to get in."

I rounded on him. "What!"

He folded his arms. "It's why I told the Heel we needed to meet. Wanted you to hear it from me." He watched me, eyes calculating. "Part of the gig. Had to prove my level of interest."

I took a step closer, prodding him with a finger. "We will have a nice long chat about that later. Maybe Alucard would care to join us."

Van pushed me back, glaring. "You want me to just waltz on in, tell him I want a job to help him abduct Freaks, run the ring where they kill each other, and then blanch at killing one to prove my mettle? That would have gone over *splendidly*." He poked me back. "Silver-spooned bastards like you might not know how to get a job, but I do." He was breathing heavily, but I kept my glare right on up, even opening my mouth to speak. "Don't even try to threaten me, boy. I've heard them all. And I'm still here." He let that sink in, and I swallowed. I wasn't scared of him, but I was... aware of his skills. And I didn't have the time or energy to fight him. After a few tense seconds, he spoke. "But knowing your weakness for harming Freaks, I kidnapped a kid instead. A werecat. Left a note telling the father to get me the money or I would give him to the Beast Master."

I felt as if a sudden weight had been lifted from my shoulders. He hadn't killed anyone. Then his words registered, and the rage came rolling back twofold. "You..." and I suddenly wanted to punch him in the mouth. It was his fault we had almost been killed at the Vaults. The werecat hadn't been talking about the kid I had seen abducted with Ashley, but the one abducted by... the man I had hired. Which meant...

I had been the cause of the fiasco at the Vaults. Because I had hired Van.

Van saw the look on my face, and frowned. "Relax. I was going to give the kid back for free anyway. My letter told him not to tell a soul. I'm meeting him tonight at a warehouse."

"You... fucking *idiot*," I snarled. "Let me tell you about my day. Really, just the most recent part of my day. I went to the Vaults."

His brow furrowed. "I heard a big fuss about the Vaults right before I came here. Some guy came running into the sandwich shop where I was eating and told his friend about it. Some robbery attempt or something..." his eyes widened, and he took a step back. "You robbed the *Vaults*?" he hissed.

I shook my head, glaring. "No, funny story. We were there to make a withdrawal, and what do you know... a *werecat* is suddenly holding the place up. Saying he needed to get some money to save his kid. From the Beast Master..." I took an aggressive step forward.

His face paled. "Oh, shit."

"Yeah. Which means the father is likely in custody at the Vaults right now, if not dead." I poked him in the chest. "If he's alive, you better get to him, and give him his kid back, and hope to whatever god you believe in that he doesn't start blabbing about a certain circus in town. He's an Alpha. They'll listen if he talks." I took a menacing step forward. "Did you even have a plan for if he had gotten the money and decided to go directly to the Beast Master with the ransom?"

Van looked horrified, suddenly realizing his own fate if the Beast Master heard about him lying about killing a kid. "Okay," he stammered. "I've got a friend at the bank. I'll get this sorted." He ran a hand through his hair. "Fuck me... I thought you would be happy I hadn't killed anyone. I never meant..." He dropped his hand and met my eyes. "Let's get this over with so I can get that taken care of."

I nodded. "Agreed. Give me the highlights on your interview, and anything else I may need to know."

"Okay, I pretended to kill the kid. With my reputation, he didn't ask for proof. He watched the father from across the street, and his grief was enough to get me in the door."

"As long as the father doesn't elaborate to the Vaults' manager..." I warned. His face scrunched up in agreement, suddenly concerned. Which distracted him from my newest bestie.

"Hi, Van. Missed you," the Huntress cooed from directly behind him. He whirled, gasping as his hand reached for a concealed knife. She planted a firm boot into his ass, sending him flying into a tower of paintball canisters, which promptly exploded onto the floor, sending out a bajillion marbles in every direction. Recognizing her, he let out a laugh, sitting on his ass.

"Good to see you too, Love," he chuckled as she helped him to his feet.

"This is fun," Alucard smiled.

Van rolled his eyes, and let out a breath.

Two employees came flying around the corner to see the four of us standing amidst the destruction. "We've had... complaints," the younger of the two stammered, eyeing the almonds and paintballs on the ground.

I smiled at them, pointing a thumb at Van. "Just got back from the military. His sister was... overexcited, and knocked over your display. And tore open his nut sack in the process. Sorry." Their faces flashed red at my choice of words, but I could still see the expectant fear of explaining this to their manager. "We'll be buying a pretty expensive bow here in a few." I pointed a finger. "Little sis' wants her big bro' to teach her a thing or two." I shrugged my shoulders, smiling adoringly at the Huntress. "Cute, really."

"Yes. I fancy a bow." She sounded as if she was swallowing rancid oil. "So that my esteemed brother can teach me." Her gaze flicked my way, and then to Van as a dark smile grew on her face. "It will have to be the most expensive one you have. I want all the bells and whistles on it. My brother offered to buy it for me for my birthday. Such a nice brother. I love him so..." Van sputtered, unable to speak, and the employees nodded once before speaking into their radios to call in a cleanup.

"Silver lining," the Huntress grinned. "I get to kick your ass – *literally* – and you buy me a new toy. Very thoughtful of you. Sorry about your nut sack."

Alucard piped up. "That was me. I just couldn't help myself."

Van closed his eyes, took a deep breath, and then opened them again. "I find that the longer I'm in your presence, Temple, the sooner I get a rapid urge to empty the contents of your stomach." He grinned. "Whoops. *My* stomach, not *your* stomach, of course…"

"I'm terrified. Now, let's get back to the BM discussion."

The Huntress frowned. "Wasn't that the reference of Van's joke? Bowel movements?"

I sighed. Alucard placed an arm around the Huntress' shoulder. "Let the big boys talk about their bowel movements. You and I will go pick out the nicest, most expensive, gaudiest, flashiest bow they have available. Because your brother loves you *dearly*. You might even find some new bracers, or a quiver, or something. I mean, what *wouldn't* your brother do to show you the depths of his love?" He winked at Van as he led her away, giving us space to talk.

"I will stake him. Very soon. And very slowly."

CHAPTER 34

I watched the two depart, frowning. "Not sure what good that will do you."

Van watched him curiously, then turned back to me with the same look. I shrugged at the unspoken question. I had seen Alucard suntan, decline high-quality blood, and eat garlic. He was something new, alright. "Any news on the Grimm?"

He shook his head. "Absolutely nothing. Which is impressive. It's almost as if she's not in town. Sure she wasn't just passing through?"

I scowled at his answer. And his question. "Call it a hunch." I let out a breath, frustrated. "So, you're in. What does that mean? What does he have you doing? Have you found the chimera?"

He held up his hands. "Jesus, man. Quiet." His eyes darted about, checking for nearby customers who might have overheard.

A wave of anxiety rolled over me. "Did they follow you here?" I hissed.

He shook his head. "No, I'm sure of that. But there are other Freaks here. Just commonplace Freaks going about their day, but still. Keep your voice down." I nodded in relief. "I haven't actually started yet, but I do know where he keeps the prisoners."

I nodded. "Yeah, already got that part."

He was shaking his head. "No, I'm confident that you don't."

"The quarry."

He blinked at me. "You bought tickets. You arrogant bastard. He'll never see that coming," he muttered sarcastically. "But in point of fact, he's not at the quarry. Yet. And neither are the prisoners. My interview process took me to two different warehouses in town, and they each had prisoners."

I blinked. "What? I thought he only had a dozen or so? *Two* warehouses?" Damn it.

"But I think he's going to have them all moved to the quarry during the fight. He'll need extra bodies to throw into the ring. Also, his whole crew will be there. He doesn't want to risk having his treasures stolen while he's otherwise occupied." I sighed in relief.

"Maybe lead with that next time, bastard."

"Or I could lead with, *I know where tonight's abduction is going down.*" He smiled.

I let out a frustrated breath, seriously contemplating murdering him. "Tell me. Pretty please. Or I'll murder you to death."

He grinned, and told me.

"I'll do my best to try and locate the chimera, and any other general info you might find helpful in your suicide attempt, but Nate... You need to hear this." His eyes grew distant as he shook his head at a memory. "He has creatures I've never even heard about. And he's had them for a *long* time. These things are feral. More beast than man. Most of them do not require saving, just killing."

I was shaking my head. "They're just kids. They need *help.*"

He gripped me by the shoulders and pulled me close, inches away. "No. Listen. These things... you stare in their eyes and all you see is wildness. Hunger. Bloodlust. No rational thought. Just instincts. He... *breaks* them, Temple. On a level that I hadn't thought possible. Trust me. I've hunted Freaks for a long time. I've never come across a Freak this far beyond the lines of madness. They are so mad that they don't even know what madness *is* any longer. They are beasts, in every sense of the word."

"Everyone can come back from madness..." I argued.

"No. Here's an example. After he hired me, he walked me to the cages. Truly horrifying monsters. I would have killed any of them, even if one had been my own son." Which was saying a lot, because Van had deep, dark issues concerning his son. As the stories went, anyway. "That's how terrible they were. And I would consider it a mercy."

"Okay, you saw them living in squalor, hungry, malnourished, injured."

He held up a hand. "The exact *opposite*. The last test was for him and I, all alone, without weapons, to stand in the center of the cages. Then he opened the fucking doors." He leaned closer. "Not one of them moved. They just watched us. And Nate... they were healthy, well-fed, and uninjured. They were in glorious shape. Their cages were fitted with more than most prison cells. Nice blankets, lamps, everything."

"Okay," I said after a shaky breath. "So, he has them in his control. They didn't attack when he opened the door. Stockholm Syndrome."

Van continued as if I hadn't spoken. "The BM made me attack him. A little girl watched us. She was with us the entire time, so I think it's his daughter or something. Or a personal favorite pet of his. He said that if I didn't try my hardest to kill him, he would kill me. Three archers with bone-tipped arrows aimed at me from above, and he started counting down from three. I panicked, not believing any of it, but let me tell you this. When he got to *one*, I attacked him with everything I had. He's good. Highly-trained fighter. But that's not the worst of it..." his eyes grew cold, dark, and haunted. "One of my punches made contact with the BM. And his beasts lost their fucking minds. Howling, clawing, screaming, destroying their cells in their efforts to get to me. I found myself suddenly swarmed by a dozen monsters with no humanity in their eyes. I was sure I was going to die."

I stared in disbelief. "You're exaggerating."

He shook his head forcefully. "No, and you know what? I know beyond a shadow of a doubt that he used absolutely no magic during our fight, or after. The BM smiled at me once, then snapped his fingers one time. The Freaks instantly halted their attack, and trotted over to stand beside him. They nuzzled, licked, and kissed his hands. Then they calmly walked back to their cages. That's when the BM told me I had the job. And *then* he used magic to heal me from my wounds."

I stared at him in disbelief. What kind of power was this? It didn't sound like mind control at all. It sounded like... Stockholm Syndrome, as I had said. And the little girl with him? Someone else to save? Or someone to use as leverage? These beasts had been under his control for so long that they looked to him as a father. "He's a wizard of some kind then?"

Van shrugged in exasperation. "I don't know *what* the fuck he is. But most importantly, he doesn't need to use his alleged beast control powers to get his pets to obey. They *want* to." He stared at me intently. "So, you may want to reconsider your position. I'm not scared of anything. Never have been. Not really." He blinked at me, letting me realize the severity of the long pause, before he continued. "I. Was. Terrified."

I let out a breath, mind racing. The dark voice in my head waited patiently, seeming to listen to every word Van spoke. "Then, why did you meet me here?"

He chuckled darkly. "Because thanks to you, I'm his employee now. The only way I get out of this is with one of us in a body bag."

"But you just urged me to get out of the situation." I frowned. "Which would basically condemn you to death."

Van nodded seriously. "Yes."

I studied him, surprised. He was willing to convince me to get out rather than to help him out of the mess I had gotten him into. "Okay. Thanks. I'm out of this. See ya later." And I turned my back on him, walking away.

He sputtered in disbelief, and I took a few more steps before grinning over my shoulder. "Just kidding." And I winked.

"You are the biggest asshole I've ever had the displeasure of meeting," he growled.

"Take care of the cat problem. Now." I glanced at my watch. "We've been here too long. I'll meet you at the abduction as early as possible. If he has as much control as you say he does with his beasts, I dare not let him get his hands on any more victims. And find a way to get to that chimera. I'll need to know where to find her when this all goes down. I need to make this as seamless as possible."

"I noticed that your wolf isn't here."

I slowly turned, leveling him with a look. "Very observant. Point?"

He shrugged, cocking his head inquisitively. "Just that you seem to be pulling from the bottom of the barrel on this one. I don't see your body-guard, your wolf, your girl, or your dragon. Bunch of new talent on the Temple bench. Hell, you even asked *me* to help, and I tried to kill you a few months ago." He flicked his chin towards the Huntress and Alucard. "As did she. And the vamp tried to kill you not too long before we showed up. All failed. All now working for you. At the expense of your original crew." He let his words sink in. "Just pointing things out to you." Before I could reply, he spoke again. "I'll get you what I can, and take care of the cat's father, but I literally can't risk being discovered, so keep your phone handy, and watch over your shoulder. In case I find anything."

I glanced at the customers around me, unaware of the dangers lurking nearby. I turned back to Van, and he was gone.

I growled. "You son of a bitch. You were supposed to buy the bow for the Huntress."

"Already did, mate..." a voice drifted from another aisle, soft enough for me to barely hear.

I raced around the corner to come face to face with an old woman who was clutching a can of pink mace. She shrieked, holding it up, aiming for my eyes. I dove clear with a shout of alarm, shielding my eyes. When nothing happened, I uncovered my face and looked up. She was grinning at me. "Just practicing, boy. This should work fine." She glanced about warily, and snuck the mace into her purse. She held up a finger to her lips, and winked before turning away, stealing the mace.

Shoplifting grandmas. What next?

I climbed to my feet to find Alucard and the Huntress striding toward me. Her face glowed with excitement as she held out her bow. Then she patted another large bag that held boxes of arrows and whatnot.

I nodded, returning a thin smile, and then motioned for them to follow me, the wooden cuff scratching my wrist with the motion. "Let's go."

CHAPTER 35

*O*thello leaned back into the couch with a curse, laptop sitting on her knees.

"Still nothing?" I asked absently, scribbling in the book in my lap. I had taken off the Fae cuff bracelet. It chafed, and it made writing all but impossible. It was now tucked away beside Ganesh's belt in my safe, where no one could get to it.

"She's good. Or he's good, considering," she growled. "But I'm better. I'll find them."

"Thanks for trying. Means a lot to me," I encouraged, mind on my work. I glanced at a clock on the wall absently, wondering why the Huntress, Mallory, and Rufus hadn't yet called. I had sent them to tail Gunnar. After all, he had obviously been at the abduction site where Ashley had been taken, which meant that he must have snuck into my office at some point after I met Baba. I needed to know what he was doing. I hadn't tried calling him, unable to lower myself to that level, but I wanted to make sure he didn't do anything stupid. Especially after hearing that he had gone to the Fight Club to let off some steam. And had bought his access to the circus. The Alpha werewolf seemed to be calling the shots lately, not my old friend.

The *only* way Gunnar could have known about the first abduction site was if he had seen the answer Baba had carved onto my desk. That was the only possibility.

Unless one of my friends had told him.

And I remembered some of the looks I had gotten recently. Was there a traitor in my midst? Someone trying to be helpful by encouraging Gunnar to go rogue, so that I could get a break? The Dark Presence inside me growled territorially, murmuring dark encouragement to my subconscious. I squashed it down, closing my eyes for a moment.

"You of all people should know better than to deface an old book," Othello said, sounding much closer. I opened my eyes and flinched. She was staring down at me now, peering at the book in my hands.

Through the Looking-Glass.

I closed it sharply, and glared up at her. "It's… complicated."

She frowned, sitting down beside me on the large chair, our hips touching. "I need a break. Distract me. What's so complicated about defacing a book? Either you're doing it or you aren't."

I ignored the familiar warmth of her legs pressing against mine, and glanced back at the book, tapping it with my fingertips. "I sort of have a pen pal," I said softly.

The room was silent for a full ten seconds. I finally looked up to see a squeamish look on her face. As if overly concerned. I sighed, understanding how that sounded, and not wanting her to feel I was meddling with a demon or something.

"Okay, this stays here." She nodded, folding her hands in her lap after mimicking a zipper closing her lips. Her smile looked sickly, but she was trying. I couldn't blame her. Magic was creepy at times. "So, a few months ago, I purchased this book. Well, stole it. From some ogres."

The look of alarm on her face kept right on growing.

"Let me back up a bit. Remember when all my friends left town and you busted me out of jail?"

She nodded. "Mardi Gras. Fun times. I died."

I smiled weakly. "Only for a little bit, ya big baby."

She chuckled at that, but motioned for me to continue.

"Did I ever tell you what happened to me that night? Right before I came to the junkyard?"

She shook her head. "No, but when you died you met the Boatman. Who brought you back. Are you saying something *else* happened that night?" she asked, incredulous.

I nodded. "Yeah. When I met Death – really met him, discovering who he was – he let me wear his mask." She nodded, remembering me showing up to the junkyard looking a whole hell of a lot like the Horseman.

"I… remember." She whispered.

"When I put on his mask, I briefly found myself in a… White Room."

"Why do you sound like you are emphasizing that part?" she asked slowly.

"Because I'm emphasizing that part," I rolled my eyes. "Anyway, I don't know how or why, but I found myself in a White Room. A *White World.* I was wearing a silver suit, nice silver shoes, but every single thing in that place was sparkling white. A cocaine palace. Couch, flowers, walls, carpets, books, art—"

"Wait. How would art and books be white? Do you mean, a white painting, or a white cover on the book?"

After a brief hesitation, I shook my head. "More than that. The paintings were white in color, but textured. As if someone had white-washed a Van Gogh, or Mona Lisa. I could feel and discern the painting beneath from the textures, as if someone had literally painted over the original with white. But the books…" I murmured to myself, taking a brief sip from the drink beside me, then setting it down. "The covers were the same. White. But embossed so that I could feel the title under my fingertips. When I opened them, even the words were all in white, so that it was essentially like I was looking at blank pages. But my fingertips could pick up that there was indeed something printed on the pages; even if it was barely noticeable."

"Weird…" she whispered.

I shook my head. "No, *here's* where it gets weird. When I looked outside, everything beyond the room was also white. Grass, trees, even the ocean was a milky white. I couldn't believe it as I gripped the windowsill staring outside at a winter wonderland of sorts. When I leaned back to resume my inspection of the room, I happened to notice where my hands had touched the windowsill." I paused, meeting her eyes. "The wood was stained a dark, sooty color where I had touched it. I looked to my hands, fearing they were dirty and that I was ruining the place, but my hands…" I sighed softly, glancing down at the book in my lap. "They were perfectly clean."

"Maybe the paint was wet?" she offered weakly.

I again shook my head. "Nope. My hands didn't have white paint on them from touching anything in the room. *I* was staining everything in the room with *my* touch. Even a book I picked up to flip through." I leaned back in my chair and took another drink. Othello eyed my other hand, which was tapping the book in my lap.

"But that book isn't white..." she said, indicating the book in my lap.

I nodded. "I know, but it's the same title. *Through the Looking-Glass.* Except it's black."

She shrugged. "I could find you a dozen copies of that book in black."

I looked at her. "Not one protected by ogres. And not an original edition."

She leaned closer, eyeing the book. "So, what, it's the opposite of the book you found in that... other place?" I nodded. She scrunched her forehead together in thought. "But... if it's the opposite, shouldn't it be entirely black? Pages and everything?"

I smiled, tapping the white paper inside. I let out a breath, closed my eyes, and then caressed the spine. The pages instantly turned blacker than charcoal. I flipped the book open, flicking through the pages, which were now entirely black paper, concealing the words inside. She gasped. The Hatter had shown me how to do it. To conceal our conversations.

I nodded. "I know."

She let out a shaky breath, and then leaned over to pour herself a drink. She took a healthy gulp, and then stared at me. "What were you saying about a pen pal?"

I let the silence build, wondering how much to tell her. But it felt nice to speak to someone I had known longer than a year. My other friends were all gone. Indie was gone. Dean and Mallory still seemed to be concerned about my mental health after seeing me with the bloody glass, and Baba Yaga supposedly giving me an early birthday present.

But Othello was mostly treating me as she always had. I had caught brief concerned glances now and then, as if she was aware that something was off, but she still spent time with me, treating me normally.

That was a true friend.

"I saw someone there. In that room."

She leaned forward eagerly. "Well, who was it? What did he want?"

"I didn't actually speak with him. Then, a few months ago, when I defeated the Grimms, I found myself back in that room. This book was sitting on the table, with my sooty fingerprints all over it. As if a pointed message that the owner knew of my previous intrusion. I didn't talk to him then, either. But I decided to buy this book on a whim. Well, kind of a whim. I heard about its origins, and the fact that it was black, and held by ogres who wanted a large sum of money for it. I stole it." I caressed the spine again and the pages turned back to normal. "The story itself is the same as any other version you would buy. But this book is also filled with spells, notes, circled words, and a whole bunch of other crazy stuff. Almost as if this was a school book that someone was studying. Then, in the back of the book was a bunch of entries where someone was talking to... well, someone else."

She frowned. "What do you mean? The owner of the book had tran-scribed dialogue?"

I shook my head. "No, at the time, it was all one-sided. As if the writer was using it as a journal. It was madness. Gibberish..." I turned to the page that had caught my attention, and showed it to her. "Except for this."

He returned! I hope he saw the book...

Othello read it, blinked a few times, and then raised an eyebrow at me, not understanding. "Who is he talking about?" I simply stared at her, wait-ing, a weak smile growing on my face. "Wait, he's talking about *you*?" I nodded. "But that... that's not *possible!*"

I shrugged. "I know. I thought it was someone having a game with me. Mallory, or Alucard scribbling in the book. So, I wrote back, and then locked the book away. When I came back to check it, the book was vibrat-ing, and... someone had responded."

I showed her the page. Only for a few seconds. She didn't need to read the entire dialogue. Especially not the most recent stuff.

She flinched when I pulled it away. She stared down at my lap intently, thinking. "Nate?"

"Mmhmm?"

"There are a lot of pages after that, and they didn't look empty. How long..." she looked very, very concerned. And very, very cautious all of a sudden. "How long have you been speaking with this... person?" I could tell that she hadn't been about to say *person* until the last second. More like *monster, creature, god.*

I understood that. I had had the same thoughts at first.

"Ever since," I answered honestly.

She shivered, rubbing her arms as her eyes grew distant. "That... that probably isn't smart... Do you even know who it is on the other end? What if he's dangerous?" she looked on the verge of tears. Whether it was from fright or concern for me, I didn't know for sure.

"I've met him. While I won't say he's harmless, he has helped me a few times already."

She stared at me, then leaned closer to grasp my hands. The voice roared inside of me, and I instinctively flinched, pulling the book clear of her reach. She sat frozen, arms outstretched, staring at me with shock. "I wasn't going to touch your book, Nate." She slowly extended her hands to grip my shoulder instead. "I don't know much about your neck of the woods, but that sounds very dangerous. Even if he is good. If he lives in a world so different from our own, he might have very different views on how things work. And... he might be using you to... escape." She finished, watching me.

I was frowning. "It's not like that. He's just... lonely."

She nodded slowly. "Okay. Just..." she took a shaky breath. "Please be careful with him. Whoever he is."

I didn't reply, not wanting to tell her the name. But I nodded. "You know me. Always careful. Plus, with my other friends abandoning me, it feels nice to have a friend to talk to."

Her face paled a bit. "I'm right here, Nate. I know things have been... well, confusing lately, but I'll always be here."

I sighed. "I've had quite a few people say that in the past." I held up my hands, displaying the entire room, comprised of just us. "And just look at how many friends I have. Almost as many fucks as I could give," I added in an angry growl.

Her eyes darted around the room, as if actually searching for people she hadn't noticed.

I furrowed my eyebrows at her reaction. "No one is here, Othello. I was referring to all my friends being absent. Present company excluded, of course..." I took a big drink, and clapped my hands. "Enough of this. We need to find out what Indie is doing in town. I don't like it. And not just for the obvious reasons. I don't quite trust Ichabod yet, and you don't stroll through an airport with a bloody sword in your hand just to see home again. Something is going on. They have a purpose."

Othello nodded, eyes still distant as they flicked to the book on the table. I had to consciously prevent myself from snatching it away with another territorial growl.

"Right. I'll keep trying," she murmured

"No need, really," a new voice interrupted.

I flinched, whirling to the sound, whips of fire suddenly exploding from my fists. Othello gasped in fright, jumping away from me. My whip struck her laptop, and it exploded into a ball of flame as it shattered into slivers of metal, glass, and burnt plastic. But no one was in the room.

Othello turned from the burning laptop to me, eyes terrified.

"You heard that, right?" I rasped.

She shook her head. "N-no…" she whispered, voice shaking.

I glared around the room, suddenly concerned that one of those albino creatures had found a way inside. I released one of my whips and reached into my pocket to pull out a decent-sized piece of the glass from the broken window.

After discovering the enchantment on the glass, I had stowed all of the broken pieces away before Dean could clean up the mess, and this piece had been the perfect size for my pocket. That way I could search for the creatures at my leisure, learn more about them. Also, to keep others away from them. If they didn't look through it, the creatures couldn't harm them.

I held the glass up to my eyes, and scanned the room. I noticed Othello staring at me in disbelief, shaking her head as her mouth moved wordlessly. I ignored her, wondering if the Beast Master was using some unknown power to speak with me. It obviously wasn't the albinos.

"This way, boy."

I swiveled toward the sound and saw Sir Muffle Paws. He was standing in the doorway, watching me, looking completely unruffled despite the whip of pure elemental power crackling on the floor at my feet. "The cat," I said, stunned. I turned to Othello, who flinched under my gaze. "Did you just hear the cat talk?"

She stared at me, then at the cat, then back at me, shaking her head sharply. "Nate…"

I turned away from her as the voice spoke again. *"Follow the filthy feline…"* Sir Muffle Paws flicked his tail, and darted from the room.

I recognized that voice. And it wasn't the cat.

"Fucking filthy feline," I growled, and strode out of the room.

"Nate!" Othello pleaded desperately, but I ignored her, my vision pulsing blue now in rage. He dared come here. In my house.

He was dead.

CHAPTER 36

I soon realized that we were headed to Ichabod's old office in the subbasement.

Which made sense.

I opened the door to find the old man sitting in the office chair, petting Sir Muffle Paws absently as he watched me. He looked old. Not frail. But hard. Like a weathered oak log. Or like those crazy writer-types. Tired, and exhausted, but still energized with a driving passion. To write that next scene. I still held the whips of power at my fists, having pocketed the glass, and I was ready to use them. Even if I had to burn Chateau Falco down to the foundation.

If it killed Ichabod, it was a price I was willing to pay.

"Speak. I'll soon be making kitty-sized snacks out of your ass, and it will be hard to understand you with all that screaming," I snarled. The Dark Presence began to chuckle hungrily.

He sighed, snapping his fingers. My whips extinguished, and the Dark Presence surged inside of me, roaring with outrage at the sudden challenge, begging for me to let him loose. I forced him back down, and then took an aggressive step forward, suddenly angry that I wasn't wearing one of the Fae cuffs. His magic would have likely rolled right off of me, and I desperately needed an advantage if I wanted to square off with Ichabod. Especially with my powers so limited. "Do you and your *friend* really want to try this again? I thought you learned your lesson at our first match. Repeatedly." The cat sprawled out on the desktop, and instantly began to snooze, as if totally unconcerned with the danger I threatened. Even the cat mocked me.

My face grew hot. "I've learned a lot since then." And I instantly regretted ever telling him about the Dark Presence a few months back.

He nodded. "I'm quite sure you have. From my book. The one I first studied. The first of *many* I studied. In effect, you are threatening me with your vast knowledge of power," he leaned forward, "that I *gave* you from my *childhood* schoolbook. Do you not think I know every line on every page, and that having studied that as a mere child, I could..." he grinned, "*school* you in the usage of such lessons? Not even considering the centuries I've spent honing my craft from the numerous other areas of study regarding our shared abilities?" He leaned back, folding his hands in his lap. "Please. You're a preschooler threatening a man with a collegiate degree."

"Using the word *collegiate* makes you sound like a douche."

"Yes, it will take me some time to get used to speaking like an uneducated peasant."

I scowled back, but knew he was likely right about a fight. I didn't let him gain the satisfaction of that though. "What the hell are you doing in my city, in my *home*, and why didn't you tell me you two were stopping by?"

"First off, if this is anyone's home, it's *mine*. Secondly, I don't find it necessary to check in with my... nephew, or whatever the hell you are. My comings and goings are my own." He grinned darkly. "As are your fiancée's, apparently."

"I will skin you alive."

"I'm growing weary of this. Cease or be deceased," He warned. Then he blinked, cocking his head as he stared at me, looking like a fox in a henhouse. "My, my, *my*. You truly *are* dangerous. To *yourself!*" and he began to laugh, hard. "You allowed a mere wizard to *curse* you? A *Maker*? I truly underestimated your vast powers."

I growled, gripping the cane at my fist, which seemed to get his attention really quickly. I glanced down to find it crackling with purple sparks. When I looked back up, Ichabod's face was no longer as arrogant. While he didn't look scared, he did look... concerned.

"Want to see my stick?" I smiled.

He studied me thoughtfully. "Enough posturing. I came here to speak with you."

"And here I thought that's what we were doing." I grinned at him with my teeth, still clutching my cane. "Well? I'm not much into harboring a criminal, so what's the story from the airport?"

He grimaced. "We were... questioned by security."

"That's just awful. Did she forget they don't allow swords on planes?"

"She didn't carry a sword. That was a construct. When she tapped into my Maker power."

I stared. "She can do that?"

"She's quite proficient at mimicking the powers around her."

"Why was it dripping blood?"

"Because she's overly dramatic," he rolled his eyes. "I can't imagine who she learned that from..." his eyes rested on me for a moment. I didn't rise to the bait. "I assure you, none were harmed... well, none were *seriously* harmed," he amended.

"Okay, why are you here, and why didn't you reach out first?"

"I thought I made that abundantly clear. You are not my parole officer. I come and go as I please."

"Fine. Would you tell me why you're here? Pretty please?" I batted my eyelashes at him.

"We are hunting for a woman. Loosely tied to the group... that Silver Tongue worked for."

I grew suddenly interested. "Oh? I haven't sensed any Syndi... any of *them* in St. Louis."

"You wouldn't."

I scowled. "No sparks, fires, or embers," I clarified.

"She is... different. She is also reclusive. And dangerous."

"Well, I'm not sure I can be of much help. Even though you did ask so nicely."

"On this we can agree. You would be of *no* help." He smiled.

"I meant that I'm otherwise engaged."

"Oh, I'm *well* aware of your *engagement*, if you recall..." he smiled like a shark.

"You know, one of these days, I'm going to have to disagree with you," I warned. "Strenuously." How dare he mock me so blatantly? If I didn't have this stupid curse on my power, there would be a pile of ash where he stood. That is, unless he whooped my ass again. The Dark Presence tried to take control again, so hungry for destruction. I fought it back down, getting better at managing his mood swings. Still, I imagined Ichabod's demise. Very visually. Details and everything, for a few seconds. I closed my eyes with a smile. "Okay, I'm better now."

He frowned at me. "Your choice of allies is… different than the last time we met."

"Don't worry about my friends. Why did you come to Chateau Falco, Ichabod? I've got more important things to do than fantasizing about your slow, painful death every time you open your mouth. Let's just wrap this up, shall we?"

He glanced at the empty room to my left. "I tried visiting the Vaults earlier, but they were closed. Know anything about that?"

"Whoops." And to be honest, I did feel kind of bad about it. Just another instance where one small action had gone so bad. Story of my life.

"This is no laughing matter." This time he pointed at the empty room beside me. "With the Vaults closed, I'll need my gemstones. Where are they?"

"You mean those really pretty ones you left in *my* house? I used them. Threw a wild party. You know, I might have even sent you an invitation. If, for example, you had let me know you were stopping by—"

I was slammed into the wall, and hung suspended a good foot off the ground, unable to breathe.

"Where. Is. My. Money?" he hissed.

"G-gone. Poof. Almost like magic." I managed.

He dropped me to the ground with a growl, climbing to his feet. "You have exactly two days to get it to me. I have need of it."

"Oh yeah? Or what?"

"I will kill you." He didn't blink. Or twitch. Or make any motion at all. It was the same tone I imagined Big G used when he said *Let there be light.*

"We'll talk about it. You never actually told me to leave them alone. In fact, you encouraged the opposite. I used them for a… side project."

"Grimmtech," he murmured thoughtfully. I nodded. He was silent for a time, watching me. "I can find other means to get funds. But you will grant me partial ownership in the company, or you will owe me my money in two days."

"I don't have time for this, old man."

"You are quite right. You don't have time to deny your ancestor. As in, you will no longer have *any* time if you do not pay me back. In two days."

He stood. "It's time I leave. I have another child to train. I don't have the patience for both of you. Even a Temple can only do so much..." he smiled darkly.

I heard a sound in the hall and whirled, ready to attack. Mallory appeared from the dark shadows, staring at me, then the room, intently. "Master Temple?" he asked, warily. Rufus stood a few steps behind him, not speaking.

I growled, glancing over my shoulder, waiting for Ichabod to snidely respond that he was the Master Temple. But he was gone. Sir Muffle Paws sat primly on the desk, flicking his tail.

I sighed. "Yes, Mallory?"

He studied me, then the cat. "Who were ye speaking to?"

I snarled as I shoved past him. "The cat, you idiot," I snapped sarcastically. "I'm not completely daft, you know."

"Of course, Master Temple..." but he didn't sound like he meant it, which only made me angrier.

"I need to go kill someone. Or hurt someone. Any ideas?"

He quickly caught up to me, shooting me a concerned glance. "No. I prefer it not be one o' us." He shot me a weak grin. Rufus made a small sound from the back of his throat.

I grunted, letting my gaze rest on Rufus for a few seconds. "We'll see."

CHAPTER 37

Othello looked up as I entered the room. Her face tightened. She was working on my computer, since I had destroyed her laptop a few hours ago. After leaving the sublevels, I had come back to growl at her to find Indie and look into Van's claim about the location of the last abduction. Then I had left, not waiting for a response. I had gone to take a shower and cool my head. I now wore a St. Louis Cardinals tee that Indie had bought me months ago, but I hadn't ever worn it. I was angry, and it was red. And Indie had bought it. Since she was one source of my frustration, I threw it on like a battle standard. Man logic. "Anything?" I asked Othello sharply.

To be honest, I was surprised she hadn't fled at my earlier rudeness. Of course, I could only admit that now because I had taken a breather.

"No. Nothing on Indie."

"The other thing, then."

She hesitated, pounding furiously at the keys. "No. Nothing on that, either. At least, nothing to corroborate Van's claim—"

There was a shouting from behind me. I spun, unsheathing the sword cane at my hip. Mallory stumbled into the hallway, carrying Van Helsing in his arms. The Huntress trailed him nervously, eyes locked on the wounded man. Blood dripped freely from his fingertips, and he looked entirely unconscious. Or dead.

"What the hell happened?" I roared, sheathing my cane.

The Huntress answered. "We were tailing the wolf, like you asked. He went inside a dark warehouse. There was a loud scuffle, gunshots, and then the wolf left, covered in blood. We couldn't follow since he had his pack of wolves with him. We went inside the building, thinking you would at least want to know what he had been doing inside." She paused, indicating the infamous Van Helsing. "This is what we found. In a pool of blood."

I shook my head in disbelief, my mind piecing together disparate facts. Van had been attacked by my best friend in a random warehouse. The same warehouse I could almost guarantee he had intended to use to return the werecat to his father.

Because I had told him to.

And as a result of my command, he had been attacked by my best friend, the once-peaceful werewolf. But how had Gunnar known—

"He's bleeding out," Mallory growled, roughly shoving past me to dump Van Helsing on my couch. I quickly swooped in and picked up my copy of *Through the Looking-Glass*, and placed it on a shelf. I didn't need anyone bleeding on it. Or asking questions about it. Othello watched me silently, taking note of my motion, although everyone else seemed preoccupied.

I studied Van Helsing. He had vicious claw and bite marks on his body, face, and arms. At least I didn't need to worry about him becoming a shifter. If he survived, that was. "Shit. Gunnar did this?" I asked out loud.

The Huntress nodded slowly. "Bone and claw are the only thing that could harm this man."

"But you heard gunshots. Van must have hit Gunnar. At least once. He's a good shot. Gunnar might be dying. We need to find—"

The Huntress gripped my arm. "The Alpha is fine. I saw his eye when he left. It danced with madness. He was unharmed. He looked only... hungry."

I stared at her wordlessly. Mallory cleared his throat. "Ye need to heal him."

I froze. I didn't know much about healing. "I... don't have enough power." A thought hit me. "Get Rufus."

Mallory studied me with a dark scowl. "Rufus is the only reason he's alive right now. He used up the last of his power to bring him this far back from death. He passed out in the car."

"Good lord. What the hell did Gunnar *do* to him?" I murmured, more to myself.

"What *didn't* he do to him, more like it," The Huntress whispered, sounding alarmed for the first time I had ever heard. I searched her eyes, and she noticed, glancing up. "I have never seen someone with that look in their eye. Van is a... formidable opponent. Gunnar exited the building looking... well, not even winded. More as if he had just finished a warm-up. He has... changed since first we met. From what I found at the scene, your friend did not even attempt to restrain himself. In fact, it seemed he rather *enjoyed* himself..."

I nodded absently, turning to Mallory. "What about you? You know how to heal."

Mallory nodded. "Aye, I do." But he continued to stare down at the wounded man.

"Is this a new form of healing where we simply stare at him?"

Mallory slowly turned to face me. "I prefer ye to do it," he said softly.

I blinked. "If your *preference* mattered right now, that would be great. But you work for me. Fucking heal him. Now. We need to figure out what's going on. Why Gunnar tried to kill him."

Mallory folded his arms. "I'm gonna need ye to do it, Laddie." His face was hard, resolved, and distantly fearful at my potential reaction.

I threw my hands up. "Would someone mind telling me what the fuck is going on? Why everyone is looking at me like I'm about to burn the house down around us? And why people keep disobeying the simplest of requests?"

No one answered, but Mallory motioned towards Van. "Please, Laddie. I'd rather not explain why... we have a history..."

Shit. "Is this something to do with your mysteriously shady background that you won't tell me about?"

Mallory lowered his eyes and shrugged.

"Goddamn it. Fine. But help me out, Mallory. I'm not familiar with healing as a Maker. Feel free to step in at any time. You know, if I run out of power because you are too much of a fucking coward to heal the dying man on my couch. The one you have a *history* with." He flinched, but knelt down beside me, eyes locked on Van, practically trembling with barely restrained fury at my scathing words. But he stayed resolute, which made me all sorts of nervous. What was so important to Mallory that he would push me like this over something he could easily heal?

I closed my eyes, took several deep breaths, and let them out, trying to calm down.

But I couldn't. I was too amped up. Gunnar had turned into a psychopath, almost killing Van, going to the Fight Club. My friends were stepping on glass around me, likely placing wagers on my sanity. And someone had to have given Gunnar the information about the abduction site. Which meant someone here was a traitor. And all this overreaction because I had seen my fiancée on the news. I wasn't that unstable. Sure, it had bothered me, but I wasn't about to fly off the hinges. I was pissed. Nothing more than any other man would be if his fiancée suddenly chose to fly to the opposite end of the world with his grandfather, not contact him for months, and then suddenly reappear in town without informing him ahead of time.

So, they thought I was a little off my game.

And they were right.

But I wasn't any more dangerous than usual. Just a little more emotional. A little less rational.

I felt Van quiver under my fingertips, and quickly checked his pulse. It was thin, barely noticeable, and I realized I didn't have time to play games. He was literally dying. Right now. And he needed to be healed, because sooner or later the Beast Master would wonder where he had gone. Why he was missing. I shot another look at Mallory, but he quickly averted his gaze. If I still trusted any of the people in the room, I would have gone to grab Ganesh's belt, but to be honest, I wasn't sure I had time to fiddle with the safe.

And... I *didn't* trust my friends any longer. None of them deserved to know about the belt.

"If he dies, it's on you. If he survives, and I don't have enough power to save the chimera, it's on you. If I save the chimera, but any of my friends get hurt because I didn't have enough magic to stop the bad guys, it's on you." I nudged his arm forcefully. "And it won't matter if I have no magic. I will go shopping at the Armory, and find the most excruciating way to end your mysterious, shady life. The one you continuously refuse to tell me about." His eyes tightened, but not in anger. More in fear, and understanding. Still resolved on whatever mad quest he had decided. I hoped it was worth it to him.

Because I meant every single word of my threat.

I closed my eyes, and reached for the cane handle. My fingers closed around the cool silver hilt, and I felt a beast rise within me as I called out to it. It felt like a dragon stretching out in my chest, eager to play after a long nap. *Greetings, Master…* it whispered.

"I need to heal this man. Help me." I felt Mallory's arm stiffen beside me, but I ignored him. I didn't have time to explain. I was pretty sure I didn't need to speak out loud, but I hadn't thought about it beforehand. I had never been in a position where I spoke with the voice while others were around, so I had spoken out loud. Rather than having a full conversation in my head.

Because it made things feel more normal to me. Less insane.

But it didn't feel that way now, with others hearing me do it for the first time.

I ignored them and focused on the voice as it whispered back to me, studying the body before us through my eyes. Tendrils of power drifted from my fingertips, my hand hovering over Van as the Dark Presence assessed the injuries. Then my chest began to pulse with an unseen pressure, my lungs growing tight as the room began to dim to a world of blue hues.

Silly mortals. Using elements to repair damaged flesh. What is flesh, if not stardust? Why stretch out an old shirt to fix a hole? Grab a handful of stardust, a kiss of moonbeam, a gut and hook of creation's chaos, and begin to weave. The void and the dust. The blood of gods, and the teardrops of the angels. A pinch of Renaissance, a dash of Crusader's marrow, and… yes, why not a Samurai's sacrifice…

The pressure inside me filled to bursting, and with his last words, I felt my mind fracture with an explosion of blue starlight, like the USS Enterprise taking off into warp speed. I kissed a woman in Venice during *Le Carnevale*, stabbed a man's throat during the Siege of Acre in the Middle Ages, and lived as a Samurai receiving his first sword – all in moments, like a montage of old movie highlights.

The power lit an explosion in the room, visible through my clenched eyelids. I cracked open my eyes as if they were covered in dried clay, and saw a smoky dark orb hovering over Van. Everyone was shouting, but my eyes were transfixed on the orb. Beyond the dark fog's sphere was a flickering rainbow of colors, like a miniature Aurora Borealis. The orb slowly descended towards Van's heart.

Reds and oranges.

Love.

Yellows and purples.

Sacrifice.

Blues and greens.

Honor.

Van gasped as the orb came into contact with his chest... and then pressed *inside* of him, disappearing from view. He lurched to a sitting position with a shout. His eyes shot open, glowing with white light as he clutched at his heart. His wounds flashed with rainbows of inner light, his eyes shifting with identically-colored flashes. Then he collapsed back into the couch, unconscious.

You're welcome, Master. See you soon... the voice whispered, spiraling into the depths of my soul. The world spun crazily, and I cracked my head on something hard before I chased after the voice fleeing deep into my soul, begging to learn the wild magic I had just witnessed.

CHAPTER 38

A muted snoring sound drifted from beyond the thick gossamer veil of sleep, and the smell of old but clean ashes filled my nostrils. Not like an ashtray, but… like a bonfire had died hours ago, leaving the crisp, purifying scent of burned wood. I also scented a pungent fur or pelt, as if I was in some sort of hunting lodge. I peeled open my eyes to find myself in a cottage. Simple shelves held wooden utensils, a few cast-iron pots, and mason jars of herbs and colorful liquids.

The faint smell of the lingering ashes tickled my nose, causing me to sneeze. Which hurt.

"He's awake," a masculine voice murmured. "Here comes the pain, boy."

But hadn't the voice just been snoring? I thought to myself.

I tried to pinpoint the sound, but groaned, only managing to turn my head a few inches – enough to see spears of sunlight drifting through a thick window in the wall. I squeezed my eyes shut at the pain of the blinding light, but was too exhausted to move. Then the intensity of the light began to grow brighter, hotter, malicious in its purification as it tore through the thin skin of my eyelids like tissue paper.

I quickly realized that this was no ordinary light as it ignited my pain receptors with napalm. Like hot fire pokers tipped with acid were slowly piercing my brain via my eye sockets. My body began to convulse against my will, rocking the surface in which I lay. But I couldn't control my body, couldn't actually pull away, despite my incessant thrashing. The light was everywhere. It was *all*.

And it was killing me.

"No. Endure," the voice cracked, startling me with its authority. I sucked in a breath, mind instantly fighting to obey such a powerful voice, despite my body continuing to spasm and shake. "Good," the voice encouraged. "It is burning away his hold. Firing away the chaff. Iron sharpens iron, after all." The voice seemed to grow closer. "You are *transforming...*" it whispered encouragingly.

The pain slowly – so, so slowly – began to dissipate, and in its place, I heard an anguished wail deep in my mind, as if someone, or something, was being skinned alive. I felt claws scrabbling at my chest, but not on my *skin...*

It was scraping at the *inside* of my chest. As if fighting to claw its way back to the surface, but recoiling as soon as it neared my sun-kissed flesh. With a final howl of rage, the voice fell.

And I was reminded how unfair the universe is.

My hands clasped onto the table beneath me as if struggling to hold on for dear life, clawing at the edge of a metaphysical cliff. My imagined fingernails tore free, and part of me fell down, down, down with the voice – as if we were one entity.

Lucky me, as part of me fell with the voice, I had the uniquely unpleasant experience of also being my *physical* self.

Which meant that as my soul fell, I simultaneously felt as if a fiery fist had struck *through* my abdomen and *out* my back. Kind of like those old Kung Fu movies where the bad guy punches through the hero's chest to grab his heart, shoving it out the back of his rib cage for a moment before ripping it back out the front to squeeze triumphantly in front of the hero's dying eyes.

Four out of five wizards don't recommend it.

The fifth wizard is the one doing the punching.

I vomited. Like a true badass.

Thankfully, my head was still twisted sideways.

I groaned, watching as my regurgitation steamed on the floor, hissing as if the ground was as hot as a griddle. The voice at the other end of the room chuckled. "That's it, boy. Let it all out." So, I did it again. Because, well, he had cheered me on. He waited a few moments, and I realized that although my mouth tasted disgusting, the pain had dissipated to nothing the moment I had finished throwing up. The sunlight now felt... invigorating.

I slowly swiveled my head as I heard a gentle clapping from the other end of the cottage. But it sounded like two pairs of hands.

The voice had hands, and they were clapping.

"I'm getting sick and tired of visits like this," I wheezed, locating the source of the voice.

CHAPTER 39

*M*y mouth immediately dropped open, awed as I saw him for the first time. I didn't even have time to consider whether my stare might have been considered rude. He was simply breathtaking.

"Happen often?" he asked in a calm, soothing tone, responding to my complaint.

A four-armed man, skin as white as bone, hovered in the air above a rug of tiger fur, legs crossed in a traditional meditative pose. Around his neck, he wore a set of rosary beads, and a freaking python of some flavor. The serpent flicked its tongue at me before losing interest to slither into a more comfortable position amidst the rosary beads. I tried to keep my face neutral, body motionless rather than running for the door. Where the rest of his skin was bone-white, his neck was a bright blue, like the color those travel commercials use to depict the ocean when selling island vacations to suckers.

His head and face were perfect, well, except for the gnarliest matted hair I had ever seen. But he made it work, somehow. His skin was as perfect and unblemished as porcelain, and he had three eyes – one centered slightly higher than the usual two. A painted crescent moon adorned his forehead like a sparkling tattoo of glittery ink. A trident was propped up against the wall behind him, looking as if made from rough, unpolished stone.

I managed to respond, regaining my composure. "You would be

surprised…" I assessed the figure thoughtfully, carefully, *respectfully*, as I swung my feet clear of the table. These types of visits didn't typically end well, but it never hurt to be polite.

He only chuckled. I was pretty sure I knew who I was dealing with, but wasn't stupid enough to say his name out loud. Some beings weren't too keen on that.

"Look… Chuckles. What's going on?"

"I just saved you from your Beast. Temporarily. He's sleeping now." And I realized that the Dark Presence was indeed asleep, practically nonexistent. And I suddenly felt free for the first time in months. Although I didn't like how he had referred to it as my Beast.

I took a few breaths, stretching my arms, preparing for some bad news. "Thanks, but I thought you were less of a helper, and more of a… *knock the house of cards down*, kind of guy…" I murmured – as respectfully as possible.

He smiled. "*Now I am become Death, destroyer of worlds…*" he recited. "I am Shiva."

I nodded slowly, unsure if I was happy or horrified to be correct. "Sweet rug." I pointed at the tiger fur below him, then scanned the cottage again, spinning in a slow circle. "Where am I?"

"Mount Kailash. My home. I astral projected you here, so, you're not really *here*, here…"

I blinked at that, but decided I really didn't want details. Astral projection was the intentional act of having your spirit leave your body. And in my case, it had been done *to* me, not *by* me. I shivered at the thought, only just beginning to realize how deep of a shit-bucket I was in.

Shiva's four arms didn't hold any objects at present, as was usually the case with him. I didn't know if that was a good or bad omen for me. I flinched as something beside the rug snorted loudly. And I suddenly remembered the snoring sound I had heard.

A huge freaking bull rested on the floor beside Shiva, dozing. It had been so motionless, and Shiva so captivating, that I hadn't even noticed the beast. The specimen was so large that at first look, I thought it might be Asterion in bull form. But upon second glance, I realized it wasn't. Horns as thick as my wrist, and tipped with a dark crimson stain, decorated his dome. This thing looked wild. Untamed. Well, untamed by anyone other than the god sitting beside him. No, *Hovering* beside him.

"He's called Nandin," Shiva said, watching me in amusement.

I grunted. "He's called a huge fucking bull."

The bull snorted, cracking open one eyelid to reveal a furnace of white fire. He took one look at my blazing red shirt, and the other eye cracked open in instant outrage.

Shit. Bull. Red shirt.

His muscles bunched up, as if ready to launch an attack at the red-shirted Matador in front of him. I promised myself that if this was how I kicked the bucket, my last words would be *Cardinal Nation!*

The bull opened his mouth as if to kill me with sound alone, but the god immediately snapped his fingers together like a whip. "*NANDIN!*" The room instantly grew thick with power, and the bull grumbled as it calmed, muscles relaxing. Then it promptly went back to sleep. The god grinned at my reaction. "One must establish dominance when necessary."

I grunted my agreement, idly wondering if it would be considered inappropriate to check my drawers for a backfire. I finally peeled my eyes away from the bull, confident I was safe.

"I hadn't considered the color of your shirt. Hindsight," he clucked. One of his hands reached up to fix his hair. It didn't work. The other hands moved absently, resting here, scratching there, stroking his snake...

Heh.

It wasn't that his arms did anything odd... there were just a lot of them. It was distracting.

He smiled, pearly white teeth peeking out from his thin, white lips. "Do you feel better?"

I opened my mouth, and then realized that he wasn't simply being socially polite. Now that I thought about it... The warm sunlight streaming in through the window no longer hurt. It was just regular sunlight.

"Yes, thank you. I feel great." I split my attention from eye to eye, unsure which one to focus on. "No disrespect, but which eye do I focus on? I'm not familiar with," and then I realized that my question could be seen as *entirely* disrespectful, even blasphemous, "your customs..." I said, hoping not to die.

He studied me for a few moments. "For all your days, with every friend or foe," he leaned forward, which must have been difficult while hovering, "always focus on the Third Eye..."

I nodded, waiting for more as I followed his advice – which felt entirely unusual, let me tell you. Try having a conversation with someone's forehead sometime. Weird. But he just continued to watch me. "Well, it's been a pleasure, but I have some important things to do today. Get my back waxed. Trim my nose hair. You know. Human things."

"Your Beast will return. You should stay for a while. Enjoy your... break."

I stared back. "You want me to stay here?" He nodded. "For how long?" I asked fearfully.

"Until you find yourself..."

My patience evaporated with his answer, and I suddenly forgot all about being respectful. I didn't have time to sit here with my thumb up my ass. "Okay, what's really going on here?"

His lips thinned at my tone, but I was done playing nice. He had a reason for bringing me here. The burden was on him. He finally answered. "I... owe my son a favor."

I waited, but got nothing else. "Nice guy, Ganesh. Loves those wieners," I said in an effort to keep the conversation going. Then I realized what I had said. And how it could be taken. But he only grunted in response. I waited a few breaths before proceeding, more conscious of my words this time. I might not have *patience*, but at least I could use a little *tact*. "How does Shiva end up owing his son a favor?"

His eyes grew distant, staring off at nothing. Or, hell, staring off at *everything*, for all I knew. In that silence, I realized that I suddenly had quite a few questions about gods. I had met Angels of Heaven who worked for the big G. But if I was sitting here, casually having a conversation with *another* god who was *also* known as the creator, well, that kind of put my brain into an impossible conundrum.

But my tiny mortal brain was saved from worrying too much about this as he shot me a dazzling smile. I couldn't prevent a smile from splitting my own cheeks. His grin was just so joyful, happy, and radiant. *Godly...* Then he answered my question.

"Well, I cut off his head, of course."

My smile fell down a trap door and died in a sickening *splat* a thousand stories below me. I realized I had stopped breathing, and was openly staring at him.

I had caused Shiva to kill Ganesh.

CHAPTER 40

*H*e burst out laughing. "Your *face*! He bellowed, slapping his knees with all four hands in a steady rhythm. This went on for a few seconds before he regained his composure, using one finger to wipe a tear from his Third Eye.

Crikey. His Third Eye could cry?

He lowered his hand, smiling at me. "Thank you for that. It feels nice to have a good cry every now and again. Been years…" he trailed off, shaking his head. Then he turned back to me. "Ganesha is fine, by the way. I meant when I originally cut off his head as a child. Boy, was Parvati upset about *that*. I had to go run and find a replacement," he snapped the fingers of all four hands like a string of firecrackers, startling me, "*really* quickly. Came back with an *elephant's head* of all things… Dumb kid was just doing as he was told, guarding the door as she took a bath. And I was only trying to get a quick peek of my wife in the nude. Didn't even know who the kid was at the time, let alone that he was my freshly-created *son*!"

And he was slapping his knees again, laughing uproariously.

I decided it was best for me to mimic his emotions. Whether I thought the topic of decapitation and transplantation humorous or not. It's a sales tactic called *mirroring*. It puts people at ease. Mirror their reactions. If they lean forward, you lean forward slightly. If they lean back, you lean back. Establish similarities. Subconscious bonds.

Of course, it got a bit more complicated too. Sometimes it was best to do the opposite. For example, if they had their arms crossed, it meant they were on guard, and it was best to open up, leaning back and spreading your arms in some subtle way.

I snapped out of it to find him staring at me. Right. Sales tactics were not important at the moment. Especially a *mortal* using them to try to psychologically manipulate a *god*.

"You have been misled," he said ominously, no longer smiling at all.

I blinked at the abrupt change of mood. "Pardon?"

"You consider yourself a Maker, yes?" he asked, hands restless again. I focused on his Third Eye as I nodded back. "Do you know what that means?"

I frowned. "No. Not a clue, to be honest."

He let out an exasperated sound. "No wonder Ganesha reached out to me." He closed all three eyes for the space of a measured breath, and then opened them, staring at me with all three of them. I felt rooted to my chair, both at the intensity and the topic. "I'll hit the highlights, if that's okay with you." I nodded eagerly. This would be the first real information I had found outside of Ichabod's book. "We made you. Gods. You were to be our enforcers. Our *Deus Ex Machina*. Our *Hands of God*. But like all creations, we failed. You were tainted. With Beasts. Do you understand so far?"

I stared as if struck in the nose. "The Dark Presence..." I whispered.

He nodded. "That *Beast*," he corrected, "is not your friend. He almost had you. You chased him down to the void, begging for him to teach you."

"Sure, he's a little demanding. But we have an agreement. We're partners," I said.

He took a calming breath, and leaned forward, explaining slowly. "You had a *temporary* agreement. During the Grimm War, when emotions ran wild. But peace never lasts, child."

I opened my mouth to argue, but closed it, truly considering his comment. The Dark Presence, or Beast, *had* been more of a struggle lately. "You're saying that this entire time... the Beast has been planning a takeover?" Shiva nodded, smiling at the fact I had accepted it so quickly. But hearing it like this, it suddenly made a whole lot of sense. "Okay." I said, discarding the emotions now rising up inside me. They would do no good here. I needed to *learn*.

Shiva didn't look best pleased at my eagerness for some reason, but I didn't care. I was going to get as much out of him as possible. "The Hatter is what happens when a Maker loses control over his Beast," he said in a dry tone, as if waiting for my reaction. He got one.

My heart stopped, suddenly horrified. I had spent time with him. Spent months speaking to him. And he was a cracked Maker? Here I was, a fledgling Maker, knowing nothing of the Beast, and I had been basically learning from a monster. A failed Maker.

Another realization struck me like a blow to the gut. I had told Ichabod about my Dark Presence. And he had said nothing about a Maker's Beast. But he *had* to have known. He had been dealing with it for centuries...

Shiva was watching me sadly. "You should probably cease speaking with the Hatter..." I nodded numbly as he continued. "Now, whether you succeed or fail in Mastering your Beast, there will likely come a time when one of us Old Ones knocks on your door. Think of it like the Draft for your military. We call. You answer. Because we *Made* you," he said ominously. "And some of us prefer the Beast over the Man." He shrugged, letting that sink in.

My mind was scattered, and I wanted to run away screaming. "Are you telling me that I have no other option? Either way, I will end up as someone's bitch? To my Beast or a god?"

He shrugged. "There is always the chance that we won't call on you. Just depends on the day of the week, really." He leaned forward. "But the way things are escalating in your world lately, I would say it's a fair bet the Draft will be called. Especially with you as one of the last two remaining Makers in existence. Not too many options left to us."

I shivered. "How long do I have?" I whispered.

He laughed, waving off my concern. "You've a long way to go before you would be of any use to *us*." I frowned at his underhanded criticism. He saw my face, and smiled sadly at me. "No offense, but you're incredibly inefficient. You've been running around, trying to be a *wizard* with your *Maker* power." He began to shake his head in disapproval. "A Maker is a *thinker*. A *doer*. He is not a *cook*. He rarely needs ingredients to make something *be*. He simply *thinks*, and it *is*. Take fire for example. Whether you know it or not, you've been using your Maker power to create the right type of air, then again for the right type of spark, then again for the right amount of force to successfully send it at your target. You've been imagining each necessary part of a spell, instead of the result itself. Like a *wizard* would."

I stared at him, unable to speak. He was right, so I finally nodded.

"That is three times the amount of work necessary for a Maker. All a Maker needs to do is look at his target, and think, *I want him to burn.*" Shiva smiled darkly, reminding me very subtly that he did not think like us mortals. "And. He. Shall. Burn." I shivered at the thought. He was right. I had no idea how to use my powers, and now that I thought about it, I wasn't sure I wanted to. Especially not if it put me on the god roster for a war. That much power... No wonder Makers had been hunted.

I sighed. "Even if I master my Beast, you just said that this isn't ever going to go away. This war. I will be sucked into it whether I want it or not. So, what's the point?"

Shiva shrugged, holding up two palms horizontal, the other two resting on his knees. "Burden of the Beast." The room was silent for a time. I wasn't sure how long. "But perhaps you've unknowingly been given the tools to latch your chariot to a different beast."

I looked up sharply, frowning. "What?"

"I sense more than two beasts inside you. They are raging against each other. Rattling the cages. Knocking screws loose. Perhaps you've noticed..." he smirked, reading my mind.

"Yeah, I've noticed. As have my friends."

"This is why my Ganesha gave you his belt. That I could find you. Help you *transform* your *obstacle*." He enunciated the two words, and I remembered something.

Ganesh was the Lord of *Obstacles*, and he had applauded Rufus cursing me. And had set things into play so that I received his belt. Nothing to do with Baba Yaga. But so I could meet his dear-old-dad, the Lord of *Transformation*.

I'd had enough. My brain felt like it was sizzling. I just couldn't do this anymore. I had fought, bled, and died to keep my city safe. Only to realize that none of it mattered. Who really cared at this point? I had no idea what the hell was going on. No idea how to save my friends.

Or the kids.

In my depression, one of his statements suddenly replayed in my ears, and I looked up at the god, frowning. "What is the third beast?" I asked softly. His face morphed into an approving grin. "You said you sensed *more than two beasts* inside of me..." My Maker power, my affinity to the Horsemen, and... Then it hit me. I remembered Rufus' idle comment right after he had cursed me. "A wizard…" I answered my own question. Shiva nodded, but I soon let out a frustrated sigh. It didn't matter. "That beast is practically dead. In fact, I don't even know why it's still hanging around, taking up space, becoming a nuisance to my *other* Beasts." I grouched.

He smiled at me, showing teeth. "Because a small part of you didn't want it to die."

I stared back. "Well, of course not. Being a wizard was my life. But the universe has never really cared too much about what I wanted. Why start now?" I complained.

"Because whether you understand it or not, you are a Maker. And part of you wanted something so badly that the Beast could not take it from you, and was instead forced to revive it, nurture it, keep it alive. Even if only barely…"

"The Beast did this for me?" I whispered, stunned.

Shiva nodded, and a small part of me suddenly loved the Beast for that one act. "He wasn't happy about it, but he did it," Shiva said.

"Wait…" I said, a thought briefly skittering across my brain pan. I replayed our conversation again. How a Maker's power worked. How it practically had no limits. "No way…" I glanced up at Shiva, who was nodding with a deep, expectant smile. "I can bring it back to life. Re-*Make* it…" I whispered. "I'm a necro-wizard."

CHAPTER 41

Shiva dashed my temporary moment of joy.

"If only you knew someone with the ability to teach you how to *Make* it so."

I flinched. "Ichabod!"

But Shiva was shaking his head already, grimacing, as if anticipating my response ahead of time. Which was probably accurate.

"Sure. The one who chose not to tell you about your Beast in the first place. Even after you brought it up to him. Even knowing the consequences. *He's* trustworthy. And I'm sure he would *love* to teach you." He leaned closer, face devoid of emotion now. "Everything he knows. In a single night." He straightened the snake on his neck absently with one of his hands. "Before the curse rips your Maker power away entirely." And I felt myself growing angry at the reminder of Ichabod's betrayal. Shiva was right. Ichabod had lied. Even if only a lie of omission, he had never warned me. Never told me about his Beast. Or agreed when I told him of *my* Beast.

That bastard. He definitely wouldn't help me. And realizing his lie, I didn't want his *help*…

I wanted his *head*.

I applied my anger to the problem at hand. "Okay, if I can't go to Ichabod, that leaves only… my Beast." I shot a look at Shiva to find him nodding, leaning forward intently. "But to do that, I need to establish dominance, like you said. Master my Beast. Then steal *his* knowledge."

"Yes…" he drummed two of his palms on his lap. "But you will need to acquire more power. The curse has taken too much already. You're close, but not close enough. Even with the Beast's knowledge, you need more power. In this state, you would burn yourself out, or die trying."

"I never thought I'd ask anyone this, but how do I get more power?"

Shiva smiled. "I've already told you. Mastery over your beasts. Domination. Beasts crave it." He held out one of his hands, showing off the cottage. "Why do you think I brought you here? *Home, sweet home,*" he said with a deeper meaning in his tone.

I frowned at the cottage. It was rather mediocre, but I wasn't about to tell him that. He folded his head into the palms of two hands, a universal sign of frustration. Right. Mind reader. But I was more concerned that he might have poked his Third Eye out. "Are you saying there is a jar of power on one of those shelves that I can borrow?"

He groaned. "Not *my home, Master* Temple." His choice of enunciation was odd to my ears, and I thought it was due to his head buried in his palms. "There is a reason your family carries the appellation, you know. Well, other than sheer arrogance," he added. I blinked again, hearing the cadence of his words, putting them together. Then I added them to the context of our conversation up to this point.

"I need to master my home…" I said flatly, not understanding the significance.

"Look out the damned window," he cursed, pointing one of his hands.

I did, and flinched. I hadn't actually looked *out* the window yet, only *at* the window. I had been too enamored by the freaking god hovering before me in a traditional yoga position.

Chateau Falco unfolded in perfect clarity. The mansion. The Grounds. The tree. Or Gateway, as the sprites had called it. Even the white lizard-men, looking like tiny ants. I didn't see anything unusual. Anything different. Well, other than the fact that Shiva had told me we were on Mt. Kailash, his traditional home, but I instead found myself now staring at my home. I had learned to take certain things in stride over the years. Then my eyes locked onto the tree, remembering what the sprites had said. They had made the tree to keep the Fae out of my life. Temporarily. Which meant… the tree had *juice.*

And seeing it from this angle, it looked like one giant, metallic lightning rod. "A power source," I whispered.

"Close enough," Shiva muttered in resignation at my dim brain.

But I was too distracted to care about his frustration. "But it's keeping the Fae at bay."

Shiva grunted. "In case I didn't say this earlier, when a god finds a Maker he wants for his own, he takes them, breaks them, and then sends them back to their home to destroy everything they once loved. Family. Friends. *Everything*. That's what lies behind door number two..."

I nodded absently. I had a decision to make. If I chose to remain a Maker, I could kill that last wizard seed inside of me, and deny my Horseman mantle. Then I would only have to worry about sharing head-space with the Beast my entire life. If I survived *that*, I got to look forward to a god making me into his personal chess piece for a future war.

Or, I could do what we had discussed. Temporarily master my Beast, tap into the Gateway – unleashing the Fae – and use that added power to restore my wizard's power. The curse would then drop, killing my Maker's power. My Beast. And I would owe Rufus a beer.

Either way, I still had to confront the Beast Master and save the kids. Ashley. The chimera.

But option two guaranteed that the Fae would join the fight. Then I thought about Tory and her gift. I shrugged. It was only a matter of time before the Fae came to town anyway. They were already stressing the boundary. Might as well do it on my own terms. Because I realized that I *needed* – not *wanted* – Tory during that fight. It was the only chance we had against keeping the Beast Master's shifters at bay. But this way, if I could time it right, I would have multiple power sources to pull from in the fight. Or at least strengthen one of them significantly.

My wizard's gift. That old, tried-and-true companion of mine.

I needed to get back to that. Back to my roots. This Maker business was too much. It had cost me too much. Had changed me. For the worse. I made my decision, not even hesitating. "I need to break the Fae out to become a wizard, so that I don't become a god or beast's bitch."

Shiva nodded, tapping a finger on his knee.

"What about those guys? I don't think they're going to approve of me plugging into their sacred tree." I said, pointing at the lizard-men. "No, wait. I think I know the answer. Dominate them." I rolled my eyes.

216

He nodded back, not catching my sarcasm. "If you time it right, you can dominate the Elders, too," he agreed. "Whatever you do, just don't feed them." I shot him a sharp look at the comment, but was more interested in their name. *Elders*. "No one may know about your power play." He leaned forward, face serious. "No one." I nodded back, swallowing. "To them, you're the same now as you were before we met."

I nodded. "What happens on Mt. Kailash, stays on Mt. Kailash."

That earned a chuckle. "Enemies are closer than you may realize…"

I frowned at his cryptic warning, but nodded. "I'm used to pissing people off."

He grunted, unsure whether I had taken him seriously or not. "There will be temporary…" he quested for the right word, "*ripples*. A result of holding all three powers simultaneously. One growing at an alarming rate, one dying, and one… on the bench. You must—"

"Establish dominance," I interrupted, grinning at his choice of words for my potential Horseman power. "I get it."

He smiled back. "Maximum effort."

I laughed. "Okay, Deadpool. Like father, like son," I murmured, mind going a million miles an hour. Planning. Calculating. Scheming. "I still have to find a way to take out the Beast Master," I murmured to myself, not expecting a response.

"To fight a Beast Master, you must first become a Beast Master. Transform. But you still have your *Home, Master Temple*. After all, what are we without our *Homes?*" He said, repeating his odd advice. I nodded absently. "But do not despair. It's in your blood. You've already taken the first step." I glanced over my shoulder, about to ask him to speak plainly.

But I was all alone in the cottage. He had even taken the rad tiger fur. "Wait, how do I get back?" I shouted.

"*Through the looking-glass…*" his voice whispered. I turned to the window with a frown.

With no other ideas, I approached the window, and stared through the glass again.

And gasped.

CHAPTER 42

I saw my friends. Standing in my office at Chateau Falco. Over my body.

Well, wasn't *this* familiar?

Charon, the Boatman to the Underworld, had shown me something similar in my not-too-distant past. But this felt different. Less final. More as if I was watching a dream given flesh as opposed to *literally* dying.

Astral projection, I remembered Shiva telling me. He had astral projected me to his home on Mt. Kailash, the place where he, his wife, and two sons called *home*.

The Hindu Gods. Well, a handful of them.

Heh, handful.

"What was that?" Othello shouted, snapping me back to the view through the looking-glass. "What was that sound? It sounded like screaming." It seemed like almost no time had passed since I had fallen unconscious after healing Van from Gunnar's attack. Which was good.

Mallory stared dumbstruck, eyes flicking from Van Helsing on the couch to me on the floor. His mouth opened and closed wordlessly several times.

The Huntress chimed in. "What is happening to him?"

Mallory turned to her, face pale. "I have no bloody idea…"

Othello stared up at him through tear-filled eyes. "You can't possibly believe that he's... look, he's not crazy. No matter what you saw, you didn't need to test him like that," she argued.

Mallory sighed in defeat. "What about the glass?"

"I'm sure... look, he's a *Maker*. None of us truly knows what that *means*!" she defended.

"Ye didn't see him at the window. Something's wrong. Ye didn't see him downstairs in the basement. He was talking to himself. Or the cat." And all three of them suddenly looked right at me in my window. I flinched instinctively. Then Mallory pointed at the melted heap that had been her laptop, but he didn't comment, just turned back to her with a condemning grimace.

She sighed, hanging her head to her chest in defeat. "Okay. I'll admit, something is off. But let's just call Gunnar. He's the only one who can get through to him. Nate just needs *help*."

Her words hurt me. The last one to defend me, was now crumbling.

"I don't buy it. He seems perfectly sane," the Huntress argued.

"As if yer opinion's worth a damn," Mallory growled scathingly. "Ye told us what happened with Gunnar in that alley..."

"That was in the heat of the moment, Old One," she warned darkly. "I'm sure you've been caught up with bloodlust a time or two. In fact, I'm pretty sure I've read about—"

"Continue speaking, and die, Lassie," he growled.

Othello threw her hands up in frustration. Then she leaned over me, laying her head on my chest for a few seconds. She gasped. "He's not breathing!" Then, without waiting for a response, she began chest compressions. Then she pinched my nose, breathing into my mouth as her tears fell onto my cheeks. I subconsciously lifted my hand to my cheeks as if I could feel her tears...

And the arm through the glass lifted slightly from the ground.

This scared the living shit out of everyone. But not Othello.

She suddenly jerked her head up to stare straight at me again, as if seeing through my window. I froze in shock for half a second, and then waved back at her frantically. She only frowned, and then resumed her chest compressions.

"What the hell was that? He's not even breathing. How did his arm move?" the Huntress demanded, gripping Mallory's arm as he stared down at my now motionless body.

He seemed to snap out of it, abruptly lifting a boot to shove Othello clear. Then a bolt of lightning appeared in his hand, and he pressed it to my chest.

In the cottage, I immediately gasped in pain, fingers splaying out as lightning shot forth from my fingertips, hammering into the shelves, the chair, the table. The lightning ceased abruptly, and I saw Mallory had withdrawn his lightning spear from my chest in Chateau Falco.

I was panting. I'd had enough of this astral projection shit. What good was it if I still felt the pain from my actual body? I was supposed to be healing, relaxing, meditating…

But Dr. Othello and Dr. Mallory had apparently studied under the tutelage of Dr. Victor Frankenstein.

She hammered my chest twice, did a few more compressions, and then began breathing into my mouth again.

In the cottage, my fingertips subconsciously rose to my mouth. I felt a… faint tingle on my lips. Then a metaphysical fist slammed into my chest, and I grunted in pain. I tensed my stomach in anticipation of another blow, wondering if Shiva had come back to evict me with his Four Fists of Justice.

But I was still alone. *Wait…*

I glanced up in time to see Othello pulling her fists away from my chest where she had escalated to pounding me rather than pressing with her palms. Mallory shoved her aside again, reaching out to poke me with his cattle prod. "No, no, *no*. This is *not* going to feel good…" I began panting as I saw the spear touch my chest in the office.

And lightning shot out of my eyes, burning Shiva's cottage to ashes as a scream was torn from my chest, seeming to shatter my own eardrums. And I was yanked out of his house, his realm, his world. Back into my office.

I lurched up, screaming.

Lightning filled the air. I instinctively grasped the tip – *just* the tip – of Mallory's lightning spear, and crushed it in my fist. A puff of crackling sparks danced throughout the room, and I heard a shattering sound like broken glass as the spear disintegrated under my touch. The lightning in the room ceased, and I realized I hadn't been the only one screaming.

The Huntress stood on top of my desk, hair standing straight up at the static charge in the room, as she aimed an arrow at me with her fancy new bow.

The one Van had bought her.

Othello was perched on Van's chest, clutching her knees in terror, cheeks stained with tears, eyes bloodshot, and panting loudly as she rocked back and forth, her hair also sticking straight up.

"That... that feels nice," Van murmured, cracking one eye open to see Othello rocking back and forth on his lap.

Her face turned beet-red and she jumped behind the couch, putting it between her and me.

Van frowned, spotted me, and then his eyebrows furrowed. "That's new..." He turned to Mallory, flinched at a few errant crackles of electricity still in the air before they evaporated to nothing. His frown stretched in deep thought.

"What's new?" I rasped at Van's comment, throat hoarse from screaming.

He turned to me. "Your eyes. Flickering like lightning. And the skin is red around them." His gaze locked onto my hand. "So are your fingers." I pressed the areas with my fingertips. They didn't feel tender or sore, so I shrugged it off as a side-effect from crying lightning bolts. He lifted his head to see the Huntress pointing her bow in my general direction, and let out a sigh.

"The bow looks good on you." He smiled before assessing us as a group. "But you people should try talking first. I feel like I walked in on the middle of a soap opera." He glanced around. "Speaking of, where's that Butler? Popcorn sounds nice while I watch the upcoming drama."

"What happened to you?" I asked Van, ignoring the looks my friends were giving me.

I didn't feel like talking to them, but I needed to know things. One, if not all of them, thought I was crazy. Or on my way there. And I couldn't confront them about it. Per Shiva's parting warning. I didn't even want to consider the long-term consequences of my astral projection. And I was pretty sure asking anyone about it would only further convince them I was clawing by my fingernails to grip the cliffs of sanity.

"I had just concluded returning the werecat. For free, I might add," he growled unhappily, "when your pet showed up and tried to kill me." He eyed the Huntress thoughtfully. "In fact, I'm pretty sure he should have killed me. One of you stupid bastards apparently saved me. Idiots." He grumbled, propping himself up to a sitting position on the couch. Sir Muffle Paws dropped down from a perch and leapt up onto his chest, where he began happily purring and clawing his chest like cats do when they are tenderizing their next human meal.

221

Othello was watching the cat with a thoughtful frown. I studied the cat for a moment, not understanding her look, but gave up with an impatient sigh.

Then I turned to leave. I had work to do. Othello's voice followed me. "You were just *dead*, Nate!" I ignored her, my vision pulsing blue as I continued on through the doorway.

I slammed the door behind me. I heard a curse followed by a solid *thunk* as something powerful slammed into the door, and an arrowhead was suddenly poking all the way through the wood. I glanced at it, frowned, and continued on through the halls.

I heard muffled arguing behind the door, but then Othello shouting back for everyone to give me some space.

They must have listened. Bully for them.

CHAPTER 43

*U*nable to find a coat quickly enough, I had grabbed a thick robe from a nearby bathroom, and thrown it on over my tee, deciding a bit of fresh air would do just the trick. To clear my head.

Before I attempted to dry-hump my Beast into submission.

And my friends thought I was crazy.

I now sat beneath the giant silver tree – the Gateway, or huge freaking lightning rod. I closed my eyes to avoid the blue tint to the world around me. Remembering Shiva's comment about the Elders, I thumbed a piece of broken glass in my palm.

The enchanted glass from Chateau Falco. *Master Temple's Home.*

I took a few deep breaths, preparing myself for I knew not what, and began to meditate.

After fifteen minutes or so, I sought out the Dark Presence inside of me. My Beast. In the darkness of my soul, I imagined myself on my knees, calling out to him, pleading, and luring him with promises. I continued this for some time, staring into the black void, fearing he knew my game.

Then, like a gunshot, a form exploded from the darkness, hurtling at me like a blazing comet. At the last second, he snapped to sudden stillness, like a kite catching the wind, but restrained by the shackles of the string.

I stared at him, my face an apologetic mask, remembering that – despite his treachery – he had kept my wizard's power alive. With a twist of guilt, I held out my arms to offer him a brotherly embrace, and a kiss on the cheek. Like Judas Iscariot.

He watched me warily, and then – ever so slowly – he met me in a spiritual bond that could not be broken.

Brotherhood.

Appreciation.

Love.

And that's when I betrayed him. In his eyes, I saw the moment that he realized my apologetic mask had not been for what *had* been done to him, but for what I was *about* to do to him.

But his understanding came too late.

Purple shackles materialized on his wrists, and he saw with horror and confusion that I had bonded them to my own wrists in identical purple shackles of crackling power. I tossed away the key, and we watched as it sailed out into the darkness, forever lost.

I wasn't quite sure what I did next, or how I was doing it, but it felt right. An instinct. I let the instinct take over, remembering Shiva's comment. *It's in your blood...*

The Beast gasped, snarled, struggled, and fought, but we were now one, and after an eternity, he quieted, watching me with both rage and trepidation. Waiting.

I dipped my head at him, and then I turned my attention back to the real world, eyes still closed as my body sat beneath the tree. I spent a single moment acknowledging the physical world, feeling the icy bark against my back, the cool, crisp smells and sounds of winter, the taste of a season dying and being reborn beneath the earth's surface – the taste of life and death. I pulled all these sensations in, relishing them, drinking them, letting them fill me to bursting.

And then I began to dismantle them. I discarded all sensation, slowly removing smell, touch, sound, taste. My eyes were already closed, so vision was by default already out, but I did imagine *seeing* nothingness – a super-black vacuum where nothing existed. I stayed like this for a few minutes until the void was absolute around us.

But my mind still ran rampant, because although I had dismantled the world around me, a human body – Nate Temple – still existed in that void. As did his Beast. I could still recall the *memories* of these things: the grass beneath me, the smells riding the breeze of cool air, the taste of blood in my mouth from my recent injuries, the replay of the conversation I had over-heard my friends having.

About my sanity.

Judging by what I was about to do, maybe they were right.

I imagined these pains, these memories, my friends, my enemies, my home, the Beast Master, the Academy, my fiancée, *everyone*, and *everything* – in full context, for the span of a baby's first laughter. For a million years' each. For *no* time. For *all* time.

And then I obliterated them from existence.

I was a Tiny God in my own tiny little void. I was *All*.

The Alpha. And the Omega.

Shiva. The Creator and Destroyer of Worlds.

Of Nothingness.

No life.

No death.

Just Nate Temple. And his Beast.

Sensing this, my Beast began to scream in horror.

Then I committed both suicide and murder, destroying those two last remaining forms of life. The screaming ceased like a snuffed candle.

And Nate Temple and his Beast became Nothingness, in *fact*.

Nothingness – an omnipotent, care-free construct – remained for an eternity.

For the duration of another Big Bang. For the single flutter of a Hummingbird's wings.

For no time at all.

Because there *was* no concept of time.

Nothingness had killed that, too.

Then, Nothingness slowly began to rebuild the world around it. First, the Gateway.

Where it had all begun.

At least for Nate Temple. The Maker that had been transformed into the Nothingness.

Then the Nothingness transformed. It sacrificed itself to build the Maker, the Tiny God, infusing his body with the elements of life: flesh, blood, bone, darkness, light, and his *Beasts*.

The Tiny God breathed for the first time, and He smiled as the Nothing-ness died.

Then the Tiny God added his own creations: love, hate, family, enemies, trust, betrayal…

Next, the Tiny God created a Prison.

Crystal bars of starlight, silver welding, golden locks and chains, obsidian floors and walls, ramparts and battlements melded together with ivory mortar. The Tiny God created raging rivers of flowing ice, formed them into impenetrable moats around the prison, made the air crackle with the pure, elemental power of purple electricity, understanding it fully for the *first* time.

Outerfire.

It was so *simple*.

Then the Tiny God filled that air with an erratic *clanging* sound, pitch, volume, and tempo infinitely random enough to drive a prisoner to madness. The Tiny God filled that same air with scents of brimstone and glaciers, ash and burnt glass, dust and disease, sand and grit, and something that was none of these. He filled his Prison with *pain*, and hints of *love*, so that any surface touched was prone to randomly bite or caress, so that a prisoner would never know which he would receive. Pain or pleasure. Forever. He instilled taste in the air – of delicious foods chased by bile and rot, savory decay.

Then the Tiny God gave the Prison its first prisoner, and the Prison growled in gratitude, hungry, sated, and *alive*. The Beast wailed.

Once complete, the Tiny God rested, and the virgin Maker opened his freshly-minted eyes.

The two had become one – Tiny God and Maker.

Nate Temple.

And he smiled, glancing down at the silver cane on his hip.

His pocket Prison.

The Beast begged and pleaded.

"Submit…" the Tiny God commanded.

And the Beast did.

"Teach me…" the Tiny God commanded.

And the Beast did.

And the Tiny God smiled, filling himself to bursting with Creation's Chaos, eyes watering with joy. The true power of a Maker. Although currently limited in strength, it now overshadowed such petty things as a wizard's curse.

CHAPTER 44

*M*y Beast begged, "Master, you don't need to do this. We were allies…"

"You are mine to do with as I please. Do not mistake my acceptance of your stained existence as affection," I whispered, twirling my fingers through gossamer strands of sunbeams piercing the tree above. "Or submission. This is called *domination. Mastery.*"

I plucked the beam of sunlight free and moved it a pace away, more to my liking.

The Beast gasped, and then flinched in pain as he attempted to move inside his Prison. "All this… for one who has assisted you. This… *hell.*"

I nodded. "Handing out candy every now and again does not constitute friendship. Or an alliance. You did what you did, when you did it, to attempt to steal my trust. Not to earn it. So that you could eventually attempt a mutiny, of my mind."

My Beast cowered in shame, but it pressed on. "Let. Me. Help. You." And the Beast collapsed to his knees, groaning in rapture as his knees touched the Prison floor. Then he began to shake as that comfort was ripped away, and true pain replaced the momentary pleasure. The chaos I had created for him. The constant ebb and flow of pain and pleasure, never consistent, never ending. Just constant, chaotic mood swings of joy and agony, famine and gluttony, war and peace, death and life, pestilence and abounding health.

Hope.

And despair.

His new home.

If he so chose.

"Please... let me help you."

I ignored his plea, studying the air around me, taking a deep breath with lungs that felt to have never tasted air. And the smells!

I touched the glass in my hand, and the tactile feedback momentarily overwhelmed me, causing my body to shudder.

I spoke softly. "We have work to do." I told him what I desired. He hesitated for only a moment before complying.

And we tapped into the Gateway behind me. Out of a clear-blue sky, a lightning bolt struck the tree, shooting all the way down through the trunk and into the roots, the leaves and twigs around me bouncing up off of the ground as a single *boom* cracked the air.

And power raged into me like a tidal wave. But I didn't move.

Because I didn't want to. And the world was *Made* as I saw fit.

I murmured a request to the Beast, and it acted, fearing any answer other than *yes, Master.*

As was right.

And I felt a small, faint, wavering heat deep, deep, deep down in my soul from a single red coal that rested on a platform of air. My wizard's power.

The coal flared brighter, hotter, and began to flicker erratically.

Then the flame came to life.

Just one flame. But it grew, and grew, and *grew*, the coal becoming a bed of embers.

Then a campfire.

Then... a forest fire.

And the blaze consumed me. I let it fill my chest as it raged, building, growing, eating...

Living. My wizard's power was still weakened, but now growing. I could feel it healing itself deep inside me, blazing old pathways free of metaphysical cobwebs. I opened my eyes, and the world *rippled*, the two Beasts fighting against each other. I sighed, releasing the connection to the Gateway. My Maker power snapped back, rejuvenated, but still weaker than it would have been without the curse.

But that was okay. I didn't need it for much longer anyway.

The Gateway hissed behind me, weakened and upset at my trespass, but still alive. I ignored this as my Beast sobbed at what he had helped me do. How he had effectively committed suicide.

I tried to use my wizard's power to ignite a small flame in my palm, but received only a staggering flash of pain. I stopped instantly, and let out a shaky breath.

Okay, no wizard's power yet. Maybe give it a minute to recover from resurrection. Perhaps it was too much to use with my Maker's power still a roommate. Because I still had *that*. And I no longer needed the Beast to use it. So, I tossed him back in his Prison mercilessly.

I felt the glass in my palm, and smiled. *It's in your blood... Master your home...* Shiva's words whispered in my ears like a lover's caress. And the Gateway was *on my property*.

Part of Chateau Falco.

I sliced deeply into the palm of my hand, ignoring the pain as I suddenly realized what I needed to do. I had given it only a *taste*. Now it was time to give it a big old *gulp*.

And take care of the Elders in one fell swoop.

I lifted the glass to my eyes to observe my home, staring at it through the crimson-stain.

My world rocked.

And my house purred a welcome.

Chateau Falco blazed like a bonfire in the distance, like Mount Olympus to a mortal. A beacon of truth, an Oasis in a desert, land after months at sea. Flickers of purple power danced from spire to spire on the rooftop.

It *spoke* to me, *welcoming* me, inviting me to come inside.

It seemed to let out a sigh of relief that it had held for hundreds of years. Finally witnessing a Master who realized she was a living creature, trapped inside the mortar of the mansion. She was eager to willingly serve a worthy lord who could see her for what she truly was.

Shiva had been right. Who else would have known that the mansion was a living entity? I had awakened Chateau Falco. My blood calling out to her, bonding us. Eternally.

The entity the first Temple had trapped here. The entity the first Temple had *dominated*.

And my blood had activated her when I touched it to the glass the first time.

But only chose to reveal her beauty *after* I had mastered my Maker's power, dominating my Beast. The house had needed a *worthy* Master. Not a man with only a whisper of magical ability.

But now that we were bonded, I knew it was for life. No matter what happened to my magic. *'Til Death do us part*, I thought with a grin.

I finally let out a sigh, and chose to acknowledge the army before me. The ones I had seen as soon as I lifted the glass to my eyes, but had ignored. The Elders.

But now that I was bonded with Chateau Falco, I no longer needed the glass to see them. The glass was a part of me now. As was the rest of the house. And the property.

And by default – an added bonus – the Gateway.

I tossed the glass down on the ground, locking eyes with the foremost Elder. He and his fellows were hunkered down on their dinosaur-like paws. One hissed and launched himself at me, ivory blades outstretched.

He died.

Explosively.

I blinked lazily, turning to the next. And dozens of them stared back defiantly, lords of themselves, lost and forgotten for so long that they had forgotten what it was to serve a worthy Master. But I was willing to show them the error of their ways. And now it was time for me to start burning off my power anyway, so I could let the curse destroy my Maker's power.

So, I, *erm*, cut loose.

The one I took for the leader watched me. Then he lifted his hands. Like lemmings, the others threw themselves at me with varying degrees of supernatural strength, speed, power, magic, and agility. And I ended them, with equal variations of chaos. Fire. Ice. Gateways. Obliterating them in such a fantastic symphony of light, sound, and concussive explosions that the scene would have given Michael Bay sweet, sweet dreams.

They.

All.

Died.

Until only one remained. The leader. I would have liked to say that he was the first one I had met so many years ago. Then I hesitated. Not *years*. *Yesterday*. My mind rippled for a moment, then quieted. I blinked at the unsettling feeling.

The creature watched me. "What does thee dessssire?" he hissed.

"Your servitude. And a headset to fix your creepy lisp," I added, grimacing. His voice sounded like nails on a chalkboard.

He cleared his shining scaly throat. "Is this better?" he asked, voice entirely normal.

I blinked in surprise, not having expected such a quick solution, and then nodded.

"You were hearing me too clearly, Maker. Too accurately. Too literally. I have corrected your senses, or your perception of reality. Whatever explanation suits you." He considered me in silence for two heartbeats before adding, "Master." The word sounded foreign to his lips, but also as if it lent him strength, as if he had been searching for a time and place to use the word again after roaming the planes of existence as a vagabond for so long. Alone.

I gave him a dark grin. "I've always liked the sound of that." I studied him thoughtfully. "I shall name you Carl. I broke your Gateway, didn't I? The Fae can now come to my world."

He nodded.

"And thanks to the Gateway residing on my property, and that I am the rightful Master of the Beast, you are now mine." I motioned towards Chateau Falco, and he shivered before nodding. "I hope there are more of you..."

He nodded again. "The Gateway is still good for that."

"Okay. Here's what you're going to do, Carl..."

And we spoke for a few moments before I bid him goodbye, and then headed back inside my home. Inside the beast that had disguised itself as my home.

It purred as I drew closer.

CHAPTER 45

I walked into my office, face calm. The Huntress jerked her head my way, watching me hesitantly, face tight, noticing something was different about me. An instinctual knowledge. A gut feeling. Van noticed her wandering attention, and turned. He squinted at me, but didn't speak. Mallory stood stiffly, warily, as if fearing retaliation of some sort. For testing me. Othello watched me with big, dark eyes, tears still dampening her cheeks. She looked ready to dart my way and hug me.

I smiled. I think.

I caressed the door frame as one would a cat, and murmured, "There, there…" The house literally groaned in reply, as a house is wont to do in the middle of the night when you are asleep, forcing you to imagine a monster creeping about in the darkness.

The sound of a house settling. Of a monster sighing in content.

My home.

Mallory flinched, eyes wide. "What have ye done, Laddie?"

I turned to him, staring as I remembered him forcing me to heal Van as some sort of test. Now I knew it was to assure himself. That I hadn't lost my marbles. But I couldn't accuse him of that, because Shiva had warned me against speaking of what I had seen through the looking-glass.

Looking-glass… My eyes briefly darted to the book on the shelf, considering the coincidence.

Then I turned to Othello and smiled, holding out my arms. She raced my way in a flash, and wrapped her arms around me. "It's okay. I understand," I murmured in her ear, smelling the tea tree shampoo in her hair.

She sobbed against my chest, a sound of relief, and the Huntress shared an intense look with both Van and Mallory, silently querying them on what the fuck had just happened, and why the house had made a noise immediately after I had supposedly spoken to it.

I studied her over Othello's shoulder. And winked.

Then I gently pried Othello from my torso, wrapped a protective arm around her shoulder, and led her to the couch. I sat in my aged Darlington, and glanced at the liquor in Van's hand. Then I glanced at the table beside me, and suddenly a glass of chilled scotch was there.

Van cursed, trying to jump to his feet, but only managing to tangle himself up in the blanket.

I held out my hand. "Peace."

He calmed, studying me acutely. "What..."

The Huntress chimed in politely. "I have the same question. Followed by *the fuck*. Also, should we be concerned about the goddamn fireworks display outside a few moments ago? Looked like you were kicking off the Apocalypse."

Everyone turned to me, eyes questioning. "That can wait. Right now, we have more pressing matters to discuss." I turned to Othello. "Did you verify Van's claim about the abduction?"

Van cleared his throat. "Othello verified it. Some charity going down at an orphanage. But..."

I turned to him, frowning. "Yes?"

He shivered, muttering under his breath as his gaze flinched away. "Tory and Alucard showed up. We talked. They might have heard about the charity. And then promptly left."

I hadn't noticed any cars entering the drive. Then again, I had been distracted. Perhaps my little show had scared them off. I leaned forward, and the Huntress' hands twitched, as if considering her bow. "When?"

"Thirty minutes ago."

"Why didn't you stop them? And what about the Reds?"

"Nate, the girls are fine, but..." Othello pleaded, suddenly kneeling before me, tears flowing freely again. "You were gone for a *long* time. We watched you." She pointed out the window at the tree. "You weren't moving.

At all. And you didn't quite leave with a... reasonable look on your face. And you had just died. Kind of." I frowned.

"How long is *long?*"

"Bloody hours," Mallory growled. "But it felt like forever." His words seemed to jar a thought into his head, and he looked at me sharply, but didn't voice his concern.

"What army were you destroying out there?" the Huntress repeated.

I turned to her, surprised that she hadn't seen the Elders I had been fighting. After all, the glass was enchanted. The Beast spoke from his Prison for my ears only. *"Because you haven't given them permission to see through the glass,"* he whispered. I blinked. Oh. *"The glass worked for you the first time because you at least had the right blood. Now you have the right power, and the right blood."* I nodded to myself, gaze snapping back to the people before me. They were staring at me, frowning. Their sense of growing alarm was palpable.

"Later. It's not important right now." I didn't have time to get into the Elders. Tory and Alucard were out there right now.

This answer did not please them. And they began to argue. I let them go on for a few seconds.

"I'll explain later. Right now, we need to go stop Tory and Alucard. And Van needs to play the ever-helpful associate to the Beast Master. Because he's probably wondering where you've been." I slowly turned to him with a hungry smile. "If that means attacking me, so be it. If you're up for that." Van nodded. "Make it appear genuine. Do your worst. No holds barred."

He cursed under his breath, leaning away. "Fine."

"We need to go save a kid. And our friends." The Huntress nodded with a glare, thinking only of Tory. "They have no idea what they are up against. A whole pack of wolves and the Huntress couldn't stop them last time. And that's not even considering how the Fae will respond when she touches her power. We've already been attacked by goblins and a troll. Their next hunter won't be so gentle." I decided not to depress them further by telling them the Fae would be coming whether Tory used her powers or not. But not using her powers might possibly delay their debut a bit longer.

"You were there too, Maker. Last time we encountered the Beast Master's thugs. And despite the mayhem, you didn't help much either." The Huntress responded softly.

"That was... *before.*"

Mallory leaned closer, lips working soundlessly. "Before *what*, Laddie?" he asked softly.

"Before *everything*." I climbed to my feet and downed my drink. "Rufus all tucked in?" I asked him.

Mallory nodded with a faint grin. "Dean might have put something in his drink."

"Good. You ready to give me a brief highlight of your past?" I asked, staring at him. The question caught him off guard for a few moments. He finally shook his head sadly. "Okay." I turned away from him, my face blank as I began to walk away, remembering something Shiva had let slip. "We leave now. At the fountain. It should only take us a moment to get there."

"After the display of magic down at the tree, I wouldn't have been surprised to see you fail to make that drink a few minutes ago." Van spoke softly, but it was left open as a question.

I didn't answer, continuing my walk instead. I didn't even bother to grab my new cuffs, I was so confident in my new powers. Or knowledge of my old powers. I heard everyone scrambling behind me, but paid them no mind, listening to the gentle throbbing of the Prison at my hip.

The Guardians about the mansion purred, shrieked, and cooed as I strode past them. Utter adoration, and pride. I had never felt that from them.

But that had been *before*.

I walked past Dean, and smiled politely. He didn't say a word, but gave me a shaky nod back. The house groaned, as if a wind had briefly meandered down the hallway, and Dean tensed.

"It's okay, Dean. I'm okay. Chateau Falco appreciates your service."

His eyes were wide as he nodded back uncertainly.

In no time, I was standing by the fountain. Van and the Huntress burst out of the house first, armed for bear. I spotted Othello and Mallory tailing them, tugging on their coats. I shook my head, and the door slammed closed between us and them. Othello needed to stay safe. And I didn't trust Mallory any longer. Van and the Huntress shared a look. I ignored the sound of fists pounding on the other side of the door. They would be safe here.

I could literally guarantee it.

"Let us be off."

Using my dwindling Maker power, I ripped open a hole in reality, a ring of blazing sparks erupting before me. The little fireflies zipped through the opening, away from us, indicating the intended direction of travel. I stepped through, not waiting for a response. Van cursed several times behind me, but I heard the familiar sound of rounds being chambered in his pistols. No crossbow this time.

I strode into a dark alleyway one block from our destination. The sounds of bullets tore through the night. Screams. Destruction.

I smiled in anticipation.

CHAPTER 46

I released our Gateway, and then created another adjacent one. I shoved Van through before he could realize it, and then zipped it closed. He couldn't be seen with us. The Huntress cursed, trying to keep up with me as I suddenly bolted away, but I wasn't planning on using the streets. I called the wind, and suddenly bounded up the fire escape until I was standing three stories above the alley, letting the Huntress find her own way. I raced to the roof's edge, and stared down at a warzone. Shifters of all flavors slammed into each other.

I made a fist, and a flying creature slammed to the ground in a wet *splat*, right beside Tory. She looked pale, eyes intent, as she murmured continuously under her breath. Raego, in full black dragon form roared at a trio of different colored werecats. A dense fog of smoke sailed from his snout, instantly turning them into obsidian statues. Two gorillas hammered into him, and Raego shifted abruptly, now a hybrid between his two forms, like Gunnar could do. He went blow for blow against the gorillas, and was doing just fine. Tory must have called him for backup after learning the location of the intended abduction. But then who was watching the Reds?

Still, I felt like letting off some steam. And I *needed* to let off steam. Burn up my Maker power. In a controlled release, so that the curse dropping didn't kill me with shock of losing too much all at once. I glanced at a nearby dumpster, and flicked my finger. The several ton hunk of metal slammed into the gorillas, flattening them against the brick wall below me, which crumbled on impact. Still, I knew they weren't down for the count. Just trapped.

Gunnar burst free from an alley with a vampire head in each claw. One of them still had the spine attached. He threw them at another vampire, who dodged it with a feral hiss. "Any more chew toys?" he roared. He was covered in blood, none of it his. And he was smiling.

I heard two more dragons screeching in the night, and the resulting lance of napalm flame. Raego had brought friends. About time. He had been dragging ass lately in the *help* department.

Then a truly horrifying monster tore through the brick wall of one of the buildings, breathing fire and spitting venom at Gunnar. He dodged it, but two of his fellow wolves caught the brunt of the poison, and then the flame. Their pelts disintegrated in an explosive hiss of acidic venom, and *then* they caught fire. The beast's cobra tail lashed out and struck one of them in the neck. As it jerked free, it tore the wolf's throat out.

Time seemed to slow as I stared in awe at the chimera. It was a little shorter than me, and stood upright as it faced the wolves. Its chest was a magnificent lion's head, complete with auburn mane, mouth open in a silent snarl at the Alpha werewolf. The monster's head was a ram of some sort, horns still seeming adolescent, but long enough to skewer anyone who got too close, and its eyes blazed with yellow light. Its green tail arched up to sway from side to side over the ram's head, the tip resembling a cobra – hood fanned out as it hissed a warning, tongue flickering ominously.

If it looked like this as a *child*, how big would it be fully grown?

Gunnar bounded forward with a howl, his blue eye glittering with revenge as he closed on the chimera. I hammered him with a blaze of ice, knocking him clear of the venomous fire-breathing chimera. "Stupid idiot," I muttered under my breath. "You trying to get yourself killed?" That thing would destroy him. Destroy *anything*.

After that pronouncement of wisdom, I jumped off the roof, and my falling momentum gave me a thought. I smiled, flicking out a hand.

A minty green sphere coalesced around the chimera, and then I gave the bubble an English spin with the snap of a finger. The chimera roared, hissed, and bleated defiance as it suddenly found itself in a zero-gravity orb, spinning about continuously, the sphere absorbing all elemental attacks cast inside of it. The surviving shifters glared pure hatred at me as I landed on the dumpster that trapped the gorillas. The metal folded in on itself, absorbing my weight as if I had landed on a pile of pillows.

But I didn't lose my footing, manipulating the metal in the dumpster to perfectly accept this new reality of me landing painlessly atop it from a three-story drop.

Still, energy cannot be created or destroyed, so the dumpster... well, died, leaving behind a broken hunk of metal, and revealing the gorillas' upper bodies between it and the wall.

They hooted in renewed fury.

I calmly stepped off the dumpster, and casually kicked the metal without looking behind me. The dumpster exploded *through* the brick wall, crushing the gorillas into a pile of broken bones and dying screams. Being a self-proclaimed badass, I walked away without looking behind me. Like that YouTube montage of badasses walking away from an explosion without looking back.

A soft clapping reverberated through the alley, and everyone rushed back to their home teams, regrouping. Again, I walked.

A bald-headed man exited the hole in the building from his chimera, frowning up at her as she spun impotently in her cocoon. He was tall, powerfully built, and sported a tattoo on the back of each hand. His face was hard beneath his bearded cheeks.

"Well played, my boy. Well played. Didn't think you would actually show. Although I assumed your crew would."

"Nice to meet you. What's your name again?" I asked pleasantly.

He frowned. "Not sure that matters, considering..."

I shrugged. "I prefer to know the names of the people I kill," I grinned, all teeth.

He didn't answer immediately. Then he shrugged. "Boris."

Boris. Boris the Beast Master. I almost burst out laughing, but somehow restrained myself.

"Okay. Thanks. Time to die, Boris the Beast Master," I smiled, taking a step closer.

He held up a hand. "Not quite. Master Helsing?"

Gunnar stiffened, mouth open in shock at hearing Van was alive, let alone here.

And Van entered the alley, shoving a young girl ahead of him, gripping her by her flaming red hair. "Here she is. Was trying to flank us. Filthy

239

bitch," He growled. My vision pulsed blue in an instant. I had told him to do his worst. Goddamnit. Gold Star earned. For Van, not me.

The Beast Master nodded at Van Helsing, studying him intently. "Not sure where you went, but don't be gone so long next time. Makes me antsy."

Van nodded. "Apologies. Had a disagreement with Cyclops over there." He waved at Gunnar with his free hand. I could hear Gunnar grinding his canines from here.

Tory chose that moment to lose her shit, and half of the shifters collapsed with a groan. Even the Beast Master blinked at that. She was quivering, and her eyes were neon fire as she stared at Van Helsing and his captive.

Because it was Aria.

Tory's adopted daughter. One of the tween dragons. I hissed at her in barely restrained rage. "What the hell were you thinking bringing her *here*? I thought they were *safe* at home."

"I didn't... I would *never*..." she whispered, staring at Aria.

The Huntress melted out from the shadows beside me. "They snuck in. Followed Raego in a separate car. I tried to stop them, but they hulked out on me, and I wasn't about to turn them into pincushions," she grumbled.

"Maybe you should have," I growled back.

She levelled a look at me, and then pointed a thumb behind her. Sonya lay behind a dumpster, an arrow through her thigh. She was unconscious. The Huntress lifted a finger to her lips, telling me to be quiet as her eyes flicked to Tory – who hadn't yet noticed, too focused on Aria. "Sonya is safe," she said, loud enough for Tory to hear.

Shit.

Tory let out a sob of relief, taking a purposeful step towards the Beast Master, eyes on fire.

CHAPTER 47

*B*oris held up a hand. "That's close enough, *Beast*." Then he hesitated as if suddenly realizing something. He cocked his head, appraising her, and then studying the fallen shifters around him. He slowly turned back, a look of surprise on his face. "Could it be? Another Beast Master?"

"Let them go," I warned. "And I won't kill all of you. As slowly."

Boris the Beast Master began to clap. "Ah, yes. The Maker come to *unmake* us. You could go right ahead…" he trailed off.

"Do it, Nate," Gunnar snarled.

"And the wolf will die." Boris finished his threat with perfect timing.

"What?" I asked, frowning.

"The little black thing I picked up yesterday." Gunnar actually let out a howl pointed at the moon, like every awful werewolf movie ever made. "Clichés," Boris agreed, frowning. "Be that as it may, she will die if I do not return safely."

I frowned. "Okay, so I will carry your ass back to the quarry, steal your toys, and *then* unmake you." I pantomimed rolling up my sleeves, and took a step. He didn't even flinch at my knowledge of the quarry. Which couldn't be good.

"Won't work. My daughter is currently watching over my… *toys*, as you say. And they will all die if we do not return safely."

His words struck me. His... *daughter?* Was that the girl Van had seen? I shot a discreet look at Van Helsing, but his face was blank. He hadn't known.

Boris glanced about at the bodies littering the alley, as if counting how many were dead. I wasn't sure how many wolves Gunnar had lost, but even one was too many. The Alpha was panting, avoiding eye contact with any of his fallen packmates.

Boris cleared his throat. "Don't fret. I will forgive you those already dead. I have spares at the *quarry.*" He smiled at me, acknowledging the location without an ounce of concern that I had already known. "But we really should be off. Big event tomorrow. Rehearsals, practice, and..." his eyes latched onto Aria, "introducing our newest *toy* to her brothers and sisters. In the arena."

Tory let out a feral cry, and I shut her down before she could harm any more of the remaining shifters. She blinked in confusion, eyes flashing back to normal. I felt a faint shiver race down my spine at the pure venomous look she shot my way. But I had another reason for shutting her down. She was drawing heavily on her powers, which would only attract the Fae. And I didn't need *that* right now. "You're not helping," I whispered, forcing an empathetic look on my face, hoping she would get my meaning. Any minute now, we were likely to have a Fae welcoming party. Then I turned away, not waiting for a response.

I opened my mouth, but Gunnar beat me to it.

"Trade me for the werewolf you caught last night. I'm sure an Alpha will fetch a bigger crowd than a fledgling pup."

Boris the Beast Master tapped his lips thoughtfully, and then flashed Gunnar a predatory grin, all teeth. "No, thank you. You're damaged goods, Mate." Gunnar roared, taking a step forward, but Alucard was suddenly there, forcing him back with one hand. This was the first time I had seen him. He must have been fighting in one of the adjoining alleys. The vampire stared deep into Gunnar's face, and the Alpha instantly calmed. I blinked. How the hell had Alucard been strong enough to stop Gunnar? Both physically and with his vampire gaze. He hadn't fed on blood for a long time now, and I had seen the after-effects of him on a diet.

This caught the Beast Master's attention. "Interesting. You're strong, vampire." Then he squinted, studying Alucard closer. "But you're not really a vampire, are you? No, you're something new. Something *fresh...*" Alucard caught the tone, and acted upon the greasy thought that had momentarily crossed my own mind.

"So, let's dicker, brown-eye."

I bit back a laugh, but the Beast Master missed the inside quip. Having referred to him as BM for a bit now, the *number-two* jokes had escalated with the immature Team Temple.

"I won't give up the girl. I don't even know what you can do, but she shows real promise. Full of fury, that wolf. I think it's the whole *love lost* thing that makes her so violent." He winked at Gunnar, who was flexing his claws, as if imagining them around the Beast Master's throat.

"Me for the child, then. You haven't even had her yet, so you're not really losing anything, but you are gaining something no one else has ever seen. A Daywalker." He took a step closer. "That. Will. Sell." He flicked a hand at Aria. "A fledgling dragon?" He stifled a hand. "Boring."

Boris the Beast Master hesitated, but Alucard sweetened the pot.

"Oh, and I belong to her." He pointed a thumb at Tory. "The other Beast Master. Never really liked her much, but she does control me pretty well. At least, until now, for some reason..." he frowned. "Is that *your* doing?" He asked Boris. The man merely stared back. Alucard shrugged. "Well, maybe it's just the conflux of events here. A Maker. A handful of true badasses." He licked his lips, eyes rolling back in his skull for a moment. "And *blood*." He opened his eyes, shooting a mocking stare at Tory. "Or maybe she's just tired. She never lets me cut loose." Then he mimicked her voice, "Nature this, balance that, trees, the Fae, sprites, blah, blah, *blah*." He leaned closer to Boris. "What good is it to be the first Daywalker in hundreds of years, if I am restrained to the Land of the Fae with a nanny watching my every move?"

"If that is the case, simply come with me. The trade is not necessary."

Alucard shrugged. "Two problems with that." He held up a finger. "One, mommy won't let that happen. She kind of likes the little runt over there, and she kinda likes me. You need to give her one of us, or she will burn this city to the ground." He held up another finger. "Two, if *she* isn't scary enough, *he* is." And he pointed a finger directly at me. The Beast Master followed his finger, frowning. "The scary part isn't that he's a Maker. The scary part is that he is not concerned for collateral damage. And he hates to lose. He's liable to destroy the whole lot of us rather than lose face. One of those silver-spooned types. Always got what he wanted as a kid. Billionaire heir." He held a hand to his mouth. "Well, *was* a billionaire heir..."

"I'm not scared of the Maker." The Beast Master said after a pause.

Alucard blinked at him. "You heard about the dragon invasion, right?" Boris nodded. "Well, that's the leader of the Dragon Nation. Now he works for the Maker." Raego gave a tight grin at the introduction, but at least he didn't outright deny the vampire's latter comment. Raego didn't work for *me*. He worked for *himself*. Alucard pointed at the Huntress. "She tried to kill him a few months back. Now, she obeys him." He whispered loud enough for all to hear. "And I don't think she has *ever* obeyed *anyone*." He looked around, then snapped a finger. "Ah, yes. The Brothers Grimm, bane to the supernatural community for thousands of years, or something. They came back. And not just any Grimms, but *the* Grimms. Jacob and Wilhelm." He paused for emphasis. "The last I saw of ol' Jacob, he was being impaled by a sword held by the Maker over there. But Nate was over a *dozen feet away*." He strode in a circle. "The Horsemen follow him. Angels serve him. And Demons flee from him. He is quite literally the most dangerous thing I have ever encountered." He turned back to the Beast Master. "And he's a sore loser. And I'm probably the only one willing to share his weaknesses. If you can protect me. And let me *fight*..." he trailed off, meaningfully. I was slightly put off. Alucard was selling this so well that even I found myself wondering if he was simply speaking the truth.

He had been cut loose from his people, and had never truly found a replacement. Even with my crew, he didn't quite fit in. And we always gave him a hard time. Was he telling the truth now? Or putting on a show? I risked a glance at Tory, and saw the same fear in her eyes. Had she truly lost control of him? Or maybe she never truly *had* control of him. He *was* a Daywalker now. Perhaps he was stronger than any of us had thought...

"You son of a bitch. I will murder you if you utter another word," And I lit up the sky with an explosion of a dozen thunderbolts that hammered into the roofs of the buildings on either side of me. This gave me a moment to consider the situation, and was not intended to *harm* anyone. But it *did* startle everyone. Was Alucard being honest, or was he simply doing whatever he needed to do to save Aria?

"Deal," the Beast Master replied, ignoring my outburst. "If the Maker allows it, of course. Don't want him to throw a fit." He glanced pointedly where I had just thrown my lightning bolts, then eyed me. "You choose. The dragon is already mine. And I already have a new red dragon in my pit. Too much of one thing..." I sighed in defeat. "If this doesn't sound appealing to you, then everyone at the quarry will die before you can even think about rescuing them. If I don't appear to my daughter and state our coded reply, everyone dies. So, you'll get your momentary revenge by killing everyone here, but you'll have over two-dozen deaths on your hands. Kids, for the most part." He folded his arms. "Decide."

"I can make it there in a heartbeat, and rescue everyone before your daughter has time to move."

He nodded. "Possible, but I have contingency plans in place for whenever I take a field trip. Which is a rare delight, by the way. I usually leave it to my crew. And after the dog's meal of last night, I wanted to oversee this one." He shook his head. "But I digress. Whenever I leave the compound, I enact a spell on my pets. If anyone enters my... *residence* before me, their cages will open, and they will be unleashed on your city. True monsters, no humanity left in them. My spell rips that right out of them, and they are only concerned with one thing. *Hunting.*"

"You're bluffing."

Boris shrugged, unconcerned. "So, call me on it, Maker. If I'm right, not only will you not save the kids, but you will also be directly responsible for hundreds, if not thousands of deaths." He held up a hand towards Alucard and Aria. "Or, you can let me keep one of my new toys." He glanced at the chimera. "And all of my old toys." He added, winking at me. "I know you already bought a ticket to tomorrow's show. Let's see what happens then. I have some... *friends* who are very interested in meeting your crew."

I cursed. "Fine." I rounded on Tory. "You got them in this mess. You decide which pet to keep."

Tory gasped, and even the Huntress shot me a murderous glare. And Tory's face broke as she slowly lifted her hand. To point at Aria.

Alucard let out a laugh. "Thank *God.*"

The Beast Master flinched in sudden realization. "You... just said..."

Alucard nodded. "Yep. Forgot to mention that. Bonus?"

The Beast Master grinned, and I could see the dollar signs in his eyes. "I think I'm going to like you." Then he frowned. "Or you will die in the pit. That part is truly up to you, but I would encourage you to strenuously disagree with anyone who has other plans."

Alucard's fangs glistened. "Understood." And he licked his lips again.

I truly couldn't tell if he was bluffing, and I was good at reading people. He looked truly... anticipatory. I shot a murderous glare at Van, who seemed to wilt, but somehow kept his composure for his boss. Alucard strode up to him, glanced down at Aria, and then leaned in.

And licked her face.

Then he leaned back and let out a harsh laugh.

Aria hissed back at him.

In response, Alucard slapped her hard enough to break her jaw. She folded against Van, unconscious. "Damn twat. Been wanting to do that forever." The Huntress was now physically holding Tory back.

I stared, power coursing through my veins, realizing that no matter what I did, countless people would die. Here I was, suddenly aware of my new powers, and I couldn't do a damn thing. And after that slap, I was pretty confident that my HR team had made a grave mistake in the vampire department.

I used a lance of air to punch Van straight in the gut, doubling him over. The man flew into a trio of shifters looming behind him. Alucard turned with a hiss, and barely dodged Aria as I drew her back to me on another gust of power. I released the chimera, who collapsed to the ground with a snarl. The cobra head hissed at me, and I flipped it the bird before turning around.

"Let's go," I snarled. "See you tomorrow, Boris the Beast Master. Get your affairs in order."

My crew followed me.

CHAPTER 48

*T*ory paced back and forth, hyperventilating. All she wanted to do was yell at the Reds. It was all *anyone* wanted to do, because they had ruined *everything*. Tory and Alucard, after seeing me sitting beneath the tree, had decided I had officially lost my mind. And had called Raego to back them up while they attempted to prevent the last abduction. The Reds, taking after me, had decided to steal one of Raego's cars. And then, just for kicks, decided to follow him to a warzone to help their adopted parents. Where Aria had been captured, and Alucard taken.

Emphasizing this, Raego stood in the corner, glaring at the Reds, looking eager to teach them a lesson. But not from a loving perspective. With the rage, power, and command of the Dragon King. The Obsidian Son. Thankfully, he hadn't done this yet, because it would have destroyed the girls, and ignited an already tense room. So, he remained silent. But it was a *tense* silence.

And with Aria so shaken up, no one else dared to scream at the teenaged dragon either.

So, Tory paced. And the rest of us fumed, turning on each other, as we had for the last hour.

Aria now sat frozen on the couch, staring off into space, cheek still red from Alucard's palm. Her jaw was swollen, and already darkening. I was entirely sure that she couldn't speak, but I knew dragons healed fast –

within hours – so I wasn't worried. Sonya was stuck to her side, staring off at nothing, eyes vacant at Alucard's betrayal. Her arrow wound would be gone soon, too. But the wound Alucard had given with his words and actions would fester. I just knew it.

I watched Tory, wanting to do the same thing. My fingers twitched with inaction and I was almost finished convincing myself to go burn the circus to the ground. It was night, so would look really cool. I had a sudden hankering for hot dogs, thinking of Ganesh's belt in my safe.

"No, Nate," Gunnar growled, sensing my mood. "We have to find another way."

"But I want *hot dogs*," I whispered desperately.

He frowned at me. "You do know that comments like that are precisely why we went rogue."

I rolled my eyes. "And you did a real bang-up job with that." I spat. His glare tightened murderously, but I waved him off. "Back to the matter at hand. My way is *simple*."

Gunnar nodded slowly. "And from what Boris told us, you'll kill a lot of innocent people. And you'll likely lose your power entirely. Which means you'll be fresh for the picking when the Beast Master's new client comes to town, wondering why his entertainment was cancelled. If you even manage to beat Boris in the first place," he sneered.

Achilles must have told him about the Syndicate. "I don't need advice from you, wolf."

He snarled back, claws bursting from his fingertips.

"Remember what happened last time?" I whispered back menacingly. The air suddenly grew heavier, and the house seemed to quiver beneath Gunnar's feet.

"Stop whatever you're doing. Last warning," he said in a low tone, single eye glittering. "I don't care how badass your house is."

"Boys," Othello warned. "This won't help get the kid. Or Ashley. Or..." she didn't finish her statement, but we all read between the lines. I had almost forgotten she was here. Mallory stood near a bookshelf with Rufus, looking none too pleased with me for leaving him behind earlier. Rufus stood beside him, very quietly. Very, *very* quietly. Thinking even quieter thoughts. Which was wise, given the circumstances. But to be honest, I was kind of glad the old bastard had cursed me. Because it had given me a once in a lifetime opportunity. But I couldn't tell anyone.

The Huntress was absently thumbing through a book, not speaking to anyone. Smart, since Tory wasn't too pleased about Sonya's mysterious arrow wound.

"Alucard," Tory finished Othello's sentence. "He's *mine.*" I couldn't tell if she meant it possessively, or as vengeance. Aria whimpered at the name, but Sonya snapped out of her daze, immediately consoling her sister.

I frowned at Tory. "Look, I know his show was pretty convincing, but I don't buy it. He was just doing what had to be done." I hoped I was right. The act of a loving father sacrificing himself for his daughter.

Gunnar grumbled. "We'll see."

"Nate's right!" Sonya suddenly shrieked, jumping to her feet, silencing us all. Her red dragon claws were out, and her fiery red eyes smoldered. "Alucard would never betray his fam—" she took a breath, closing her eyes for a moment. "His *friends,*" she corrected, still looking angry as she opened her eyes, daring anyone to say otherwise.

"Regardless, as much as we might need her, Tory should probably sit this one out." I threw this out there because it was a typical Nate thing to say, and I was trying to mask my true plans. I knew Tory was going to come with me, but old Nate would have resisted this out of fear of the Fae. New Nate understood that the Fae were going to visit either way.

And I wanted the Fae to show up right where I would be, so I could better defend everyone. Otherwise the Fae could abduct Tory while I was out taking on the Beast Master, and I wouldn't be able to stop them. Which meant I needed her close. To keep her safe.

"No!" she snapped. I threw a hand at her, nullifying her before her eyes could shift green.

"Queens take King. Checkmate," I murmured in warning, implying she was the King.

She let out a scream of frustration. "They didn't come last time!"

"We were lucky. Doesn't change anything. Do we have any other ideas?" I asked the room, wondering the same thing. The Fae had no more wall holding them back, and Tory had used her powers big time in the alley. Maybe it would take the Fae some time to realize the Gateway was low on juice. The electrical fence down. The room was silent other than Tory's pacing.

"We have to go to the Circus," the Huntress said, setting down her book with a *thud.* "Thanks to Van doing exactly as Nate asked him to do."

Gunnar and Tory turned to me with a look of surprise. Aria snapped out of her daze to shoot me such a hurt look that my heart broke into a million pieces. "Great job, Maker. Genius, really. Even I can't understand your master plan." She looked up, frowning at me. "You did have a master plan, right? You're just stroking our egos right now, trying to make us little people feel important beside your holy Maker God Complex."

"Shut it, Huntress," I growled.

Tory's tone was arctic. "No, I want to hear what the *hell* she's talking about. Van did exactly as you *asked*? You..." she took a deep breath, "asked him to kidnap Aria?"

I shot a desperate look at Aria, who stared back at me as if she had never seen me before. A look of such betrayal that the already broken pieces of my heart burned to dust. Sonya, on the other hand, looked ready to remove my innards. Slowly.

I began shaking my head adamantly. "May as well have," Mallory chimed in, voice clipped, obviously still furious I had made him play babysitter to Tory.

The Huntress turned to appraise Mallory. "There you are. Thought you had lost your spine there for a while, Old One." I cringed, growing angrier at her words.

"It's right where it always was, Lass. Right behind my throbbing stick." His eyes seemed to welcome a response, anything to release the aggression eclipsing his reason.

"Whip out your throbbing stick, old man. I dare you," Sonya defended the Huntress.

I didn't have time to laugh though. "Nate," Tory demanded. "What did you tell Van?"

I cast my eyes down in shame. It didn't matter what I said. She was out for blood.

"He said to do whatever it took to convince Boris he was trustworthy. *Pull no punches. Do your worst.* Something along those lines." She smiled at me. "Lucky us, Van's a good listener."

I shot to my feet, leveling a finger at Gunnar. "And I wouldn't have had to do that if Gunnar hadn't tried to kill him to get information on the next abduction. And Gunnar wouldn't have had to resort to *that* if he hadn't lied to me about the *first* abduction. The one that got Ashley taken."

Gunnar roared, smashing a table as he slammed his paw down. "Say that again. I dare you."

"You got your fiancée killed!" I shouted at the top of my lungs, my world suddenly blanketed in a blue haze as my Maker power screamed in anticipation, begging to be used. My vision wavered, the world wobbling for a second, but I continued to glare at my once-best-friend.

Mallory was suddenly pointing a spear at each of us. "Stop, both of you."

The door swung open to reveal Achilles and Dean. The Myrmidon was holding Sir Muffle Paws, scratching his back. "Oh, I *love* spears!" he grinned. No one spoke. "Bad time?" he asked.

"You could say that," I mumbled, taking a deep breath and running my hand through my hair.

He shrugged and waltzed on in, squeezing the Huntress' shoulder with a roguish grin. The Huntress barely noticed, eyes only for Tory at the other end of the room. Achilles muttered under his breath, "Always the Bridesmaid, never the bride..."

Gunnar blinked, and then barked out an incredulous laugh.

I couldn't help it. So did I.

Tory blinked at us, not catching the comment, but the Huntress turned red from the neck up.

I nodded at Achilles, and he winked before addressing everyone. "Sounds like the Beast Master had a disagreement with a group of vigilantes tonight. But he came out on top." His gaze scanned the room. "Got a shiny new Daywalker." He locked eyes on Gunnar. "Find Van?"

Gunnar grimaced, nodding.

I frowned. "What do you mean?"

Achilles turned to me. "Mr. Big Chest came my way trying to find the location of the next abduction. I didn't know, but knew you had planned to meet Van about something urgent." He shrugged. "I put two and two together. Sent Gunnar towards my good friend, Van. He deserved it." He turned to Gunnar. "I take it you got the information you needed?"

I couldn't believe it. "You sent *Gunnar* after *Van*? What the hell is wrong with you? Were you trying to get them both killed? And what the hell were you doing telling him about the *other* crew? The ones who like embers and sparks!" His face clouded over with instinctive anger, but I caught a small flicker of guilt at mention of the Syndicate.

But I didn't wait for an answer as I rounded on Gunnar. "And *you*! You stupid son of a bitch. You could have ruined *everything*. Van was working for *me*! To get me *information*! He's my inside man at the circus! If he would have died, the Beast Master would have *known* something was wrong." I was panting, vision now a storm of blue shards, like sheets of glass shattering over the world around me.

Gunnar flared up. "How the hell was I supposed to know *that*? If you hadn't been acting like a psycho lately, I would have been right here with you to help. But instead of trusting your *friends*, you're trusting your old *enemies*."

"I did warn you of that," Achilles added.

I took a step towards the wolf, flipping the bird at Achilles. My fists crackled with purple flame. I didn't even care anymore. They had almost ruined everything. "If my best friend was worth a damn he would have simply shared his concerns with me. You know, during one of those times I came to him for *help*."

"I. *Did*." He clenched his fists, knuckles popping. "And you tried to *kill* me!"

Tory flung up her hands, changing the topic. "I'm going. And no one is going to stop me!"

"Sit. DOWN!" I roared at her. The house groaned in response, and she sat her ass down.

Achilles glanced up at the rafters. "That wasn't ominous..." he eyed me thoughtfully.

Gunnar answered his unspoken question. "Nate married his house. Or woke it up. Or something. He hasn't exactly been *clear* on that. Probably because we're such good *friends*."

"It doesn't matter!" I turned my back on him, pacing. "We need to find an army. An army the Beast Master can't take away from us. Which means no shifters. One we can sneak inside—"

"As a matter of fact, it *does* matter." Gunnar shouted. "Why do you think we've been keeping you out of the loop? You're certifiable." He began ticking off fingers. "Talking to yourself. Babbling on about creatures speaking to you. Creatures that no one else can see. Magical glass. Going on a vision quest—"

I spun around, staring at him as my anger winked out, but not in surprise at his mention of my vision quest. Even though him admitting that verified that he had insider information. Because that had only just happened, so he shouldn't have known. But I already knew who the culprit was, because I had seen Othello through the looking-glass from Mt. Kailash, admitting that they needed to ask Gunnar to get through to me. But I couldn't admit that to anyone here.

No, I stared at him because of something else he had said. "Magical glass..." I whispered.

Gunnar threw his claws up in the air. "See? You've lost your marbles! This is *exactly* why we've been working behind your back!"

But I was staring out at the tree, the Gateway, mind flying. It glowed in the darkness. Achilles spoke over Gunnar's panting breath. "Give him a minute. This might be good. Or fucking insane. Either way, entertaining." He added. In the reflection on the glass, I saw him prop his feet up on a table, nuzzling Sir Muffle Paws' face with his beard.

I shoved my hand in my pocket, turning to face everyone. "You guys need to follow me."

I darted to the office door, and opened it. And I came face-to-face with Ichabod. "What in blazes have you done to my house, boy?" he spat, eyeing the rafters anxiously. "With all due respect," he added.

"Oooh, family drama," Achilles chuckled. "I knew I liked having Nate around. It's like my very own *Desperate House-Freaks of St. Louis.*

I stared at the traitor through a blue haze, imagining his death over and over again. But not yet. I needed things from him. For now... I forced a tight smile. "Please, won't you come in?"

CHAPTER 49

*I*chabod's eyes darted about wildly. "I repeat, what the hell have you done to my house?"

I leaned back in my chair, absently fidgeting with the sliver of glass. "Nate's heart stopped. Then he went on a vision quest and spoke to a tree. Sat under it for a while too. Not forty nights or anything, but at least forty minutes." Gunnar said. "Then he cut loose with a magic show that terrified everyone. Like he was mowing down an army. He came back as a married man. To his house." He arched a brow at me. "Does that about sum it up, or did I miss something crazy?"

I scowled at him. "No, Othello told you correctly," I said softly, turning to cast a forgiving look her way. "It's okay. I overheard your concerns when you were... bringing me back to life. Thought it had been a dream until Gunnar opened his big fat mouth about my vision quest. Which he could only have found out from one of you three." I indicated Mallory, Othello, and the Huntress. They stared at me, mouths open. Everyone else was staring at me. Well, except for the Reds. Every now and then, I caught them ogling Achilles as the manly man stroked the cat.

"The house?" Ichabod pressed, voice eager.

I suddenly felt self-conscious at my answer. And at how much had already been shared. I wanted to make sure it didn't mess with Shiva's warning to not tell anyone about my plan. But this wasn't part of *that* plan.

This was just a facet of my new life. Shiva had also said that my plans would upset some people. People who might be in this room with me.

Right now.

I allowed a brief thought to flicker across my mind, *phoning a friend.*

Then I turned from face to face, assessing them to discern the unlikely enemy, but pretending to think on how to answer the question. I knew it wasn't Othello, because she was a Regular, and her betrayal had been in my best interest, like Achilles had brought up in the bar yesterday. But I had no idea who Shiva had been referring to, so I played it safe.

"Coincidentally, I was just going to show everyone something." I glanced at the doorway and smiled. Everyone turned on reflex. "Made you look," I chuckled. They didn't find it humorous as they turned back to me. "I thought it would require a walk, but I was wrong."

The house groaned again, but to my ears it sounded like an approving purr as I teased them.

"Show us, you crazy bastard, or we're leaving," Gunnar said, doing his best to ignore the groaning sounds of the mansion.

I sighed. "Alright. If you run screaming like frightened children, know that I tried to warn you ahead of time." No one moved, but it felt like they had all leaned closer. I turned to Ichabod. "Okay, first off, a little house cleaning." He frowned as I stared at him, face blank. "So, the Dark Presence we talked about..." I unbuckled the cane at my hip, and handed it to him.

He stared at the silver eagle-headed cane handle warily, not accepting it. "I remember."

"Here, hold it for a second." I waved it encouragingly.

He shook his head after a few beats. "No thanks."

I shrugged. "It's not just a cane anymore," I said softly. "It's a *Prison.*"

"For the... Dark Presence, as you named it." He was staring down at it thoughtfully. I nodded, watching his eyes. He was a Maker. He knew all of this already. I let the silence stretch, giving him a last chance. But he remained steadfast.

"You really should have warned me about the *Beast* ahead of time." His eyes flashed to mine, stunned. "You may leave. Now."

"How..." he asked, staring at me in disbelief.

"I read good," I said, flippantly. He didn't move, a thousand questions on his face. "In case you didn't hear me correctly, I asked you to *leave.*"

And Chateau Falco fucking *growled.*

He jumped to his feet, staring up at the rafters. "Okay, okay. But we must talk. After... you've had time to think."

"I don't need time to think. Buh-bye."

"But—"

"The only way I won't kill you where you stand is if you have some news on how to take down the Beast Master."

His face froze at the abrupt topic change. "What?" he whispered incredulously, forgetting all about his argument. "You're taking on the *Beast Master*? You can't do that," he warned.

"Of course I can. I'm Nate Fucking Temple," I smiled arrogantly.

He was shaking his head, practically pleading. "No, you don't understand!" He ran a hand through his hair, eyes wild. "Indie is in the pit!" he finally whispered.

My world halted.

The house creaked, rattled, and moaned. And I found myself unable to move.

"What... did you just say?" I whispered. And I suddenly realized why he had wanted his gems. He had needed to buy tickets to the circus.

Gunnar tackled me to the ground as I unleashed a blast of air at Ichabod without even realizing I had formed it in my fist.

But he was long gone.

CHAPTER 50

*N*o one moved in my peripheral vision, but I could feel them watching me as I sat on the floor, staring at nothing. The hole in the wall was a glaring reminder of their fear.

That I had temporarily misplaced my sanity.

And I had been hoping to relieve them of that fear.

I took a slow breath. Then another. Then I climbed to my feet, dusting off my pants restlessly. I lifted my eyes to meet theirs. "Talk about a game changer…" I said softly, unable to smile, but managing to look a bit guilty, chastised, or ashamed. Humble was not my forte, but I tried.

Achilles grunted. "You could say that."

I saw Dean peer through the hole in the wall from the hallway, eyes concerned. I waved at him, and was rewarded with a grimace of disapproval. Then he was gone.

I sighed. "Okay. Before my crazy ancestor decided to show up, I had something to show you. But there have been a few hot heads lately." I faced them, face serious. "I want to forgive you."

Gunnar abruptly turned on a heel, heading to the door as he growled over his shoulder. "You miserable son of a bitch—"

"No, Gunnar, he's *smiling!*" Aria burst out laughing for the first time since her injury.

Which made it all worth it in my eyes.

Gunnar froze, and then slowly turned to face me, face slightly red from his temper tantrum. I flashed him a grin. "I maintain my previous statement," he growled.

"I make a motion." Raego spoke for the first time. I squinted at him in mock anger.

"Seconded," Tory growled, playfully.

"All in favor?" Achilles continued.

Every single person said *Aye*. Even Rufus, the bastard.

I met each pair of eyes with a significant pause, maintaining my smile. "I thought we could all use a good laugh," I said softly. Nods responded from everyone. "But in all seriousness, I'm sorry." A chorus of soft apologies filled the room. "Thanks. Now, we have some friends to—"

"Wait, we're not even going to *talk* about it?" Othello asked, tone incredulous.

I shrugged, turning to see her face. She stared at me, dumbfounded. "What would it matter? We need to game plan. I have some things you need to see. Because we need to save our friends. Indie *chose* to go into that pit. And she's working with Ichabod. A betrayer."

"Can ye elaborate on that last bit, Laddie?" Mallory asked.

I shook my head. "Maybe later. Right now... I can't," I answered honestly, meeting his eyes with a desperate look. He studied me for a few beats, then nodded.

"Good enough for me." He shared his glare around the room, hitting everyone. "Should be good enough for ye too," he threatened.

Rock-solid nods answered Mallory, and even though none were happy about the situation, I could see that they were all behind me. "We probably all need to take a seat. I have someone you ought to meet." I kept my face serious. After a few odd looks, everyone complied. "Thanks. Before I proceed, I need everyone to promise that if I show you this, you will ask no questions. I understand that, given the circumstances, it's a tall order, but that's how it has to be. If you're not okay with that, I get it, but that means you don't get to see this next part. I need you to trust me."

The room was tense for a good ten seconds. After a few exchanged looks, everyone gave me a nod of some kind or another, agreeing to my terms.

I let out a breath. "Thanks. For trusting me. Now," and I smiled a mischievous grin, "shit's about to get weird." Then I looked up at the rafters, and said, "Would you be so kind as to let my friends see through the..." I grinned to myself, suddenly hearing how I had phrased it, "looking-glass?" Othello glanced at me sharply, catching the word combination, remembering our talk.

The house groaned in response to my question.

"Thanks," I replied cheerfully. I met Gunnar's confused look, and then tossed him the piece of enchanted glass. He caught it, then frowned at me. I pointed at the glass, and then turned to my left as I spoke. "Say *hello* to Carl," I grinned.

Gunnar followed my look, saw nothing, and then scanned the rest of the room, even sniffing. I burst out laughing, which didn't make him give me a happy face. "Who the fuck is Carl?" he asked, not amused.

The Huntress looked at me, then up at the rafters. "Did you name your house *Carl?*"

Achilles leaned forward curiously, frowning at the glass in Gunnar's hand. "Hi, Carl," he said politely to the glass.

I burst out laughing even harder, which gave everyone constipated faces as they shot each other silent, meaningful looks. I grasped my knees, listening to Carl grumble impatiently. "I know, Carl. Just give them a minute. They will eventually get there."

Everyone looked considerably alarmed now, and Tory was clutching the Reds to her chest.

"Here, watch." I snapped a finger, and one of the Guardians entered the room. "Say *hello* to Carl," I commanded the griffin. Everyone turned to the stone construct to find it staring intently at the empty space to my left, exactly where I had looked a moment ago.

The griffin purred, and forcefully nudged the air with a shoulder... where it struck something unseen. Raego hissed. The Guardian flicked its tail in the air, nuzzled the space with its beak, and then glanced at me. I nodded, and the Guardian prowled out of the room.

"Okay, his house caught his disease, or this is some kind of prank," Raego grumbled.

I motioned Gunnar to hold the glass up to his eye. He did so slowly, until he was staring at me through the makeshift lens. I pointed at the empty space, and he slowly turned to look.

Then he jumped backwards with a shout of alarm, dropping the glass on the carpet. "Fuck me," he whispered, staring at the now empty space. "I mean... Hi, Carl," he corrected.

"Carl, meet Gunnar. Please don't eat him." I remembered Shiva's advice.

Achilles abruptly picked the glass back up and stared through the lens at the empty space, his jaw dropping to the floor. "H..." he cleared his throat. "Hello... Carl."

Carl had sensed my earlier telepathic summons right after Ichabod had shown up, and had entered the room when I pulled the *made you look* joke. He hadn't appreciated the intruder in my home, which was now *tied* to Carl, thanks to my... *vision quest*.

Carl stood beside me, glaring with disdain and impatience at the crowd, which was now alternating turns with the glass, and murmuring *hello, Carl's*, in startled surprise.

He turned to me. "Why did they not believe you?"

The Huntress flinched, as it had been her turn when Carl spoke for the first time. I shrugged in response. "They do not hold me in high esteem at the moment. To be fair, you didn't believe I could see you the first time either. Then you and your pals tried to kill me." I shrugged, holding up a hand as if to prove a point.

He nodded. "That's true. But it's been a long time since we last made contact with mortals."

I held up my hands, capitulating towards my friends. "Same story, Carl."

He finally nodded in acceptance.

I turned to the crew. "Everyone satisfied that I'm not insane now?"

Achilles watched me thoughtfully. "Either that or you yanked us all down the rabbit hole."

"What about the house?" Sonya asked softly.

It groaned in response, as if joining in the introductions. Everyone quieted, waiting to hear my explanation. I addressed them with a small frown. "That one is going to have to wait. Possibly for a long time. As are any questions about Carl..."

They didn't look happy, but they accepted it. With only a few mutters.

I turned to Raego. "Since you've been so talkative, you're on daddy duty in the porcu-shine's place. They need a firmer hand, judging from recent events..." The Reds instantly flared up with arguments, but Raego cleared his throat. Lightly. They flinched instinctively at the sound of the king of their people. Then they shot desperate looks at Tory, but she was shaking her head, too.

Their shoulders sagged as they silently admitted defeat.

Problem solved, Raego spoke. "I'll do it. Someone needs to keep an eye on them. No more Grand Theft Auto. But I don't like leaving you unsupervised either, Temple." He smiled.

I pointed at Carl. Then the rest of the room. "I think they can handle it."

The Reds opened their mouths for one last rebuttal, but Raego snapped his fingers, eyes flashing black – iris and all. Which looked startling. Since he was an *obsidian* dragon, his irises and pupils were the same color when he was in black dragon mode. Two black holes. The Reds sighed in resignation, gathering up their nonexistent things, stalling.

"Don't worry, girls. We'll get him back," Tory whispered, smiling sadly at them.

The Reds mumbled something back, and then the dragons left.

I carefully crafted my lie as I thought through the basics of my game plan for tomorrow night. As far as everyone was concerned, I needed Rufus to get to the chimera so that I could get my Maker's power back. Gunnar would join him, giving him the chance to also free Ashley and Alucard. Who would then free the kids. Mallory and the Huntress would stalk the crowd, keeping an eye out for threats. Tory and I were taking on the Beast Master, because none of it mattered if we didn't take him down. Nothing would be said about me really wanting the curse to succeed. That was a surprise.

It was all about timing.

Othello would remain behind, of course, having no magical powers. She had work to do anyway. A meeting with Tomas about his recent trip to Germany.

The only wildcards were Ichabod and Indie. I shook my head. Nothing was ever perfect.

"Alright. Here's where we stand. Carl wants to make some new friends. And I want to help him…" My friends began to smile.

So did Carl.

CHAPTER 51

I fidgeted with the glasses on my nose as everyone else geared up for the circus.

I had spent the morning wandering the halls, getting to know my mansion more intimately. The secrets she had shared with me were mind boggling. And some of my dad's past comments began to make much more sense. But I knew I was the first one to bond the house in a very long time, so I wasn't quite sure how he had known.

I had spent the rest of the day trying to decide exactly how much power I wanted to bring into my fight with the Beast Master. I needed the curse to rip away the last of my Maker's power, but couldn't risk having so much power taken from me all at once that I fell into unconsciousness. Similarly, I couldn't go in there with nothing, or I would be useless to help.

So, I guess-timated. I'd been forced to go on a few walks to get away from everyone, burning through my power in calculated bursts without their knowledge. As I burned through my Maker's power, the odd ripples had diminished in both frequency and intensity. I had also paid close attention to my budding wizard's power, which seemed to be healing in direct proportion to the drain on my Maker's power.

Which was good. But I still couldn't *use* it. At all. Which was concerning, making me doubt the entire plan.

So, I had packed some toys in my pockets.

I had even considered heading to the Armory, but with all the powers inside of me already threatening to crack my brain open like an egg, had decided it wasn't wise to tempt myself. Sure, taking the Golden Fleece with me would be fun. But not if it broke my sanity.

On one of my walks, I had found the spectacles I now wore in one of the cabinets of curiosities my dad displayed near the entrance to Chateau Falco. Nothing special, but they looked old. Which was all I had really needed. An ace in the hole.

The remodeled Vilnar Range Rover – not unlike the one Gunnar had driven for a short time back when we had met Raego – ticked and purred as it wound down behind me. Here was where things would get dicey. I had about one big burst of energy left, but that was it. And to be honest, I wasn't sure if it qualified as *big*. But it had been the best I could come up with. I needed the timing to be perfect.

And I couldn't tell anyone what I was doing. Even though they were risking their lives right alongside me. Which sucked. Especially after working to regain their trust. Only so I could break that trust tonight. Purposefully.

As requested, Raego was watching the Reds – against their will – so that I only had to worry about Tory. I knew I wouldn't have been able to handle three overly-emotional women as we tried to rescue their dad. Especially with Ichabod in the mix. And Indie. And the Beast Master. And the Fae.

I shook my head from the dark thoughts. This would *work*.

"Maximum effort," I murmured. Gunnar glanced at me with a frown, but I ignored him.

I *needed* the curse to take my power.

And bring me back to my roots. A wizard. Master Temple.

No more possession for me.

Rufus fidgeted guiltily, and I realized I was staring at him with an angry look – not because of him, but because of my thoughts. I had my war face on. "Did I ever tell you *thanks*?" I asked, tone icy, playing my part.

Gunnar gripped the wizard's shoulders. "Don't worry, I'll tell him how thankful you are. Rufus and I are going to be spending quite a bit of time together tonight." His lone eye glinted in the moonlight, and Rufus flinched.

Tory spoke from beside me. "What about Ichabod? Or the Fae?"

I kind of hoped the Fae made an appearance. I had something I needed to tell them. A suspicion I needed to verify. And increasing the chaos never hurt. At least in my experience. "It will all work out. Let them come." And I shot her a suicidal smile. It didn't convince her, because I could see her thoughts were all about one man. Not in a romantic way, but in a responsible way. Alucard was *hers*. "We'll get him back. He didn't mean it."

She let out a small sob. "What if he did?"

"Then he's an idiot, and he and I will have a long talk. Either way, we're getting him back."

"Okay…"

The Huntress stared at me. "I don't remember you ever wearing glasses to battle."

I shrugged. "These ones are lucky. And they make me look intimidating."

She squinted doubtfully. "If you say so…" Dean would kill me if he saw them missing from his cabinet. Well, *my* cabinet, but he didn't seem to ever consider that part.

A huddled mass of monsters stood outside the group. The ones only I could see at the moment. "Hey, Carl. And Carl's friends."

They merely stared back, eyes bottomless pits of woe in their albino faces.

"Right. Not much for small talk." I turned to my friends to find them staring at me with sick expressions, having not known that Carl and Company were beside them the whole time. "Like I told you, Carl is here on a friend-finding mission. Because I killed a few of his old ones." I shot him a guilty look. "Sorry about that." I had killed dozens of the Elders, but Carl had a good reserve team. There were at least a dozen standing beside him.

Carl smiled back at me, black fangs glistening against his albino scales. "Just gave me less mouths to feed, Master." His compatriots grinned, nodding, which made me shiver.

"You know, comments like that make it hard to find new friends."

They only smiled, and my friends shivered, imagining his response. "Okay, give me a minute and we can head out. Like I told you, until that curse is broken, I'm going to be less than useless."

Gunnar growled. "We're used to it," he grinned. I scowled back. "You're the Trojan Horse…" he smiled darkly in anticipation. "So I can go reclaim my Helen."

I sighed. "You do recall that Helen's husband was kind of one of the bad guys."

Gunnar shrugged. "So was Achilles, by that logic."

"You say the sweetest things. You should tell the Heel that. I'll buy drinks."

"Is every Temple an asshole?" The Huntress asked me.

I nodded. "It's in our *dunnah*."

The Huntress turned to Gunnar with a confused look. "Dunnah?"

Gunnar shrugged, frowning at me with concern.

"DNA. It's pronounced dunnah, phonetically," I answered.

Rufus laughed, slapping his knees.

Gunnar frowned at Rufus. "I don't get it. That's not how you say it."

"Don't tell me what I know, Travis!"

Rufus roared in laughter. "That's Camilla's favorite movie!"

I turned to him, frowning. "Camilla... the *chimera*?" I asked in disbelief.

He nodded, wiping his eyes.

Gunnar simply shook his head, turning to the Huntress with a resigned sigh. "Nate is apparently fine. Let's go save some monsters."

"Not monsters," I held up a finger. "*Beasts*." And we headed towards the circus entrance.

Tory spoke softly, for my ears only. "Nate, you should recall that the Trojan Horse didn't survive the invasion." I frowned at her. "Let's not repeat that mistake." And she gripped my hand, giving me a quick squeeze as we continued on.

CHAPTER 52

$\mathcal{T}$he guards grinned in recognition as we approached a table blocking the entrance. Shifters of some flavor. We had split up, in order to be less noticeable. I ignored them, peering past their shoulders to see a large tent in the distance, and a line of people headed towards it. I smiled back at the guards, ready to fight my way inside since we didn't have enough tickets. Instead, they waved me on through with anticipatory grins.

It was obvious Sir Deuce had told his crew we were coming to crash the party. But that wasn't what had me on edge. Somewhere in this stink of flesh and blood was Indie. And Ichabod.

And it was all I could do to not start a war.

Indie's life was in danger if she was in the pit.

Just like Ashley.

And Alucard.

And Camilla, the chimera.

I took a calming breath, adjusting my spectacles, and led Tory by the elbow towards the tent. I just hoped I could find a way to get Indie out. If not, Gunnar and Rufus would try when they went for Camilla. The Huntress was mingling in the crowd with her bow – craftily concealed by magic – so that she looked like nothing more than a young girl. Of course, Van had likely given the Beast Master and his crew descriptions for each of us, and likely expected all hell to break out, so if they knew anything about the Huntress, they probably knew she had a bow with her. And that she was sneaky.

Mallory was playing third wheel to Tory and I, but remaining a discreet distance away to spot trouble, hoping that we could handle ourselves from any immediate danger – at least for a few seconds until he could get to us.

"Let's follow the crowd."

And there was a very large crowd. All flavors of Freaks, mostly leaning towards the overlord persuasion, or at least the deranged. And they smelled of money. A lot of money. And dark hungers danced in their eyes. Those finding no problem with watching fights to the death for casual entertainment. Possible members of the mysterious Syndicate. And I might as well have been wearing a neon sign that said, *Nate Temple, #NotMySyndicate*, judging by all the angry looks I got. I just smiled back. Nothing else I could do, really.

Kids fighting to the death.

We traveled down the rocky slope to the main tent, which was fifty feet tall, and filled with raucous shouts at the fight already taking place in the ring. Canvas walls hung to the rocky floor, and as I stepped through the entrance, I saw the tent was erected around an even smaller pit, a good twelve feet deep from the quarry floor, and judging by the claw marks on the walls, the BM's pets had either dug it, or they had held numerous training sessions in the last few days.

My Beast was silent at my hip, and my vision began to pulse blue as my rage grew. Tory grabbed my arm, a look of concern crossing her face. I overcame the feeling, and shot her a grim smile. "It's okay. I got it."

But I didn't know if that was true. I was gambling. Sure, my plan sounded great. But plans could always go wrong, and I began to find numerous holes in mine as we approached the ring. If Gunnar and Rufus couldn't find the girl soon, bad things were going to happen. Because even though I could always force the curse to burn through my Maker's power, I didn't dare do that until I knew the girl was safe. And a small part of me realized that my whole plan was predicated on my wizard's power being strong enough to take out the Beast Master.

When even the Academy was leery about confronting him.

And the Fae were likely to show up at the worst possible time

And I hadn't used my wizard's power for a *long* time.

There was also the very likely chance that Boris the Beast Master – since he likely already knew I was here, or at best, on my way – would throw my captive friends into the ring just to be a dick, and to keep me occupied, forcing me to try and stop a fight that over a hundred powerful, paying customers were eager to watch.

Indie.

Ashley.

Alucard.

Camilla the Chimera.

I shook off the feelings of doubt. Too late for second-guessing. None of these scenarios were ideal. But I knew one, if not all, would happen tonight. They just needed to happen at the right *times.*

"Don't worry. They'll find her, and we will lay waste to this hellhole," Tory murmured, squeezing my hand.

A nearby patron scowled at us, and I managed to grin sheepishly, rolling my eyes at Tory. "Women, don't know a thing about fun," I grinned at him.

"Disrespect me again and I'll rip your heart out," Tory growled at me.

After a tense silence, the man nodded, and turned back to the fight, satisfied we were fellow sociopaths.

Turns out, there were no seats. Standing room only. Tory followed as I tried to get as close as possible to the ring. I would need to act fast if things went south. Which they were going to do at some point. Fighting to get through the crowd, only to fight to get *into* the ring, would waste valuable seconds. And the contestants might not have that precious commodity. So, I risked bruising a few egos, and pissing off a few – no doubt powerful – strangers, to get us close. There was no need for hiding, because the BM had to know we were here already.

We got right up next to the ring, no doubt thanks to my arcane spectacles letting people assume I was next to blind. The glass wasn't prescription, but it did make my vision a little distorted, what with the ocean of magic ebbing and flowing before me, a result of the myriad of Freaks here. This added to the sense that my vision was indeed impaired, and it worked – people letting us pass without much fuss. Of course, in a place like this, one never knew who exactly to be rude to. Growling at a person for cutting in line could very well be the last thing you ever did.

So, overall, the crowd was warily polite. And hungry for blood.

We were just in time to see one werewolf sink his claws deep into the stomach of another werewolf. I flinched instinctively at the sudden intense violence, and also in fear that one of them may have been Ashley, but they were both brownish in color.

I let out a nervous sigh, and Tory did the same.

Two gorillas entered the ring, one pointing at the winner, and then at the exit. The winner complied, eyes vacant as he and the gorilla headed back to what I assumed was the direction of the cages outside the tent. The other gorilla picked up the loser, and carried him over a shoulder – also towards the unseen cages. I was pretty sure I saw werewolf intestine outside the body, and shivered. The ring was soon empty, and a large make-shift door of pallets boomed closed behind them. A voice called out from the opposite side of the pit where a disheveled grandstand stood, like where royalty would sit at a jousting event for Knights. Except, grungier.

It was Boris the Beast Master and his entourage. I wondered what kind of money he made on this, and how much of it he got to keep after expenses. I shook my head after a second. Who cared? I was about to destroy it all.

Van Helsing stood beside him. He locked eyes with me for exactly one second, but it was enough to let me realize something bad was about to happen, and that he couldn't stop it. Then his gaze continued about the ring critically, like any faithful bodyguard, watching, assessing for threats.

"Thank you for coming! You paid a high price for entry, and the Beast Master does not disappoint!" Boris grinned at the crowd, standing in front of his chair to grip the bannister overlooking the ring. Two hulking gorillas flanked him and Van, and a young woman – possibly even a teenager – sat behind him, looking distracted. His daughter. Her face was a scarred mess, and her body also looked to be physically mangled. Not a cripple, but a *survivor*, for sure.

I frowned at that. The BM hadn't mentioned her injuries.

Apparently, he hadn't always had such control over his beasts.

My mind raced with possibilities, wondering if this was information that could help in the upcoming battle, but my thoughts were interrupted.

"Next up is a truly... *unique* specimen. One I've wanted to acquire for ages. Thanks to a favor owed to me by an ex-Justice," he winked as the crowd hooted in derisive laughter, "we have some fresh meat to initiate..." I growled at his mockery of Rufus' plight. And his knowledge of Rufus in the first place. Boris held out his hands, and the pallet doors to the pit opened again, this time revealing two women. One was a girl, a teenager at most.

Her eyes darted about wildly, panicked for a few seconds at the loud cheers and shouts. Then she flinched, shoulders locking rigid. Her face went slack, and a look of calm took over. I almost growled out loud. The Beast Master controlling her fear.

But Tory *did* gasp out loud.

I turned to her quickly, only to find her staring at the next fighters. I turned back, and truly saw the other fighter for the first time. And my brain temporarily shut down.

"Misha…" Tory whispered, voice stunned and haunted.

"That… isn't possible," I whispered. But it *was*. Tory's old flame – no pun intended – stood beside the small child. A full-grown woman with red hair, and red eyes. The mother to the Reds. A fiery red weredragon. I remembered that a red dragon had been abducted, but I had thought it to be another kid. No wonder Raego had known nothing about it. Because we had all seen Misha die in the Grimm War. But I stared at her now. Impossibly alive. And…

She. Looked. Pissed.

I latched onto Tory's arm as she placed a hand on the bannister overlooking the ring. "It's not her, Tory," I hissed under my breath. "It *can't* be her. This is a trick. No doubt meant for us."

Then Misha-not-Misha let out a very familiar laugh, and Tory's spine locked rigid. It was uncannily accurate. But that just wasn't *possible*. We had all seen her die while fighting the Grimms. Had we been mistaken? Had she *survived*? Dragons *did* have remarkable healing abilities… No way. I looked up to see the Beast Master staring directly at me. He let out a nod and a triumphant grin. As if to say, *your move*.

I shivered, but couldn't do anything. Not yet. It was too soon. We didn't have what we had come for. We couldn't fight his enforcers, his pets, the crowd, and find the victims at the same time.

The two contestants strode to the center of the ring, encouraged by the hulking gorillas. They stood facing each other, no longer concerned with the crowd. The gorillas stepped away, and Misha let out another laugh. "A child! This will be fun. Roasted children taste so delicious. Extra crispy. My favorite." Tory was shaking, whether in horror at her words, or at the realization that it just might actually be Misha.

The child smiled back, and then exploded from her clothes, and I gasped.

Camilla. The chimera.

Misha exploded into her own dragon form, crouched low, and then breathed a lick of fire at the chimera. Tory let out a shout, but it was drowned in the roar of the Beast Master.

"A dragon and a chimera. This ought to be *fun*." And he shot me a wink as the crowd went wild.

CHAPTER 53

*C*amilla, now a horrifying monster, let loose a blast of venom at Misha, who deftly avoided it with a duck of her scaled head. The chimera roared in frustration from her lion-headed chest, the tail hissed, and her goat head bleated.

Simultaneously.

I shivered.

I physically restrained Tory from interfering, squeezing her arm hard enough to bruise. We couldn't do anything yet. We needed the chimera back in Rufus' hands, and that meant that the fight must go on. But at least we now knew where she was. And that she was safe.

If she survived. Against our pal, the resurrected weredragon.

But my heart was pounding as the two monsters flew at each other, because I found a fatal flaw in my plan. We effectively now had opposing goals, Tory and I. I needed Camilla saved. She wanted her lover saved. Which was probably exactly what Boris wanted. To keep me distracted. All he really had to do was throw my friends against each other, and watch my torment, knowing I couldn't do two things at once. Couldn't challenge him *and* save my friends.

I glanced back to see Mallory staring at me with wide eyes at the change in situation. Or maybe it was because Misha was alive. Didn't matter which, really. I dipped my head at Tory, grimacing, and he nodded, slicing through the crowd to get to us. No one seemed to notice or take offense, much too engaged in the fight down below. Mallory stepped up, and wrapped his arms around Tory as if in an affectionate embrace.

But it wasn't affection.

It was restraint.

I let go of her, hands shaking from exhaustion.

In case anyone had forgotten, Tory was *strong*.

But so was Mallory.

Not *as* strong, but stronger than me, and I hoped strong enough to keep her restrained. Still, seeing the love of your life suddenly back from the dead, suddenly in harm's way from the child we *had* to save in order for any of us to walk out of here alive...

Let's just say it was a test in resolve.

And I didn't think it was going to end well.

The red dragon was throwing up a good fight, but it was essentially like she was fighting three opponents. The chimera would switch from a charging horned goat on all fours, to a bipedal fire-breathing lion, to a striking cobra, and the child was *fast*. Sometimes managing to successfully attack with all three forms in rapid succession.

I suddenly saw for the first time why these things had been eradicated.

And this was an untrained *child*.

Which possibly made her more dangerous. She showed no restraint, a wild, reckless abandon, and Misha wasn't faring well. The goat head slammed into her, goring her stomach with its horns, causing her to momentarily shift back to her human form as she rolled to safety, now a much smaller target. She clutched her stomach, scooted clear, and then shifted back into dragon form, a powerful sweep of her wings launching her a dozen feet away.

Blood flowed freely from her scaled abdomen, and she wobbled as she landed.

Dragon scales were tough, but the chimera had torn through them like crepe paper.

The chimera rounded on her with a triumphant roar, and the Beast Master held up a hand. For a moment, the chimera didn't seem to notice, and then her shoulders locked rigid and she stopped. The Beast Master

273

called out. "I don't want to lose any of my new pets..." he winked at the crowd. "Yet. Looks like the infamous chimera is truly as magnificent as they say. Perhaps we will bring her out later, against more *even* odds." The crowd had been roaring – at first in disappointment, and then renewed vigor at the thought of seeing an even *better* fight later. "Unless my ringmaster has anything different to say..."

Van Helsing.

He assessed the two fighters, and held a hand pointing at the chimera. The crowd screamed with renewed frenzy at the official winner, and I could see bookies suddenly overwhelmed with bets for an upcoming fight with the chimera. Several patrons simply watched Van with deep, thoughtful eyes. Syndicate members, or just people who had crossed paths with him once before?

I growled under my breath, cursing my choice to get Van Helsing involved in this.

Misha wobbled again, licking her stomach with her dragon tongue, and staring with pure hatred at the now adolescent girl. She was cradling one arm as if it was broken, but I couldn't be sure. I had once seen Tory snap a dragon's arm practically in half, only to see her entirely healed the next night. Misha – if it truly *was* Misha – would be fine. I let out a sigh of relief, thankful that dragons healed fast. I just hoped it was fast enough to be of assistance when we made our move. Because there was no question that we now had to save her, too.

But then Misha suddenly shot me a significant, desperate look, as if trying to tell me something. Then she glanced pointedly at Tory.

I stumbled back a step. *What the hell?* How had she known I was here, what with fighting for her life? And what had she been trying to tell me?

Tory hadn't noticed, struggling and arguing with Mallory, and Misha's look was over before I could second-guess it.

Misha *was* alive, and knew I was here.

Then another thought entered my brain.

Had she... *thrown* the fight, knowing I needed the chimera?

I had seen Misha fight before, and... now that I thought about it, I wasn't entirely sure the fight should have gone the way it did. Misha was balls-to-the-wall crazy in a fight. She had even been Raego's primary guard, and that wasn't an occupation one got for seniority.

And my mind began to fumble around with new thoughts, considering, as the fighters were escorted from the ring. "Two minutes to place bets on the next fight. An all-out fight to the death this time, with *teams...*"

And I suddenly couldn't hear a thing as Mallory shot me a desperate look, mouth opening and closing as he shouted something at me.

His arms were empty.

And Tory was gone.

CHAPTER 54

*M*allory and I met. I grasped his shoulders as he shouted at me. I almost didn't hear him over the screams of the crowd. "She's gone!"

"Where is she?" I hissed. "You were supposed to keep her occupied!"

He looked embarrassed, and very, very angry. "I damn well know that, Laddie. She's fecking strong! And a wee bit emotional at the moment!" he snapped, face a thunderhead.

I nodded, gritting my teeth.

I spotted the Huntress in the crowd, cloaked in shadow.

But she was staring at me with a desperate look on her face, clutching a phone to her ear. She must have found Ichabod. But I didn't have time to go beat down my ancestor. Not Yet. I needed to find Tory. I shot her a look, silently telling her to keep her eyes on Ichabod. She shook her head urgently, fighting to move through the crowd, closer to me. I shook my head adamantly, and turned my back on her.

Mallory and I began mingling through the crowd, searching for Tory. But it was no use. There were too many people, and they were all milling about like it was a High School party and the parents had left town. All too soon, we heard Van Helsing's voice pierce through the din, casting the tent into an eerie silence. And we had seen no sign of Tory yet.

"Say *hello* to our new contestants! They may be a little shy, but not

276

for long..." he added darkly, and I thought I imagined a slight undertone of guilt, as if apologizing to me for the display, and asking me for a sign so that he knew when to end the charade. But I didn't know if there would *be* a sign. Not if Gunnar and Rufus couldn't get to Camilla in time.

And I wouldn't even blame him if Van threw in with the BM if things seemed to be going his way. After all, I would no longer be a threat, and he did want to live, even if under the rule of a psychopath. At least he would live. I craned my neck to see the ring, and groaned.

Alucard, skin seeming to glow, as he turned his back on his competitors, waving at the crowd.

Ashley, eyes on fire, challenging everyone.

And then I gasped. Sonya stood on battered legs, looking shaken and terrified as she stared at Alucard's back.

"What the *fuck?*" I roared, panting in horror. How? How the hell had they gotten to Sonya?

Then it hit me. *Alucard. She went to save Alucard. The next best thing to her father.* She had argued in his defense, but none of us had seemed to back her up. And her sister had been hurt. And she was a rebel. So, she must have decided to save him herself. To save her family. To escape Raego's supervision.

Goddamn it.

I saw the Huntress – closer now – staring into the ring, face frozen in horror. Then she began frantically looking for someone. Tory. Of course. She would want to be there to support Tory. But she looked to be torn between saving the woman she had a crush on, and saving that woman's daughter. Consequences be damned.

Mallory groaned. "This is a right clusterfuck, Laddie."

I could only nod as Van chimed back in. "Now, rules are simple. Last man... well, last *beast* standing." He held up his hands dramatically, eyes discreetly scanning the crowd as if looking for me, and masking it as building anticipation. With a breath, he dropped his hands. "FIGHT!"

A woman screamed. And a dozen monsters in the crowd suddenly collapsed in a ring of unconscious bodies.

Tory stood in the center of them.

Then she was moving, casually striding towards the ring, walking like a puppet on a string. And dozens around her collapsed to the ground as she approached. Those lucky enough to remain conscious within her proximity simply stared up at her adoringly.

Mallory suddenly had twin lightning spears in each hand, revealing them for all to see, having been invisible up until now. They sizzled, causing shouts of outrage and confusion as the crowd around us jumped back. I clenched my fists.

Well, shit.

CHAPTER 55

*T*he beasts in the ring flew at each other while Tory climbed the bannister and dropped into the pit. Mallory shot me one pained look, and then tore after her. I shoved clear a path, hand on the hilt of my sword cane, knowing it was now next to useless as a magical totem, but hopefully as a physical weapon it would be useful against fang and claw.

The fangs and claws of my friends as they tried to kill me for trying to save them.

Because they were under control by Boris the Beast Master.

What a stupid fucking name, I growled to myself as I reached the bannister around the pit.

My spectacles almost fell off as I swung myself over the ledge, using the bannister to carefully drop into the pit since I didn't want to waste the last of my Maker's power to break my twelve-foot fall. I didn't want to enter the fight physically *and* magically crippled.

Talk about a dead Maker.

I landed on the rough, rock floor, and scanned the area leading to the cages, hoping to see Gunnar riding a pony as he led Camilla to safety. Of course, this wasn't the case. I saw only hungry faces staring back at me, faces suddenly starving to see not only death from the contestants, but also the three idiots stupid enough to enter the pit uninvited.

With no knight in shining armor to announce Camilla's safety, and one

– or all – of my friends about to die, I gripped my cane in a sweaty fist, and tapped into that last shallow pool of my Maker's power, ready to burn it to ashes in one final – hopefully fruitful – act.

So that my wizard's power could come roaring in, and hopefully be enough to save the day.

But my Beast had other plans, having meekly waited in his Prison long enough.

The moment I touched my Maker's power, my Beast ripped it away from me.

And I nearly collapsed from a sharp, spiking pain in my chest.

And my cane began to glow in my fist as my Beast used his centuries of knowledge to fight back. Resist suicide. To fight for his life.

No...

I fell to my knees as he bulged against the weakened Prison walls, hammering my mind with fists of molten lava. They weren't strong, but I was helpless. He had wrestled control of the Maker's power from me, and I still couldn't tap into my wizard's gift – although I felt it deep inside me, pulsing with a warm, healthy glow. Like an Oasis just out of reach in a desert of despair.

There just simply wasn't enough room in my limited head space to simultaneously access both powers. Both Beasts.

I lasted only moments before gasping, palms crashing to the rock floor, the cane flashing ice cold before it tumbled free from my grasp. The Prison crumbled away to pulverized dust, and thanks to my spectacles, I saw this clearly – even though no one else could. Screams tore at my ears as my friends continued trying to kill each other. I barely managed to raise my head, and found an apparition standing before me.

The Dark Presence. My Beast.

He looked not that different from me, although ragged, beaten down, and malnourished from his sojourn in my Prison. My eyes latched onto the cane handle lying a few feet away from my palm. Amazingly, it hadn't been destroyed upon his escape.

This thing wanted payback, revenge, and freedom. At any cost. He knew my plan. Knew *me*. Knew I had been willing to sacrifice his existence to go back to being a wizard. And this displeased him.

Greatly.

He glared down at me, smoky eyes seeming to burn with black fire, and he snarled. A lightning spear suddenly sailed through his chest and he gasped in shock.

I blinked in surprise, seeing Mallory off to my right, hefting his other spear to a shoulder. I turned back to my Beast, wondering how the spear had harmed him, if even a little.

And how the hell had Mallory seen the apparition?

Wasn't he just in my mind?

Then it hit me.

My Beast, my Dark Presence was *physically* here, having broken free from my Prison, and with me no longer controlling my Maker's power, he was quite literally... a free spirit.

"Want to make a deal?" I whispered weakly. His frown deepened, seeming to be only annoyed at the spear-wound now. I threw up a hand as Mallory prepared to launch his other projectile. "The way I see it, we're both about to die unless we team up." He continued to watch me with those ageless eyes. "You're weakened, injured, and still only a spirit. One more spear and you're fairy dust."

"You are in much the same position. And your plan was to murder me anyway."

I nodded in shame. I could still feel my wizard's power inside me, but for some reason could not access it yet. Which meant we were still connected somehow. And seeing him before me, a physical entity, but knowing that we were still somehow connected, I suddenly had a crazy thought. "*Exactly*. But together... we may just stand a chance."

"Explain..."

And I told him my crazy plan. It didn't take more than a few seconds. And although it sounded impossible, I pointed at him now. "Kind of puts proof to the possibility."

"Freedom..." he whispered longingly. But then he frowned, looming over me. "I was bound to partner with you, and then you caged me. Lied to me. Why would I trust you?"

I cast my eyes down. "You tried to change me. I don't like change. I want to go back to being me. A wizard. Not someone's pet. And I'm hoping... that maybe you do, too." This didn't make him happy, but at least he seemed to appreciate my honesty. And his curiosity was piqued. "I'm not just saying that so you won't kill me." I crawled up into a crouch, slowly, so as not to startle him as the arena continued to build with the sounds of violence. I shot a quick glance out of the corner of my eye. Alucard looking to tear out Ashley's throat, and Sonya looking to help him, even though it was to kill another friend. Anything to win her... *father* back.

"What if I simply choose to inhabit another body? Give them my gifts for a time before I'm strong enough to overcome them."

I nodded slowly. "You could try." I pointed a thumb at Mallory. "He'll stop you though. Even if he doesn't, I'm pretty sure that without my help, everyone here is going to die, and you don't look strong enough to switch from body to body while you bet on a winner..."

He growled, leaning forward aggressively. Mallory reacted.

I threw up a hand at my bodyguard. "No! Give him the chance to decide for himself! That's all he's ever wanted..." I whispered the last, still cringing in pain from the loss of my power.

My Beast flinched as if struck. "Don't presume to know my motivations, child. I've been around for *eons.*"

I nodded respectfully, trying to ignore the sounds of battle raging beyond us, knowing it was my friends. Tory screamed, and my friends fell to their knees, shaking their heads in pain. Then another voice shouted, and they shambled back to their feet, looking dazed. As if they were being forced to listen to two different masters. "But I imagine most of that was as someone's bitch," I said softly, spotting the Beast Master and his daughter glaring down at the ring from their royal stand.

The Dark Presence quivered at my words, but finally let out a sharp, frustrated nod of agreement.

I reminded him what lay in store for us if we continued as we had. Judging from his reaction, Shiva had been right. A god would indeed gobble us up in the future. He had obviously experienced it before. My question was how it worked. If he was centuries old, and had experienced that before, how did he truly exist? Was he attached to some physical totem – not my cane, because I had made that – or after his host died did he just roam the earth looking for a new vessel to inhabit? A new Maker to be born. I shook my head. It didn't matter. I looked up at him. "None of us truly wants that. I propose a temporary... partnership."

And I watched him think about it. There really wasn't a choice, to be honest. With the curse in play, he was going to die unless we freed Camilla. Which wasn't looking likely. He could fight me, but he would still die. But with my plan... the curse might not affect him. It might just be enough to *free* him. I glanced at the cane pointedly, then back to him.

"There is no guarantee this will work..." But I could see he knew his other options were guaranteed *death*.

I nodded. "But we can *try*. And we'll have fun doing it..." I smiled. I glanced around the ring, adjusting my spectacles a bit. Then I very discreetly tapped my belt, and clicked on the two wooden cuffs I had stolen from the goblins. As they snapped into place, my forearms hummed with power for a moment, letting me know they were still functioning. I knew nothing about them, so didn't know if they regularly needed to be charged, or if they just worked. His eyes widened. "And people have a bad habit of underestimating me. Never ends well. For them." I winked.

My Beast... my *partner* studied me for a good long time, and I began to twitch in concern that he was either going to deny me, or that his decision would come too late.

He finally nodded.

And slammed back into me, no longer restrained by the Prison, no longer dominated, but no longer trying to coerce control from me either. A partnership. A *true* partnership.

In case you're wondering, a true partnership feels an awful lot like your soul being flushed down a toilet.

But the sickening feeling faded, and I felt a sharp warmth replace it deep in my chest. Nothing really, power-wise, but enough to maybe pull one last trick. And possibly kill myself doing it.

I climbed to my feet to find Mallory staring at me in astonishment, mouth opening and closing wordlessly. I gave him a sharp nod, and turned to the warriors fighting each other.

Mallory was suddenly a blur, racing to jump between Ashley and Alucard, who looked on the verge of killing each other. Tory was wobbling on her feet as she tried to pull Sonya from the fight. But apparently, Sonya didn't want to leave.

The teenage mutant ninja dragon lashed out with one razor-sharp talon, biting deep into her adopted mother's leg. Tory gasped, and then threw the unruly child a good dozen feet to slam into the wall of the ring. Then she collapsed to her knees, clutching her head as she screamed.

And green fog washed out from her, over the pit, striking the beasts.

Ashley the black werewolf – airborne in mid leap to attack Alucard –

crumpled into human form. Alucard fell to his knees, clutching his head just like Tory. Ashley slammed into him, knocking them both sprawling.

Tory fell onto her chest, unmoving, and the fog dissipated.

The Beast Master was now in the ring, and striding towards Tory with a murderous gleam in his eyes. Mallory threw a spear at him, but the man merely flicked his hand and the spear sailed harmlessly away. Two more spears appeared in my bodyguard's hands, and were cast just as rapidly, but they didn't faze the Beast Master as he also flicked them away, and finally reached Tory.

He grabbed her by the hair, and yanked her to her feet.

Tory groaned – struggling weakly, bleeding heavily, and eyes dazed.

And then I saw the Beast Master's little girl was also standing in the ring, holding her head as she concentrated deeply on something. Perhaps she was some flavor of beast shifter? And Tory's power was still affecting her? It would explain all those claw marks. She had been attacked by a shifter, and had been infected by the gene.

And a wacky thought hit me as I watched her familiar actions.

They looked an awful lot like when Tory…

My Beast murmured in my ears. *Just now figured it out, did you…?*

"You *knew*?" I shouted at myself, well, the Dark Presence. The Beast Master glanced at me sharply, frowning in confusion at my random comment. The crowd was silent with rapt attention. This was way more than they had paid for.

Of course… Males cannot control beasts… My own Beast said as if speaking to a particularly slow child.

I…

Blinked. Then stared at the bald-headed psycho.

Boris was the hologram face in the Wizard of Oz movie. He wasn't the Beast Master. And I suddenly realized who the… *man* behind the curtain was.

Out of nowhere, Van Helsing sucker-punched Boris, knocking him a dozen feet away. A good chunk of hair was torn from Tory's scalp, which seemed to wake her up, pain receptors activating a boost of adrenaline.

Alucard was suddenly beside her, helping her to her feet. He ripped off part of his shirt to tie a make-shift tourniquet around her leg. Mallory threw a spear at Boris' back, intending to kill him on the spot. The spear jerked to the side, and the wizard – or whatever flavor of magic user he was

– slowly unfolded from the floor, turning to glare at Van Helsing with sheer outrage.

"You dare bite the hand that feeds you?" He shouted. "I should have known better than—"

"Die, Beast Master!" Mallory interrupted, launching both of his spears at Boris, and then sprinting at him in a dead run, fists aglow with a golden nimbus of power.

"It's not him," Tory whispered weakly, and Alucard began nodding furiously, staring at me pointedly before pointing a finger at the child who stood with her head down, hands slowly rising in the air as if lifting a great weight to either side of her. Her hands reached a crescendo as Tory slammed her eyes shut, mimicking the gesture in a last-ditch effort. The girl threw her hands down, and every shifter in the ring collapsed.

The crowd roared, but this time, not in joy, but terror.

After all, a good chunk of them were beasts.

Mallory was suddenly sideswiped by a gorilla. He struck the wall of the ring with a *crack*, rock splintering out from his back in a spider web.

The gorilla reached down for one of the spears that had magically reappeared in Mallory's hand, and tried to take it away.

The smell of burnt hair filled the air of the pit as he turned into a pile of ash and monkey dust.

I lifted my voice to the crowd, shouting as loud as I could as I rounded on them with an insolent grin. *"ARE YOU NOT ENTERTAINED?"*

And, yes, it felt exactly as awesome as I had hoped it would.

"Whoever stays behind will die," I added, smiling up at those in the crowd still standing.

CHAPTER 56

I used the moment of incredulous silence to scan the crowd for the Huntress or Gunnar.

But all I saw was a sea of angry faces.

One voice shouted back, mockingly. "Oh? You're going to do that all by yourself, Maker?"

I found the man behind the voice, and shrugged. "You're probably right. That wouldn't make any sense. One guy, killing everyone here... kind of ridiculous when you say it out loud like that," I admitted.

Several more in the crowd belted out dark laughter, backing up the first challenger.

"What I *will* do is pick up a pile of new toys. As spoils of war."

A hushed moment of silence met my words. Then a low growl replied. "No toys here, boy. Just grown-ass monsters excited to see you taken down a peg. It's more than we paid for. I came here to see death, not the death of a *legend*. But no complaints!"

I grinned back, smiling. "You see yourself as monsters, bloodthirsty killers, no doubt dangerous folk. Beasts, as a matter of fact."

Their silence was beautiful.

"But you know what? I've got a Beast Master of my own. If I win, I get a bunch of new chew toys to take home and play with. You heard I'm a

Maker… one of those dangerous, mythical, juiced-up, elusive creatures that were once hunted to practical extinction by the Brothers Grimm."

I paused, slowly addressing each face.

"Took care of that nuisance, didn't I? Now, there are no more Grimms to keep you safe from me. Because, well, I had a *disagreement* with their business plan," I shrugged. "So, here I am, a freshly-minted Maker, with no Grimms to keep me in line. No targets to practice on. Because, well, all my targets have met unfortunate ends lately."

I shrugged with a dramatic sigh.

And then I took a page from Alucard's earlier speech, ticking off my fingers. "The Brothers Grimm. The old Dragon Lord. A gaggle of geese – or Angels, if you prefer. A smattering of demons. Hell, even the Four Horsemen think I'm cool," I leaned forward, "and owe me a few favors. They even offered me a temp job once. Haven't taken it yet. Kinda have my hands full being a badass already. Let's see…" I tapped my lips thoughtfully, smiling as my Beast purred in approval. "Oh, that's right! Rumpelstiltskin, the Academy… their Justices *and* their Grandmaster. Man, it sounds so impressive when I list them all like that. Almost as if," I smiled out at them, squinting hungrily. "I shouldn't be fucked with…"

A few dozen of them snuck out, but a dozen of the more hardcore remained, dancing on their toes, trying to decide whether to leave or not. To save face or call my bluff. I didn't know which party the Syndicate would include. Those pretending to be scared, or those rightly pissed, calculating the odds. But I had openly disrespected them by mentioning Rumpelstiltskin.

On purpose.

"Here's how it's going to pan out. One of us is going to win this showdown." I pointed at Boris, then myself. "And the other will die a truly horrifying death. The winner will then be looking to recoup his losses. Rebuild his army. Pick up some new toys. So, how about it, ladies and gentlemen? You paid to watch a show…" I paused dramatically. "But all that's left are openings to participate in the *next* show… Who wants to be someone's bitch next week?"

They fled. Some even helped drag an unconscious body or two with them, not wanting their friends to wake up collared to one of the psychos in the ring.

Boris had approached during my speech, and was glaring at me. "You didn't need to tell them all that."

I shrugged. "I kind of felt like killing less thugs than I had to tonight."

"You really think your fledgling Beast Master can out-control *me?*" he growled.

I shook my head. "No, but she can out-control *her.*" And I pointed at the girl in the ring.

His daughter.

The man flinched.

And with a roar, Alucard, Ashley, and Sonya latched onto Tory. Her eyes shot wide open, literally spitting green fire. My three shifter friends – beasts – slumped to the ground, releasing Tory, but I saw tendrils of power now snaking out from them, boosting her with what seemed like limitless power. Her wounded leg didn't seem to bother her at all. Green fog suddenly swarmed her, and I heard roars from deeper within the quarry.

Where the other beasts waited to kill everyone.

And the ground beneath my feet began to thump as if a heartbeat the size of a locomotive had suddenly awoken some truly large and terrible monster.

The Fae? What the hell kind of monster had they sent this time? Or was it simply Tory's power? Or was there some uber-beast under the child's control.

The Beast Master child slumped to the ground, struggling to fight back, but it was no use. Her eyes winked out, no longer glowing with green light. The thumping continued to shake the ground, which could mean only a few things. Either the child had lost control of her secret beast…

Or the Fae were galloping in.

Boris considered the quaking ground with a thoughtful frown, but when nothing seemed to happen, he shot a look at his daughter. She was awake, but barely, breathing heavily. "Enough!"

I grinned at him. "I had really expected more from you. Once again, role models letting you down. One thought from me, and my Beast Master will make this place Ground Zero."

He took an instinctive step closer, practically foaming at the mouth. "You forgot one thing, Maker. No matter how powerful you," he glanced at Tory, "or *she* is, I have broken their minds. Sure, I didn't control them, my daughter did. But *I* broke their spirit. Release them, and your city will be torn to pieces. Your Beast Master can never let that control go. Ever. For even a moment. It will consume her. But at some point, she must *sleep*." He smiled. "Even still, my daughter has to use only the faintest of her powers, or lose consciousness, or fall *asleep*, and the guard will open the gates. He already has his orders. Because the moment she falls asleep, the beasts will respond, no longer under control. This will alert the guard, and he will unleash them. Such horrors will visit your city that even *I* can't comprehend it. And it will be all." He took a step closer. "Your." Another step. "Fault."

I glared back. "You're bluffing."

"Try me," he grinned, eyes twinkling with madness. We stared at each other for a time, waiting for the other to break. And the thumping beneath our feet continued, increasing in speed, as if the heartbeat was growing excited. Finally, he spoke again, seeing that I wasn't willing to back down. "Or, you can tell your Beast Master to stop. I will let you live, and you can take your friends away. We shall never have to cross paths again. Although my employer will not be pleased about the situation. Might even want to talk to you about it in the near future."

The Syndicate.

He continued. "I am curious… how do you control your Beast Master? I hadn't thought it possible for a man to control beasts, let alone a man to control a Beast Master."

I really hoped Gunnar and Rufus were almost finished. If not, things were going to go very badly for me. With his threat, I couldn't think of a way to use my last spell to Maximum Effort. With no other choice, I entertained him, tapping my spectacles. "These. Been in the family for generations."

"That's not possible. Nothing can control a Beast Master."

I shrugged. "Well, it's nothing like what you're doing. Manipulating your own child."

He seethed, eyeing my spectacles for a moment. Then he began to laugh, a dark, foreboding sound. "You truly have no idea why I do what I do, do you…?"

I shook my head. "Kind of obvious. You're a psycho who gets off on power. Even at the expense of using your own daughter," I answered, disgustedly.

"No," he said softly. He glanced sadly at her. I motioned Tory to ease off, but she had heard his words, and hadn't knocked her unconscious. She released the girl, and the child gasped, climbing unsteadily to her feet as she regained her bearings.

The girl took one look at me. "You can't take my toys!" And she stomped her foot.

I blinked. "They aren't *toys*. They're *people*."

She was shaking her head violently. "No, they're my toys. I brought them to life. Tell him, Daddy!"

And a flicker of unease danced right down my chest and flicked me in the nuts.

She was insane.

Her father flashed her an enabling smile, a practiced gesture. "There, there, Honey. Let me talk to this man here and explain. He doesn't understand magic like you do," he pleaded.

She folded her arms impatiently. "I want my toys back. She took them away. They're *mine!*"

I turned to Boris, frowning. "She was… abducted by a gang of shifters. They… broke her. They had her for hours. All night. They picked her up from the street outside our home, where she had been playing with her toys. I had been inside, working. Her mother outside with her. Normal day. I heard the screeching of tires, and a scream that I will never forget." He took a deep breath, eyes distant.

"I'm not going to fall for your sob story, old man."

But he didn't seem to care, lost in the memory. "I ran outside to find my wife dying in the street, her throat exposed. She had used her last strength to scream my name. I saw a van racing down the street, and suddenly realized that my girl was… gone." A tear streamed down his face.

"Stop it, Daddy! That was just a nightmare," the girl warned. "I don't have a mommy. Just a guardian angel."

"I know, Honey. I'm just telling the man about your nightmare. How strong you are. How you managed to wake up from the bad dream."

My mind was racing. What the fuck was going on? Tory was staring at the two of them in shock. Mallory groaned from his position near the wall, and I saw that my friends still lay in a circle around Tory, like the spokes of a wheel. Eyes open, staring up at nothing, but breathing. Where was the Huntress? Gunnar? Ichabod? The tent was empty for all but us, as far as I could tell.

Boris lowered his voice, trying to keep the child from reliving the nightmare, apparently. "The trio of shifters beat her to a pulp. Raped her. Tried to force a change. Three different strands of lycanthropy. When they couldn't force a change, and grew tired of their sport, they hit up a convenience store before seeking another victim. Just so happened that a witch was nearby. She heard the men bragging about their conquest, and went to the nearby warehouse where they had kept my daughter." His voice was a dull rasping sound, like grave dirt on a coffin. "The witch tried to save her, but there wasn't much left. The witch tried to console her pain, telling her stories that the men had only been a nightmare. Not real. They were actually naughty toys, but the witch had taken care of them." His breath caught.

"No, no, no, no..." the girl began to sob, stomping her feet and shaking her head. "Naughty toys. Never again... I will *fix* you. Make you better. Let you fight each other when you want to be naughty..."

And I shivered. Holy crap...

Boris met my eyes and nodded. "In her pain, my daughter managed to ask the witch one question. A single word. And I don't even know how she managed that, dying, mind broken after crying and calling out my name for hours as they raped, tortured, and abused her in a dirty warehouse..."

"What did she ask?" I whispered, ignoring the soft whimpers coming from Tory.

"*How?*" The man was staring down at the ground. "My daughter asked the witch *how* she had taken care of them." He took a deep breath and met my eyes. "The witch then tried to heal her with her powers. Show her how to control the beasts. And... it worked. Thanks to the trio of conflicting lycanthropy genes in her blood, and the witch's spell, something... *new* was born from the tragedy. My daughter. A Beast Master. The witch later found me, and told me what she had done. And... I couldn't bring myself to tell my daughter the truth. I spent months caring for her, trying to help her heal, and soon realized that I didn't have time to make money." He glanced at his daughter sadly. "We happened upon a werewolf in a park. A bum. Begging for change. My daughter grew terrified, and before I knew it, the beast was under her thrall. A mugger happened upon us as we frantically tried to fix what she had accidentally done. But my daughter had other plans. She commanded the werewolf to save our lives. And he did. Dying in the process, but he did save us."

He looked up at me, eyes a million miles away. "And that's when I realized how much I hated shifters. I felt not an ounce of pity for the dead werewolf. And I realized I had found a new way to make money. Collect some beasts... some toys, for my daughter. I could let her false memory come to life, and gain my vengeance upon the monsters who had ruined my family."

I stared at him in horror. "That..." I cleared my throat, struggling to find a response as I risked a glance at the girl. "That doesn't make it right. You can't condemn a whole race for the actions of a few."

The man shrugged, turning cold, hard eyes on me. "I don't give a damn about *right*. I wanted blood. And I got it. And my daughter got her toys back." He shot me a challenging look. "So, now you know our story." Then he glanced back at my spectacles thoughtfully. "Again, how is it that she obeys you? How do those glasses work?"

Realizing I couldn't stop him, I took a risk, letting him think I was granting him my trust in exchange for his honest story, but I saw Mallory climb to his feet, hand twitching, ready to kill the man if he did anything dangerous. "Here. You can see for yourself. Granted, you agree to let us go." The man nodded. I took them off, and strode up to him. I handed them over, and then folded my arms.

He stared at them a good long moment. "I would do anything for my daughter..." and I began to grow very uneasy, even though I had anticipated this. "You really shouldn't have given me these. I never intended to let you leave." Then he stabbed me in the stomach.

I fell to my knees with a grunt and my friends shouted in alarm. Well, Tory didn't. Boris watched me for a moment, satisfied. I felt an oily warmth wash over me, only to be replaced by a queasy feeling in my stomach, then a flash of cold. I kept my face hard, not revealing anything.

Boris flicked a finger, and his daughter snapped her fingers. My friends halted as we heard a shout from deeper within the quarry, and then the metal clang of dozens of locks disengaging.

Then a miasma of feral roars, and the padding of many large feet filled the air.

A moment later, a horde of monsters tore through the pallet gate leading to the pit.

Coming straight for us.

CHAPTER 57

*M*y friends tensed, and I did my best to look beaten, dying. I saw Boris slowly raise the spectacles to his face, frowning as he turned to his daughter, staring at her as he tried to figure out how to make them work. My smile began to stretch as I saw Van frowning at me, then at Boris.

Boris suddenly flinched, instinctively casting a ball of fire at thin air as he dove to the ground.

Well, *thin air* to everyone but me. I could see Carl clearly. And about a dozen of his friends. It had been difficult not acknowledging them as they followed me through the circus. The fire fizzled to nothing before them, I know not how. And they grinned through inky black fangs, chortling in a nightmarish laughter at the puny wizard at their feet. And his stupid spectacles.

Because I had used my powers to replace the lenses with enchanted glass from Chateau Falco.

I climbed to my feet. "Hold it, Carl."

Boris was panting. Then he noticed me standing, brushing off my stomach and his eyes grew as big as saucers. "How?" he stammered. My friends – except Tory, who was glaring at the horde of monsters, waiting – looked equally incredulous, which surprised me. I would have thought she had told them.

"Tums." I grinned. Then I turned to Tory. The Beasts were closer than I had thought. "Now!" I roared at her. The green fog erupted around her again, and the murderous beasts almost upon us skidded to a halt, groaning and whimpering in confusion.

Boris swung to face me, eyes wild. Seeing he couldn't harm the albino lizards before him – and that no one else seemed concerned or even aware of them – he attacked me. A frantic ball of fire struck me in the chest, igniting my shirt, and burning like the dickens. I fell on my ass, the flame eating away at me like acid. Then I felt it.

The sensation of warm oil again flowed over my wound, dousing the flames on my chest, and then I felt my skin tugging, itching, healing as the wound closed back up. Then a cold tingle flashed once, and the heat evaporated. I glanced through the burned hole in my shirt, and even though I had hoped for it, was amazed to find totally healed flesh beneath.

Boris gasped as he saw me climb to my feet again, but his eyes darted in every direction as the Elders surrounded him. He began to scream. "Say *hi* to Carl," I snarled. "And his friends."

And I watched as Carl stalked up and stabbed Boris right in the forehead with his milky white knife. White fire erupted from his skull, shooting straight into Carl's open mouth. The other Elders rocked back on their heels, eyes rolling up into their skulls for a few moments as they moaned – as if having sampled a particularly flavorful wine – thin tendrils of the white fire shooting straight for their mouths, also. Then they tore him to shreds like a school of piranhas.

I looked up to stare at Alucard, remembering how he had told me never to use a forehead strike in a fight. Of course, he couldn't see the Elders. He just saw the aftermath, and must have thought *I* had done it. He didn't even look at me, so horrified by the sight of Boris' death.

The Beast Master let out a piercing scream, unable to stop the madness of seeing her father torn to shreds by invisible monsters, suddenly reliving the nightmares her father had saved her from years ago.

I actually felt... sorry for her as I walked over to Tory, checking her wound. With Boris dead, now all we had to do was deal with the psychotic daughter. I hadn't had to use my last shred of Maker power yet, but judging by the horde of monsters before us, I knew that might change any second.

I shouted loud enough to be heard over the Beast Master's screams, keeping with the white lie I had told everyone. That I needed them to break the curse. I still didn't know how I was going to do the next part, both Shiva's plan and my promise to my Beast, but I needed to keep up appearances, or else everyone was going to start asking questions about how I was suddenly able to use my power even though I was cursed. "Gunnar, you better get that chimera to Rufus right fucking now! The whole cage is going to kill everyone here in nanoseconds. Tory can't keep using her power, or—"

"Nate!" Tory screamed. I flinched, spun to face her, and my heart stopped.

A massive claw of pure ice, like icicles given life, clutched her head like it was a basketball.

And another claw of glowing coals gripped her thigh, burning through her pants.

From *beneath* the quarry floor, which now resembled quicksand for a good several feet around Tory, stopping right next to the tip of my boots.

And I realized that the thumping I had heard earlier was indeed a monster beneath us.

The clawed hands began to drag her... *away*. Not across the ring, but back into the very rock itself, pulling her through the floor.

Even though I had no idea what the hell – exactly – was happening, I reacted.

As did Alucard.

We dove for her.

As our fingers made contact with her, we were sucked deep into the quarry.

Before the sound of the real world faded away entirely, I heard a chorus of beasts let loose cries of freedom.

And bloodlust.

And outrage.

And a little girl suddenly began to laugh.

My friends were all going to die.

And what was about to happen to Alucard, Tory, and I...

Well, that would be a worse fate.

CHAPTER 58

We entered the Land of the Fae much as everyone comes into the world: kicking, screaming, and covered in blood. Because we crashed through a stained-glass window, and fell a good thirty feet straight into a pool of water that must have been a balmy 32.1 degrees Fahrenheit. Just a hair over freezing.

I gasped, frantically thrashing to get out of the water as my chest tried to instantly shut down in shock. If you haven't ever jumped into water this cold, I'd advise you against it.

It is literally worse than being hit by a bolt of lightning.

I can tell you this from experience.

Medically speaking, your body instantly *freaks the fuck out*.

And the *pain*. You have no idea. It's as if every millimeter of your body was suddenly slapped with the flat of a ruler that had been covered in acid. It stings, its arctic chill actually burning.

Burning with pure shock at such cold temperatures striking you everywhere. Simultaneously. It's blinding. Shocking. Your breath is instantly expelled, and you only have seconds – if you're lucky – to continue even a marginal control of your *anything*.

Your body instantly diverts all brain power to keeping your core warm enough to keep that ticker of yours ticking. Which means that you quickly lose control of your motor functions, preventing you from saving yourself.

Catch-22, right?

Yup.

Luckily, the water wasn't deep, and my head exploded from the water at about the same time as my friends' heads. Gasps of pain, shock, and terror echoed in the icy cavern around us.

We jerked left and right, standing only in chest-deep water, and we all began clamoring to get out on jerky, aching limbs, momentarily forgetting the dangers of what had brought us here in the first place. Like I said, that level of cold murders your mental capabilities as well as your physical ones.

We crashed to the frosted rock embankment outside the pool, panting as clouds of vapor filled the space. The air felt like razors in my throat. I reached out to touch my friends, and the sensation of tactile feedback stung like I had reached into a beehive, an explosion of pins and needles at the pressure against my skin. But I verified that all of us were alive before I crashed onto my back. It wasn't long before the familiar inner warmth began to spill through me, moments later replaced by a flash of cold. Like magical Icy Hot.

But my friends didn't have a magic belt, so were not as lucky.

And the party had only just begun.

A heat wave like the Sahara suddenly struck us like a charging bull, and we all hissed in pain as we suddenly felt parboiled, our skin already overly-sensitive from the arctic bath.

My heart shuddered, skipping a beat, then double-timed to make up for it.

My beast whimpered deep inside of me, unable to help, loudly cursing his poor choice to ally with me. I ignored the whiny bastard.

You would think that heat would have felt good after our ice bath.

You would be grossly incorrect.

It hurt more than anything I had ever experienced, and I had just received a new top score on pain thanks to the ice bath. I gasped, unable to breathe properly, clothes steaming as I seriously contemplated jumping back into the pool.

You know when you're cold and you try to step into a lukewarm bath? And it makes you cry out in agony as your skin explodes with pins and needles?

Well, that's *lukewarm* water. After being *slightly* cold.

This was an exponentially higher form of torture than that.

After a second or two that felt like an eternity, my steaming clothes literally began to burn me. I frantically began tugging at them with numb fingers, afraid I was about to get third-degree burns from the steam trapped against my skin.

The belt began working overtime, struggling to find out exactly how to heal such rapid, conflicting injuries. Which made me want to throw up.

Just as we regained strength enough to renew our screams, the heat vanished, throwing us back into the cold... but this time, just the natural cold of our new home.

Soft clapping filled the silence, reverberating off the walls like a steady drumbeat. The sound hurt both the frozen interior of my eardrums, and the tender, burned flesh of my earlobes before Ganesh's belt had time to begin doing its thing.

We stood in darkness. Alucard stared wild-eyed, tugging Tory to her feet, and placing himself in front of her as he silently asked me *what the fuck was going on* with only his eyes.

Good friends could do that, and I found myself silently relieved to have been right about his loyalty. He hadn't chosen the Beast Master out of desire to kill. But a desire to save his adopted daughter. The best kind of father material. But we didn't have time to get sentimental.

I let out another shiver, shoulders and ligaments still twitching spasmodically as I assessed our surroundings.

We were in a dark cave. The darkness was broken up by glowing hues of icy blues, purples, and greens in several places. The stalactites and stalagmites – I never knew which was which – glowed and pulsed, throbbed and breathed as if we were inside the gut of some giant ice-beast. I glanced up, and up, and up... to see a shattered stained-glass window in the ceiling of the cave. Dozens of feet or more above our heads. I hadn't imagined it.

And I realized that we were officially fucked, because there was no other way out.

"Fubar..." Alucard murmured, following my gaze.

We *were* in the Land of the Fae.

And I had one decent boost of power left. My Beast began murmuring dark ideas to me. I listened, but was distracted by the kaleidoscope of colors in the cave, and didn't quite follow how any of his ideas might get us out of here. I very discreetly accessorized my wrists.

And that incessant clapping kept right on clapping.

I slowly turned until my gaze rested on a throne. A figure sat upon it.

The Winter Queen had decided not to draw from her B team any longer, and had apparently decided a more... *direct* approach was required.

Her skin glowed a pale, pale blue. Like the faintest-hued sapphire catching sunlight. She smiled at us, fangs glistening in the moonlight that pierced the broken stained-glass window above, and the tips of her pointed ears were covered in hoarfrost. Frost also coated her eyelashes, and icicles hung from the bottom of her earlobes.

She wore furs of purple, green, white, and blue. Which, of course, wasn't possible.

Then again, Fae.

And her furs hadn't been designed to keep her warm. More like furry lingerie.

She was beautiful. And cold. And merciless.

But more than one claw had grabbed us...

As if my thought had been a summon, I got my answer. Instant gratification rocks.

A second figure stepped out from behind the throne, looking smaller, younger, and more fragile. Not sickly or anything, just less powerful than her sister. Which didn't really mean anything, relatively speaking. The Summer Queen, and since it was Winter, she was at a slight disadvantage to her sister.

For all that, she was healthily naked, and wore a cloak of living fire. The sharp clacking of her molten lava high-heels emitted sparks that burned through the icy cavern beneath her feet. Sprouts of green life tore through the cavern floor in her wake, and her fingertips dripped embers as her eyes of fire stared at us hungrily.

"Welcome home, hounds. It seems you have taken gifts without proper repayment. That shall be rectified this night..." the Summer Queen leaned forward with a lava claw as if to pet us, "and for all nights to come," she cooed, urging us closer with a beckoning motion.

The Winter Queen nodded excitedly. "Come, come, my pets. You are still mine until the Summer Solstice." She frowned as none of us moved.

"Nate?" Alucard whispered urgently.

I glanced over my shoulder to see that we were suddenly surrounded by dozens of pairs of crystalline eyes, flickering like glowing sapphires from the darkness around us. One form moved a bit closer to a glowing stalag-whatever, and I noticed it had a white, shaggy pelt, not unlike Gunnar.

"White Walkers," Alucard whispered.

"The night is dark, and full of terrors..." the Winter Queen quoted, smiling to reveal icy – dainty, but still needle sharp – fangs. I opened my mouth in surprise at her pop culture reference, causing her to laugh lightly. "Do you not think we pay attention to your mortal entertainment? Where do you think Master Martin came upon such monsters? He visited our lands, and was allowed to adapt some of our tales."

"Jesus..." I whispered, more to myself, now realizing why it took the author so long between books. He was visiting the Land of the Fae between stories...

CHAPTER 59

*T*he Summer Queen laughed. "That God is of no use to you here, Maker…" Her eyes then shifted to Alucard, and they looked suddenly ravenous. "Ah, a Daywalker… How sweet he feels," and her fingers reached out as if to brush his hair, even though we were two dozen paces away. Alucard flinched, and I saw his locks shift as the scent of burnt hair struck me in the nose. He slapped his hand to his head, jumping back as he pushed Tory further behind him. She stumbled a bit from her bleeding leg, but remained upright. My brain moved like molasses, as if slowed by the chill of the Fae Realm. Still, my Beast continued offering, then discarding, ideas like a machine gun.

The Summer Queen pouted. "This hound fears the touch of his Lady. Does he not know the taste of our love?"

"He has not sampled yet, my sister."

"You!" I finally managed to speak, pointing in disbelief. I didn't want to use names. We had pissed them off enough already.

"I," she responded flatly before turning to her sister. "I've heard of this game, from the little folk, although I do not fully understand its purpose."

"Such mortal toils are beyond our comprehension. They shall be much more content as our hounds, discarding their putrid iron-kissed skins." The Summer Queen's eyes rested on my sword cane, and her brow furrowed with disapproval. "Thee shall have no need for iron teeth. Thee shall have claws of fire—"

"And fangs of ice," the other queen added.

That didn't sound pleasant. But a very small part of me came to the same conclusion as my Beast. We didn't have enough power to get out of this. That we were, in fact, helpless to stop them from doing whatever they desired. Then I remembered that my friends were dying in our world. With Tory gone, the Beast Master was no doubt cleaning up house, avenging her father.

And none of my friends would be able to stop her. They were primarily all shifters. Unless Ichabod decided to help, but I hadn't seen hide nor hair of him. Which meant that only Rufus, Mallory, Van Helsing, and the Huntress – wherever she had gone – were present to withstand an army of over two dozen bloodthirsty beasts.

And that my shifter friends would likely be turned *against* my non-shifter friends. And I couldn't do a thing to stop it.

"I taste Grammarie," the Winter Queen hissed.

"Spiced with Glamourie," the Summer Queen spat.

I nodded. "I used my powers to—"

"*Faen* powers, not *yours*," they hissed in unison.

I nodded, swallowing slowly. "Yes, that. I tried to protect her from her enemies—"

"We are not her enemies," the Winter Queen snarled, taking charge of the conversation. "We are her *Masters*."

I shook my head. "No, in our world, we were under attack—"

"Ah, by the failed father and his Beast Master. The broken puppeteer. The entertainer. The ringmaster. He was going to host our solstice in a few weeks." Her brow drew down, a few tiny icicles snapping off her eyelashes. "But you have taken them from us." And I gulped.

"Yeah… about that," I said in my best apologetic tone. "Sorry?"

"All will be forgiven when you are collared."

And they began striding towards us, hands held out as if calming wary dogs. I tried to back up a step, but warning growls behind me halted my movement. We were entirely boxed in.

"Anytime now, Rufus. I thought you said you were good at this type of stuff…" I whispered to myself, full of panic. Alucard shot me a look, confused at my words. Because he thought I was relying on

Gunnar saving the chimera in time to give me my full Maker powers back.

But that wasn't what I really wanted.

I wanted the curse to *drop*, burning up the last of my power forever.

I had been hoping for it to happen by now, because I didn't dare proactively use my limited Maker's power to attack, burning away the last of it. Even if I only used it to free my Beast, because that wouldn't accomplish anything. The Queens would still have us.

As soon as I tried to use my Maker's power, the Queens would kill me on sight. And I didn't know how long it would take for my wizard's power to unlock. Hell, now that I thought about it, I wasn't sure what would happen. Would I pass out? Then wake up hours or days later, only *then* having access to my wizard's power? Fat lot of good that would do me.

"This Rufus will not save you. You belong to us, now, Maker…"

And I suddenly realized that we had been here for some time now. And that at any moment, Rufus could touch hands with Camilla, giving me all of my Maker's power back, and with my newfound wizard's power regrown inside of me, I would likely become a vegetable on the spot.

Alucard struggled, pressing Tory further behind him. "Nate…" he cried out, terrified. "Do something!"

Then he went rigid, and the Summer Queen stepped up to him, grinning hungrily. "Mmmmm, my pet. Lick my hand, like an obedient little beast."

And, seemingly against his will, he opened his mouth and obeyed.

My mouth ran on autopilot. "How many licks does it take to get to the center?" I asked, panting, the stupid Tootsie Roll Pop commercial replaying in my mind as I panicked.

They chuckled, dark, throaty purrs of anticipation. "We shall get to that later, boys…" the Summer Queen considered Tory hungrily, "and girl."

Despite how stupid, how reckless, how suicidal, I needed to burn up that last shred of power.

Right freaking now. I had no idea how much time had passed in the mortal world. Could be seconds, years, or no time at all. Then again, nothing had happened yet. Maybe they were all dead. I sighed, realizing it was my only option, even though there was really no upside. At least I could die knowing I hadn't given up.

I really had nothing to lose.

"Pah! You wear our cuffs, hoping to defy our power?" The Summer

Queen belted out, eyeing the bracelets I had stolen from the goblins. Being closer now, she must have finally sensed them. "See how well they work against me, Maker." As I prepared to do something drastic before she could stop me, I felt the combined power of the Queens of Fae hammer me like a million-pound blanket, settling over me, pressing me down, down, down, forcing my hands to my sides...

To rest on the hilt of the sword cane.

I gripped it, barely, my muscles not working properly as a faint click reverberated through the cavern. Alucard's eyes went vacant, and he suddenly spun, latching onto Tory, a stupid grin on his face. "It feels so nice..." he whispered, his fingers slowly rising to the intricate silver collar around his throat. "No more pain. Here, just try it..."

She shouted, eyes lighting with green fire, but they faded almost instantly as the two queens' eyes also lit up with fire – blue and orange. The Winter Queen slowly clasped a collar around her throat, too, and a peaceful smile slammed into place like an iron portcullis on a castle fortress.

Then the four turned to me, and began to saunter closer.

No, no, no, no... don't let them lock me away again. Please, please, PLEASE! The Beast begged in my ears, panting frantically.

I responded in my mind. *I can try to release you now, but we're still toast. It's suicide. They'll take us both no matter what we do...* he whimpered in response, fully realizing that his brief hope for freedom was now dashed.

My mind raced as I backed up another couple steps. I felt a sharp lance of fire bite down into my leg, and I hissed, spinning, to find that a hound the size of a Great Dane had bitten me.

The familiar warmth slowly began to pour over my wound, followed by the icy flash as it healed. I wondered how many times it would work.

Or if it could bring me back from the dead.

My only choice was to honor my promise to my Beast. He needed me in control to free him. He couldn't do it on his own. I had given him a Prison... a home. The cane. Hopefully a safe place to ride out this storm. And there, he could possibly recover from this. Heal. If it took him years, so be it. At least he might live. I was dead either way. As were my friends. Or we were mindless hounds. Same thing, really.

We were going to die.

My only choice in the matter was whether to be a martyr – freeing the

Beast as I had promised – or as a victim – under the control of the Fae Queens.

I accepted this truth, and smiled for the first time in what felt like years.

A soul-deep smile.

And my fist squeezed around the cane.

"Stop! Kamikazee time!" I shouted at the advancing group, preparing to burn up the last of my power in two simultaneous spells: a quick, dirty attack on the Fae, and severing the tie connecting me to my Beast.

The Queens frowned as I opened myself to my power for the last time.

CHAPTER 60

*B*ut I was slapped down at the last second.

And not by the Queens.

My turn, my Beast roared in my ears, wrestling one of the two spells right out of my metaphorical hands. Right as I was trying to unleash a fireball at the Winter Queen's heart.

But instead of fire, my cane tore free from my belt, a kiss of hard iron, and it glowed bright yellow as it abruptly screamed through the air, and my Beast was riding the metaphorical bullet.

Remember me... I heard him say in farewell.

But the Beast hadn't been strong enough to stop *both* of my spells.

And as time seemed to slow, I realized what he had just done.

He had sacrificed his life to possibly save mine. Not likely to work, but he had still done it.

The Winter Queen threw up her hands to block the sword, but the sacrificial power of my Beast was apparently too strong, because it didn't slow down, only flashed brighter in retaliation. I frantically sliced through the cord connecting us, my world exploding in a shower of sparks as the last of my Maker's power severed the tie right before the blade pierced through the Winter Queen's outstretched arms, and right into her chest.

She flew from the force of the impact.

On her way, she shattered right through several stalag-whatevers, before slamming into the wall, pinned like a butterfly a good ten feet above the ground, which was just terrible.

I fell to my knees, screaming as my wizard's power suddenly filled my skin to bursting. I cried out in relief and pain.

I was *back*.

Next, I may or may not have indulged myself.

Bolts of lightning suddenly hammered into the cavern floor around us, and I realized I was laughing like a maniac. Everything with a heartbeat went sailing off into the darkness, even my friends, hammering into yet more of the stalag-whatevers. Then each hound was stabbed by a bolt of lightning, and the collars around my friends' necks snapped open. Then, silence.

And my fading laughter.

The scent of blood filled the air.

Alucard and Tory were sitting up, dazed, covering their ears as they unsteadily waved back and forth.

The Summer Queen lay draped on the throne, whimpering in pain, but the Winter Queen was impaled on my cane, still hanging high above the floor, embedded in the rocks of the cavern wall. She gasped, bloody tears dripping from her eyes, only to freeze into crimson snowflakes as they drifted to the ground below her thrashing feet.

The Summer Queen's eyes saw her sister, and she howled.

My eardrums shattered, but I felt no pain, only the sensation that something had broken inside of me. Then a warm band around my waist began to throb, steadily, stronger, faster, until sounds slowly returned, and the wailing of the Summer Queen was more of a sob.

"I will not be collared," I spoke in a low, authoritative tone.

"You have no idea what you've done..." the Winter Queen whispered back.

"You tried to collar a Temple," I replied. Then, for dramatic reasons, and to give her pause, I leaned closer. "A future *Horseman...*" I added in a menacing whisper.

"We had only... rumor of this," the Summer Queen was on her knees, one of her lava heels broken, and her cloak lying on the ground behind her, smoking as it slowly burned through the ice floor. She looked like a candidate for the worst walk of shame ever. "But you have doomed us all now. Without her, the world will burn to ashes..." She glared daggers at me, eyes full of hatred, doom, and... defeat. "You have won, and ultimately lost..." she sobbed.

My belt throbbed at my waist, and I glanced down, a sudden revelation.

"What do you mean, burn to ashes?" I asked softly.

She was staring at her sister as she answered. "Life requires balance. Dark and Light. Glamourie and Grammarie. Beasts and Masters. Fire and Ice. Life and Death. Your retaliation has doomed us all..."

I stared down at her. "Thanks a lot, my Beast," I said to my old room-mate. Both as a eulogy for his sacrifice, and a frustrated realization of my luck.

I heard a faint whisper from deep inside the cane. *Always so dramatic, the Fae...*

I almost gasped, but seeing that no one else had heard it, I kept my outburst internal.

You're alive? I asked in disbelief. But I heard no response. The cane – his *home* – had protected him. It had *worked!*

I studied the Summer Queen, and then the dying Winter Queen. "I propose a bargain."

The Winter Queen spat bloody slush onto the cavern floor. "Denied. Reap what thee has sown..." she managed in a feral hiss.

But the Summer Queen was watching me, considering. "Bargains will soon be null and void, when the void of Creation's Chaos reigns supreme..."

"Well, I don't know what the hell that means, but... I can heal her." I pointed casually.

Alucard groaned from his position on the floor, thrashing weakly in an effort to find Tory. His fingers touched her chest, and power began to pour out of him into her, waking her. Her fiery green eyes shot open, tiny flames lancing up an inch into the air, and she sucked in a huge gulf of oxygen. But they seemed dazed – not deaf, at least – from the Summer Queen's initial shriek. Maybe because I had seen them covering their ears.

"*Speak!*" the Summer Queen commanded.

I blinked at her lazily, arching a condescending eyebrow. "Perhaps you misunderstood the situation. I do not obey you. I thought I made that perfectly clear..."

"Wretched swine," she hissed back, stumbling to her feet with lava claws as she took an aggressive step my way. "I will strip the skin from your bones for bacon to break my fast."

I flicked a hand, and she went flying into the cavern wall. "Manners, my Queen. Always, manners. Lest, we are but beasts." I think it was the shock and fear that allowed me to get away with it. After all, I didn't think a wizard would be able to go toe-to-toe with her. Then again, I did feel stronger than I remembered with my wizard's power. I strode up to the Winter Queen, staring at her with merciless eyes. She stared right back, but no longer with fury. Her gaze was calculating, dying, desperate for a taste of hope.

"What is your bargain, Mak—" she corrected herself, "Horseman?"

I waved a hand. "That's just a temp job. I seem to have an affinity with them, but I wouldn't go around pretending to be one. Consider that a... job offer." But I wasn't truly certain about my words. I hoped they were true.

I really didn't want to be a Horseman. That had just been me putting them on edge. In fact, I was entirely sure that it wasn't possible to be a fifth Horseman of the Apocalypse. It would mean the Revelations Chapter in the Bible was effectively full of typos and that Big G needed to fire his editor.

I met her immortal eyes, unflinching. "We leave with no obligation, commitment, or promise to return. We are entirely free from Fae entanglements. And you are obligated to return any and all property brought here to its rightful owner. Oh, and no more child abductions," I added, remembering the numerous Amber Alerts recently. Her eyes glittered with fury. I couldn't think of anything else, so continued. "And in exchange, I will heal thee," I added gently.

"Child abductions?"

I scowled. "Don't play coy. I know you've been taking children from my world lately."

She blinked at me, and then wheezed in laughter. For a good twenty seconds. It looked like it hurt her, but she didn't stop. "Lately?" she asked. "We've been taking your children since the Grimm War, impudent mortal!"

I simply stared. That... was almost a year ago... She greatly enjoyed the shock on my face.

I finally shrugged. "We're all going to die if you don't take the deal."

"How could you do such a thing?"

I shook my head. "That's not part of our bargain. Accept, and thee shall see."

An eternity stretched before us, and I watched as her chest began to crack and crumble like baked clay, pieces of it falling away to shatter to dust. Her arms, where the cane had pierced them, did the same. She groaned, fighting to draw breath, but she set her lips in a hard, defiant line. "I shall not dicker with—"

"Agreement made," the Summer Queen whispered directly into my ear. I flinched, rounding on her instinctively. But she was hunched over in pain, eyes fixated on her dying sister, as if sharing the touch of steel that was buried in her chest, eating her alive.

"Agreement made," I repeated, and then began to slowly, dramatically unbuckle my belt.

Alucard let out a surprised, but weakened laugh, pointing animatedly at my crotch. "*Sexual heeeaaalling*," he sang.

I couldn't help it. I chuckled, but continued to take off my belt.

She obviously recognized it, eyes staring in disbelief as I stepped up on a large, broken stalag-whatever to reach her. I then pressed the snakeskin belt to the Winter Queen's chest. Everyone watched in awe as the skin began to heal before our very eyes. The Summer Queen gasped beside me, stepping up closer to inspect the belt. After a few moments, I met her eyes, and placed my palm on the hilt of the sword cane. I arched my brow in question. "I told your sprite that *I had some hard iron for* you. Didn't she tell you?" She quivered with outrage, but could do nothing, because she couldn't pull the sword free from her sister without harming herself. It was iron. Or at least it had enough iron in it to matter. "You didn't want me leaving this here, did you?" She grimaced, and gave me a weak shake of her head.

I heard Tory and Alucard climbing to their feet behind me, and I mentally ran back over my bargain. I hid the sudden terror as a thought hit me.

I hadn't made them promise we could *leave unmolested*.

And I also realized that like Baba's Familiar, this healing would take more than a single touch of the belt. I had to leave it. With a frustrated curse, I withdrew the blade, kicked the Summer Queen in her chest, right between her stupid Fae boobs, and then dove for Alucard and Tory. The Summer Queen shrieked as she flew. Then I heard her lava claws scraping the icy cavern floor as she scrabbled to pursue us. "You shall never leave the Fae realm!"

I slammed into my friends, latching onto them with my fists. Then I Shadow Walked our happy asses right out of the Land of the Fae.

As the world winked to darkness, I wondered how badly I was going to pay for losing Ganesh's belt. But this thought was trumped by me wondering how many years had passed since we had been in the Fae Realm.

One always heard stories about such things. Time to find out.

Maybe I would get to wheel Gunnar around in a nursing home for a few years.

CHAPTER 61

*T*he air crackled like shattered rock as we slammed back into the center of the quarry. I absently verified the cane handle was secured to my waist, a habitual gesture. I caught a swift motion off to my right, and instinctively flung up a hand, calling upon my wizard's gift. It answered, almost making me want to cry. Something heavy came to a sudden halt directly before my hand, and then neatly fell into my palm. I turned to find an arrow resting there.

I followed the trajectory to find the Huntress staring at me, open-mouthed.

But I didn't have time to explain.

"Nate!" Gunnar roared. "They're right behind us!"

And I saw the Huntress suddenly loose three arrows in quick succession, right over my shoulder. Grunts of pain and agony erupted from her targets as I spun to find shifters dropping like flies as they tore after Rufus, Gunnar, and Camilla – who was unconscious and slung over the were-wolf's shoulder. Rufus had three ragged claw marks on his face, right down to the jaw and cheekbone, his face a crimson mask. He saw me, his eyes widened, and he put on a quick burst of speed, finally slapping his hand onto Camilla's dangling palm – the weakest high-five I had ever seen.

I frowned, and then suddenly remembered they still thought I needed the two to touch hands for the curse to drop. But so much was going on that I didn't even try to pretend I felt anything.

I just began unleashing fireballs.

I noticed Alucard helping Tory to her feet. I lowered my hands, the onslaught slowing for a moment as Gunnar and crew skidded to a halt near us. Gunnar unceremoniously dumped Camilla into Rufus' arms and raced to Ashley, still lying unconscious on the ground. He was not gentle in tugging her back closer to us, more concerned with her safety than any new scrapes he may give her. I realized everyone was now staring at Alucard. I turned to see him, eyes closed, squeezing Tory's shoulders from behind. His skin erupted in golden light, fainter than before, but still brilliant.

"Porcu-shine power!" I shouted, laughing.

And spears of luminescent green erupted from Tory's eyes, hammering into the oncoming horde of monsters like a machine gun. But instead of mowing them down to their deaths, they simply skidded to a halt, blinking a few times as if having just woken up.

"Help…" Tory whispered, hand vaguely pointing to her right. And I saw similar, if weaker bolts, suddenly flash out from another direction, hammering into the monsters, but this time suddenly filling them with irrational fury. The exact opposite of Tory.

I stared hard at the child, seeing that she held a weregorilla's head in each palm, squeezing hard enough for bone to crack, and blood to pour freely from their skulls. Purple power filled her, growing weaker as the gorillas died, but that didn't seem to bother her in the slightest. She had already taken the power she needed to battle Tory on an even playing field.

Except she had needed two shifters to match Tory's *one* Daywalker. I now knew beyond a shadow of a doubt that he was bonded to Tory. If not before, *definitely* now. Because I could see power flowing both ways between them, feeding off each other, not just Alucard powering Tory, but the other way around, like a supernatural circuit.

I just wondered how long it would be before they burned each other out.

With a reptilian roar, a red dragon slammed into the ground beside the Beast Master, and nuzzled her with a bloody snout.

Misha.

Tory screamed loud enough to make the army of shifters stumble on their feet, struggling against the conflicting powers battling to control them.

Out of the corner of my eye, Sonya suddenly sprinted into view, and threw herself closer to Misha, shifting in midair so that a much smaller – but no less deadly – red dragon landed beside her mother. Misha snarled at her in warning, but to me it seemed more like a reprimand. *Don't get in the middle of your parents' fights.*

Sonya ignored this, walking warily on all fours until she was close enough to sniff her mother, as if testing the veracity of what she could see with her eyes. She tensed for a good three seconds, abruptly crouched lower, and then let out a soft whine, tail flicking back and forth to slam into the rocky floor in an agitated motion. Then she arched her neck to glance at me, then Tory, and then she slunk to stand beside her mother, staring at me intently. The Beast Master smiled, patting the new dragon on the forehead.

I blinked, ignoring the two figures stealthily moving about in the background.

Shit.

Two red dragons, an army of beasts, and my ragtag crew of wounded warriors. Most of whom would fall under the spell of whichever Beast Master prevailed. I noticed my spectacles lying broken in the center of the ring, and sighed. Not that they would have done me any good, but maybe Carl knew of some revelation that would get me out of this mess. I could see them standing all around the ring, watching, waiting, impotent to help.

"You have taken my father. Tried to steal my toys…" the Beast Master hissed, eyes dancing wildly in her scarred face. The two dragons crouched lower, Misha emitting a lance of fire up into the canopy of the tent above, punctuating the child's words with a final condemnation.

Canvas and wood began to burn in a concussive *whoomp.*

None were going to survive. Whether by battle or fire. We were all dead.

"Time for me to clean up my mess, take my toys, and go to bed. Nighty night, Maker," she hissed, raising both hands towards the stunned crowd of beasts. Tory let out a shout, throwing her own hands at the monsters, and I watched as they were literally hammered back and forth, swayed by whichever Beast Master managed to hit them first.

"Yeah, nighty night, toots," I smiled sadly at her. She risked a quick glance my way, expecting an attack with my magic.

But this wasn't my fight.

I had done enough.

Killed enough.

Failed enough.

So, she saw me standing still, arms folded, frowning sadly as I watched.

And Van Helsing's sword suddenly erupting out the front of her chest from behind caught her entirely off guard. As did the two arrows that suddenly tore through the palms of her hands.

The dragons let out fiery roars of surprise, but Tory threw her hands into the air, and a shockwave of green fire expanded out from her in all directions, like a crashing tidal wave.

Van, having survived the brunt of the conflagration by the Beast Master's body protecting him – ah, irony... – gave one last twist of his blade, then shoved the child off, sending her crashing to her knees, wounded palms slapping into the quarry as she gasped in agony.

Rufus had collapsed to the ground, as did everyone else too close to the blast. Even though we weren't all beasts, the physical force had been violent, enough to affect all of us. Even Alucard lay a dozen feet away, smoking with glittering, golden dust. Gunnar lay slumped over the naked Ashley, protecting her.

Well, except for Tory of course.

And me. A ring of black fog clung low to the ground around my feet in a perfect circle, seeming to have gobbled up Tory's outburst.

The only other person standing was...

Misha.

Wait... that doesn't make any sense...

Misha took one single step, and I spotted a single dark scale on an otherwise sea of red scales on her front leg. She growled, shaking her head as she approached Tory, tail lashing. I noticed a flicker of motion on the ground, and murmured, "Strike one..." Misha ignored my warning and took another step, purring hungrily as fire danced across her snout, eyes battling for dominance against the weakened Beast Master. Talk about old flames... "Strike two," I whispered.

"You ruined everything, Tory..." the dragon cooed, licking its razor-sharp fangs hungrily. "Control your beasts, woman..." I began shaking my head at Misha, but hesitated as her words tickled my memory. Tory was frowning as well, but shook her head once, and finally lifted her arms, green orbs of power abruptly flaring up around her outstretched palms.

Pointed directly at Misha.

But the red dragon didn't take heed as she took another step, only six paces away now. "Strike three..." I said loudly, voice saddened.

Arrows suddenly sprouted up across her stomach in rapid succession, *wham, wham, wham*! They were strong enough to pierce even the thick scales of a dragon, which was goddamned hard to do. The Huntress was growling, lying on the ground with what looked like an injured leg, bow levelled at Misha. I nodded at her in gratitude. She grimaced back in pain, but her gaze quickly flashed back to her victim, and then Tory, making sure she was okay.

Even though she had been the instrument of Tory's impending pain – having shot Tory's lover – she still cared more for Tory's safety than she feared her wrath.

The dragon let out a terrible roar, shooting more flames into the air, this time fully igniting the tent around us. It began to rain down around us, burned poles, supports, and canvas. I dove to the side, dodging a particularly large piece of fiery detritus, and shouted, "Tory, we need to get everyone out of here! Wake them up!" But Tory stood, face pale as she stared at Misha. First, in horror, but then...

And I risked a glance at the wounded dragon.

My heart stopped as a figure calmly strode across the ring, staring down at the woman now lying on the floor, stomach perforated with three arrows.

Except the woman didn't have red hair.

A shimmering stone was embedded in her forearm, glinting like a shiny black diamond. Like the single black scale I had seen on the dragon's skin.

I couldn't move.

It was Indie.

And Ichabod was somehow crouched over her, whispering something to her. My grandfather. I began to shake, and fire suddenly engulfed my fists.

Instead of sparks, snowflakes of fire – perfect crystalline patterns – fell to the ground around me. The power grew in intensity, shifting to white as the heat intensified, but I didn't feel a thing.

Well, physically.

But inside, I felt a whole hell of a lot.

"You..." I began, panting hoarsely. Ichabod slowly turned to assess me, a hard line on his face, waiting. "You've been here this whole time. Sitting. Drinking. Being... entertained."

The flames shot up my arms, engulfing my shoulders, and I saw Van's face go pale as he scooted further from Ground Zero. "It was a necessity..." Ichabod replied softly, angrily.

"Your hunger for the Syndicate is strong enough to watch mentally abused children fight to the death..." I hissed, the ground around me suddenly sheathed in hoarfrost. Spikes of the frost grew taller, almost as if watching a fast-forward of the Winter season passing us by. The daggers of frost curved away from my feet, leaving me unimpeded, but surrounded by a small circle of knee-high frosted knives.

"The Beast Master was going to host the Syndicate's party during the Winter Solstice. Do you have any idea what we could have accomplished if you hadn't ruined everything, you petulant child?" he roared, fists clenching at his sides. "Yes. In war, there are casualties. I don't like it, but I care more about the big picture. Sometimes a pawn must be sacrificed to take the queen."

The rock quarry began to shake, a steady hum of power as rocks rumbled down from the heights surrounding the fighting ring. And I realized I was causing it, my wizard's power way stronger than it had ever been before. "Kids..." I took a step closer, crystalline ice crunching under my foot. "Are not pawns. And neither..." my eyes fell on Indie, stirring lightly on the ground, "...is my *fiancée*!" and I leveled everything I had at him.

CHAPTER 62

$\mathcal{A}$ wall of water identical to the temperature of the pool from the Fae Realm suddenly roared twenty feet tall, barreling towards Ichabod. I slashed an opening in the wall for Indie, so that the water surrounded her but didn't actually touch her.

It felt *good* to use this again. No more hesitation. No more confusion.

Back to my roots.

And right now, those roots wanted to make up for lost time.

Ichabod's eyes widened in confusion for all of a second as he stared at me, but he threw up a hand in a defensive gesture against the water at the last moment.

I dropped the temperature a single degree, and cast a blast of air behind the now frozen water, effectively turning it into the world's largest shrapnel grenade.

Right at my beloved ancestor.

A fire monster instantly coalesced before the explosion, a giant horned beast complete with a trident blazing like lava – the surface constantly cooling and crackling to solid rock upon each hit of the thousand shards of ice, only to be replaced by yet more oozing lava a moment later.

First round over, I found Ichabod staring at me as his fire-construct crashed to the rock floor in a shower of white-hot coals. I vaporized the rock beneath him with a thought, and flung up my hand to the sky. He

318

disappeared with a shout, only to fall from three stories above, pummeling to the ground at three times the speed of gravity.

I had never thought to use a Gateway offensively before.

I wasn't sure where the knowledge was coming from. Maybe it was my brief experience as a Maker forcing me to rethink how magic worked. Even though I had been a horribly inefficient Maker. Regardless, it was fun to finally not feel clueless in a fight.

Before Ichabod could slam into the earth, hopefully breaking every bone in his body, wings abruptly sprouted from his back – inky black, and dripping blood as they flared out, showering the air above us with purple rain. *Purple rain...* come on! Then I panicked, throwing up a last second dome of air around my friends. The rain struck the dome and hissed like water on a hot griddle. Because it wasn't rain. It was freaking acid. I threw my hands at him, casting razor-thin wires of air in rapid succession, almost too thin to see.

They severed Ichabod's wings, and he finally hammered down into the ground. He scrambled to his feet, face crimson with rage. I grabbed my knees, feigning exhaustion.

My wrists chafed.

"Time for another lesson, *wizard...*" Ichabod hissed, obviously picking up on the fact that I wasn't using my Maker's power.

And he threw everything he had at me.

A wave of souls flew at me, claws of shadow and bone, nightmares and despair. They struck me, and disappeared in a puff of smoke. I dusted off my shoulders with exaggerated motions, and then met his eyes. He stared at me incredulously.

"One move, Ichabod... one move, and all my dreams come true..." I smiled, staring into his eyes. I strode over to him, panting with rage. "Everyone, prepare to kill him. He'll block half of us, so I want to make sure someone gets through if I so much as *desire* him to die." His eyes tightened. The idea was actually very smart. He was powerful. Strong. And a Maker who knew his stuff. But with so many instruments of death aimed at him, at least one would get through.

The sounds of weapons filled the air. Sounds of death.

Ichabod had literally stood in the shadows, doing nothing as innocents lost their lives, and as Indie... I shook my head, clearing it. My anger was out of control.

I leaned forward. "We're through here. You're not taking her from me this time. I've seen your true colors. Your Beast. And I've learned a few things since last we wrestled." I leaned closer, allowing a bit of madness to dance in my eyes. "And I've come to the realization that I prefer battling in *this* world over the Dueling Grounds." I winked ominously.

"Nate..." a familiar voice whispered from behind me.

I slowly turned, limbs suddenly leaden.

Indie stared at me, shaking as she tried to support herself on one arm, the other clutching the arrows. I turned to Mallory, mouth open to command him to heal her.

"No!" she hissed. "Don't touch me." My mouth remained open, and I realized after a few seconds of staring, that she wasn't just whispering in pain... but whispering in downright *fury*.

"I don't understand. Let us heal you," I began, pleading.

"No." Her tone was an iron fist to my stomach. "You don't get to do that anymore." She leveled fiery eyes at me, then turned to Ichabod. She scowled a bit, and I saw her eyes shift to the smoky, coalescing dark depths of a Grimm. Her arm almost gave out as she turned. I instinctively took a step to help her, and was hammered with a fist of raw power.

Except, thanks to my cuffs, nothing touched me. But by the venomous look in her eyes, I knew beyond a shadow of a doubt that she had just tried to kill me.

"Lucky you," she spat blood onto the floor. With grunts and groans, she climbed to her feet. An arrow slammed into the ground between her and me, a warning from the Huntress. Indie chuckled in dark amusement, but other than that, didn't acknowledge the threat. She stood facing me, finally lifting her head to meet my eyes. They still shifted with the smoky darkness, little flickers of light like distant lightning in those murky depths. "You ruined everything."

I couldn't help it. I let my emotions fly. All the rage from knowing she was in town. She not calling. Me loving her. She disappearing for months. Pain. Sadness. Confusion. And white-hot rage. "What are you talking about?" I shouted back, torn between outrage and love. "I saved that kid's life!" I pointed at the chimera.

"And indirectly killed how many more?" she shouted right back. "Basically guaranteeing that thousands more would die in the years to come. *Months* to come."

I shook my head. "It doesn't work like that…"

"It works *exactly* like that. You're so used to being the hotshot. Getting your way. Thinking yourself a hero." Her leg almost gave out as she clutched her abdomen in a spasm of pain. "But, you are *wrong*."

"Indie, listen. I might not know everything you're talking about, but you don't know what he's done!" I pointed a finger at Ichabod. My hand was shaking.

"At least he can make the hard decisions."

I wanted to hit something. Hard. But I took a deep, calming breath. This was Indie. She had been misguided, led astray by Ichabod. "Look, we can figure all that out later." I took a cautious step closer, letting out a small smile. "You came back…" I began.

"Stay away from me!" she screamed. I froze, stunned. "I have more important things to do than play *house*." Her glare was frigid, like the Winter Queen had looked at me. "Or was me not calling you upon my arrival somehow unclear?"

I stood there, lost as I stared at my fiancée. "Indie—"

"No. I choose *him*. At least he's trying to do the right thing, the tough thing. Take care of the big picture, and not just put out small fires. We could have *stopped* them, Nate. The group Rumpelstiltskin worked for. But you *ruined* that. To save *one* life." And she stumbled over to Ichabod. I wrung my hands in frustration, not knowing what to do. What to say. I scratched at my chafing wrist absently as my mind stumbled for anything I could say to convince her of the madman before her.

Ichabod's gaze settled on my cuffs, and he grimaced. He flung one hand up at the canopy above us, and touched Indie's arm. The ceiling of the tent made a large *cracking* sound, and the two were suddenly gone with a second crack of power that signified him Shadow Walking.

And I howled in outrage as the circus tent finally came down around us.

My friends screamed as our world exploded in flames and sparks.

And the beasts were now all unconscious, or under Tory's thrall.

Defenseless from the rain of fire and embers falling down towards us.

I flung my hands up into the air to cast consecutive blasts of air into a dome protecting every living body in the pit. The spherical force expanded until it hammered into the falling tent around us. The canvas, support poles, and cables tore free, snapping free from the quarry floor, and vaporizing to ash. Then two more domes of light – even stronger than the first – flew out of my hands, until the fire was entirely gone, and only the night sky hung overhead. Stars like shiny diamonds rested on a bed of dark velvet, faint gossamer clouds like transparent cotton candy drifted lazily by.

And I realized I was lying on my back, finally exhausted, or over-whelmed with grief.

Or something.

A broken heart, perhaps.

I heard a horse's hoof stamp down by my head, and then a sharp, hard object wedged itself underneath me like a fulcrum, propping me up. I didn't react, simply staring up at the sky as voices shouted all around me. Shadows of motion flickered around me, but I refused to focus on them, admiring the simple beauty of the cosmos above. The hard fulcrum suddenly flung me up into the air, and I landed on hard, but yielding, feathered flesh, my world tilting crazily for a second. I didn't allow myself to focus on the montage of shapes and colors that represented the pit, my friends, and the horse. I heard more feathers snap out, rattling in the wind as a lamenting *neigh* cracked the night, silencing the protesting voices of my friends all around us.

I wrapped my arms around my ride, and decided to rest, closing my eyes for a moment.

I felt reality shatter to pieces around us as the horse bolted forward, and only silence resided where we now traveled. I cracked an eye open, mildly curious, and realized we were in the stars. In the darkness. In the cosmos.

In moonlight and sunbeams.

And I felt at peace for the briefest of moments before closing my eyes again. I heard four more sets of hooves racing up beside me, and my level of comfort increased. An honor guard…

CHAPTER 63

I opened my eyes to a dystopian world of fire.

I sat on the heights of a mountain that didn't exist in the real world. And I could see all of St. Louis. Not just *a lot*, but *all*. I climbed to my feet. I could see for miles – *dozens* of miles – and what I saw made me want to empty the contents of my stomach.

Fires raged through my once great city, smoke cloying the air. No electricity illuminated the cityscape – only flame. The St. Louis Arch was now twin jagged spires of twisted metal. I let my gaze wander. Pulverized skyscrapers. Rivers putrid with the rotting bodies of both man and beast. The earth oversaturated with blood, like a nightmarish swamp. But the fires still raged on, many in colors that were not possible... well, not *humanly* possible.

Abandoned vehicles filled roadways: tanks, sedans, and even wreckage from planes. A nearby train lay on its side, grain spilling from its torn cars. The grain was rotten.

Bodies lay everywhere. And weapons of all types lay discarded and forgotten near those bodies: guns, swords, knives, spears, shields, riot gear, and shell casings. A shitload of shell casings. Only one building stood unharmed.

A church.

And crows blanketed the earth, filling the air with hungry *caws* as they feasted on the buffet of death.

Millions of them.

Someone cleared their throat behind me and I flinched in surprise, spinning.

A flickering white campfire crackled in a small pit, and four figures sat in a circle around it – all hooded, and leaning forward. Despite the bright fire, their faces remained shadowed. Five large beasts stood silhouetted in the shadows of the fire, a dozen or so paces away, calmly munching on a fresh deer. I bit my tongue. They were horses. And one of them was Grimm, my unicorn. Eating raw flesh.

Understanding dawned, and my sense of alarm doubled.

The Four Horsemen.

Then memory came whispering back to me.

They had escorted me from the quarry.

And they obviously wanted to talk.

I approached them warily. "Thanks," I said, sitting down on a vacant log. "I wanted to get away for a minute anyway. Clear my head. Find something positive to ponder." I flicked my head to my destroyed city. "That's just not doing it for me though," I muttered.

Pestilence spoke. "It's a vision. Of what will be. Or what could be."

I stared at his three Brothers, waiting for them to back him up, or clarify the cryptic comment. None of them did.

"Very helpful," I grouched. We sat in silence for a time, watching the fire. As I stared closer into the flames, I realized I could see a tiny winged warrior fighting his counterpart – an Angel and a Demon. Dozens of nearby humans were mowed down as a casualty of being in the wrong place at the wrong time as the two battled above. Then a figure on horseback galloped through the fire, mercilessly destroying the Angel, the Demon, and the surviving humans, leaving no one behind. Then the apparition faded away, leaving a normal campfire once again. Well, a normal *white* campfire.

I lifted my gaze to find the four figures staring at me intently.

"There is a storm coming," Death murmured softly. "Or has already come, depending on how you look at it," he amended, waving a hand dismissively. "The girl warned you once."

I frowned at him for a moment, then turned back to the destruction below our mountain. "The Apocalypse?"

Another voice piped up, a bit too cheerful. "Our first day on the job," he chuckled.

I shot him a look, finding his jovial attitude misplaced. But a mask of lava stared back at me from within the cowl of his hood. Obviously, no expression was found there. "What girl? I have a lot of girls warning me of one thing or another," I complained, memories of Indie creeping up like poison in my ears.

"Pandora," Death answered. "She warned you of the storm. And the embers. The sparks."

I nodded. "Oh, right. I nudged that down on my to-do list. Because I wanted to go take care of some other things. You know, less obscure, more obvious necessities."

He leaned closer. "There *are* no more obvious necessities." He waved a hand at the death and destruction blanketing the world below, proving his point.

"Fine. And what does that have to do with me, exactly? I'm just a man."

"You're a *vessel*," War corrected, his mask flowing with moving lava beneath his hood.

"A vessel for *what?*" I asked, recalling Shiva's conversation.

The Horsemen grew silent, and I scowled at all Four simultaneously. Pestilence spoke. "Well, that's yet to be determined, Firestarter... But let's just say a vessel to begin this... or end it. Or prevent it." Then Pestilence chuckled. "How's that for obscure?"

"Grimm! We're leaving." I stood to leave, having no patience for humor. Or word games.

The figures grew agitated, arguing animatedly as they climbed to their feet. I had forgotten how tall they could appear, easily ten feet tall. And horrifying wings that resembled their persona poked out from their backs, all different.

War, with his red and white samurai mask of molten lava. The spines of his wings like red-hot branches tearing through his robes of burning coals. No skin stretched between the spines, so that they more resembled fiery branches. But they probably worked.

Pestilence, with his *The Walking Dead* zombified mask that oozed with pus and phlegm, disease and parasites. His robes were rotten, full of holes and green stains. His pale wings shot out from behind him, rotten skin riddled with maggots and vermin.

Famine wore his scarecrow mask – complete with bloodstains on the torn and ravaged burlap sack-textured surface – and his robes were seemingly made of dead corn husks, desiccated branches formed claws that reached out from the sleeves. Wings like dried cornstalks sprouted out behind him.

And Death, with his traditional bone mask, skeletal wings flaring out behind him, again with no skin between the spines. His robes were a death shroud. Like one big great black doily.

And me. A reborn wizard. A temporary Horseman. No wings. What a crock of shit.

I pointedly began searching the area immediately around the fire, pacing. "What are you doing?" Death asked, softly.

I glanced over my shoulder. "Looking for a bush," I snapped, turning back to my surroundings. The Four shared a concerned look, as if fearing I had lost my marbles. I'd had just about enough of that from my friends over the past few days. "If I'm a Horseman, I'd really like to meet my employer. Hear it from Him. So, I'm looking for a *Burning Bush*."

Death rolled his eyes, finally understanding. "It doesn't work like that..." he sighed.

I shrugged. "Then I decline. I like to meet the men I work for. Before I go kill people for them. Eliminates misunderstandings."

Death grabbed my arm, but not with hands of flesh.

A skeletal claw that felt like frozen steel gripped my shoulders, and squeezed urgently. "You must go talk to her. She is outside of..." he glanced up at the skies of flame, "His purview. She can give you some of the answers you seek."

I locked eyes with him, studying the flickering purple flames behind the haunting skeletal mask. The bone was aged ivory, with scratches, claw marks, cracks, and what looked suspiciously like a bullet impact. But they were just cosmetic damage. Whatever weapons had hit that bone had no doubt shattered on impact, leaving only small scrapes in its wake. Which was a bit alarming. Who had attacked him? And what had happened to *them*? And if Armageddon hadn't started yet, how had he been attacked? And what was the bone made out of? I had heard once that a Maker had made the masks for the Horsemen.

I shook off the bone claw, and made as if to leave. "You must be careful with your choices, Brother. You have many before you. You're full to the brim with them." I turned to see Famine staring at me through his scarecrow-like mask.

I burst out laughing. "That's rich. Famine, telling me I'm *full*. Jesus…" I muttered, shaking my head.

He nodded at the irony, lifting his hands in a defeated gesture. "You have eliminated one path to destruction. Freeing your Beast." My Maker's power, I thought to myself, hand checking my hip for the cane. It was still there, although the connection was gone. The Horseman saw this, but didn't comment. "But many more choices lie before you. Or behind you, considering."

I frowned at him. "What are you babbling about?"

Famine shook his head one time, staring at me meaningfully. "Talk to the girl." Before I could question him, he turned away, speaking over his ratty-robed shoulder. "Tell her I said, *hello*."

I laughed again, great big belly laughs. It was just too much. I wiped my eyes with a sigh after a few seconds. "I'm not too good at talking to women, apparently. I can't even keep one around for longer than a few months. I'm worthless. Just a helpless man, fumbling around."

"And a butterfly in Los Angeles sets off an earthquake in Tokyo. A ripple in a pond can still reach the shore," he said, still walking away.

I grinned at his back. "Goodkind said something kind of like that once."

Famine paused, then shared a pointed look with his Brothers before turning back to me. He approached slowly until he stood only inches away, leaning close, practically having to fold himself in half to do so. "Is he a Scribe of God?"

I shook my head, trying not to flinch under the intensity of his mask. "No. Never mind."

Famine straightened back up, cocking his head at me. "Just be wary of your powers. I smell Elder on you."

"Wait, you can *smell* Elders? What the hell are they?" I begged, thinking of Carl.

But Famine was finished. War approached, holding out a hand to lead me to Grimm. I complied, studying his mask of living fire out of the corner of my eye. "We see things," the Horseman finally murmured.

I flinched. "You can see them?"

"Aye. We can see everything. Those white bastards are dangerous."

"Really," I replied dryly. "I know they're dangerous. I've seen them kill.

Those knives..." I shivered, remembering Boris' fate. "I have them under control."

A lava claw latched onto me, and white crackles of energy lit up at the contact, apparently preventing the fire from burning me. War frowned down at it, and then smiled, nodding in approval. "Horseman, alright." He met my eyes. "Back to the Elders. When every supernatural nation in the world – Angels, Demons, Gods, Beasts, Makers, Witches, and Wizards – teams up to take out a group of... *things*, you might want to pay attention."

We walked another few steps before I finally cracked my knuckles in frustration. "Pay attention to *what?*" I roared. "How the hell am I supposed to know these things? There's no record of half the creatures I'm warned about. I just find myself in the middle of it all."

I sensed him smiling. "No, you *put* yourself in the middle of it all." He turned his fiery face my way, and I felt the heat, a soothing glow. But I was entirely sure I should have felt second-degree burns. Yet more proof that something was happening to me. Something I couldn't explain, but that many other people seemed to intimately know. "I truly can't decide whether you are the unluckiest son of a bitch God ever created, or..." he trailed off, staring up at the sky.

"Or *what?*"

"Or if someone else made you for another purpose. A catalyst."

I watched as he departed my side to approach his own mount, a fiery steed not unlike Gruff – Death's horse. I didn't know all the horses' names, but I knew Gruff. War's horse was a true nightmare of a creature with literal armor covering his frame. Horns, spikes, and even blades seemed to be braided into his thick, shaggy fur, like dreadlocks. He shook his head under War's touch, and sparks cascaded from his mane like dandruff. I turned to my mount, Grimm, the unicorn. Although deadly, and carnivorous, he was rather lacking when compared to his fellow beasts. Here I was, a drafted Horseman, and...

I rode a freaking unicorn.

Might as well get some rainbow-colored robes and a bedazzled mask.

"If I'm to be a Horseman, who do I talk to about upgrades?" I asked, pointing at Grimm. The unicorn stomped a hoof disapprovingly.

Pestilence spoke from behind me, and I suddenly *felt* the presence of decay. I didn't dare look inside his hood if his mere presence gave me such unease, apparent immunity to the Horsemen's powers or not. "You *earn* them."

And he, too, walked past me to mount up. Onto a bedraggled, decaying horse. I could see the veins beneath the skin pulsing with faint light, and I shivered. Rheumy eyes glanced at me, milky white, and the horse peeled back a rotten lip to show me a palate of black, rotted teeth.

I didn't dare study the other horses. "You guys suck. Just for the record." I turned to Grimm. "Please take me away from this place. This vision." He dipped his horn, like a begrudging nod. I climbed atop his back, and he reared up on his hind legs, roaring into the night.

A sound that a horse should not be allowed to make.

Then we were galloping, the Horsemen at my side, and the world warped to a realm of shadows. The only light came from two sources. The sparks erupting from each strike of hoof on unseen floor, but even those sparks of green, white, blue, red, and purple faded almost immediately. The other source of light were the four sets of eyes, flickering beneath the hoods in identical flames as their horse's hooves.

"We bring the terror," they murmured in unison, and I shivered.

Because I had said something very similar when fighting Gunnar in the alley a few days ago.

CHAPTER 64

I sat in my office at Chateau Falco, Othello sitting across from me and petting Sir Muffle Paws in her lap. I frowned at the cat. Othello had told me that while she had been trying to bring me back to life, she had felt as if the cat had been communicating with her. Her staring at the looking-glass at me on Mt. Kailash… had really been her staring at the damned cat. It watched me now with intelligent, calculating eyes. I looked away first, and it began to clean its belly in triumph.

The silver eagle-headed cane handle rested on a nearby coffee table, and although it felt odd not to carry on my hip anymore, it also felt like a big weight had been lifted from my shoulders.

The cane – the Beast inside – had yet to speak to me again. Resting. Healing. I looked away, happy that he at least had a chance at freedom now.

Tory sat in a nearby chair, watching in silence, her eyes glazed over in deep thought, almost appearing to nap. She had told me about the Reds tricking Raego – how Sonya had called the FBI to tell them that Raego was harboring a fugitive at his home. Indie.

Jeffries had shown up with the cavalry, and Sonya had escaped in the chaos. To join the fight at the circus. Raego had called the Huntress, telling her the news. Which was why I had seen her talking on the phone at the circus before we had entered the pit. She hadn't found Ichabod. She had been trying to warn me about Sonya.

Luckily…

"I'm glad everyone made it out alive." I shot a look at Tory. "And that you were able to save so many."

Tory nodded. Slightly. She was still deeply shaken from seeing Misha. From mentally deciding to *fight* Misha. Even though it hadn't been Misha, but Indie – the Sister Grimm – using her powers to shapeshift into the dragon from memory. Wilhelm had been able to do that. Shapeshift into people. Right before I had killed him.

Even though I knew Indie had used Misha's appearance as a disguise to sneak into the circus, it still felt like a betrayal. Misha had been my friend. Our friend. Our ally. And she had saved us numerous times in the past, before ultimately laying down her life in the Grimm War.

But her lover had seen her again. Had chosen to fight her. And had to watch her hurt by the Huntress. That topic hadn't been broached yet. The Huntress had kept her distance.

Othello broke the uncomfortable silence. "The other thing is complete, too. Tomas had some very… interesting news to share."

I nodded absently, waving a dismissive hand. "Any word on Indie?" I asked softly.

She shook her head, shooting a sharp look at Tory's motionless body, a pained look dancing in her eyes before she rounded on me with a disapproving glare for bringing the memory of Misha up, even in an indirect way. "I don't think anyone needs to be worrying about *Indie*," she said climbing to her feet and approaching me. She finally walked up behind me, and placed her hands on my shoulders, giving me a light, gentle, friendly massage, as if trying to help me relieve the weight dragging me down, down, down.

I reached up and placed my hand on hers. "Thanks, Othello."

She continued massaging my shoulders, and I let my eyes close, breathing deeply. "You ready to meet Ganesh again? I can't imagine he's going to be pleased that you left his belt with the Fae," she said softly from behind me. I had told them everything now that it was all done. How I had given up my power. That I was a wizard again. They seemed relieved.

I smiled tiredly at her question. Ganesh. "No, I imagine not." I just couldn't find the energy to care. I had tried my goddamned hardest to appease everyone. Sometimes it just couldn't all work out. And I still had Baba Yaga to worry about, too. I had promised to heal her Familiar – her house. Without Ganesh's belt, I had no idea how to make good on that promise.

But first, I had to survive Ganesh's wrath. I had lost his belt. Or given it up to save my hide.

At least Asterion would be there with Ganesh, and he was a stickler for non-violence, now that he was Buddhist. And it would be right outside my home, at the tree dominating the grounds. I glanced through the window over my shoulder, and spotted about a dozen white figures strolling the grounds, openly now, no longer concerned with stealth. To me they now looked stronger, more real. More... vital.

Othello shivered, following my gaze, able to see them through the glass now. "I still can't believe you aren't insane, and that there really are semi-invisible people outside."

We didn't talk about her working behind my back. I had forgiven her. She'd had the best intentions.

I chuckled at her comment, nodding as she pressed harder into a partic-ular knot, causing my laugh to shift into a groan of pleasure as my eyes closed. I deserved to smile at least one last time before Ganesh and Baba Yaga fought over who was going to kill me. I had lost Indie on an epic scale, and still didn't understand how. Or why. So, yeah, I was going to sit my happy ass down and enjoy a friend comforting me for a few minutes.

"Am I interrupting something?" an icy voice hissed from the doorway.

I opened my eyes to see Tory jump to her feet, spinning with a fire poker in her fist. Murder shone in her flickering green eyes.

Indie stood in the doorway, face utterly emotionless. "I see your old... *friend* is already cleaning up the table scraps." Her eyes rested on Othello's hands on my shoulders.

Othello tried to jerk her hands away, but I gripped them tighter. "This isn't what you think."

And Indie flipped her shit, pointing a finger at Tory. "Don't try that again, Beast Master. Your little tricks no longer work on me."

And Tory grunted, the fires winking out of her eyes as Indie's irises shifted to a smoky black.

"What is *wrong* with you, you freaking psycho?" Othello shouted.

"Don't *ever* use that tone with me again, *child*," Indie warned, taking an aggressive step forward, smoky eyes locked on the Regular. She took a breath, and shifted her glare to me. "Perhaps my decision to leave with

Ichabod was right. I had misgivings upon healing my wounds. But now…
You look pretty content with the Regular."

"I was rubbing his goddamned shoulders, you stupid bitch!" Othello's
tone was venom, disgust practically spraying out like a physical substance.
"Not that it's any of your business now, anyway. You made your choic—"

And Indie flung up a hand.

A pencil thin bar of the purest white light I had ever seen struck Othello
in the forehead, barely missing my own. The heat sizzled like a hot poker,
and I was afraid my hair was about to catch fire. Maybe the cuffs on my
wrist had just saved my life.

Othello flew back into the window with a groan. The bar of light
winked out, and Indie looked momentarily sickened at what she had
instinctively done. Purple flecks hung in my vision where the light had
been, and the house growled a warning at the intruder. Because even
though I had lost my Maker's power, the house and I had formed an
unbreakable union. We were still married. Indie's startled eyes darted up to
the house, wary, but I didn't care about that at the moment. I spun,
surprised I hadn't heard Othello crash through the window or explode into
a pile of dust behind me.

She stood behind me, eyes wide as she shook her head.

No more impeded than if someone had thrown a Nerf ball at her. I
stared in disbelief. She nodded back at me, slightly dazed for a moment
before her face morphed into fury at the Grimm.

I didn't understand how the hell she had survived Indie's death ray, but
if she could walk that off, perhaps she had a few other tricks. More *offensive*
tricks that would reduce my home to rubble and kill two women I loved.
Tory stared at the two women, eyes wide.

I rounded on Indie, jumping to my feet. "What the fuck is *wrong* with
you?" And I hammered her with everything I had, feeding my grief, and
slamming her through the open doorway to crash through the bannister
and down onto the first floor through twenty feet of empty air. Well, except
for the chandelier she crashed into. And the second chandelier. She disappeared from sight amidst an explosion of glass shards and splintered wood.
I stood frozen for a moment, panting. Then I was racing towards the
destruction in sudden fear.

What had I just done?

I reached the bannister, Tory and Othello hot on my heels. The

Guardians were screeching in alarm, stone feathers ruffled in confusion. After all, Indie had been a friendly. The house was practically quivering now, groaning and creaking like a hurricane was right outside the walls.

The floor held a liberal pool of blood amidst the broken crystal and metal chandeliers, but other than a long smear of blood, and a few crimson footsteps, the floor below was empty. I stared for a good long time, and the house calmed, no longer groaning.

She was gone.

Off the property.

Othello gripped me by the shoulders, turning me to face her. Tory and Othello wore terrified expressions. I stared back, my heart a dried husk inside my chest. I frowned at her as a thought broke through the surface of my inner struggle. "How are you alive right now?"

Othello's hand went to her chest, clutching something beneath her shirt. Tory was frowning at her hand. "I…" she took a step back. "Hemingway gave me something to keep me safe," she whispered. "It's mine," she warned, face hard.

I slowly held up my hands, remembering the satin box I had seen Death give her at Friendsgiving. Sneaky Horseman. "Easy, Othello. I'm not going to take anything from you."

"Maybe you should inform your face of that."

I blinked. Then nodded slowly. "Okay. I just… wanted to make sure you were okay. Sorry if I alarmed you." She gave me a clipped nod. "That's a hell of a gift." My sluggish mind began to work in fitful jerks. "You shouldn't tell anyone else about it. Let them underestimate you."

A small grin cracked her cheeks, breaking through the previous anxiety. "I seem to recall someone else teaching me that lesson." Her eyes grew distant. "Long ago. But then he became an asshole." She glanced past me at the carnage. "Who beat up his ex-girlfriend." Then she grinned. "To protect his other ex-girlfriend. But I heard that the bitch deserved it." Then she turned around, walking back into the office. "We need to talk about Grimmtech…"

"I don't really care to talk about that right now. If ever. Call…" my mind wandered for a minute, thinking. "Ashley. Call Ashley. I've got other things to worry about." Like my death.

She turned to stare at me in disbelief. "Do you have any idea how hard I worked to get it for you?" she whispered. I nodded. "And, what, you're just going to hand it off to Ashley? I bent so many laws trying to hide this transaction that even a lawyer wouldn't follow my trail. Because you *asked* me to!"

I still hadn't moved, noticing Tory watching me thoughtfully. "I have... other things on my mind at the moment. I think I need to go take a walk..."

The look of hurt on her face almost crippled me. "What?" she whispered.

I dropped my head to stare at my shoes. Then, before she could argue, I turned to walk away, leaving the mess behind me, and ignoring Othello's arguments echoing on the walls of an empty office.

Dean rounded the corner, and I shoved a thumb over my shoulder. "I made a mess back there. You should clean it up. The house gets persnickety about messes now."

And I walked past him, ignoring his concerned look.

I realized that Tory was a pace behind me, following silently as I finally approached the front door. "You should leave me alone right now, Tory. I'm not... myself."

She chuckled darkly. "And I am? I'm a train wreck. Where's the next stop on this crazy journey?"

I smiled to myself, nodded, and placed my hand on the front door.

Someone knocked on the other end, and Tory forcefully shoved me out of the way with her super strength. I crashed into the cabinet of curiosities, shattering the glass as Tory tore the door from the hinges, growling menacingly, and eyes on fire.

CHAPTER 65

I lay in the rubble of the priceless artifacts with a clear view of the now open doorway. Rufus stood there, eyes startled at the sudden explosion of wood and hinges.

"Christ!" and his eyes instantly darted to the small tween at his hip before shoving her clear of the vengeful Beast Master standing between us. He took another step back, ushering Camilla behind him further as his eyes darted to me with a desperate look.

"Tory, it's fine. Give him some breathing room."

Tory turned to me, eyes still glowing, and then slowly nodded before turning back to the pair outside. "Sorry. Instinct."

"Rufus, Camilla, welcome to Chateau Falco. As my *guests*," I said, watching Tory.

Tory turned to me, nodded apologetically, and finally stepped out of the way.

"Mom?" two voices called out in unison from the hall behind me. "What was—"

I arched my neck, and felt several small pieces of glass fall from my hair as I turned to look behind me. The Reds stared at me, faces tight. I casually waved back. Sonya and Aria took one look at me, turned to each other, and then cautiously walked past me. They didn't wave back, simply acted as

336

forcefully calm as if they had encountered a rabid dog on the streets and simply wanted to be past it.

The girls froze as Rufus and Camilla nervously entered the Chateau. The house rumbled slightly, an ominous purr, and Rufus and Camilla tensed. Then the Reds stepped forward, and each took one of Camilla's hands. The tween shot a look at Rufus, who shot a look at me.

I shrugged. "I just work here. Them's the real bosses. Ever tried to tell a teenager what to do? Or a redhead? Or *two of them*? They know *all*," I stated, soberly. I remembered something my mom had once told me. *Raising a teenager is like nailing Jell-O to a tree.* I smiled to myself.

Sonya piped up. "It's true. Just like I knew that the dragon wasn't really our…" her voice trailed off, suddenly remembering Tory was right there. Tory's eyes were pained, but she nodded, as if telling Sonya that she was okay.

Aria backed her up. "It's all in the scent," she added softly.

After a moment of silence, the three young girls giggled as if at an inside joke, and then left to explore the house.

I climbed to my feet and led Rufus and Tory into the living room where I had first met the wizard. "So, how are things?" I asked him sarcastically.

He shot me a dazzling smile. "You're the best kind of crazy."

"I guess so. Camilla's alright then?"

He frowned for a moment, peering off at nothing as if able to see through the walls to his daughter. "I think so. She has nightmares. Those monsters hurt her. I don't know if she will ever be the same. But I don't know how to help her." He cast his eyes down into his lap, sighing. Then he chuckled darkly. "At least I can help carry some of her burden now," he said, rubbing a hand over the claw mark on his face, where a shifter had attacked him during his rescue attempt.

I blinked. "What flavor?" I asked curiously.

Tory answered, suddenly smiling. "Chimera," she murmured approvingly.

Rufus nodded. "Aye. It will take some getting used to, and I'll likely be *her* student in that regard. At least for a time. Not sure what that's going to do with my magic, but we'll find that out as we go, I guess."

"Perhaps I can help both of you," Tory offered.

We both turned to her, curious.

"I've been feeling the same way about the others we rescued. They need… rehabilitation. And, after all, I *am* a Beast Master. I'm already training two red dragons. And I feel slightly responsible for the others. I could help you two. Or at least try. I'm friends with a lot of monsters. Thanks to him." She pointed a thumb at me, smiling.

"Tory," I began, "that's a big responsibility. There are over two dozen of them."

"Enough for a classroom," she argued.

"Okay, Professor X. Where are you going to train them?"

She smiled darkly. "I was meaning to talk to you about the old Temple Industries property. The one scheduled for demolition."

I felt a smile begin to creep onto my face. "Interesting…"

A sudden tingle raced down my arms. A warning from the house. I instantly feared for the children, but as if sensing my alarm, the sensation faded, and I felt a flare of power, a beacon, coming from outside. Sudden realization dawned on me. I looked up to see Rufus and Tory staring at me. "You okay, Nate?"

I nodded, climbing to my feet, and replying over my shoulder as I headed back towards the now door-less front entrance. "Discuss this proposition. I need to see an elephant about a belt."

I left the room and saw Dean clutching a broom in one hand, staring at the crushed cabinet and the door lying a dozen paces away on the marble floor of the foyer.

I sighed. "Yeah. I didn't do this one. Need some Pledge or something?"

Dean scowled for a moment, and then in an impeccable accent, said, "*I clean…*"

It was exactly like the Hispanic cleaning lady from Family Guy. His eyes twinkled with a faint, grateful smile to see me somewhat back to normal. I bowed formally to him and left.

Time to go meet a god and a monster.

CHAPTER 66

I glared at the uninvited third party leaning lazily against the tree.

"Your Brothers are all assholes, but *you*…" I began, scowling at the Pale Rider. He merely nodded. "Nice gift. Would have been even nicer if you had told me about it beforehand so I didn't have a heart attack when my ex-girlfriend tried to kill my other ex-girlfriend."

Death dipped his head, grinning like a shark. "No fun in that."

I scowled one more time for good measure, and then appraised the two giants sitting on the ground before the tree, away from Death.

They were having a duel. Or napping.

I shot a look back at Death, who merely shrugged, and then suddenly whipped out his scythe. The air screamed with the sound of a million lost souls crying out in agony before he settled the butt of the weapon in the earth. Then he began to sharpen the blade with practiced motions. The glowing runes seemed to absorb energy from the tree. He noticed it at the same time as me, and hastily re-holstered the weapon behind his back so that the crescent blade hung over a shoulder like a single-winged Angel. Then the blade faded from view so that only an ornate handle – much like my sword cane used to do – rested on one shoulder. He grimaced at my interest, and folded his arms.

Interesting. Our blades were similar. But I was getting a little annoyed at the amount of similarities between myself and the other Horsemen.

I turned back to Ganesh and Asterion. The elephant and the bull.

They knelt in traditional meditation poses.

Ganesh sat much like every statue of him you've probably seen, this time with no shirt or robe. Three of his hands were empty. The last held the jagged end of his broken tusk.

Asterion sat opposite him, a good six feet away. Eyes closed, nose ring faintly swinging back and forth with each bellow of breath. His prayer beads hung free, and I noticed runes dotting each bead, but couldn't get close enough to depict them without startling him.

An intricately knotted silk scarf sat between the two.

I waited a minute. Then two. Then another, before letting out an impatient sigh.

"I guess I'll just come back later."

"No patience in kids these days," Ganesh grumbled, cracking an eye open. "You think after everything that happened, you would be less impatient for your own death." Asterion chuckled, opening his eyes also.

I shrugged. "I guess I don't feel like spending my last moments standing out here, freezing my ass off, while you two meditate on a knotted scarf."

"Knotted scarf?" Ganesh asked, sounding amused.

Asterion abruptly snorted in frustration, "Dirty cheater."

I glanced down to see that the scarf was now perfectly untied, not even wrinkled where a few moments before, it had been knotted. In fact, it faintly steamed as if just pressed at a dry-cleaners. And it was folded in a perfect little square.

I stared in disbelief at the fact that neither of them had moved to untie the scarf. Yet I had clearly seen it knotted, and then unknotted. And I had sensed no magic to untie it.

Asterion noticed my look and grinned. "A meditation practice. You try to mentally untie the knot, focusing on it so intently that it happens in the real world." He leaned closer, whispering. "Without magic."

I frowned. "That sounds... astoundingly useless."

Ganesh arched a brow at me.

And then I was suddenly naked. Magically nude. Except... *not* magically. I hadn't sensed a thing. My hands shot to cover my crotch, and Death burst out laughing. "Hey!" I shouted, skin instantly pebbling as my danger-zone threatened to mutiny and climb up inside my body. "What the hell?"

"Astoundingly *useless*, you say?" the giant elephant grinned at me. "Meditation is not to be trifled with, boy." He studied my face thoughtfully. "Yet another feather to add to your cap one day, possibly," he murmured, cryptically. And my clothes were suddenly back. I jumped up and down a bit, trying to regain some warmth as I shoved my hands in my pockets.

"Okay. It was kind of cool." I stared at the scarf, thinking. "But a knot? Seems like with all your practice, a single knot might be cheating."

Asterion smiled. "Tell him."

Ganesh held out two hands at the neatly-folded scarf, his two other hands resting peacefully on his knees. "That knot was folded 77 times. That was the first part of our duel. Which of us could add the last knot." He pointed a thick sausage finger at Asterion. "The Minotaur won that one. Apparently, the Greeks are good with knots."

I smiled. "I prefer Alexander's method."

Asterion rolled his eyes, but Ganesh frowned, drawing a blank.

I flung my hand down, and slashed the scarf in half with a blade of air.

"Alexander's solution to the Gordian Knot," Asterion grumbled.

I nodded. The scarf had split into two pieces, each with a single word written on the silk.

Asterion leaned closer to read it. "Team. Temple." He frowned up at me.

Ganesh was smiling and I scowled at his subtle use of power to write the words there. "Perhaps that is more symbolic than you intended…"

I stared at the words. *Team. Temple.* And a frayed gap between the two, breaking them up. Breaking up the dynamic. The single unit it had once been.

Team Temple was indeed fractured. Indie, for one. But at least the others seemed to be coming around. After hearing my iteration of events behind the scenes.

I grunted unpleasantly. "It's just a stupid scarf."

"Much like my property is just a stupid belt…"

And my heart did a little two-step at the warning in his tone.

"Nice knowing you, Temple," Asterion had stood, and was patting me on the back, inadvertently shoving me closer to the angry elephant god. Then Asterion was gone, speaking in soft murmurs to Death. The two glanced about thoughtfully, and then Death pointed at Carl standing a dozen paces away. Asterion flexed his fists and nodded. They both cast me a look of deep concern, and then huddled closer to speak in light whispers.

"My father warned you not to feed them," Ganesh murmured.

I turned back to him with a start. "Yeah…" I fumbled for words. "I only fed them a little. And not on purpose." Ganesh merely watched me. I sighed. "Well, long story short. I lost your belt."

And I prepared to be skewered by his single remaining tusk. And then, perhaps, eaten like a hot tofu dog.

CHAPTER 67

Ganesh studied the air around us, and then motioned for me to sit.

"I'd rather die on my feet."

He looked at me. And I was suddenly sitting before him.

Wow. I patted my chest to make sure I still had my clothes, which brought out a faint chuckle from his great big bare belly. The quivering red elephant skin had a pair of words branded into it.

Om Life.

Exactly where Tupac had tattooed *Thug Life.*

I burst out laughing, pointing at his belly. "Copying Tupac? *Really?*"

Ganesh shrugged with a smile. "Perhaps *he* got it from *me…*"

I let out a breath, still smiling. It didn't really matter, given the circumstances. "So, how are you going to kill me?" my gaze wandered, taking in the sights, sounds, smells.

Life.

He didn't speak, so I decided to fill the silence. "I'd like you to know that your belt saved the Winter Queen. I was trying to do the right thing. Everything just…" I fumbled for words, "went sideways," I finally said.

He studied me patiently. "Oh? And why did the Winter Queen need saving?"

I sighed. "Yeah, okay. Even that was my fault, I guess." I looked up at him.

"I've been calling you Ganesh, but your Dad called you Ganesha. I didn't mean any offense."

He nodded absently, not looking at me. "He says *hello*. That you were particularly pleasant company." I nodded as his eyes continued to roam the grounds. "Seen any ravens lately?" he asked, staring up at the silver canopy above us, catching me off guard at the abrupt change in topic.

I frowned at him, beginning to shake my head, then stopped. "Yeah, now that you mention it… But it was a long time ago. During the Grimm War."

He frowned at me. "Grimoire?"

"No. Grimm. War." I paused between each word, enunciating the separation.

"Ah, that." He pondered my words, staring back up at the tree. "Not since then?"

"I'm not saying they haven't been there, but I haven't seen them." Then I remembered something that hadn't seemed important at the time. "Well, I heard ravens the other day. When I… well, when I was meditating." When I had been Making the Prison for my Beast.

His face hardened. "I… see."

"Why? Was Odin paying me a visit?" I teased. His sharp look shut up the laughter I had been about to expel. Instantly.

"Do. Not. Speak. That. Name." He was leaning forward now, all four palms pressing into the frosted earth. And it steamed beneath those red leathery palms.

"Okay," I whispered meekly, staring up at the silver branches, suddenly concerned.

And a fucking raven tore free from the branches, speeding off into the distance. I lowered my wide eyes to Ganesh, and he shot me a single nod. "Take heed," was all he said.

"Take heed of wh—"

"Mab returned my belt," he interrupted casually.

I flinched, glancing down at his waist. It wasn't there. "Wait, *what?*" I threw up my hands, wanting to break down and cry in both relief, and frustration. "Maybe lead with that rather than letting me contemplate my death for the last few days!"

He cocked his head at me, frowning, as he tapped his jagged broken tusk with one finger. "I often meditate on my death. *Memento Mori.*" He smiled. "Well, maybe not, *remember you are mortal*, because, well," he held out all four hands, encompassing his entire self. *"Hello, not mortal."* He winked. "But it is good for one's health to consider one's death. Often, and with great attention. You never know what you may learn…"

"Maybe you can give me the fortune cookie version here. Asterion's already offered to teach me meditation. Not really my thing," I lied, preferring not to speak of my own vigilant form of meditation. The one I used for my Memory Palace. To organize the almost eidetic memory that threatened to overwhelm me with useless information.

"Yes, this is quite different from your Memory Palace. That is child's play."

I rolled my eyes, forgetting that he could read my mind.

"Did you honestly think you won the race?" he asked casually, eyes distant. "I'm curious."

I frowned. "You mean when we first met?" He nodded, still observing the grounds, almost as if he wasn't paying attention. "Yeah, I tricked you. Brought Tory along to mess with your ride."

He was nodding thoughtfully as he turned back to me. "I knew of your Beast Master, Temple. Even if you did not entirely understand her powers." He leaned forward, grinning at my frown. "I'm good at winning races, boy. I can see that you read *that* story about me, at least."

I sighed. "You immortals are no fun," I grumbled, causing him to chuckle lightly. "Speaking of stories, what's the deal with your tusk?" I pointed at the broken tusk in his hand.

He frowned down at it. Another hand absently rubbed the jagged tusk near his mouth. "Ah, that."

I nodded. "I heard you were once challenged to copy a story, but that if your pen stopped, you lost." He nodded absently. "But your pen broke, so you broke off your tusk, using it to continue, and ultimately win the bet."

"Seems you have the gist of it," he murmured.

But I shook my head. "I don't want the *gist* of it. I want the truth." He turned to assess me with hard eyes. "You didn't even hesitate. If you would have, you would have lost the bet. Which means you must have known it would happen beforehand." He finally nodded. "But why? It was just a stupid bet…"

He was silent for a long time. "I don't like to lose."

I rolled my eyes, leaning forward. "The truth. You've played me long enough, elephant man. I'll at least have that out of you."

He smiled at that, was silent for another spell, and then studied my face very intently, as if encouraging me to read between the lines of a language I did not speak. "Someday, I hope you realize that there is no such thing as a stupid bet…"

"Go on…" I pressed.

He sighed in resignation. "Perhaps there was more at stake than the story tells. Or that the story led to future decisions that wouldn't have been possible if I had lost the *stupid bet*…" His eyes were deep and foreboding for a few seconds, as if seeing things that weren't there. Then he glanced past my shoulder. He looked up at the sun, and then nodded to himself.

"Ah, right on time," he said, staring past my shoulder again and waving.

I hadn't noticed the sensation from the house, but now that I focused on it, I sensed it was practically shouting a warning at its stupid, ignorant, apparently deaf, Master.

CHAPTER 68

$\mathcal{B}$aba Yaga stalked up to us, and I almost jumped out of my skin in alarm. Ganesha didn't have the belt on, and Baba was going to kill me. I began filling myself with magic so that I could survive the Russian Witch and her hulking Familiar.

The stench of decay and slaughterhouses wafted closer, seeming worse than before. Perhaps because the Familiar was actually dying again. The two figures stumbled wearily, both in obvious pain, and both looking ready for a fight as they stared at me, practically bursting with magic.

Wizard's magic. Not Maker's magic. And I could see they sensed this difference.

Ganesh waved a hand, and the stench evaporated. "I hate that smell," he said. I blinked at him. I hadn't felt any motion of air to push it away, so had he simply made it not be? He noticed me full of magic and frowning at him. He held up two hands. "Easy, boy. I summoned her here."

And a tense feeling crept up my spine. "Wait, actually *summoned*, or do you mean you simply arranged for her to be here?"

Ganesh frowned. "Why would I do anything *but* summon her here. I am Ganesh. She is a witch. I do have my dignity, you know."

He turned back to Baba, and her pain suddenly made more sense. Not only were the two injured, but they had also been summoned here against their will.

347

"Wait, when you summon someone, it's practically instantaneous. We've been sitting here talking the whole time..."

"You've been talking with *one* of me. I used another part of me to summon her. It grows quite boring to focus all of my personas on a single topic for longer than a few heartbeats," he replied flatly. "I'm sure my father shared some of this with you." Then he turned back to Baba, who was now only paces away, eyes on fire.

I dropped it, idly replaying my conversation with Shiva, wondering what the hell he was talking about.

I was entirely confident that Baba wouldn't want to hear the specific details of how she had been summoned against her will – to meet the man responsible for her already fatal injuries.

Ganesh nodded politely at them, then his eyes locked onto the Familiar. "Come,"

And the Familiar hulked closer on chicken feet, claws stubbornly, but resolutely dragging through the frost, as if knowing this was its only chance for salvation.

Ganesh touched the Familiar, and its face shot upwards as if receiving an uppercut from an elephant. It gasped, clawed hands stretching wide, and the purple cracks of power began to fade from its bone mask, fading to nothing in mere heartbeats. Baba gasped in response, clutching her abdomen, her tear-stained face staring hopefully at the Familiar, despite her own very intense pain. But I didn't see his belt anywhere. Perhaps he didn't have to wear it. Or he could transform it into one of his earrings or something.

Within moments, the healing was done, and both figures stood panting, their breath making tiny clouds of fog in the cool air.

Baba finally lowered her head, and thanked Ganesh between sobs.

She shot me one harsh glare through tear-filled eyes, gritting her iron teeth. Then she froze, cocked her head, and glanced at Chateau Falco behind me, sniffing the air. Then she smiled a grim smile, meeting my eyes. "About time you made peace with your Beast, boy. It's been a long time since there was a true Master of the Temple Clan." And then she turned away without another word. She held hands with her Familiar, and they disappeared in a puff of smoke.

I turned to Ganesh, frowning at her words. Temple Clan? I hadn't thought about my house being similar to her Familiar. On further thought, I didn't think I wanted a mansion following me around as a shadow. Inconvenient. I shook my head, saving it for later consideration as I addressed Ganesh. "Why would you help me?" I thought about that. "Help *her*?"

He shrugged. "What are we without our homes?" he asked, glancing pointedly at Chateau Falco behind us. He let out another breath as Asterion and Death approached, listening politely. "I am the overcomer of obstacles, boy. Thought you would remember that..."

Then all three vanished, leaving me alone at the base of the tree.

I sighed, thinking about the crazy adventure behind me, and those hinted at to come. I quickly dropped that line of thought, already too depressed to consider more dangers coming in the years (hopefully) ahead.

I was single, having unwittingly destroyed the relationship with the woman I loved.

But I had saved a kid that no one else had been willing to save.

My last family member had betrayed me.

But I had saved my friends. And made new ones. Ganesh, Rufus, maybe even Shiva.

I had poked a stick in the eye of some pretty big enemies: the Fae, and the elusive Syndicate.

And then I thought about Baba and her Familiar. But I had *healed* some past enemies too.

I had made some new friends, both physical, and metaphysical. I glanced up at Chateau Falco, thoughtfully.

I took a calming breath, slowly nodding as I turned to the tree. To find Carl standing a foot away from me, sharpening a milky blade in his fist. My heart practically exploded in my chest.

"Fucking Carl! You trying to scare me to death?" I roared, panting.

He kept right on sharpening his blade for a few moments. "Now, what did the red one say about Ravens?" and he winked darkly at me.

I felt myself smile...

I hadn't lost everything. Sometimes you needed to take what you can get.

"Carl, I think I'm going to go play with my new toys."

"Yes, Master. Which new toys are you referring to?"

"Grimmtech..." I glanced at his blade. "Perhaps you have some ideas on weaponry."

A smile even darker than the first split his face. "Oh, yes. I have *many* ideas..."

We turned to head back to the house, and I saw that Othello was standing in the driveway, staring at me.

I blinked at the stunned look on her face. "What's wrong?"

She just stared at me for a few more moments. "Do you have your cane on you?"

I frowned, and glanced down at my hip. I remembered setting it down on the table. Before...

I looked up sharply. Whatever she saw in my face made her shoulders sag in despair. Then she spoke, but I already knew. "She took the cane. She didn't come back to make *peace*. She came here to distract us. Get us out of the office. So she could take your cane..."

I couldn't think of an expletive foul enough to express my emotions, so I just stared back.

Indie had stolen my cane. My Beast. Likely to give to Ichabod...

But to what end?

Ichabod, the last Maker on earth, prime candidate for some god to recruit for the upcoming war that I knew nothing about, had not only *one* Beast.

Now he had *two*...

～

～

350

*Nate Temple returns in **TINY GODS**. Turn the page for an excerpt! Or **get the book ONLINE!***

TEASER: TINY GODS (NATE TEMPLE #6)

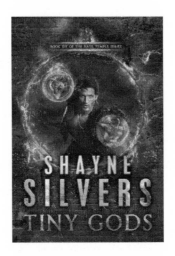

*B*ullets shattered the back windshield of the Tahoe, but I had already been ducking down in the front passenger seat.

"What part of *lose them* was unclear to you? And you're *still* going the wrong way," I shouted, peeking over the back of my headrest. "You girls okay?" I asked, loud enough for the Reds to hear me over the sudden street noise and roar of our engine, let alone the van chasing us. They nodded, slowly climbing back into their seats from the floor.

"I *know* I'm going the wrong way, but I had to go the wrong way to lose the first two vans!" Alucard snapped, tires squealing as he jerked the wheel to avoid another barrage of pistol fire. "You didn't have to break his damned arm! We could have just agreed to disagree."

"They surrounded me! All while you stood there doing a whole lot of *nothing*!" I argued.

"It's what weregorillas do when threatened! And you told me you needed a *driver*, not a *thug*!" he shouted right back, turning down a side street to get us going in the right direction.

Bullets sprayed the buildings beside us, their shots going wide as we changed course. "In my world, they're the same thing!" I snapped. "Just drive. Lose them. We'll sort this out after we escape the angry monkeys," I growled.

He just shook his head angrily, glancing in the rearview constantly, trying to predict their shots and keep us bullet-free. I turned around, watching the van chasing us. It seemed to be getting closer, and I could see a man leaning out the car window. "Tory is going to be so pissed. We're going to be late," Alucard whined.

"No, we're— Ah!" the man had pulled out a shotgun, aiming it our way. "Get down!" I shouted at the teenaged weredragons in the backseat, and let off a few shots from the pistol in my fist, trying to deter the van. The man ducked back inside instantly. One of my shots went wild, but one struck the front wheel, blowing their tire – just like in the movies.

The chasing van lost control and swerved right into the only parked car on the deserted street. I grunted satisfactorily, trying to both hide my astonishment, and maintain my devil-may-care reputation in front of the Reds. "Okay, you can get up now, but be ready to duck again." I changed my voice to the Count from *Sesame Street*. "Because like Sparkula said, there are *one, two, three vans of gorillas chasing us! Muah, ha, ha, ha.*" They just stared at me, probably not getting the reference.

Kids.

"I do *not* sound like that," Alucard snarled. "And don't call me Sparkula!"

I chuckled, searching the floorboards now that we had a moment of respite. "We're not going to be late to the Gala. I have a—" I cut off, staring at the floor in disbelief. "Shit," I whispered, quickly leaning over the center console to check the floorboard in the back. The Reds moved their feet, confused looks on their faces. *Nothing.*

"What are we going to do when the other two vans find us? *Hmm?*" Alucard persisted. "You know they're circling the block. This is their neighborhood. And what the hell are you looking for?" he hissed, annoyed that I seemed to be ignoring him.

"I must have left it at the office," I said, feeling like an idiot.

"What are you *talking* about?" he yelled, eyes scanning the streets as we zipped by.

"My satchel. Our way out of here."

"Your man purse?" Sonya asked. "I saw it on the table. You left it there when Greta began showing you those pamphlets."

"Religious tracts," Alucard shuddered, saying it in the same tone someone else would use to describe a platter of steaming dog feces. Because he was a vampire. Although the whole religious thing didn't seem to bother him as much anymore, he'd still been zapped one too many times by them. Because vampires and religion got along like a dog peeing on an electric fence.

"It's not a man purse," I argued, pulling out my phone to call the office. "It's a *satchel.*"

A harried voice answered the call, sounding annoyed. "Grimm Tech."

"Greta! This is Nate. Did I leave my satchel there?" I asked desperately, fear clawing at my insides. The contents of the satchel were unstable. Lethally unstable.

"Your man purse? Let me check," she responded. Alucard burst out laughing.

"You are literally the only one who calls it that. Just admit it," he said. Then he jerked the wheel hard to the right – almost making me drop the phone – and ducked into an alley. He had flipped off the lights before we even stopped. A van flew by on the street where we had just been, racing towards their stranded pals, most likely. I flashed him a smile as Greta came back on the phone.

"You left it here on the table. Yahn said he would take it to you at the Gala after his dance class in the old warehouse district. The Gala I'm trying to get ready for. The one *you* are supposed to be hosting..." her annoyance was blindingly obvious, because Greta didn't waste time on *feelings*. At least not when it came to me. "He said he called you."

"Dance class," I repeated dumbly, but my fear was slightly diminished by relief, because at least we were *in* the old warehouse district. "Okay. Thanks,

Greta. See you there," I blurted, hanging up as she began reprimanding me about something else.

Because fear still gripped me. Yahn was just *walking around* with my satchel? Did he have any idea what was inside? One wrong move and he could blow up a building! I quickly scrolled through my phone, Alucard tapping the steering wheel anxiously.

"We can't just sit here, Nate. They're bound to find us. We need a way out. Now. Or we're going to be late to the Gala," he warned. "Or dead. I would rather get dead than be late," he added. The Reds chimed in their agreement from the backseat.

I saw the missed call, and realized my phone had been on silent. I immediately dialed it back, ignoring Alucard. "Fucking wizards," he muttered as I waited for Yahn to pick up.

"He's carrying around a freaking *bomb*, man!" I snapped. Alucard's anger evaporated.

Yahn answered. "Ya, this is Yahn," he said in a thick, cheerful Swedish accent.

"It's me, Nate. Hey, did you pick up—"

"Master Temple! *Alriiight!*" he shouted happily, voice laced with enthusiasm, happiness, and unicorn farts. His accent was so strong, so flamboyant, and so overly enunciated, that it was sometimes painful to talk to him for very long. He was Greta's grandson – a foreign exchange student – and she had convinced me to hire him as an intern for my new company. "I *toe-tah-lee* have yer man purse—"

Even the Reds burst out laughing at that.

"Satchel, Yahn. *Satch*—" I cut off my argument abruptly. "Never mind. Where are you?"

"Just leaving dancing class, we are putting on this show, and like, it's going to be toe-tah-lee awesome and stuff!" he answered, excitedly.

"Address. What *address?*" I pressed.

He told me. Alucard pulled it up on the screen, face going pale. It was back the way we had come, right through gorilla territory.

Yahn began speaking into the phone again, but I interrupted him. "Yahn, listen. I need you to get my... purse, and wait outside by the curb. Be very, very careful with the bag. Don't jostle it. We will be there in," I glanced at the GPS unit, "two minutes. Be ready to jump in. Fast."

He was quiet on the other end of the line as Alucard put the car in gear, backing up quickly and turning around. "Yoo want to, like, give me a *ride* and stuff?" he repeated, almost whispering, but sounding as if he had won the lottery. "That would be *toe-tah-lee cool!*" he squealed, piercing my ear canal with Swedish cheer. "See you soon!" and he hung up.

Alucard shifted back into drive, shaking his head the entire time, but he took the first left, running parallel to the street we had originally been on, sending us straight back to monkey-town. "This better not blow up in our faces, Nate." He realized his words after the fact, and shot me a sickening look. "Figuratively or literally, I guess."

"Just drive, Glampire. And avoid the weregorillas, or I'm blaming it all on you."

The Reds clapped in the backseat, as Alucard pressed the gas pedal harder.

"Call me Glampire all you want, but just remember which one of us has a pet unicorn…" he offered casually. The Reds sniggered in the back seat as I bit back a growl…

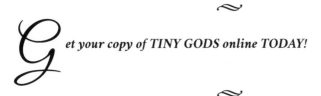

~

G *et your copy of TINY GODS online TODAY!*

~

Turn the page to read a sample of **UNCHAINED** *- Feathers and Fire Series Book 1, or* **BUY ONLINE**. *Callie Penrose is a wizard in Kansas City, MO who hunts monsters for the Vatican. She meets Nate Temple, and things devolve from there…*

(Note: Full chronology of all books in the Temple Verse shown on the 'Books in the Temple Verse' page.)

TRY: UNCHAINED (FEATHERS AND FIRE #1)

$\mathcal{T}$he rain pelted my hair, plastering loose strands of it to my forehead as I panted, eyes darting from tree to tree, terrified of each shifting branch, splash of water, and whistle of wind slipping through the nightscape around us. But… I was somewhat *excited*, too.

Somewhat.

"Easy, girl. All will be well," the big man creeping just ahead of me, murmured.

"You said we were going to get ice cream!" I hissed at him, failing to compose myself, but careful to keep my voice low and my eyes alert. "I'm not ready for this!" I had been trained to fight, with my hands, with weapons, and with my magic. But I had never taken an active role in a hunt before. I'd always been the getaway driver for my mentor.

The man grunted, grey eyes scanning the trees as he slipped through the tall grass. "And did we not get ice cream before coming here? Because I think I see some in your hair."

"You know what I mean, Roland. You tricked me." I checked the tips of my loose hair, saw nothing, and scowled at his back.

"The Lord does not give us a greater burden than we can shoulder."

I muttered dark things under my breath, wiping the water from my eyes. Again. My new shirt was going to be ruined. Silk never fared well in the rain. My choice of shoes wasn't much better. Boots, yes, but distressed, *fashionable* boots. Not work boots designed for the rain and mud. Definitely not monster hunting boots for our evening excursion through one of Kansas City's wooded parks. I realized I was forcibly distracting myself, keeping my mind busy with mundane thoughts to avoid my very real anxiety. Because whenever I grew nervous, an imagined nightmare always—

A church looming before me. Rain pouring down. Night sky and a glowing moon overhead. I was all alone. Crying on the cold, stone steps, and infant in a cardboard box—

I forced the nightmare away, breathing heavily. "You know I hate it when you talk like that," I whispered to him, trying to regain my composure. I wasn't angry with him, but was growing increasingly uncomfortable with our situation after my brief flashback of fear.

"Doesn't mean it shouldn't be said," he said kindly. "I think we're close. Be alert. Remember your training. Banish your fears. I am here. And the Lord is here. He always is."

So, he had noticed my sudden anxiety. "Maybe I should just go back to the car. I know I've trained, but I really don't think—"

A shape of fur, fangs, and claws launched from the shadows towards me, cutting off my words as it snarled, thirsty for my blood.

And my nightmare slipped back into my thoughts like a veiled assassin, a wraith hoping to hold me still for the monster to eat. I froze, unable to move. Twin sticks of power abruptly erupted into being in my clenched fists, but my fear swamped me with that stupid nightmare, the sticks held at my side, useless to save me.

Right before the beast's claws reached me, it grunted as something batted it from the air, sending it flying sideways. It struck a tree with another grunt and an angry whine of pain.

I fell to my knees right into a puddle, arms shaking, breathing fast.

My sticks crackled in the rain like live cattle prods, except their entire length was the electrical section — at least to anyone other than me. I could hold them without pain.

Magic was a part of me, coursing through my veins whether I wanted it or not, and Roland had spent many years teaching me how to master it. But I had never been able to fully master the nightmare inside me, and in moments of fear, it always won, overriding my training.

The fact that I had resorted to weapons — like the ones he had trained me with — rather than a burst of flame, was startling. It was good in the fact that my body's reflexes knew enough to call up a defense even without my direct command, but bad in the fact that it was the worst form of defense for the situation presented. I could have very easily done as Roland did, and hurt it from a distance. But I hadn't. Because of my stupid block.

Roland placed a calloused palm on my shoulder, and I flinched. "Easy, see? I am here." But he did frown at my choice of weapons, the reprimand silent but loud in my mind. I let out a shaky breath, forcing my fear back down. It was all in my head, but still, it wasn't easy. Fear could be like that.

I focused on Roland's implied lesson. Close combat weapons — even magically-powered ones — were for last resorts. I averted my eyes in very real shame. I knew these things. He didn't even need to tell me them. But when that damned nightmare caught hold of me, all my training went out the window. It haunted me like a shadow, waiting for moments just like this, as if trying to kill me. A form of psychological suicide? But it was why I constantly refused to join Roland on his hunts. He knew about it. And although he was trying to help me overcome that fear, he never pressed too hard.

Rain continued to sizzle as it struck my batons. I didn't let them go, using them as a totem to build my confidence back up. I slowly lifted my eyes to nod at him as I climbed back to my feet.

That's when I saw the second set of eyes in the shadows, right before they flew out of the darkness towards Roland's back. I threw one of my batons and missed, but that pretty much let Roland know that an unfriendly was behind him. Either that or I had just failed to murder my mentor at point-blank range. He whirled to confront the monster, expecting another aerial assault as he unleashed a ball of fire that splashed over the tree at chest height, washing the trunk in blue flames. But this monster was tricky. It hadn't planned on tackling Roland, but had merely jumped out of the darkness to get closer, no doubt learning from its fallen comrade, who still lay unmoving against the tree behind me.

His coat shone like midnight clouds with hints of lightning flashing in the depths of thick, wiry fur. The coat of dew dotting his fur reflected the moonlight, giving him a faint sheen as if covered in fresh oil. He was tall, easily hip height at the shoulder, and barrel chested, his rump much leaner than the rest of his body. He — I assumed male from the long, thick mane around his neck — had a very long snout, much longer and wider than any werewolf I had ever seen. Amazingly, and beyond my control, I realized he was beautiful.

But most of the natural world's lethal hunters were beautiful.

He landed in a wet puddle a pace in front of Roland, juked to the right, and then to the left, racing past the big man, biting into his hamstrings on his way by.

A wash of anger rolled over me at seeing my mentor injured, dousing my fear, and I swung my baton down as hard as I could. It struck the beast in the rump as it tried to dart back to cover — a typical wolf tactic. My blow singed his hair and shattered bone. The creature collapsed into a puddle of mud with a yelp, instinctively snapping his jaws over his shoulder to bite whatever had hit him.

I let him. But mostly out of dumb luck as I heard Roland hiss in pain, falling to the ground.

The monster's jaws clamped around my baton, and there was an immediate explosion of teeth and blood that sent him flying several feet away into the tall brush, yipping, screaming, and staggering. Before he slipped out of sight, I noticed that his lower jaw was simply *gone*, from the contact of his saliva on my electrified magical batons. Then he managed to limp into the woods with more pitiful yowls, but I had no mind to chase him. Roland — that titan of a man, my mentor — was hurt. I could smell copper in the air, and knew we had to get out of here. Fast. Because we had anticipated only one of the monsters. But there had been two of them, and they hadn't been the run-of-the-mill werewolves we had been warned about. If there were two, perhaps there were more. And they were evidently the prehistoric cousin of any werewolf I had ever seen or read about.

Roland hissed again as he stared down at his leg, growling with both pain and anger. My eyes darted back to the first monster, wary of another attack. It *almost* looked like a werewolf, but bigger. Much bigger. He didn't move, but I saw he was breathing. He had a notch in his right ear and a jagged scar on his long snout. Part of me wanted to go over to him and torture him. Slowly. Use his pain to finally drown my nightmare, my fear. The fear that had caused Roland's injury. My lack of inner-strength had not only put me in danger, but had hurt my mentor, my friend.

I shivered, forcing the thought away. That was *cold*. Not me. Sure, I was no stranger to fighting, but that had always been in a ring. Practicing. Sparring. Never life or death.

But I suddenly realized something very dark about myself in the chill, rainy night. Although I was terrified, I felt a deep ocean of anger manifest inside me, wanting only to dispense justice as I saw fit. To use that rage to battle my own demons. As if feeding one would starve the other, reminding me of the Cherokee Indian Legend Roland had once told me.

An old Cherokee man was teaching his grandson about life. "A fight is going on inside me," he told the boy. "It is a terrible fight between two wolves. One is evil — he is anger, envy, sorrow, regret, greed, arrogance, self-pity, guilt, resentment, inferiority, lies, false pride, superiority, and ego." After a few moments to make sure he had the boy's undivided attention, he continued.

"The other wolf is good — he is joy, peace, love, hope, serenity, humility, kindness, benevolence, empathy, generosity, truth, compassion, and faith. The same fight is going on inside of you, boy, and inside of every other person, too."

The grandson thought about this for a few minutes before replying. "Which wolf will win?"

The old Cherokee man simply said, "The one you feed, boy. The one you feed..."

And I felt like feeding one of my wolves today, by killing this one...

∾

Get the full book ONLINE!

∾

*Turn the page to read a sample of **WHISKEY GINGER** - Phantom Queen Diaries Book 1, or **BUY ONLINE**. Quinn MacKenna is a black magic arms dealer from Boston, and her bark is almost as bad as her bite.*

(Note: Full chronology of all books in the Temple Verse shown on the 'Books in the Temple Verse' page.)

TRY: WHISKEY GINGER (PHANTOM QUEEN DIARIES # 1)

*T*he pasty guitarist hunched forward, thrust a rolled-up wad of paper deep into one nostril, and snorted a line of blood crystals—frozen hemoglobin that I'd smuggled over in a refrigerated canister—with the uncanny grace of a drug addict. He sat back, fangs gleaming, and pawed at his nose. "That's some bodacious shit. Hey, bros," he said, glancing at his fellow band members, "come hit this shit before it melts."

He fetched one of the backstage passes hanging nearby, pried the plastic

363

badge from its lanyard, and used it to split up the crystals, murmuring something in an accent that reminded me of California. Not *the* California, but you know, Cali-foh-nia—the land of beaches, babes, and bros. I retrieved a toothpick from my pocket and punched it through its thin wrapper. "So," I asked no one in particular, "now that ye have the product, who's payin'?"

Another band member stepped out of the shadows to my left, and I don't mean that figuratively, either—the fucker literally stepped out of the shadows. I scowled at him, but hid my surprise, nonchalantly rolling the toothpick from one side of my mouth to the other.

The rest of the band gathered around the dressing room table, following the guitarist's lead by preparing their own snorting utensils—tattered magazine covers, mostly. Typically, you'd do this sort of thing with a dollar-bill, maybe even a Benjamin if you were flush. But fangers like this lot couldn't touch cash directly—in God We Trust and all that. Of course, I didn't really understand why sucking blood the old-fashioned way had suddenly gone out of style. More of a rush, maybe?

"It lasts longer," the vampire next to me explained, catching my mildly curious expression. "It's especially good for shows and stuff. Makes us look, like, less—"

"Creepy?" I offered, my Irish brogue lilting just enough to make it a question.

"Pale," he finished, frowning.

I shrugged. "Listen, I've got places to be," I said, holding out my hand.

"I'm sure you do," he replied, smiling. "Tell you what, why don't you, like, hang around for a bit? Once that wears off," he dipped his head toward the bloody powder smeared across the table's surface, "we may need a pick-me-up." He rested his hand on my arm and our gazes locked.

I blinked, realized what he was trying to pull, and rolled my eyes. His widened in surprise, then shock as I yanked out my toothpick and shoved it through his hand.

"Motherfuck—"

"I want what we agreed on," I declared. "Now. No tricks."

The rest of the band saw what happened and rose faster than I could blink. They circled me, their grins feral...they might have even seemed intimidating if it weren't for the fact that they each had a case of the sniffles

—I had to work extra hard not to think about what it felt like to have someone else's blood dripping down my nasal cavity.

I held up a hand.

"Can I ask ye gentlemen a question before we get started?" I asked. "Do ye even *have* what I asked for?"

Two of the band members exchanged looks and shrugged. The guitarist, however, glanced back towards the dressing room, where a brown paper bag sat next to a case full of makeup. He caught me looking and bared his teeth, his fangs stretching until it looked like it would be uncomfortable for him to close his mouth without piercing his own lip.

"Follow-up question," I said, eyeing the vampire I'd stabbed as he gingerly withdrew the toothpick from his hand and flung it across the room with a snarl. "Do ye do each other's make-up? Since, ye know, ye can't use mirrors?"

I was genuinely curious.

The guitarist grunted. "Mike, we have to go on soon."

"Wait a minute. Mike?" I turned to the snarling vampire with a frown. "What happened to *The Vampire Prospero*?" I glanced at the numerous fliers in the dressing room, most of which depicted the band members wading through blood, with Mike in the lead, each one titled *The Vampire Prospero* in *Rocky Horror Picture Show* font. Come to think of it...Mike did look a little like Tim Curry in all that leather and lace.

I was about to comment on the resemblance when Mike spoke up, "Alright, change of plans, bros. We're gonna drain this bitch before the show. We'll look totally—"

"Creepy?" I offered, again.

"Kill her."

∼

Get the full book ONLINE!

MAKE A DIFFERENCE

Reviews are the most powerful tools in my arsenal when it comes to getting attention for my books. Much as I'd like to, I don't have the financial muscle of a New York publisher.

But I do have something much more powerful and effective than that, and it's something that those publishers would kill to get their hands on.

A committed and loyal bunch of readers.

Honest reviews of my books help bring them to the attention of other readers.

If you've enjoyed this book, I would be very grateful if you could spend just five minutes leaving a review (it can be as short as you like) on my book's Amazon page.

Thank you very much in advance.

ACKNOWLEDGMENTS

First, I would like to thank my beta-readers, TEAM TEMPLE, those individuals who spent hours of their time to read, and re-re-read Nate's story. Your dark, twisted, cunning sense of humor makes me feel right at home…

I would also like to thank you, the reader. I hope you enjoyed reading *BEAST MASTER* as much as I enjoyed writing it. Be sure to check out the two crossover series in the Temple Verse: The **Feathers and Fire Series** and the **Phantom Queen Diaries**.

And last, but definitely not least, I thank my wife, Lexy. Without your support, none of this would have been possible.

ABOUT SHAYNE SILVERS

Shayne is a man of mystery and power, whose power is exceeded only by his mystery…

He currently writes the Amazon Bestselling **Nate Temple** Series, which features a foul-mouthed wizard from St. Louis. He rides a bloodthirsty unicorn, drinks with Achilles, and is pals with the Four Horsemen.

He also writes the Amazon Bestselling **Feathers and Fire** Series—a second series in the Temple Verse. The story follows a rookie spell-slinger named Callie Penrose who works for the Vatican in Kansas City. Her problem? Hell seems to know more about her past than she does.

He coauthors **The Phantom Queen Diaries**—a third series set in The Temple Verse—with Cameron O'Connell. The story follows Quinn MacKenna, a mouthy black magic arms dealer in Boston. All she wants? A round-trip ticket to the Fae realm…and maybe a drink on the house.

Shayne holds two high-ranking black belts, and can be found writing in a coffee shop, cackling madly into his computer screen while pounding shots of espresso. He's hard at work on the newest books in the Temple Verse—You can find updates on new releases or chronological reading order on the next page, his website or any of his social media accounts. **Follow him online for all sorts of groovy goodies, giveaways, and new release updates:**

Get Down with Shayne Online
www.shaynesilvers.com
info@shaynesilvers.com

BOOKS IN THE TEMPLE VERSE

CHRONOLOGY: All stories in the TempleVerse are shown in chronological order on the following page

NATE TEMPLE SERIES

FAIRY TALE - FREE prequel novella #0 for my subscribers

OBSIDIAN SON

BLOOD DEBTS

GRIMM

SILVER TONGUE

BEAST MASTER

BEERLYMPIAN (Novella #5.5 in the 'LAST CALL' anthology)

TINY GODS

DADDY DUTY (Novella #6.5)

WILD SIDE

WAR HAMMER

NINE SOULS

HORSEMAN

LEGEND

KNIGHTMARE (TEMPLE #12) — COMING SOON...

FEATHERS AND FIRE SERIES

(Also set in the TempleVerse)

UNCHAINED

RAGE

WHISPERS

ANGEL'S ROAR

MOTHERLUCKER (Novella #4.5 in the 'LAST CALL' anthology)

SINNER

BLACK SHEEP

GODLESS (FEATHERS #7) — COMING SOON...

PHANTOM QUEEN DIARIES

(Also set in the Temple Universe)

COLLINS (Prequel novella #0 in the 'LAST CALL' anthology)

WHISKEY GINGER

COSMOPOLITAN

OLD FASHIONED

MOTHERLUCKER (Novella #3.5 in the 'LAST CALL' anthology)

DARK AND STORMY

MOSCOW MULE

WITCHES BREW

SALTY DOG

CHRONOLOGICAL ORDER: TEMPLE VERSE

FAIRY TALE (TEMPLE PREQUEL)

OBSIDIAN SON (TEMPLE 1)

BLOOD DEBTS (TEMPLE 2)

GRIMM (TEMPLE 3)

SILVER TONGUE (TEMPLE 4)

BEAST MASTER (TEMPLE 5)

BEERLYMPIAN (TEMPLE 5.5)

TINY GODS (TEMPLE 6)

DADDY DUTY (TEMPLE NOVELLA 6.5)

UNCHAINED (FEATHERS... 1)

RAGE (FEATHERS... 2)

WILD SIDE (TEMPLE 7)

WAR HAMMER (TEMPLE 8)

WHISPERS (FEATHERS... 3)

COLLINS (PHANTOM 0)

Made in the USA
Monee, IL
12 June 2020

32942468R00222